She opened the sec_____ the air conditioner to turn it on. The room was stifling. And then she stopped stock-still, staring at the single page. It was a Xerox copy of an old lurid pulp-magazine cover: a crude drawing, everything exaggerated. A woman was being strangled by a madman. You could see he was insane by the bulging eyes and the slavering mouth. The woman's mouth was wide open in a scream. And she was a nurse, wide-winged cap still on her head, starched white dress unbuttoned just enough to show cleavage.

Oh Christ. She couldn't move, couldn't really breathe. Only one person in this hospital knew her past— Dr. Zee—and Julia Zachary-Felsen was more than a colleague, she was a friend. They were close friends, in spite of the thirty-year difference in their ages. Dr. Zee knew everything about Marty . . . well, *almost* everything. But Dr. Zee could never have even *thought* of this nastiness.

Then who . . . ?

By Marcia Rose
Published by Ballantine Books:

NURSES

Marcia Rose

BALLANTINE BOOKS • NEW YORK

Copyright © 1996 by Marcia Kamien

All rights reserved under International and Pan-American Copyright Conventions. Published in the United States by Ballantine Books, a division of Random House, Inc., New York, and simultaneously in Canada by Random House of Canada Limited, Toronto.

http://www.randomhouse.com

Library of Congress Catalog Card Number: 96-95366

ISBN: 0-345-39001-6

Manufactured in the United States of America

First Hardcover Edition: February 1996
First Mass Market Edition: June 1997

10   9   8   7   6   5   4   3   2   1

This one's for
PAM STRICKLER,
Marcia Rose's editor and cheering section
since Book One.

ACKNOWLEDGEMENTS

The author spoke to many nurses and appreciates being told their thoughts and experiences—most particularly Sally Davis, R.N., Mary Ann Camporeale, R.N., and Sheryl Rosenfield, R.N.

Thanks are also due to Judy Panitch, Julia Hechtman, Loretta England, and Martha Truglio for research and background . . .

A special thank-you to Maureen Baron . . .

And last but hardly least, many thanks to Gabriel S. Zatlin, M.D.

Excerpted from the *New York City Health Care Directory*

ALL SOULS WOMEN'S HOSPITAL
Van Dam Avenue Triangle, New York City

Beds: 201
Deliveries: 1,230
Services: (for inpatient and private medical care)
OBSTETRICS/GYNECOLOGY • FAMILY PRACTICE •
PEDIATRICS • PSYCHIATRY • NEONATOLOGY •
GENETICS • ICU • CCU • Neonatal ICU • Substance Abuse
Programs • Voluntary Inpatient Mental Health Unit • HIV
Services • Oncology Services • Birth Defects Unit • HIV
Children's Unit • Pediatric Surgery • Parenting Program

Nurse-run COMMUNITY CARE CLINICS, entrance on
Hamilton Place (for outpatient and public medical care) •
Birthing Center • Certified Nurse-Midwife Services • High
Risk Maternity • Family Practice • Birth Defects • Family
Planning • Mother/Child Nutrition • HIV Family Services •
Genetic Counseling • Pediatrics • Obstetrics/Gynecology

Information Hotline: (800) 555-0110
Hospital Telephones: (212) 555-0000

Milton D. Messinger, MD, Vice-President for Hospital
Administration
J. Zachary-Felsen, MD, Chief, Family Practice
Dennis Dinowitz, MD, Chief, Ob/Gyn
Joel Mannes, MD, Chief, Psychiatry
Len Fassbinder, MD, Chief, Neonatology
W. Clayton Cranford, MD, Chief, Pediatrics
Aimee R. Delano, RN, BBA, Director, Nursing
Marta D. Lamb, NP, Ph.D., Director, Community Care Clinics

COMMUNITY CARE CLINICS
Marta D. Lamb, Director

The Birthing Center   open 24 hours
with nurse-midwives   Clinics G and H

General Gynecology and Obstetrics (with physicians specializing in OB/GYN)*	MON - TUES - THU 9–3 Clinics C and D
High Risk Pregnancies (with physicians as needed)*	MON and FRI 9–1 Clinic E
General Pediatrics (with physicians specializing in PEDS OR FAMILY PRACTICE)*	TUES - THURS - SAT 9–4 Clinic B
Mother-Child Nutrition with nurses and nutritionists	WED 9–Noon in the nursing office
Birth Defects & Genetic Counseling	TUES and WED 9–3 Clinic E
Family Planning*	TUES and FRI 9–4 Clinic H
HIV Family Services*	TUES EVENING 7–10 Clinic D
Family Birth Training Lamaze Method	THURS EVENING 7–9 Clinic C
Family Practice (non-private patients)	MON - WED - FRI 9–5 Clinics A and B
Family Practice (private patients) Julia Zachary-Felsen, Chief, Family Practice	by appointment

Nurse-Practitioners and Nurse-Midwives see patients by appointment throughout the week, as needed.

---

*Attending physicians from All Souls Women's Hospital are available on these days during the hours of 11:00 A.M. to 3:00 P.M.

1

If you came off a spaceship into the Community Care Clinics of All Souls Women's Hospital in the middle of the day this Monday, you would probably think you had landed in a war zone. A restless crowd milled around, with babies crying, people shouting, children squabbling, arguments erupting, telephones ringing . . . and over it all, the intermittent outburst of gabble from the loudspeakers. Since four of the clinics were open this Monday—including one for the most difficult patients—the commotion was *not* the final throes of anarchy. It was just business as usual.

So no one noticed the silent figure, furtively looking about, then sidling into one of the offices, dropping an envelope on the desk. Out quickly, fading back into the normal traffic, the figure moved on, with a satisfied smile. Neatly done, and nobody the wiser. One more drop of poison . . . one more nasty little secret exposed . . . one more proof of who was *really* in control around here.

Marty Lamb, making her final rounds of the day, caught something out of the corner of her eye—a movement, a door opening, she wasn't quite sure. But when she turned, everything was normal—which, on Monday, meant chaos. The trick was to keep the chaos under control, and fortunately, she was pretty good at it. She'd better be, since she was in charge. *Marta D. Lamb, N.P., Ph.D.,* it said on her dove-gray business cards. *Director, Community Care Clinics. All Souls Women's Hospital.*

Thirty-four years old and boss of the first and the only nurse-run health facility in the entire city of New York, now into its fourth year. Not bad for a gawky, redheaded girl from the

1

wrong side of the tracks, Marty decided. As she passed each of the clinics—there were eight clinic areas, each one a collection of examining rooms, storage spaces, and offices—she could hear babies' cries, voices, sometimes an argument and sometimes even laughter. Moving down the main corridor, she peered into each waiting room as she went by, admiring the practically new paint jobs, a different color for each clinic, and checking for any unusual activity.

She had to keep her eyes open, including the ones in the back of her head. *Especially* those. New York was in the midst of a major heat wave, with temperatures well over ninety day after steaming day. That kind of weather tended to make people crazy, and today the High Risk Pregnancy clinic was open. High risk, in this hospital, was a nice way of saying prostitutes, teenagers, and junkies, a group with a high degree of nuttiness to begin with. It didn't take much to ignite a major battle.

Today, though, when she walked into Clinic E, sullen silence greeted her. Two of the mothers-to-be were stoned and therefore out of it. The only other patient in the waiting room was engrossed in a comic book romance. Marty hoped it was one of the special comics she had ordered, where the heroine kicked her pimp boyfriend out, always insisted on a condom, and was wonderful to her children. Vain hope: it was one of the more lurid offerings from the local stationery store.

Just as Marty turned to go back to her office, Nurse Kenny Rankin came out of the examining room, his arm around the shoulders of a young, too-thin, very pregnant woman. It was Peggy Armstrong, once a glamorous receptionist at Saatchi and Saatchi, the hot downtown ad agency . . . but that was in another time. Now Peggy was mostly in another world. She was a crack addict, thirty-three years old, and this was her third pregnancy.

"Hi, Doc!" Peggy said when she saw Marty. Her smile was sheepish. "I know, I know. I said I'd make them use a condom. But I'm a sucker for a pretty face, you know that. And Lance was awful pretty. I just couldn't think straight." Peggy shrugged. Whoever Lance was, or had been, he was nowhere to be found now. Peggy was on her own, as usual, earning her meager way by turning tricks.

"But look, I'm eating and I'm not smoking . . . well, not cigarettes . . . well . . ." Her voice trailed off.

Marty looked her over. Peggy was pale and thin, but today, at least, she was clean. And she was trying to smile. Maybe, finally, they'd reached her. Maybe. In any case, they had to keep trying.

"We're here for you, Peg," she said. "Remember that, okay? If anyone hassles you, gives you a hard time . . . call us. Or just come in. We'll always find you a bed." She took the woman's hand in hers, amazed at how frail and bony it was, like the hand of a very old woman. "And be sure to come in next week, okay?"

"Yeah, yeah, sure, Doc."

"I'm a nurse, Peg, a nurse-practitioner."

"Yeah, Doc, I know."

"Peggy knows who takes care of her, don't you, darlin'?" Kenny gave her shoulder a squeeze. "Now you make sure you take those vitamins I gave you."

"Yeah. Sure." Marty and Kenny exchanged a look. They both knew she'd probably forget the vitamins within moments of leaving the building; either that, or she'd claim they were hallucinogens and hawk them on the street.

"How pregnant is she?" Marty asked, watching the scrawny figure shuffle out.

"Five months, as near as we can figure. She's not very good at remembering dates."

"Five months! She sure doesn't look it. The fetus?"

"Small, but a good heartbeat."

"Has she been coming in regularly? Never mind," Marty added wryly. "I know the answer." There was no regularity in a crack addict's life. The surprise was that she showed up at all.

"This was her first visit. And, yes, we talked to her about her choices. It's funny, Marty, she can hardly think straight enough to keep from starving, but if she thinks you're talking about abortion, she starts crossing herself and talking about mortal sin."

"Well, we can't force her to do anything. Still, it's a shame, considering . . ."

"Yeah. Considering." They were both remembering Peggy's

last infant, born skinny and quaking with his drug addiction. He was still in the nursery upstairs, waiting to be placed with foster parents. But nobody wanted to deal with problem babies of any kind anymore.

"Look, the next time she comes in, call me. Maybe she'd agree to have her tubes tied. Let me talk to her. Maybe we can do something. Anything else?"

"Nope. I thought for sure we'd have trouble . . . the full moon."

"Wait. The day isn't over yet." They both laughed but it wasn't really a joke. Every hospital staff knew what happened when the moon was full. Psych wards became zoos and even normally sane patients behaved strangely. Between the heat wave and the moon, anything could happen—and probably would.

Kenny turned, to the sounds of raised voices in the back of the clinic. "Gotta get back to work," he said. It was three-thirty, and the High Risk clinic was supposed to close at one. It never did; there were too many risks nowadays. "Watch out for werewolves," he added as he left.

Marty shook her head, laughing a little; and from behind her a familiar female voice, loaded with irony, said: "The work we do here is *not* a laughing matter, Ms. Lamb." It sounded amazingly like Milton Messinger, M.D., the chief administrator for the hospital; but it was Dr. Julia Zachary-Felsen, head of Family Practice, better known as Dr. Zee.

"Please," Marty said, turning around with a smile. "Messinger haunts my nightmares as it is."

Dr. Zee's white coat was not buttoned—she probably hadn't had ten free seconds to do it—and her short white hair was sticking straight up, from her habit of pulling it whenever she was deep in thought. What Marty noticed most, though, were the dark shadows under the doctor's eyes, like sooty thumb-prints. Lately she'd been looking like what Marty's aunts had called "ganted," and it was worrisome. Dr. Zee was not a young woman, but she was still working the hours of doctors half her age.

"Sorry. Anything new in your young life?" Dr. Zee's eyes

bored into Marty's and she grinned. It made her look a whole lot better suddenly.

"No. Why? You look mischievous. What do you know that I don't? Come on. Give."

"Nothing. I tried to call you several times, that's all."

"You know I'm never in my office. And now I'm afraid to go in because the paperwork will get me."

"Paperwork is going to be the death of us all," Dr. Zee said, beginning to move on.

"Wait. Julia. Why were you calling me?"

Dr. Zee took a step, stopped. "Well, you probably don't want to hear this, since you're so shorthanded, but they put a new line in for Family Practice. I can have another doctor. Just in the nick of time, might I add."

"Meaning?"

"Meaning I'm hoping to retire one of these days soon."

"Don't make me laugh. Dr. Zee—retire? I don't think so."

But Dr. Zee did not grin back at her. "We'll see. In the meantime, I've been putting feelers out for months, and a highly qualified doctor, board certified in Family Practice, is coming to look us over tomorrow." She was already moving on as she talked, another of her habits. "So don't go anywhere."

"Like I have somewhere else to go," Marty said as Dr. Zee disappeared into her clinic.

Marty continued briskly down the hallway. Her plan was to stop at each clinic area for ten or fifteen minutes, dealing with whatever problems might come up, saying hello to the patients—after three years, she knew most of the regulars by name—handling any emergencies, changing assignments if necessary. That was always the plan; but it rarely worked out that way. It frustrated her that she could never really finish anything. She'd get into one problem, and right in the middle, something else would come up and she'd be off and running in another direction.

As she made her way down the corridor, people called out to her, sometimes "Mrs. Lamb" and sometimes "Hi, Marty!" Much more often, though, it was "Doctor! Doctor!" Peggy wasn't the only one who refused to see the difference. It made most of the M.D.'s nuts. They felt so noble, coming downstairs once or twice a week, giving their time to the poor peasants. They didn't want any mere *nurses*, no matter how capable or with how many degrees, getting the credit for being physicians!

It would certainly give Dr. Dimwit a fit, Marty thought. Dr. Dennis Dinowitz was chief of Ob/Gyn and was probably quite bright, but everyone on staff called him Dr. Dimwit. Dennis Dinowitz was tall and muscular and ... there was no other word for it, he was gorgeous. But he was an asshole, pure and simple. Unfortunately for his image, when he got all huffy, as he did frequently, his face flushed to a bright plum and his voice rose to a countertenor squeak.

Speak of the devil. There he was, purple face and all, emerging from the entrance to Clinic D, General Obstetrics and Gynecology. Well, at least he had deigned to show up today; that was nice.

"There you are, Marty!"

"You noticed."

But he wasn't in the mood to kid around; he was definitely on the warpath.

"I know I'm considered politically incorrect, Marty, but there *is* a limit. Your nurses are taking entirely too much onto themselves!" He was trying very hard to be stern and aggressive; quite a feat when his voice kept rising to the soprano level. With great effort, Marty kept herself from smiling.

"What seems to be the problem, Doctor?" *This time*, she added silently.

"Isabelle had the temerity to tell me I had prescribed the wrong medication for a patient."

She kept her face as bland as possible. "Had you?" She couldn't wait to hear Isabelle's version.

"Had I what?"

"Prescribed the wrong medication."

"Well, as it happens ... Well, how was *I* to know the woman is at risk for cancer? She came in complaining of hot flashes, so I put her on hormone therapy, of course. But that's not the point."

"Oh, really, Dennis. What *is* the point?"

"The point is, Marty, that a nurse is *never* supposed to call down a doctor in front of the patient! She was *yelling* at me! You want to know the trouble with your nurses?" Without waiting for an answer, he went right on: "Your nurses think the patients are *their* patients. They're *our* patients. We're the doctors."

"Dr. Dinowitz, surely you remember that CCC is nurse-run? Isabelle Molina is a Nurse Specialist, and that woman is her patient." Adding silently, *And if you ever bothered to read the chart or—what a concept—talked to the patient, maybe you wouldn't have made such a dumb mistake.*

"Now don't get me wrong, Marty, your nurses do a really good job, but there's a limit! They're only nurses, after all." His eyes shifted quickly; he *knew* he shouldn't have said that. She decided not to blast him, though. Not after he'd just gotten a tongue-lashing from Isabelle.

"Since your nurses want to be doctors so badly, let them go to medical school!" And away he stomped, looking triumphant.

Marty knew it wasn't worth arguing with him. He was hidebound, and he had always had an attitude. Especially where she was concerned. When they both were new at the hospital, eight years ago, he had decided to favor her with his amorous attentions. Her lack of interest had astonished and offended him. It still did. Every once in a while he'd try again. She was aware that every *no* made him even more resentful. She was also aware that he was the darling of Administration. But she was damned if she'd try to stay in favor by letting him screw her on the burgundy leather couch in his office! Even though the rumor was that he was quite the sexual athlete, and her love life lately left a great deal to be desired—pun intended.

Anyway, he was not the only doctor around who longed for the nursing staff to go back to the old ways, standing behind the physician, meek and submissive, handing out instruments and sexual favors with equal alacrity. And with hospital accreditation looming, the medical staff had a perfect way to keep the smart-ass nurses in their place. Just stall the necessary improvements to the Community Care Clinics, so they'd fail to meet the criteria. They'd be closed down in a New York minute, and the one and only nurse-run program in the city would be history.

Although lately, she'd begun to fear they'd be jinxed out of existence first. For the past couple of months strange things had been happening. There was no other way to put it. Blood tests got mixed up; supplies of painkiller didn't match the records; and their new dove-gray "greens" simply walked away in the night, never to be seen again. Well, greens were always being snitched . . . but the rest of it was odd, to say the least. Not to mention the poison pen letters.

Her clinics were supposed to solve problems for the hospital, not *make* them. And lately there had been definite signs that management was looking for ways to quote contain costs unquote. Translation: What can we get rid of? She had to make sure the answer wasn't Community Care Clinics, and Marta Dauber Lamb, Director.

She'd had to fight like crazy to get the hospital to adopt a nurse-run program in the first place, even though she had raised the grant money. It should have appealed to them; after all, like it said, engraved in stone over the front entrance, they were *All Souls Women's Hospital*. They specialized in women. Having nurses take over the overcrowded public clinics should have made the medical staff jump for joy. But hospitals in these troubled times were just not interested in the special health needs of poor, often immigrant, often ignorant, women.

She'd needed help, and she'd gotten it—from Dr. Zee, who'd been around so long and was so popular with the people who gave money that she was just about untouchable. Marty was sure Dr. Zee had bullied the Executive Committee into giving Community Care Clinics a shot. So far, so good . . . but God only knew how long before it got scuttled.

A lot of doctors still refused to admit that mere nurses were capable of giving examinations and advice, not to mention prescriptions. Some of them couldn't handle nurses doing simple procedures, or *any* procedures at all. They saw it as a usurpation of their role as healer. And maybe it was, but tough. All her charge nurses had a master's degree; she had a master's *and* a Ph.D. We can take care of patients just fine, thank you, she thought. The old fogeys were pathetic, but unfortunately, they outnumbered her. She was just glad she had Dr. Zee on her side.

At the Birthing Center there wasn't anyone in labor, but there were two new mothers with their infants. Marty stopped in to admire the beautiful babies and talk to Crystal Cole, the head midwife. Where was she? Crystal was a friend of hers, but lately Crys always seemed to be somewhere else whenever she looked for her. Oh well. She'd see her later. Virgie Nesbit was covering, and Virgie was terrific.

That was the last clinic. A whole day, a Monday at that, and no major problems, no knife fights, no drunken husbands, no mixed-up X rays, no missing bloods. Unbelievable. Marty checked her watch and stretched her back. Only five-fifteen. She might even be able to go back to her office and look at the accreditation files. Or, since that was bound to be depressing, maybe the budget, another joy and delight. Or—

"Ms. Lamb, Ms. Lamb, front desk, please," squawked the loudspeakers. "Ms. Lamb to the front desk, please."

Marty ran, her red ponytail bouncing on her back. Something bad must be happening or Carmen would have left her a message on the answering machine in her office.

She could hear a woman sobbing hysterically and repeating something over and over. It was hard to make out. And a baby screaming. Marty ran faster. Carmen had stepped out from behind the reception desk and was trying, vainly, to get the disheveled young woman to calm down.

When Marty came into view, the woman took one look at her and rushed forward. The word she was shouting was "Dyink!" and she held out her shrieking infant to Marty. "Doctor! My baby dyink! Help, pliss!"

Marty took the red-faced infant into her arms. The baby was almost scrawny, much too thin, the little neck so skinny it looked like it might snap. This baby was *starving*! She squelched her anger quickly. "Where's Isabelle?" Isabelle Molina was not only chief pediatric nurse, she knew nutrition.

"Search me," Carmen said. "I beeped her but she hasn't answered. That's why I called you. What do you need?"

"Get a bottle of formula for this baby. There should be plenty in the Birthing Center . . . never mind." Grateful, she spotted Isabelle hurrying in, her usually cheerful face a study in concentration. "Izzy, feed this child."

"Oh my God! Poor baby! What's with the mother?"

"I'm about to find out."

The skinny young woman was still weeping uncontrollably, but she had stopped hollering. That was good. Marty put an arm around her and led her to a chair, making her sit.

"What's your name?"

"Dyink. So sick. Maybe poison? Oh . . . !" She began to cry loudly.

Marty took the woman's hand and looked into her eyes. "No," she shouted. "Not poison."

"No? No poison?"

"No." Well, at least they were getting *somewhere*. "Hungry! Needs to eat!" Her answer was renewed sobbing.

"What is your name? *Votre nom? Deine nomen?*" Was that right? Her foreign languages were running out rapidly. She pointed to herself and said, "Marty Lamb."

"Ah." Pointing to herself. "Anna Pretikin."

"No English?"

Sniffling but much calmer, the young mother shook her head sadly. "*Nyet.* No. Ukraine." She pointed to herself. "Soviet Union."

Ukrainian. Oh Christ. Who in the clinics had people from Russia? Besides herself, of course, but she'd never learned the language. Her father had rarely spoken—in any tongue.

"Anna," Marty said, "are you hungry?" She mimed eating, and the girl—for that's all she was, a girl—burst into tears. "Yeah, I guess you are. Carmen . . ."

"I'm sure there's half an eggplant hero in the staff fridge. Hang on. I'll be right back." Carmen hurried off to the staff kitchen.

A few minutes later, while Anna devoured the sandwich and gulped some heavily sugared iced tea, Marty went searching through the big book of community resources that sat on Carmen's desk. Where in New York was there someone who might speak Anna's lingo? "Aha," she said after a moment, her finger lighting on a listing under Family Services. *St. Nicholas Ukrainian Church,* it said.

"The very thing," she murmured, although she wasn't sure. Maybe the woman was Jewish, a lot of Russian emigrés were. She might have no religion at all. Still, it was Ukrainian.

"Call these people, would you, Carmen? Anna Pretikin is

her name, she speaks almost no English and she needs help. Badly. First food and, I'd guess, a place to stay . . ." She would bet that mother and baby had spent at least one or two nights sleeping on the streets of Manhattan, maybe even in the back of the clinic building amongst the garbage cans. It wouldn't be the first time. Still, the thought of it made her shudder. "And a translator."

"Yeah, that part I figured." Carmen was already on the phone. "Hello, this is the Community Care Clinics in upper Manhattan. We have a Ukrainian woman and her baby here. Homeless, I think. She doesn't speak English and none of us speaks . . . uh-huh . . . uh-huh . . . oh, good . . . Yes, I do . . ." And Carmen's pencil began to fly across the paper, punctuated by "uh-huhs." Without looking up, she held up her thumb and forefinger in the A-okay sign.

By this time Isabelle was back with the baby, who was now in clean diapers and a little pink nightie. So, she was a girl baby. "Crystal has a whole drawerful of baby clothes, did you know that? We fed and bathed this dirty little girl and cleaned her up, and look how happy she is."

"The mother thought she was dying."

"Excuse me, Marty, but a couple more days, and who knows. I wonder why she's not breast feeding?"

"I'll bet she is," Marty said. "And I'll bet the milk's dried up. I think it's been a while since the mother ate what you and I might call a meal. But I found a Ukrainian church, and I think Carmen is getting her fixed up."

"Carmen is a saint."

"So she is," Marty agreed. "One minute," she said as Carmen gave her a signal.

"They have a program, at the church, for new immigrants. You want to speak to Mrs. Holub, who seems to be in charge?"

"You bet." Mrs. Holub, it turned out, could place the mother and baby with a family, on a temporary basis.

Marty explained the situation. "I have a feeling she may have been eating out of our garbage cans." The woman on the other end of the line made a sound of pain, and Marty said, "Yes. It's awful. But now we've found you, at least. If you'll give your name and address to Carmen, we'll put her in a taxi and send her down to you. Have somebody make sure to get her back up here tomorrow, to our Pediatrics clinic. Nine to four, and the earlier the better."

"Yes. Of course. And thank you so much. Not too many big hospitals care," Mrs. Holub said.

"Well . . . we do." Marty glanced over at the mother, cuddling her baby and looking less like a waif herself. "I'm going to put her on now. You can explain what's happening. And thank you, Mrs. Holub. I don't know what we'd do without all the wonderful volunteers who help take care of people in this city."

It was a little embarrassing when Anna got off the phone, grabbed her hand and kissed it fervently—Marty could feel herself blushing—but on the whole, she was pleased. She watched with a smile as one of the orderlies took mother and baby to get a taxi.

"Izzy, was Crys there when you took the baby to the Birthing Center?"

"Sure. That's how I got the sweet little nightgown."

"How'd she strike you?"

"How do you mean?"

Marty laughed. "Oh hell, Izzy, I don't know why I'm beating around the bush. Crystal hasn't been . . . herself lately, that's all. Moody. Temperamental."

"You worry too much about Crystal, you know that? Anyway, it's probably this weather. Marco and I are snapping each other's heads off lately. The heat gets to you . . . well, it gets to *us*."

"Oh, that hot Latin blood!"

They smiled at each other, and then Isabelle said, "Oh God, it's time I was on my way. They'll be waiting for me." Isabelle made a particular point of being home with her whole family— husband, mother, two sons, and daughter—every night for dinner. "Mama said she was making something special."

"How *is* your mother doing? I guess okay, or she wouldn't be cooking." But the shadow that passed over Isabelle's round, big-eyed face told Marty that Mama was *not* doing okay.

"If you want to talk, Izzy, call me later. I'll be home. As usual."

"I keep telling you, Clive Moses is after you, and seeing as he's a hunk, I don't know why you won't even—"

"Isabelle. Think what you're saying. Clive Moses is a *public relations* man." They both laughed.

"Excuse me. I forgot. So stay home and watch 'Murphy Brown.' I'll catch you tomorrow."

Marty's office was in the far corner of Community Care Clinics, but at least it was in a corner. That meant two windows, and two windows meant you had Made It. Both windows were, of course, tightly shut because of the air conditioner, which had, of course, been turned off by some miserly soul.

The messages on her machine were from Dr. Zee and from her friend the shrink, Dr. Joel Mannes. Nothing important. She gathered her papers together, shoving them into her nylon briefcase with the shoulder strap, and then nearly dropped it when she picked it up, it was so heavy. The damn thing was stuffed with budgets and lists and duty rosters and her notes for a new article on nurses as executives—not to mention all the memos that kept falling onto her desk—hundreds of papers, *thousands* of papers, and no end in sight. She'd gone into nursing to take care of *people*, not papers.

As she was about to leave she noticed a plain gray hospital envelope in her in-box. It hadn't been there earlier. Her heart started to thump and she just stood there, looking at it, unwilling to reach out and take it. Two of her nurses had received plain gray hospital envelopes with anonymous messages in their mailboxes, hateful, cruel things.

One, brought to her by the hysterically weeping recipient, Angela Buonanotte, a sweet young woman with an ethereal air, had the cutout picture from a soap advertisement, a plump pink-and-white baby splashing in its bath. When Marty saw it, icy fury had gripped her. She had reached out to the young nurse, but Angela was huddled into herself, bent almost double, her arms tightly wrapped around her stomach. Angie's baby girl had accidentally drowned in the bathtub a year before. What fiendishness! And, in God's name, *why*?

Marty shivered again at the memory. It was spooky, knowing there was someone on staff, someone completely crazed but clever enough to hide her sickness under a veneer of

smiles and casual conversation. Was it fair to assume the
poison pen was a woman? She didn't care; in her heart, she
knew it was. Someone working here was smiling, sitting down
to lunch in the hospital cafeteria with everyone, joining in on
the gossip, while her sick mind planned the next attack.

Was it her turn now? She licked her lips and decided what
the hell, ripped it open and began to laugh. Folded into a sheet
of hospital stationery was a copy of one of her favorite car-
toons. For years she'd had a yellowed and tattered copy of it
in a frame above her desk, and one day recently it had disappeared. She'd been annoyed—who the hell would *want* it,
besides her?—and had mentioned a couple of times that she
missed it.

She didn't have to look at the illegible signature on the sheet
of paper to know who had dropped it on her desk. Joel Mannes,
of course. She punched out his extension on her phone—where
in the world had he found it?—but he'd gone already, so she
left him a brief message, thanking and blessing him.

She felt silly that the sight of an envelope had made her
panic. When it had happened to Angie, she'd assured herself
and the victim that it was a random thing, some sick soul's idea
of a joke. If it happened again, she'd call the cops. Or talk to
management. *Something.* If it happened again.

And then it *had* happened again, to another nurse, this time
Kenny Rankin, who was one of the sweetest men in the world.
The other nurses said he'd gone absolutely *green* and then had
ripped the paper into a million pieces. But had she called Security? No, she had not; she wasn't sure why. Well, yes she was.
She didn't want to go public with this, not yet. She'd like to
solve this problem herself. Still, she'd already lost Angela,
who'd quit on the spot. . . .

She was tired, ready to go home. With a last look around,
she turned out the lights, closed the door, and left. Like Scarlett
O'Hara, she'd think about it tomorrow.

2

Early the next morning, Marty was racing round her apartment, feeling like an idiot. Where had she put that duty roster? She'd just had it, right in her hand, and now it was nowhere to be found. Not here. Not there. Where the hell *was* it? She decided to just retrace her steps, and of course *then* she saw it, on the windowsill right where she'd left it when the phone rang. Whoever was calling had breathed into the phone for a few seconds and then hung up. She hated that, especially when she was in a hurry. Which was *always*. There just weren't enough hours in the day.

Stuffing the roster into her briefcase, she went out the door at a run, locked both locks—this was, after all, the Big Apple—and charged down the steps, full speed ahead. And screeched to a halt. The heat hit her like a wall, and it was barely six-thirty! She squinted up at a bright blue sky, searching in vain for a cloud, any kind of a cloud, something to cover up that brassy glare. But no. The worst heat wave to hit New York City in a dozen years showed no signs of letting up.

Oh well. Six blocks wasn't *that* far. She set off, slowing as she passed under the imposing green awning of 1186 Van Dam Avenue, a large brick apartment building. She hoped to see Shayna Brown sitting at her window in the far corner on the ground floor. Sometimes the heavy velvet drapes were pulled tightly shut. Like Shayna's life. But today, there she was. The girl's lovely face, the intelligent dark eyes edged with thick lashes, the luxuriant black hair pulled up into a topknot, was framed in the open window. She was wearing new earrings, Marty saw, silver cascading bells that tinkled as Shayna waved to her.

15

"Good morning, Shayna!" she said, walking over to the window. "Love your earrings!"

"Hello, Marty! A gift from one of my suitors!" The last word was tinged with sarcasm. Shayna had just turned sixteen, and already her father was haggling over betrothal terms with the fathers of suitable young men. Beautiful Shayna had never had a date, of course, had never even been allowed to be alone in a room with a man, much less converse with one. The rules and regulations of the Survivor Orthodox congregation didn't allow it. Only Marty knew how much the girl dreaded the inevitable betrothal, the inevitable wedding, the inevitable humiliation.

"How're you doing?" A shrug answered the question. How should I be doing? it seemed to ask. And anyway, you *know* how I'm doing.

She was right. Marty was the only medical person who saw Shayna regularly. It was important that *someone* keep track of what was going on, because Shayna had many physical problems. But God forbid Rabbi Ezekiel Brown, Shayna's father, should let Shayna go into the hospital for checkups, where everything could be done for her. First of all, a *man* might have to put a hand on her, and that was forbidden. But the real truth was something different. Rabbi Brown didn't even like having Dr. Zee, who was definitely not a man, seen coming into his apartment. Dr. Zee was too well-known in the neighborhood and someone might guess there was something *really* wrong with Shayna.

How could he do this to his only daughter? Keep her a prisoner in the house this way? But Marty knew the answer. Rabbi Ezekiel Brown wanted nobody to guess the truth about her . . . not until he had arranged her engagement, and probably not until the vows had actually been exchanged under the marriage canopy, when it would be too late for anyone to back out of the contract. Poor Shayna. Poor ignorant bridegroom.

There was no convincing Zeke Brown there might be another way. Once his mind was made up, there was no changing it, and his mind had been made up since the day this child was born. Dr. Zee had been there, and she had described the incredible scene: Miriam, Shayna's mother, her long hair in its thick braid, the tears pouring down her cheeks; the rabbi, his handsome face so set that it might have been carved from stone, repeating, "No one must know, is that understood? Nobody must ever know."

And nobody ever did. No one in the cult's congregation knew exactly why Shayna Brown did not walk and run and play with the other children. There were rumors, started and fed by the rabbi, that it had something to do with her heart, all very vague, nothing serious, but why not be careful.

"Are you in any pain?" Marty asked now.

"Just the usual. My neck."

Marty said, "Maybe we should have the orthopedist come over—"

"Sneak over, you mean. What good will it do? *He* won't let them do anything." Shayna's eyes flashed with anger, and Marty thought, Watch out, Rabbi, she's not going to sit back passively forever, waiting for you to run her life.

"Let me bring you some painkiller, at least."

Shayna scowled. "I'm sorry, Marty. I know I'm a pain in the tush." She shook herself, as if to throw off her bad mood, and smiled. It was a beautiful smile, but sad. Marty felt a kinship with the girl. There was something so ... lonesome about Shayna, even though her mother made sure she had tutors and books and plenty of company. None of it mattered; she was isolated from the rest of the world . . . from her own life, in fact. It reminded Marty of her own painful childhood. But she wasn't a miracle worker, and Shayna had a good mother— although what Miriam Brown really thought, who could tell? She kept a cheerful face and a closed mouth. Miriam never complained though every year she looked increasingly thinner and more worn, while her energetic and handsome husband seemed to grow more expansive, more electric. Marriage of Dorian Gray, Marty thought, and then scolded herself. It wasn't any of her business.

"Around lunch," she told Shayna. "I'll bring the pills then. Unless you really need something right now. I have a few in my case. . . ." She patted the big shoulder bag. "Yes?"

"Yes. Okay." Shayna pushed aside the screen in the window and held out her hand for the capsules. "Thank you."

"Shayna, never hesitate to call me, at any hour, even at home, if you need something."

"Oh, I could have asked *him* and he would have brought me some aspirin. It's just . . . I don't know . . . we seem to be in a contest to see who can be stronger, tougher . . . who can withstand pain longer without crying out. A strange kind of father-daughter relationship, no? Whenever he comes into my room, I feel that we are strapping on our swords." She laughed. "Can you tell I've been rereading *Ivanhoe*? Thanks for the pills. I know you have to get to work. But if you have time later, come by and help me with my bridge lessons, okay?"

"I'm only going to coach you until you can beat me, you know. . . ." They both smiled.

If only she could open up to the girl, if only she could tell her. "I know what you're going through, Shayna. I had a stubborn, difficult father, too. I had to live a secret, too, a different secret, but it closed me off from the rest of the world, just as you're kept isolated in your room."

But she couldn't. Shayna was her patient. Shayna didn't need true confessions from Marty, she needed help and care—more help and more care than her father was willing to let her have. It was important to maintain a professional position. It was never a good idea to get too emotionally involved with your patients. But sometimes she just couldn't help it.

Marty always hated to leave Shayna; she always felt she hadn't done enough. But—consulting her watch—if she didn't hurry, she'd be late for her staff meeting. This morning, Dr. Zee was coming by to talk to the staff about handling crack cocaine patients, of which they had too many.

"So," Marty said. "I'll call you after I see if there's time for a bridge lesson."

"If there isn't, not to worry, Marty. I taught Mama. I'll make her practice with me." Again they smiled at each other, and this time Marty continued on her way.

The neighborhood was an early rising one. As she came to the last two shop doors on the block, she could smell frying peppers and marinara sauce already. The first door was Proto's Apizza, and next to it, the hospital's favorite hangout, Protozoa. Originally it had been Proto's Italian Ristorante; then some wiseguy doctor had called it Protozoa, and now there was the nickname, spelled out in neon. Inside, there was everything a tired doctor or nurse could want after work: dim lights, a huge polished bar, music, and many booths. You could relax over a drink, meet someone, hide from someone, if that's what you needed.

Aldo Protozone, one of the two brother-owners, was out front, sweeping the sidewalk.

"Yo, Doc! Loretta, she dropped!"

"Congratulations! It won't be long now!"

"I can't wait to see my son! My girls, I love them, but a man needs a son, know what I'm sayin'?" She gave him a wave and kept walking. She had tried—they had all tried—to convince him that boy babies didn't get born just because Papa wanted a son. He couldn't be budged. He did have a fifty percent chance of being right. And he wasn't going to throw it against the wall if it turned out to be another girl.

Unfortunately, not all the men who turned up with their pregnant wives and girlfriends were quite that reasonable. Violence was never far from the surface at the clinics. Marty always had to hope that someone young and strong, preferably male and *large*, would be around to wrestle with crazed patients who might have weapons, or worse, might have AIDS. Administration kept promising more security for the clinics, but another burly uniformed guard with a gun was not what Marty wanted. What they really needed, she told herself for about the millionth time, was a first-class Crisis Intervention Officer, preferably a nurse, maybe a Nurse Clinical Specialist in Psychology. But there was no money in the budget for a new job line.

Across the street, All Souls Women's Hospital loomed over the scene in all its Victorian brick splendor. This corner was peculiar—the crossing of Van Dam Avenue, Riverbank Drive, and a strange little alleyway called Hamilton Place, with nothing on it except the entrance to the clinics and, on the other side, the blank brick side of the buildings on Van Dam. The hospital sat in solitary splendor in the middle of this isosceles triangle, a grassy island in the middle of the traffic.

All Souls Women's Hospital looked like a church. In fact, it had been built in the 1830s at the height of the popularity of the

Gothic Revival style. The front entrance, up a shallow flight of steps, was a set of heavy wood doors in the shape of a Gothic arch, set back into an ornately carved stone surround, the name chiseled for eternity into the granite amidst the quatrefoils and trefoils.

The entrance to the clinics, around the corner, was less imposing, consisting of glass doors within a frame of glass brick. Community Care Clinics had been put into a modest, one-story addition, known as the New Wing, though it was neither a wing nor new. In fact, the facilities were sadly out of date.

When she had finally gotten funding and the hospital administration agreed to give the nurse-run clinics a try, COMMUNITY CARE CLINICS had been painted in large gilt letters on a blackboard and nailed, "temporarily," above the double glass doors. That was four years ago; and, like all the makeshift temporary measures at All Souls, it had become permanent. The staff almost never used that entrance, preferring the shortcut through the main lobby, which brought them out in the back, with the food machines, cartons of overflow paperwork, and a couple of ancient orange plastic chairs.

She paused at the busy, three-part intersection. Every time she came to work it struck her again how the five-way traffic lights—go, stop, wait, turn left, turn right—seemed symbolic of medical decisions: *sort of, maybe, wait and see, no*, and every once in a while, *yes*.

At last the signal blinked WALK, and she crossed to where, marching listlessly up and down in front of the building, a few Life Saviors were praying aloud, hoisting their LIFE ABOVE ALL placards. They were always in front of the hospital, doing their right-to-life thing, although only half a dozen of them had showed up this hot and muggy morning, three of her patients among them. And a new guy . . . at least she thought he was new; she'd never noticed him before. Nice-looking, young, short blond hair, neatly dressed. There were always a lot of men protesting abortion; she supposed with them it was religion or politics. It was the women marchers she didn't get. Especially since several of the regulars had *had* abortions.

At least, she thought gratefully, they could no longer protest in front of the clinic entrance. There wasn't enough room. The law said they had to stay fifty feet from the sidewalk, and Hamilton Place wasn't quite thirty feet wide.

And there was another familiar figure—Rabbi Ezekiel Brown himself, Shayna's father. He always showed up at least once during the day, often with women from his congregation bearing homemade cookies and jars of fruit punch for the demonstrators. He never actually marched or picked up a sign, nor did any of the Survivors.

As soon as he saw her, the rabbi gave Marty a big hello, gesturing that she should come talk with him. "So, Marty." He grinned at her. He was one of the most utterly self-confident people Marty had ever known. He met your eyes and kept your gaze, and he had no little tics, like most mortals, no throat-clearings or foot-tappings or eyebrow-raisings.

"So, Rabbi. Here again, giving aid and comfort."

"Isn't the rest of that phrase 'to the enemy,' Marty? Surely, you don't consider *me* your enemy . . . or any of these well-meaning people, for that matter."

"I know. They're all salt of the earth and highly moral. . . ."

"Right. And I am here to give them moral support."

They were just about the same height, so she was looking directly into his surprising pale gray eyes. Surprising because he was so dark, with olive skin and thick black hair.

"Really? I thought you were here just in case Channel 12 showed up." She smiled to show she was just kidding; but she wasn't. The rabbi loved being in the spotlight.

"Oh that would be good, too," he admitted. "My father, may he rest in peace, always said take whatever pulpit God offers, and for the Almighty's sake, don't be shy."

"Your father said that?" Marty had seen Zeke Brown's father, Rabbi Shalom Brown, a few times. He had been a tiny white-bearded man who never spoke above a whisper.

The rabbi laughed. "More or less. Actually, he didn't say that, *I* said that. He was such a passive man, so forbearing and quiet . . . I'm told I take after my sainted grandfather, may his name be blessed, the founder of our little group. *He*, I understand, was not averse to putting himself forward. When I was growing up, Marty, I found myself feeling ashamed of my father. *Ashamed*. That's a terrible thing. He was a good man, a saintly man, certainly not a father to be ashamed of. But when the Orthodox rabbis refused to acknowledge us, and then the Conservative movement turned us away . . . when we became the outlaws of Judaism . . ." Here, his voice rose and took on that singsong tone, like a chant, which Marty always thought of as his Rabbi Voice. ". . . it killed him. It destroyed him. He didn't have the courage of his convictions. I watched him wither away, his heart broken. What he *should* have done is defied them, said to hell with them and their rules—"

"Which is what *you* did," Marty supplied. She'd heard this story several times.

"Which is what *I* did. I said to hell with mainstream Judaism. If they won't have us, we won't have them. But why am I telling you all this?" A bark of laughter. "You know us."

She didn't think so. She knew the rabbi—sort of—and Shayna and Miriam, pretty well. But she understood practically none of the Survivors' rules and regulations. Rabbi Brown's congregation of 250 families was directly descended from a group of thirteen Holocaust survivors. When she had first heard the story of the founding of the Survivors, from the rabbi, she had blurted out, "Thirteen? Really? Like the Last Supper?" Abashed, she had covered her mouth. But Zeke just put his head back and laughed.

"Do you know, I hadn't thought of that? But it's wonderful! Maybe thirteen is the Lord's number! Maybe I should make a bet on thirteen!"

She had been shocked, back then, to hear such talk from a rabbi. He found *that* funny, too. "Don't be fooled by our Orthodox trappings," he had told her. "We're very open and modern, in certain ways."

In certain ways they were, although all the open-and-modern stuff seemed the province of the men only. Their women were always covered, up to the neck, down to the wrist, and below the knee, even in a heat wave. Zeke Brown, on the other hand, wore pretty much what he pleased. Today, he was in chinos and a T-shirt. Only the small circle of velvet held on the back of his sleek hair with bobby pins indicated his religion. It was apparently too hot for his blue and white satin athletic jacket embroidered with *Rabbi Zeke*, in gold.

"Ah, and here come the ladies with iced tea. Will you stop and have a drink with me?"

"Oh, I couldn't, not with a married man." This made him laugh, too, more heartily than the small joke was worth, she thought. She gave him a smile and started up the walk with a purposeful stride. A childhood spent as often as possible at the movies had taught her that a good exit was worth a thousand lines.

Gilbert the guard gave her a big hello at the entrance. "Hey, congratulations are in order, I hear. That's great, Ms. Lamb, that's just great!"

What? "Congratulations?"

"Jeez. I thought for sure you knew. Maybe I spoiled the surprise."

"Well, you may as well tell me, now that you've let the cat out of the bag."

"You're on the Executive Committee."

She couldn't keep the pleased smile from spreading all over her face. So she'd made it. Finally! A chance to make a real difference at All Souls, to sit with the real power and make real decisions. *Yes!*

"I am, hey? Well, thank you, Gilbert. Thank you!"

She sailed on into the high-ceilinged entry, for a change not averting her eyes from the huge mirrors with their carved gilt frames that were set into every wall. She hated the damn things; she'd suggested a million times that they be taken away. But they were original to the building, and someone in Administration liked them. So the mirrors stayed, reflecting everything and everyone and each other, over and over again, into infinity. Usually, she found it rather creepy. But today, who cared? She was now a member of the Executive Committee! Gilbert had said so, and Gilbert always knew everything. So she knew it was true!

Past the mirrors she went, past the elevators, ignoring the signs that said COMMUNITY CARE CLINICS USE ENTRANCE ON HAMILTON PLACE, through the double swinging doors that said NO ADMITTANCE, and ta-*dah*! She was energized, she was full of life, she was on the Executive Committee, and tomorrow the world! Past the food machines she went, past the cartons, down the back hall, humming a happy little tune—not aloud; she was among the singing-impaired. She danced into her office.

Two gray hospital envelopes were waiting on her desk. One was from the Office of Hospital Affairs, her name emblazoned on the front, with all her degrees—R.N., N.P., M.Sc., Ph.D.— so she knew what *that* was. The other was blank. Another cartoon from Joel? But first things first. She ripped open the official envelope and there it was, just as Gilbert had said it would be: "I am pleased to invite you to join us as a member of the Executive Committee," and so on, signed in Dr. Messinger's neat round schoolboy script.

She opened the second envelope as she walked to the air conditioner to turn it on. The room was stifling. And then she stopped stock-still, staring at the single page. It was a Xerox copy of an old lurid pulp-magazine cover: a crude drawing, everything exaggerated. A woman was being strangled by a madman. You could see he was insane by the bulging eyes and the slavering mouth. The woman's mouth was wide open in a scream. And she was a nurse, wide-winged cap still on her head, starched white dress unbuttoned just enough to show cleavage.

Oh Christ. She couldn't move, couldn't really breathe. Only one person in this hospital knew her past—Dr. Zee—and Julia Zachary-Felsen was more than a colleague, she was a friend. They were close friends, in spite of the thirty-year difference in their ages. Dr. Zee knew everything about her . . . well, almost everything. But Dr. Zee could never have even *thought* of this nastiness. Then *who*? Marty had never told anyone about her marriage; it just invited their unwanted questions and her uncomfortable evasions. Anyway, it was no one's business!

Apparently, someone felt differently, someone who *wanted* her heart to pound and her mouth to go dry. Someone who seemed determined to undermine every nurse in CCC.

She had to get to her meeting. She had to put this thing right out of her mind; but the primitive drawing was indelibly imprinted on her brain. Who in this place had found out about Owen? And how? How could anyone know that one horrible evening, eight years ago, her husband had tried to choke her to death? She had never pressed charges, had never even called the police, had actually managed to put it behind her. Owen was a sick man, a psychotic; he couldn't help it. She'd known for months before it happened, but hid her knowledge, covering for him, keeping it her own terrifying secret. That night, she realized the charade had to end. And she'd had him admitted to the hospital where she was working—as a psychiatric nurse, wasn't that a scream?

Clutching the page, she licked her lips and told herself to calm down. It wasn't important, the person who did this was sick. Quickly, she folded the photocopy and shoved it deep into her handbag. Why was she saving the horrid thing? Who in the world would she ever show it to? She should rip it up and flush it down the toilet. But what was the use of *that*? she thought mournfully. The loathsome message had already brought it all back. . . .

3

She heard about Owen Lamb long before she met him. He was eccentric. He was a character. He was a hoot. He was terribly fey, but it was all part of his charm. She was bound to meet him, sooner or later, since he was part of the loosely organized group of young people in Middletown, Connecticut, who laughed at each other's jokes, threw parties for each other, and called themselves the Crowd. The Crowd was a mix of academics, advertising people, and doctors. "Oh, and an occasional nurse, too," Joel Mannes told her. "As long as she's cute and redheaded and knows she's not nearly as good as a doctor. *Just kidding!*"

It was 1983, and she and Joel were new friends. They worked together at Middletown Mental Hospital. He'd been there for three years and she was new, he was a doctor and she a rookie nurse, but already they were good buddies. They were both ready to laugh at anything and everything. There wasn't even a hint of a romance there because Joel was a newlywed and she was still carrying a torch bigger than the Ritz, as she had informed him.

"Not to worry," he'd said. "We'll get you back in the swing of things. We know lots of guys." Actually, it was Alice, his wife, who first suggested Owen Lamb. "He has everything a girl could want. He's a professor, he's cute, and very, very rich." Alice rolled her big brown eyes and laughed.

"Rich or poor, it's nice to have money," Joel added. "But maybe Alice is on to something, Marty. Owen's not a professor yet, my darling Alice, but neither is he your usual Wesleyan English teacher. He's famous for leaping up on his desk to declaim, or wrapping himself in a silk shawl and acting out one of Elizabeth Barrett Browning's lovesick sonnets. He also cuts his own classes—often without rhyme or reason, excuse the pun," Joel said. "The students, of course, think he's really cool. So you can understand why Owen Lamb's classes are always the first to fill up at registration. I think they love him because he's more of a kid than any of them. If a professor never has to grow up, maybe *they* don't have to, either. I can see the appeal."

"Never mind that," Alice teased. "Owen's really cute, Marty, with golden curls down to his shoulders, and he rides around on a big black Harley-Davidson hawg."

"My dreamboat!" Marty laughed, but she was shaking her head as she spoke. She knew that Alice and Joel meant well and, actually, this Owen Lamb sounded . . . what? Intriguing, maybe. But she was nursing a broken heart, and even the thought of going out on a date, or trying to make conversation with someone she didn't know . . . It was just too much for her. "Maybe after I settle in more," she said.

But it happened anyway, at one of the parties. It was given by one of the young doctors, with a wife from New York who was determined to make a salon out of their cheap rental apartment. She never served enough nibbles, but plenty of alcohol, so that most of the guests left smashed, convinced they'd had a wonderful time.

"And this is Owen Lamb. Owen, Marty Dauber, psychiatric nurse. Owen's an English professor at Wesleyan and an eligible bachelor. Quick, grab him before you end up with, God forbid, a doctor!" their hostess burbled and moved on.

He was just as Alice had described him, except he was more than cute. He was really handsome in a movie-star way, and he was looking at Marty as if he'd like to eat her: dazzled, delighted, enamored. She was flattered.

"You're beautiful, do you realize that? You look like . . . a medieval maiden . . . like the French Lieutenant's Woman. All that wavy red hair . . ."

Well, it was the era of hair, and she had let hers grow until she could sit on it. At work it was primly rolled up, but for parties she let it down, and it curled down her back and around her face. She knew it was attractive, but Owen was positively fascinated. That night, he kept touching it. And later, after they had started to date, he always had his hands in her hair, smoothing it or braiding it, twisting it, curling it around one finger. It could get annoying. Once, she pulled away and said sharply, "What *is* it with you, Owen, didn't they let you play with dolls?" His face fell and he looked so hurt that she quickly added, "I was just kidding, Owen, honest, just kidding." She even found herself saying, "I *like* when you fuss with my hair."

He was that way about everything. Very intense, very wired. But he was so obviously smitten; maybe that was why he held her hand too long, why he couldn't seem to take his eyes off her, why he needed to see her every day, all the time, if not for dinner, lunch; if not for lunch, how about breakfast? It was like being swept along by a hurricane. Owen Lamb was like an act of God, single-minded and tireless. And, she *was* on the rebound. It was balm for her bruised spirit, to be so desperately *wanted*.

His devotion did have its charm. Once, dozens of roses were delivered to her little studio apartment, filling the entire dining area. Young men in tuxes or costume appeared at the nursing station, with a message to sing to Miss Dauber. Another time, the entire tape of her answering machine was filled with Owen's voice reading love poem after love poem.

In the end she found herself melting. He was pretty irresistible. She'd never known anyone like him, never. He was like . . . she didn't know what he was like, but he made her giggle and he made her feel so lovable. They began to date regularly. They danced in the moonlight on the Wesleyan lawn with bottles of champagne waiting nearby in a cooler. He took her on his motorcycle to the deserted beach at Hammonasset at dawn with a packed picnic basket. A dinner date might mean a pizza joint, a hotel in Newport, or Chanterelle in New York. He changed his classes, or cut them, so he could be with her, no matter what shift she happened to be working.

He was so fevered, she hardly knew what to do with him. But when she tried to tell any of her girlfriends how uneasy it made her sometimes, they all swooned and said, "Are you nuts, Marty? You think this is *awful*? God, I'd give my right arm to have some guy come after me that way."

There was something of the fairy tale about his courtship, simple and pure, the stuff of teenage fantasies. And that's exactly what appealed to her so mightily, she realized at one point, the unsullied romance she'd never had as a teenager.

He even asked her if he might kiss her, the first time. No man—no boy, either—had ever *asked*. "Yes," she said. "Yes, of course you can kiss me." She braced herself; she was so afraid it would turn her off. It was sweet and gentle, but it never heated up; he didn't push his loins into hers, his hands did not roam.

When he finally pulled away and said, "I'm in love with you, Marty," she was astonished.

Two months went by, and still he hadn't dragged her to bed. He hadn't even asked. So one night, while they were necking on the couch in her little apartment, she said to him, "Look, Owen, we can sit here and hug and kiss. Or we can go to bed."

They went to bed. It was slow and sweet and gentle, almost shy. His eyes were tightly closed and he constantly whispered words she couldn't make out. She was not sure when he came, because he made no sound, but he held her all night long. If she turned to her other side, he turned with her. It was so loving, her eyes filled with tears.

Still, she sometimes wondered what was wrong because it wasn't like . . . Oh, forget it! she told herself a hundred times. That part of her life was over, gone forever! Obviously, it hadn't meant much to begin with. She had thought that other kind of lovemaking was true love. He'd been randy and wild, pulling her into a closet sometimes in the hospital; once, they did it in an empty examining room where they were nearly caught. Or, if they had to wait too long, he would take her standing up, the minute they got to the apartment, right against the door. As soon as it had closed, they'd be grabbing each other, their open-mouthed kisses avid. She always had bruises from where he dug his fingers into her soft flesh, where he bit and sucked at her.

Maybe there was something wrong with *that*. What did she know? Maybe every man didn't roar with pleasure as he came, his buttocks pulsating, sweat covering his chest and back, his lips pulled back tightly against his teeth. Maybe Owen was the normal one with his silent, intense orgasms, followed by deep sighs of satisfaction, soft kisses all over her face and neck, and fervent declarations of love eternal. Maybe *this* was the way it was supposed to be, she told herself.

One day one of the patients, someone she'd grown fond of, a woman her own age, managed to sneak a razor blade into her shoe and slit her wrists in the shower. Just before the end of the shift, the word came down. She had died. Marty was distraught; the girl had a borderline personality disorder, and she cut herself from time to time, little cuts to ease the psychic pain. She didn't seem to be suicidal. Had the patient really managed to fool them all? Or, Marty wondered, had she allowed her feelings to get in the way of her judgment? Had she relaxed her guard? Was this suicide *her* fault?

That night, she couldn't sleep. Her mind kept circling around the terrible thing that had happened. If she were in any way to blame . . . She sat bolt upright in bed, shivering. She had to talk to somebody. She called Joel, but Alice answered and said he was sound asleep. "You want to leave a message?" she whispered, and Marty just couldn't say "Wake him up, I need him." Alice was nice, she was a friend, but there was a limit.

So Marty called Owen, she was never sure why, except that she knew he would come. And he did. He made her tea and then he loosened her hair from the French knot and began to brush it while she sat in a chair, weeping silently. Brushing and brushing and brushing until her tense muscles began to relax and her heavy eyelids started to close. Just for a minute, she told herself, just for a second. And the next thing she knew, she was being kissed awake by Owen, who was still fully dressed. She could see the blond stubble on his jaw by the morning light that poured in the window. After carrying her to her bed, he'd sat vigil over her all night long. "To make sure you didn't wake up and find yourself all alone."

Such tenderness touched her. Without thinking about it, she lifted her arms and drew him down, close to her, and kissed him with passion. He pulled her closer, wrapping his arms around her and then his legs. She could feel him getting hard.

"Owen," she whispered into his ear, "you're so good to me."

"I am good, aren't I, Marty? Because I love you so much."

"Yes," she said, surprised because he was breathing very fast, his eyes were wide-open, and he was reaching down, pushing the pj bottoms off her hips, two fingers shoving into her, hard. She gave a grunt of surprise and excitement because this time he wasn't neat and sweet. He pushed his jeans down to his thighs and put his fist around a cock stiff and purple with engorged blood, holding it out like an offering. It looked huge. And then he pushed into her, pulled her legs up onto his shoulders and began a rhythmic, relentless thrusting that kept accelerating, her heartbeat keeping time with it. He came in a rush, throwing his head back. Marty looked up at him, Owen still on his knees, breathing very hard. Her heart was pounding from her own orgasm and she wanted him to open his eyes and *look* at her.

He shook his head from side to side. "No, dammit," he cried. "I won't! I can't!"

She stared at him. "Owen! What is it?"

He opened his eyes and stared at her. She thought for a split second that he was surprised to see her. An instant later he said. "My . . . my back seizes up on me sometimes. That's why I'm so careful when we make love. But not this time. I won't let it! I won't!"

Was that all! A wave of sheer relief ran through her. "My poor darling," she said tenderly. "Come lie down next to me and I'll rub your back." There was nothing wrong with him, just a bad back, and nothing wrong with her, either. He really did want her. Everything had changed.

"You *have* to marry me, Marty. I love you. You *have* to marry me." He always said that. But this time she said yes.

They had a beautiful wedding, on a gray and dismal Valentine's Day. In his usual extravagant way, Owen had hired the Opera House, the whole place, complete with kitchen and serving staff. He'd had it filled with white roses, every rose in Middletown, he announced proudly, as well as in Haddam, Higganum, Killingworth, Hartford, and New Haven. She sipped champagne and danced with everyone, and sipped champagne and danced with Owen, and sipped champagne and posed for photographs and sipped champagne. Everybody they knew came, and everybody said what a stunning couple they made, what a smashing party it was, what a wonderful beginning to their new life together. And it was. It *was*. She was married to a man who thought she was the most wonderful woman God had ever created. He told her so, all the time. He loved her. He wanted to give her everything, and he had the money to do it. They took a honeymoon trip to Italy, and when they came back, there was a house waiting for them, filled with beautiful things. His parents had bought the place for them, as a wedding gift. And yet—this always surprised her—his mother and father did not intrude upon them. They kept their distance. It was quite ideal. What a lucky girl she was!

Owen left their bed almost every night. She knew because she would wake up, aware of his absence, and her heart would begin to speed up. On his nighttime excursions, he would go downstairs, into the kitchen. But she could always hear his voice. Who was he talking to, in the middle of the night, in their kitchen? Once or twice, when she heard him shout, loud and excited, she jumped out of bed, running down the stairs, calling his name. There was always an explanation. He had stubbed his toe, or a cupboard door had slammed on his hand when he reached for a glass. But she knew that wasn't it. Didn't she? She knew and yet refused to know.

One night, it was around Christmas—she remembered that because she'd hidden herself in the dark living room behind the huge, decorated tree, watching everything blink in and out of sight with the lights—she listened, filled with fear, as Owen, agitated, yelling, arguing, pleaded for mercy. All she had to do was move a few inches and she could look into the kitchen and see for herself that Owen was all alone. That he was pleading and begging with absolutely nobody. She could not move that foot. She stood behind the tree, holding her breath and squinching her eyes tightly shut, telling herself it was not what she knew it was. And then she tiptoed back to bed. He didn't come back to bed that night. She knew, because she didn't sleep, either, just lay in the dark with her eyes wide open, trying not to think, waiting.

It escalated quickly after that. When she came home from work, she often found him staring at nothing, his lips moving. Once or twice she found him curled into a ball, cowering in the corner of the laundry room, whimpering like a child.

One terrible day, she let herself in and nearly tripped over a pile of trash in the middle of the entrance hall. A moment later Owen came in carrying two large plastic garbage bags. When he saw her he grinned, came to her and gave her a kiss. "Here, help me with this stuff, would you?"

"What *is* this, Owen?" She was chilled.

"All our radios and TVs."

"How did they all get smashed?"

He was very pleased with himself. "*I* did it."

She bent to help get the pieces into the plastic sacks. She didn't want to look at him. "Why, Owen? Why did you smash the televisions?"

"The radios, too, Marty."

"Why did you do it?" She had to stay very calm, she realized. She must not show the least little bit of panic.

He looked all around, making sure nobody was spying. "Somebody wired all of them to read my thoughts. I had to get rid of them." He looked around again and lowered his voice to a whisper. "And I think the fluorescent lights in the kitchen, too."

She swallowed, painfully. "The lights in the kitchen are reading your mind, Owen? Is that what you think?"

His voice became sharp. "It's what I *know*, Marty."

She should have done something right then. But then, he went back to being his old charming self, coming home with a kitten, or a group of his students and a stack of pizzas. Surprising her with a diamond bracelet or a weekend in Aruba. And, a week after he had destroyed them, he replaced all the radios and television sets. "Oh yes," she would agree with their friends, "life with Owen is one surprise after another. I never know quite what I'll find when I come home."

On the night that everything changed, she had found the front door locked. That was a surprise. Owen was very careless about such things. She let herself in with her key, and, thinking he might have gone away for the day, looked for a message on the hall table. Out of nowhere, he'd lunged at her, his hands curling around her throat, pulling her down to the floor, where he knelt over her, his teeth bared. She hadn't realized how strong he was. He was so slender, almost frail-looking, and always so gentle with her.

At first she thought it must be a grotesque joke. But looking into his crazed, dazed eyes, she began to fight back. Desperate, panting, she'd scrabbled around on the floor with her hands, finally found a metal doorstop, an antique in the shape of a house. She grabbed it and slammed it against his head. His hands loosened from her throat and he fell back with a crash. She'd knocked him out. She could hardly breathe, from shock, from fright, and from the pressure of his angry hands choking her. Tears were streaming down her face, and her nose was running as she freed one trapped leg and scrambled to her feet.

She looked down at him. Oh Christ! She'd just had to knock unconscious the man she had promised to love, honor, and cherish only months before. There he lay, his mouth open, a line of saliva slipping down his chin. And blood! Blood seeping from a wound in his head. The man who loved her so desperately, he had sworn to kill himself if she wouldn't have him . . . and he had just tried to choke her to death. She was sobbing as she dialed the hospital to ask for an ambulance. His eyes had rolled back and she was terrified that she had killed him, and then instantly wished that she had. That was the worst shock of all.

As soon as Owen was safe in a bed in the hospital, Marty grabbed a cab and went home. Her hands were shaking uncontrollably but her mind was empty and calm. She felt emotionally frozen. She had to tell his parents, that's all she knew. She tried three different residences until she found them—in their thirteen-room cottage in Palm Beach, California.

She spoke to Owen's mother, Beatrice. Of course. She could

count on the fingers of one hand the number of times she'd even *seen* the man Owen referred to as "the pater." The pater! Really warm and intimate! Beatrice listened without comment until Marty finished her recitation. Then she spoke.

"Middletown Mental? That dreadful place? Oh, no, my dear, not there, not for Owen!" In fact, it wasn't a dreadful place, and furthermore, Marty worked there, but she didn't argue.

Marty realized, with a shiver, that her mother-in-law was not at all surprised by her news. So Beatrice had known that Owen's "little quirks," as she liked to call them, were far more serious than that. The self-serving bitch! She'd just been looking for a way to have someone else be responsible. I must have looked like manna from heaven, Marty thought, on the verge of hysterical laughter—while Beatrice Lamb's voice went on and on—a *nurse* to take care of Beatrice's little problem child!

". . . not a good place for him, Marta, as I'm sure you'll agree." She forced herself to focus on her mother-in-law's voice.

"Just what do you suggest, Beatrice? An associate professor's salary, even added to mine, won't *begin* to pay for a private hospital."

"Oh, my dear Marta, not to worry! We will pay. Of course we will pay. I couldn't expect you to—no, no, you needn't worry about the cost. He can go to the Mansion, it's not far from Middletown. And then you can visit him just as often as you like."

Marty had heard of the Mansion, above the Connecticut River, in the hamlet of Cold River. The Mansion, with its discreet bronze marker out near the entrance drive, its discreet and intricate iron gates, its discreet entrance in the exact middle of the gray stone edifice. No one would ever guess this elegant home was a hospital for the insane. Not until they noticed that every door had a strong lock, every window strong iron bars, and every corridor several attendants. The cost of a short stay at the Mansion would pay the national debt of a small African nation.

"Well, of course. The Mansion is quite wonderful, but I understand their waiting list is two years long."

"Oh, not to worry, my dear. They . . . we've . . . dealt with the Mansion before. Perhaps Mr. Lamb sits on the board of trustees . . . I never can remember. He sits on so many."

Mr. Lamb might or might not sit on the board, but Marty was now certain of one thing: Owen had already spent some time at the Mansion. And they hadn't had the kindness to tell her, not even a little hint. But how could they have? She might not have taken him off their hands!

Well, they could just go to hell, she had thought, furious. "That's very generous of you, Beatrice. I'll tell them at the hospital that Owen is back in his parents' care and you'll be arranging for his transfer." And before his mother could say another word, she had hung up. Then she began to cry.

Now Marty roused herself. Dwelling on the past was not her way. And this was *very* far in the past. She'd seen Owen very little in the eight years since he went into the hospital, and on those occasions, he was generally not quite in his right mind. He was no longer part of her life. In any case, it was time to get upstairs to her meeting, in the bubble on the Family Practice unit. She'd tell the staff the good news, that she'd be part of the allocation of money decisions from now on. Hear what Dr. Zee had to say about the growing number of ill drug addicts and especially their sick babies. Take reports on any clinic patients who'd been put into hospital beds. And then she'd go to Security and tell them about these letters. No, she wouldn't. She'd wait and see. She would bury that horrid picture somewhere in her files where nobody would ever be able to find it. Maybe there wouldn't be any more hate mail; maybe this was the end of it. She could always hope.

4

The first person Marty saw as she got off the elevator on the fourth floor was Norma McClure, head nurse in the Family Practice clinic. Instead of heading to the nursing station for the meeting, Norma was bustling down the hall, hot on the heels of Doug Lavoro, Mason Pharmaceutical's slick, good-looking drug rep, who reputedly had laid half the nurses in the hospital over the years. Doug must be in his late forties by now, Marty thought, and had begun dyeing his wavy iron-gray hair. She found it pathetic, especially because the color came out a brassy, unreal red. But the younger nurses twittered like little birds whenever he was around. Maybe his reputation *was* deserved! In any case, this morning he was laying on a big breakfast spread for the pediatricians—his company had a new baby antibiotic on the market. So he'd be there, handing out brochures and free samples, along with the bagels, Danish, and muffins. And that reminded her: she hadn't even had coffee yet.

"Norma!" Norma didn't pause in her chase after free breakfast. She was such a wispy little thing, you'd never guess how much food she could cram into her greedy maw. Marty had seen Norma at these drug company things. She'd circle the table like a bird of prey, thrilled at the idea of all those freebies. And she was not shy about stuffing a shopping bag with samples, either.

Doug Lavoro was walking very fast; doubtless he was trying to outpace her. Fat chance. Norma on the scent of something-for-nothing was an unstoppable Norma.

Marty caught up with her, putting a hand on her shoulder. "Come on, Norma," she said. "We'll be late to the meeting."

"Meeting? Oh. Sure, Marty. As soon as I get some goodies for my girls."

"We'll give them our leftovers."

"Huh! You people never leave over *anything*."

Marty hid a smile. "Well, as long as you're chasing Doug, could you get me a bagel and some coffee?"

Norma was annoyed but she nodded. What else could she do, except give up the chase? She stomped away with a toss of her head.

Marty headed down the hallway. It was a mystery to her how people could come into any unit in the hospital and ask, "Where's the nursing station?" It was always in plain sight, where all the people were, where all the action was, with a loud buzz of mingled conversations above the wide counter. The Family Practice station was no different. Right now, three nurses and two doctors conferred behind the counter, and two residents in their dove-gray scrubs leaned over the front. She hoped that one or two of them would be interested in helping out with the abortions. It was getting to be a dangerous occupation, and some of the older doctors shied away from it.

At the station, she stopped, holding her hand out for last night's reports. She had two patients up here. One was Aldo Protozone's mother-in-law, who often had "palpitations." The tests had never showed a thing, but she insisted on them anyway. When the meeting was over, Marty figured she'd drop by and take a look at the chart. And then there was Susanna Feldman, from Rabbi Brown's congregation. Fifteen years old and a lump in her breast. The biopsy report was attached. Shit. It was not benign, just as Dr. Zee had figured. Old Mrs. D'Amico could wait; it was more important to see Susanna. When the meeting was over, she'd run over and see how the girl was doing and learn how much she had been told. They'd have to find a female surgeon, probably from Harmony Hill.

Marty gave a wave to her crew in the bubble, the glass-walled inner sanctum where the floor nurses took their breaks, if any. This morning's meeting, called by Dr. Zee, was clinic head nurses only, and they were all there, stuffing their faces and talking a mile a minute. Virgie Nesbit, who was in charge of Ob/Gyn in the clinics, had pulled an emergency double shift in the Birthing Center last night. She looked as if she'd love to go to bed. Crystal Cole, head nurse-midwife, however, was bright-eyed and bushy-tailed; nothing seemed to faze her, not even staying up all night. How did she do it? Kenny Rankin and Emilio Chavez were having an argument, as usual. Isabelle was handing out the food and pouring the coffee. She was such a mama, which was probably why Marty was so fond of her. But hell, everybody got along with Isabelle, in spite of her feistiness. She didn't have an enemy in the world. Surely *she* would never get one of those poison pen letters. But, Marty reminded herself, she was not going to think about that particular problem right now. The floor nurses, of course, were nowhere to be seen. Their shift started at seven, and it was ten after. And Dr. Zee hadn't yet made it, so Marty knew she wasn't *too* late.

Crystal made intense faces at Marty through the bubble's glass wall and waved a piece of paper—something was up— but a first-year resident came up and just started talking to Marty. It was amazing; he'd only been a doctor for a few weeks, and already he thought the world would stop to listen to him.

"Yes, Doctor." She gave him a smile, even though she considered him a major pain—a regular Dr. Dimwit wannabe. Every time he worked at the clinics, you could hear his voice, whining about something. She'd asked Dr. Zee how in the world they'd ended up with him. Julia shrugged and said, "He looked good on paper and he interviewed well. You *never* know who is going to be the pain in the butt, Marty."

"I was on duty last night," the resident said, "and one of your patients was scheduled for an EKG, and your nurse on duty refused to take her up."

"Surely you didn't expect her to leave the patients."

"Him," the resident corrected. "And I was on call."

"Did my nurse explain why he refused?"

"Well . . . he said he didn't have the time, but he only had two patients."

"You'll find, I think, that even two patients need to be watched, Doctor. The hospital could get sued." He had the look of a man who hadn't had his entire say. "Yes?" she prodded.

"And he yelled at me because the last time I was in the clinics I left a few things. Said I should have put them in the dirty room. Isn't that *their* job? Nurses, I mean."

"Not these days," she said, keeping the pleasant smile—she hoped it was pleasant—on her face. "Not at *this* hospital. Nurses are professionals, too, Doctor, and I would suggest you try to remember that. Sorry, I really must get to my meeting." He didn't like her answer. Well, they were even; she didn't like his attitude.

Crystal was looking impatient behind the glass, so Marty hustled into the bubble. The door hadn't even closed behind her when everyone began to sing in a kind of ragged unison: "Congratulations to you, congratulations to you . . . !" to the tune of "Happy Birthday."

Virgie leaped up and kissed her, and then they all took turns, bussing her cheek and telling her how great it was that she was finally on the committee and how much she deserved it. She sat there, in a warm glow, gazing upon them, her motley crew—the closest thing she had to a family.

"Thank you, thank you. I richly deserve it." That got the laugh she had hoped for. "And I would like to say—"

"Excuse us, Marty, but there's another announcement we all think you should see." Crystal waved her piece of memo paper again. Then they all erupted into speech. "The nerve . . . !" "And we can't get enough bandages . . . !" "How can they even think . . ." "What's going on around here, anyway?"

"Hold it, hold it! At least show me what you're talking about."

The paper was pressed into her hand. For one heart-stopping moment she feared it was more hate mail. But of course it wasn't. It was a copy of an official memo to the medical staff from Dr. Milton Messinger. A purloined copy, she was sure.

"And how did we get this?" she asked, not really expecting an answer. Somebody had "liberated" it.

"Never mind, never mind." Emilio's face, as usual, was creased with concentration. "Just read it. Aloud would be good."

So she read aloud:

After long discussion at the last Medical Staff meeting, we have set into motion the following changes:

1. House staff will be required to put in only six hours per week at Family Center clinics.

2. Patients sent from Community Care Clinics to the hospital will not be admitted without examination by a physician.

3. Such examinations will be billed to Community Care Clinics at the rate of fifty dollars per hour, payable directly to the physician.

4. Attending physicians will have yearly vacations extended to three weeks with pay.

5. There will be additional support staff hired for the following units: Gynecology/Obstetrics, Pediatrics, Psychiatry . . .

She stopped reading. Additional support for the M.D.'s, and more vacation time, but the nurse-run clinic was suddenly

required to submit its patients to scrutiny by doctors! And then
pay them for the insult! Where were the nurses she needed so
badly? Last night was not the first time her people had been
forced into double shifts. A wave of anger swelled in her
throat, making it hard to breathe. Cutting back on the doctors'
clinic hours! Had Dr. Messinger ever seen the hundreds of
people who crowded into the clinic waiting rooms? Most
clinics were only open one or two days a week; and for poor
people, there was no other way they could get to see a doctor
or a nurse. But she knew the reason. The administration was
cutting back. *They're getting rid of everything that doesn't
make a profit. Me. Community Care Clinics. My clinics. Indi-
gent patients. All of the problems, all of the eyesores. So they
can sell the hospital.*

Community Care Clinics was separate and unequal in too
many ways, a little hospital for second-class patients. But
dammit, they were doing a fine job—a better job in some cases
than all the high and mighty M.D.'s upstairs with their expensive state-of-the-art machines.

"Those shits!" she said, with feeling. She sat down hard.
The other nurses in the bubble laughed and applauded. Much
good *that* was going to do! "Wasn't Dr. Zee there to stop this?"

"She was with a dying patient," Crystal said. They all were
careful not to look at each other. Dr. Zee helped a lot of people
in extremis to leave this vale of tears ... or so everyone
believed. It was one of those things that everyone "knew" but
didn't really know. Even Marty was not so sure.

"I guess when Dr. Zee didn't turn up at the staff meeting, the
rest of those bastards took advantage," Virgie said. "Men are
so vicious and self-serving." She patted her already-perfect
blond pageboy. Virgie was a fine nurse, very exact and effi-
cient; but she did tend to rearrange herself a great deal, forever
patting and smoothing and stroking herself into shape. She was
old-fashioned in a lot of ways, prim and even a bit prissy.

"The point is not how men are, Virginia," Emilio said.
"Even though you take every chance you get to badmouth us.
You wanna talk about sexual harassment? Nobody ever thinks
it could work the other way around! Well, dammit, I feel
harassed!"

Virgie glared at him but did not deign to answer. From the way they looked, Marty expected them both to stick out their tongues, like a couple of ten-year-olds.

"If you weren't a female, I'd show you what I mean. But seeing as you're female, I guess I gotta give you some respect."

"You don't 'gotta' do 'nuttin'.'" Virgie's imitation of his heavy Brooklyn accent was dead-on, and Emilio reddened. He had a short fuse and Virgie knew it.

"Okay, okay. Enough squabbling," Marty insisted. "The point is, can we do anything about this nasty new state of affairs? Our Medical Staff, as we are all aware, is holy. What they say, goes. But . . ." She paused, smiling at them. "Maybe now that I'm on the Executive Committee, we'll have a chance to be heard. I give you my solemn promise it won't be for lack of trying."

"We know how good you are, Marty," Kenny said. "We're just proud the guys upstairs finally got a clue."

She could feel herself blushing: the curse of the redhead. "Okay, people. It looks like Dr. Zee has been held up on rounds, so let's talk a few minutes about JCAHO before we go to work."

A loud groan went up. JCAHO: the dreaded Joint Commission for Accreditation of Health-related Organization. It sent its eagle-eyed scouts to every hospital in the city and state every couple of years, to see if they were up to snuff. The last time they had been here, three years ago, All Souls had been threatened with a loss of accreditation if it didn't shape up. No accreditation, no Medicare. No Medicare, no hospital. So promises had been made, tons of paper had left the hospital, with "Plans for the Renovation and Enlargement of the Birthing Center in the Family Care Center" . . . "An Outline for New Postoperative Techniques" . . . "A Blueprint for Medical Staff Reorganization" . . . "A Price List for New Plumbing" . . . a plan proving they could afford new machinery for fetal examination. Most of it was bullshit. There wasn't enough money to do anything but diddle; and so for months both buildings had been crawling with men in coveralls, diddling with the wiring or the pipes, or the plaster, or the tiles, accomplishing very goddamn little. It was the way you dealt with accreditation when you were running out of dough.

"I can't believe they're picking *now* to give the doctors more vacation time, for Christ's sake," Kenny complained. "And fifty bucks an hour to give examinations we can do just as well!"

"So what's going to happen when the committee people see that the Birthing Center is pretty much the way it was?" Crystal asked. "Didn't we promise it would be enlarged and given more toilet facilities? And let me tell you," she added, "we need the space. You know we're the only twenty-four-hour clinic around, and lately, people are trying to use us as an Emergency Room. I don't have the room and I don't have the staff to take patients in, even if they *are* hurting! Not unless they're having a baby."

Marty sighed. "I've sent a dozen memos, Crys, saying we really have to open another twenty-four-hour clinic—" She stopped as everyone in the bubble laughed. She was known to some people in the hospital as the Memo Queen. Well, she believed in putting ideas in writing. That way, people couldn't quote forget unquote. "Maybe now that I'm on the Executive Committee, magic will happen. And of course . . ." Her voice faded as she looked out into the hall and spotted Dr. Zee's cropped white head turning to talk to a man walking briskly beside her. They were headed for the nursing station. "But wait. Here comes Dr. Zee. I'll bet she's mad, too. You know the Medical Staff hates to buck her. Between the two of us, they just won't be able to get away with this garbage anymore—"

Marty broke off suddenly. The blood drained out of her head, leaving her dizzy. The person chatting with Dr. Zee was Paul Giordano. It couldn't be! But it was! Of course it was Paul! He hadn't changed a bit in ten years—except that the wavy black hair was now touched with gray. Paul Giordano, here, in his white coat, gesturing, talking, smiling, damn him, looking right at home! His eyes, the blue eyes she remembered so well—too damned well—met hers for the space of a heart-beat. But then something happened out in the hall and every head turned. Both Dr. Zee and Paul swerved abruptly and began trotting in the opposite direction, toward the elevators.

"Yo! Emergency!" Marty ran out of the bubble, out of the nursing station and down the hallway. She could hear footsteps pounding behind her. Norma, bearing an enormous tray heaped with food, was coming carefully toward her. The nurse stopped, bewildered, her head turning from side to side as people streamed by her. As she passed, Marty leaned over and grabbed a bagel from the top of the heap. "Thanks, Norma."

"Wait, Marty, what's—"

Too late; she didn't have time to answer. She ran to the stairs. She couldn't bear the thought of finding herself next to Paul in a crowded elevator. Paul! Here! Her thoughts were whirling. How could he *do* this, just appear, after what he had done to her? There had been a number of years—yes, even after she was married—when she saw him everywhere, years when she would run down the street, her pulse pounding, sure she had just spotted him—only to have the person's features shift as she came closer, to become someone else, a stranger. She had thought she'd *never* get over him.

She ran down the stairs, cramming pieces of bagel into her mouth, barely tasting it. For a brief moment she allowed herself to remember Cape Cod. They had been all alone because it was May, well before the season opened. They were making love on a blanket on the empty beach, naked in the milky sunshine, his hands in her hair, his mouth all over her. . . .

She stopped herself. She'd put all that away, where it would never hurt her again. Still, there it was, back again, as clear and vivid as if ten years hadn't passed. It hadn't been long after that magical weekend that Paul had left her. He hadn't said goodbye—just disappeared one day, leaving not a single trace. Today was the first time she'd seen him since then, and she didn't know if she could bear it. Well, she had to! She didn't have the time or the energy to ponder her long-ago, long-gone lover. What in hell was he doing here, at *her* hospital, with *her* Dr. Zee? And then, of course, she knew. Paul Giordano was the nice young doctor applying for a job in Family Practice.

Well, Dr. Zee had a lot of questions to answer, that was for sure. Not to mention Paul . . . but he was another story. Later, Marty promised herself. Later she'd deal with it all.

5

No one with normal hearing could miss the racket outside. It was like the roar of the surf, rising and falling. Marty stood on tiptoe, but she couldn't see a damn thing—except the van from Channel 12 and the reporter Ham Pierce, his blond curly head towering above everyone. At six-foot-six, Pierce could hardly be missed. Everyone had converged at the bottom of the brick walk, and there was no way to see through the throng.

Then she heard Dr. Zee's voice behind her. The elevator door had opened and heading toward her was Dr. Zee, with Paul Giordano right behind. He was smiling broadly, the bastard. He looked so great! Like a rocket, Marty zipped out the door, pretending she hadn't seen them, catching just a glimpse of Paul's smile as it swiftly faded, and willing her heartbeat to slow down.

Traffic had come to a standstill, and behind the general roar, car horns bleated, sounding frustrated. It certainly was sound-bite time. And there was the rabbi, cozying up to Pierce, looking ready to make trouble on the local news. She saw Clive Moses on the other side of the crowd, fighting his way forward, too, probably hoping to keep the hospital off television. Right! Like he had a chance!

She pushed through the thicket of curious onlookers, yelling "Medical personnel!" at the top of her voice until she got close enough to see what was going on. The Life Saviors had got ahold of one of the clinic's patients and were praying over her. The victim—or convert, depending on your point of view—was Jessie Trudeau, not even sixteen. Not to mention that the father of her baby was heavily into substance abuse. The very girl who should *not* be talked into having a baby. She should get rid of the fetus, get rid of the boyfriend, and try to have a life. And that had been the plan. So what had made the girl stop to listen to the Life Saviors? They couldn't have been more pleased with themselves. They were all smiling and talking a mile a minute. Ham Pierce's camera must be eating this all up, Marty thought with a groan.

As was Rabbi Brown, she noted. His pale eyes were shining with excitement and a little smile curled his lips. What was with the rabbi, encouraging these people to make trouble? All right, he was a bit of a fanatic, a right-to-lifer who always looked right into the eye of the camera to say how he would never even step on an ant if he could avoid it. All life was sacred, *all* life. All life was equal, but some life was more equal than others, Marty thought sourly. As far as she was concerned, he cared more about his imagined ant than he did about his daughter. Or his wife, for that matter. But since his entire family came to All Souls for their medical care, you'd think he might try to protect the hospital. He was an enigma.

Pushing her way through the thicket of bodies, Marty finally emerged at the front of the crowd. Now she could see that Jessie Trudeau was not quite the willing convert; in fact, she was struggling with the loving arms that held her, looking around wildly for a way to escape. As soon as she spotted Marty, she began hollering for her, "Mrs. Lamb! Mrs. Lamb! Get me outta here!" Were the cameras *still* running? Marty hoped so. She elbowed her way to the girl. The moment she appeared, looking official and angry, the Life Saviors released Jessie. The girl ran to Marty, grabbing her and holding on for dear life.

Marty turned to find herself facing a trio: Ham Pierce, Clive Moses, and Zeke Brown. And the camera, of course, held by Pierce's favorite camerawoman. Marty composed her face. Might as well look as intelligent as possible for the six o'clock news. "Excuse me, but aren't we witnessing a Class B misdemeanor here? Didn't you hear this young woman calling for help?"

"Now, Marty . . ." Clive Moses spread his hands.

"Don't Marty me, Mr. Moses. I'm sure people twenty blocks away heard Jessie yelling for someone to get her outta there! Would you care to explain why you ignored her pleas?"

Moses turned to the TV people. "Hold it!" he yelled. What did he mean, "Hold it"? *She* wasn't finished. She turned all the way around, to the sea of faces. "You heard this girl calling out, didn't you?" she shouted.

A voice called back, "Yo! She said someone help her!" There was a chorus of yeahs and right ons and a spatter of applause.

"You see, Clive? Other people heard her." She turned to the demonstrators, who had clumped up around them. "Jessie and I are going to leave here, so back off. *Now!*" she snapped when they didn't move. Reluctantly, the line of Life Saviors fell back, leaving a small space. Jessie, apparently feeling safe, began to talk a mile a minute. Since she was chewing gum and spoke very rapidly anyway, it was hard to understand her.

"Hold onto that thought, Jessie, and get rid of the gum, okay?" It was instantly swallowed. "I want you to tell it to Ham Pierce. Mr. Pierce . . . ?" She raised her voice.

He put on a big grin and came toward her, mike in hand.

"Mr. Pierce, this is Jessie Trudeau and she'd like to make a statement."

"Oh, it was awful! They grabbed me, they started talking so fast. They say I'm killing my baby! That I'm a murderer!" Jessie burst into nervous tears.

"They're doing something that's against the law, Jessie," Marty said, for the benefit of the six o'clock news. "And they're wrong. You're saving your own life." Marty turned to the newsman. "Are you aware, Mr. Pierce, that this child was being held against her will?"

"Child?"

"Jessie is fifteen. And we have enough babies having babies in this city, wouldn't you agree?" Without waiting for an answer, she went on. "In any case, Jessie has an appointment with me—"

"And you are . . . ?"

She looked right into the camera. "Marta Lamb, Nurse Practitioner, and the director of Community Care Clinics. I have been very patient about the constant demonstrations by the Life Saviors in front of our building, but if this sort of harassment of children continues, I shall have to consult the hospital attorneys." She took in a deep breath and added: "If you want to discuss anything more with this patient, why don't you interview her on her way out? Can't you see she's pregnant? We can't keep her out here in this heat . . ." and as she talked, she began to move. Arm around the girl's shoulders, Marty marched them across the grass toward Hamilton Place and the clinic entrance.

The Life Saviors did not touch them, but pressed close, walking along with them, shouting, "Don't kill your baby, miss! Please don't kill your baby!" Marty did not look their way and she hoped Jessie was also keeping her eyes straight ahead. But they were unable to make much headway in the crowd. This scene was just too good for anyone passing by to miss. As soon as one group drifted away, another curious cluster came crowding in.

And then up ran Rich Lionheart. Not exactly Charles Atlas, with his glasses and round baby face, but he was male, he was wearing a white coat, complete with stethoscope folded in the pocket. Even though someone called out, "There's the *real* killer!" the rest of them fell silent, made uneasy by the arrival of Medical Authority. As the demonstrators paused, not sure what to do next, Marty and Rich were able to whisk Jessie away.

Now the Life Saviors fell to their collective knees and started to pray aloud for God in heaven to show the wicked of the world the Way. Behind her, Marty could hear Clive Moses's rich voice going on and then the rabbi's impassioned tones. She couldn't be bothered to listen. She'd catch them both on the evening news, that she was sure of. When they got to the CCC entrance, someone opened the door for them and Marty let go of the girl, saying, "I'll be in by the time you're prepped, Jessie."

"No, that's okay, Mrs. Lamb. My mother's coming."

"Oh, I'm so glad she changed her mind."

"Yeah. So am I." Finally, a smile.

Marty watched Jessie turn the corner, then consulted her watch. God, was it only ten o'clock? Already she felt as if she had been going for a whole day; no, make that a whole *week*.

When she turned back to look, the crowd was breaking up and the Channel 12 van was pulling away from the curb. And there was Dr. Zee. Marty's heart speeded up as she scanned the heads nearby; but Paul seemed to have left. Crystal was making her way over to Dr. Zee. Marty had a thought: maybe they'd both like to come over to her place for some pizza later, and watch Ham Pierce's show to see what he had done with this spectacle.

She joined her friends. The other two said they were free tonight, and they all promised each other to give Ham Pierce hell if he twisted *this* story around. They were known as the Odd Trio or the Odd Triage—medical joke—and she supposed they *were* a rather strange group: the almost-elderly doctor who always wore pants, her white hair cut short; the tall, lanky redhead with her ponytail; and the gorgeous mocha-skinned black woman. It was hard to tell Crystal's age. Blacks seemed never to wrinkle. No zits, either. Marty sometimes mock-griped about this to Crystal, who found it funny. But once, she'd snapped. "Well, we gotta get *something* good to make up for all them troubles you white folks done put onto us for so long." The slave-talk bit was chilling; but a moment later Crystal was smiling, saying, "That was a *joke*, Marty!"

Crystal was a nurse-midwife, and a very good one, empathetic and laid-back. Usually. But she did have these lightning-flash changes of mood; and in private she often made derogatory comments about her patients. Crys was the first staff member Marty had hired when Community Care Clinics opened. Crystal had just left the Birthing Center at St. Francis Assisi, renowned throughout the city. At her interview she had explained that it was a great job but it was too far downtown, and here she could walk to work. To leave a prestigious teaching hospital for a small, unknown place that was always on the verge of closing? It seemed odd. However, St. Francis had given her a good recommendation; so why question a windfall? Just shut up and be grateful, Marty had told herself.

Dr. Zee was something else again. She'd taken Marty under her wing when Marty first came to All Souls, as a Family Practice floor nurse. She was twenty-seven at the time, still stunned from her ill-fated love affair and then the sudden end of her brief marriage: a double whammy of a particularly nasty sort. Since there was a jinx on her relationships, she figured, she

might as well get a master's degree and become a Clinical
Nurse Specialist or maybe a Nurse Practitioner—if she ever
had time. As she worked alongside Dr. Zee, they talked, and
then they met after work to eat and talk. Pretty soon they were
good friends. Dr. Zee was easy to talk to because she listened
carefully and made no judgments.

One day, when Dr. Zee had asked her for the millionth time
why she didn't just go get an advanced degree, Marty burst out
with it: "I'm in limbo. I can't divorce a poor sick man, not
yet—what if he gets better?—and I feel I can't move on to anything else. I'm frozen."

Dr. Zee had looked her straight in the eye and said, "Marty,
you've had a lousy break. But you're too smart to let it keep
you down. You're not frozen. You're fine. Go back to school.
Get as many degrees as you want. If you need help, I'll help. If
you need money, I have it. And don't worry about making a
mistake. You'll always have a job with me." Dr. Zee had
changed her life. Marty admired the hell out of her . . . loved
her, in fact.

The Executive Committee, as everyone knew, felt a bit differently about her. "They think I get away with murder," Dr.
Zee liked to say. Then she'd laugh and add, "In both senses of
the word," because of the recurrent rumor that she helped some
of her private patients to die. But she was such a popular
doctor, it was impossible to fire her without causing a riot, and
the Executive Committee knew it. Hey, Marty told herself with
pleasure, now *I'm* part of that committee, and just let them try
anything!

Suddenly, Dr. Zee grabbed Marty's arm. "Quick! Look!
The big black limo!" Marty whirled around. The crowd had
thinned out to almost nothing so it was easy to spot the well-
dressed group getting into the back of the shiny stretch limo
parked in the triangle. The uniformed driver stood at attention,
holding the door open. Marty just missed the first man, catching only a glimpse of navy-blue suit as he climbed in. And
right behind him, none other than Aimee Delano, Vice President for Nursing . . . you couldn't miss her tightly encased,
neat rump. Nurse Aimee was not your ideal choice if you
wanted to be nursed. What she was good at was crunching

numbers, making management charts, and impressing important visitors with her good looks and designer suits. She was
very tall, thin, and blond. You expected her to be cold and distant, and guess what? She was.

The last passenger Marty recognized as Dr. Eliot Wolfe, an
imposing figure of a man and the president of Harmony Hill
Hospital, downtown on 100th Street.

"I'm surprised Dr. Messinger is out in the daylight,"
Crystal remarked. "I thought vampires melted in the sun, or
something."

They all laughed. Milton Messinger, M.D., kept himself
nearly invisible, rarely emerging from his office and never
appearing in the hospital cafeteria. His predecessor, a big
hearty Irishman, had roved the halls, glad-handing everyone.
There had been a great deal of conjecture about Dr. Messinger
when he first came, and rumors had abounded—the more fan-
tastic, the better. But Marty was much more interested in the
tall slender figure of Eliot Wolfe. Maybe it was true, the rumor
that Harmony Hill was thinking of buying All Souls. That
would explain this sudden urgency to show some kind of
profit. And, she worried, if Harmony Hill sucked them in,
they'd probably fire everybody except the very top brass. Then
they'd cut the "expensive frills."

Good-bye, Community Care Clinics, she thought. She did
battle with the budget every month. When almost all your
patients were poor, most of them without insurance of any
kind, there was no way to make money, no way in this world.
Not showing a profit was how you became a "frill" in the world
of hospital management.

"Penny for your thoughts," Crystal said.

Marty gave a bitter laugh. "They're worth a lot less. Like
everything around here." Out of the corner of her eye she
thought she saw Paul Giordano approaching, and she added,
"Oh, my God, I almost forgot. Gotta run. Date with Dr.
Mannes."

"A date? As in, a *real* date?" Crystal was all ears. She loved
to dish.

"No, no, Crystal, retract your romance antennae, if you

don't mind. Joel's still happily married." She moved away quickly. She did *not* want to see Paul Giordano face-to-face.

Dr. Zee shook her head. "You're going to give yourself an ulcer if you don't learn to relax, kiddo."

"I'm relaxed! And, Julia, tonight, while we're pigging out, would you please remind me I have to ask you a couple of questions."

"Such as . . . ?"

"Well . . . why Dr. Paul Giordano is here at All Souls, all of a sudden." One of Dr. Zee's eyebrows shot up in surprise and interest.

"Dr. Who?" Crystal instantly wanted to know. "Someone new?"

"I used to know him . . . years ago. . . . Never mind," Marty said. She tried for a casual smile and, mumbling something vague, ran back to the front entrance, pretending she had something to do that needed her *immediate* attention. She could feel those two pairs of eyes fastened on her back the whole way. What a stupid thing to do. Why the hell had she asked about Paul? And in front of Crystal, who would now not rest until she had dug the story out of her. Well, Crys wasn't getting anything, not even a hint, not this time!

Safe inside the lobby, with people moving purposefully on *real* business, Marty decided she might as well go to the cafeteria and pick up something to take back to her desk.

The cafeteria was buzzing even more than usual. Probably gossip about the scene outside. The lines at the cash registers barely moved as people discussed what had just happened. She could just forget the whole idea of eating, she thought, except that she was starving. The hospital had put in a health food bar with a vast array of bean sprouts, twelve kinds of tofu, and multigrained breads; but it didn't appeal. She needed comfort food, and there was *just* the thing: egg salad on rye, potato chips on the side . . . or how about macaroni and cheese? That looked good. And the corned beef hash smelled heavenly.

A voice at her elbow said, "For shame, Nurse. Hanging out on Cholesterol Corner. Is this the sort of thing you tell your expectant mothers to eat?"

"Speak of the devil, Dr. Mannes."

"You were speaking of the devil?"

"I mentioned your name a few minutes ago. And what are *you* doing here?"

"Just sniffing. It's better than glue, for giving you a high." Neither of them reached out for any of the prepared plates, and a moment later they both moved on, to the salad section.

"Joel," Marty said, laughing, "do you realize we just psyched each other out of eating what we really wanted?"

"What are friends for?" he said, munching on a carrot stick. "You sitting down or lunching at your desk?"

"Lunch! This is my breakfast, Doctor."

They both picked rather weary-looking salads and styro-foam cups of coffee and headed for the shorter of the two lines. Marty was glad she'd bumped into him. Joel Mannes was one of her favorite people. After Paul had done his disappearing act, back in '83, she'd run off to Middletown, Connecticut, not to join the circus but—as Joel had said at the time—"pretty damn close! When you work at Middletown Mental," he used to joke, "you're in the biggest three-ring circus in New England."

She and Joel had discovered each other right away, and had remained friends through all the years. His zany sense of humor was like medicine to her aching heart. He was forever acting the clown, throwing out quips and making faces until you laughed. But if you ever really needed something—a ride, a shoulder to cry on, or just some advice—he was always there, unlike some other men she could name. She had called him the minute she heard All Souls was looking for someone to head up their Psychiatric service, and here, thank God, he was.

"So you can't lunch with me in the Plastic Pavilion," Joel said. "Pity. I wanted to hear all about what went on out there in televisionland. I was on rounds and couldn't join the party. But I heard that the nurse who runs CCC gave the right-to-lifers hell."

She blushed. "The Life Saviors took a prisoner. I made them let her go. Yes, I'm a hero. Call me later. Maybe we can grab a drink or something."

"Anything to get close to a real live hero." They grinned at each other and parted.

She wasn't paying attention to where she was going. She

was in her usual hurry, racing down the hall, and plowed right into somebody, and the somebody, she saw when she looked up, was Paul Giordano. The flood of automatic apologies died in her throat. He was holding her by her arms, to keep her from falling, and they were only inches apart. For a moment it felt as if they would kiss, naturally and inevitably, and all the long years in between would just melt away. She came to her senses and pulled back. There was no way, however, to pretend she didn't know who he was.

"Well, Paul. Long time no see."

"What's wrong?" The smell of him was the same, like fresh grass. It wasn't fair!

"What's wrong?" she repeated stupidly. "After you went out for a quart of milk and never came back, you want to know what's *wrong*?"

He flushed. "Actually, what I was referring to was your headlong drive down the hall and the scowl on your face. But—"

She waved off his words, feeling the heat climb in her face. How humiliating! "It doesn't matter. Excuse me, I'm in rather a hurry."

When she tried to push past him, he held onto her arm. "Please, Marty. I do want to talk to you about . . . that time . . . about what happened."

"Well, I don't want to talk to *you*."

"We have to, Marty. I know what I did was stupid and horrible, but—"

"No buts, Paul. Please, spare me the buts. I won't talk to you and that's final."

"Marty, please. I'm going to be working here, with Dr. Zee. We have to straighten this out."

Finally, she was able to look directly at him. That was a mistake, though, because once she looked into his eyes, all she wanted to do was cry. She kept her voice ice-cold and steady. "There's nothing to straighten out. You have your job. I have mine."

"Please. Just meet me this evening—in a public place, anyplace you say—so I can explain—"

"No." This time he let her go without protest. That was good. So why the sudden feeling of emptiness that assailed her?

She plunged down the hall, around the corner to the lobby, and through the back entrance. This brought her out by the cluster of food machines and the motley collection of plastic chairs that passed for the lunchroom/staff recreation area at Community Care Clinics. They really didn't have enough room. The so-called New Wing that housed the clinics had gone up after the flu epidemic of 1919, when it had served as the repository for women who were infectious—a kind of quarantine building.

Before CCC, various departments—Accounting, Medical Records, then Computers—had moved in and quickly moved out. Everyone found the space lacking. So of course it was the very thing for a bunch of nurses and their welfare mothers! The examining rooms might be minuscule and the waiting rooms insufficient, but a lab was already in place—yes, and a small operating room, too. Dr. Messinger had been delighted to put her "little program" into the space because very little money needed to be spent. And I am here to tell the world, Marty thought bitterly, that very little *was* spent.

But come on. They were lucky to have a home at all. They were a pioneer program, the wave of the future. And what was a little crowding, compared to being trailblazers?

An orderly was getting lukewarm coffee out of the machine; otherwise, the space was empty. Marty checked the mailbox, a wooden honeycomb mounted on the wall. There were half a dozen mailboxes in CCC, and *still* things fell through the cracks. She found two things in her cubbyhole. One was a single sheet, printed by hand for a TEEN MOTHERS SUPPORT GROUP, LUNCH INCLUDED!!! The second informed her there would be a lecture on "The Nurse as Executive," next Tuesday, lunch included. She made a mental note to put it down in her calendar and try to go, since she was working on an article on the same subject.

She stuffed both papers into her bag, walked past the staff offices and into the clinic lobby, where Carmen's big desk faced the front doors. Nobody got into the clinics without signing in with Carmen. She was there now; Carmen was always there, her unbelievably black hair piled high in an ever-changing elaborate do, her rhinestone-sprinkled, cat's-eye glasses twinkling. Carmen was of indeterminate age, loyal, organized, sane, and *smart*. She had to be, to do her job. It fell to Carmen to explain how to fill out all the forms, make sure she had the records—for patients with appointments—or send for the records of drop-ins. She had to know all about the different kinds of insurance, and she had to make everything clear to people who might or might not speak English. Somehow, she managed it all.

As soon as Marty appeared, Carmen leaned forward and beckoned her closer. "There's a woman here, Marty, been sitting in Clinic A since we opened. She's Haitian, and my Creole isn't too good but I do know she wants to see *le docteur* because she's going to have *le bébé*." Carmen gave a little laugh. "She doesn't have to tell anyone—she's showing."

"Didn't you send her to Dr. Dim—Dr. Dinowitz?"

Carmen's lips twitched. "Dr. Dimwit left long ago—due in the O.R. upstairs, he said, for another of his famous D and Cs—and the other doctor on clinic duty, some new resident, said she couldn't handle any more than she had right now. Mark my words, she'll take herself off on the dot of three, when her hours are over."

Marty didn't comment. Clinic was something the doctors were forced to do, but they didn't have to like it and they didn't have to give a damn. And they *didn't* give a damn, mostly. That left the nurses to do all the real work.

"I have a little French. I hope," Marty said. "It's been a while since high school."

"They say it's like riding a bike. You never forget."

"They also say you're only as old as you feel. They lie!"

They were interrupted by a stream of curses, in French.

"That her?"

"No," Carmen said. "Yvette," and Marty instantly went into high gear. She ran all the way to Clinic D.

Yvette Pierre was the thirty-two-year-old mother of three, six months pregnant, and a crackhead. Sometimes she didn't come to the clinic at all. When she did, she might be okay, nodding and listless but okay, or she might be raving. Today she

sounded hysterical rather than furious. Crack did horrible
things to people. Marty had known Yvette when she was in her
twenties and going to secretarial school. Then, she'd been a
perky little woman with brains and determination. But she got
mixed up with a dope-dealing creep, and good-bye to her life.
They were seeing too much of that around here.

Yvette was shouting unintelligibly in French—and English,
too, if you counted the word "fuck" used as noun, verb, and
adjective. Her cheeks were streaked with tears and black eyeliner as she struggled against Crystal, who was holding her. A
little crowd of other pregnant women had gathered to watch.

Quickly, Marty stepped up, very close to Yvette, grasping
her shoulders and shouting, "Yvette! Yvette! *Faites attention!
C'est moi, Madame Lamb!*" For just a moment the woman
stopped her struggles. Good thing, too, Marty thought, since
she had used up most of her French.

"Bon." Excellent, she had another word. "Yvette, you must
be calm, *comprenez*? You know I am your friend. *Votre ami.* I
will put you to bed . . . *un lit?*" She started to flounder. How the
hell did you say *I'm going to put you to bed for a little while,
until you sleep off this jag*, in French? "And after you have slept,
you can tell me what's bothering you. Okay? *Comprenez?*"
Yvette stared at her with stuporous eyes, swaying a little.

"Excusez-moi, madame . . ."

Marty turned, and found herself looking directly into the
dark almond-shaped eyes of a very lovely young woman,
whose head was swathed in a bright printed turban.

In a heavy French accent the girl—for surely she was no
older than twenty—said, "If I may 'elp *madame le docteur*? I
can speak in Creole to this *femme*, I shall tell her . . . *quoi,
madame?*"

It took Marty a moment. "Oh. What should you tell her?
Please tell her she has too many drugs in her body. Tell her . . .
detox, *vous comprenez?*" The young woman nodded, listening
intently. "We will send her upstairs, to sleep. Tell her now, *s'il
vous plaît*," she added as Yvette began once more to swear and
struggle.

Fearlessly, the young woman marched up to Yvette and
took Yvette's face gently in her hands. Into the sudden, sur-

prised silence she spoke rapidly in French, and, miraculously, Yvette listened. She actually said, *"Oui, oui"* and then slumped so suddenly, she'd have fallen if Crys hadn't still been holding her.

"Madame. I 'ave tell her you will be able . . . *trouver* . . . to find for her . . . baby-sitter, yes, that is *le mot*. You will find the baby-sitter and . . . explain."

Baby-sitter. Oh Christ. Yvette must have taken something just before she came in for her appointment.

"Crys, does Yvette have a phone?"

"A phone? I'm not sure. It'll be in her records. Which are back in the examining room. Why?"

"There's a baby-sitter with her kids."

"Sitter," Crystal said sarcastically. "Probably some nine-year-old from the building."

At this moment, Virgie walked in from the back. The very person! "Yvette needs to be put into a bed," Marty said. "And watched, Virgie. Call one of the residents to okay an admission, all right?"

"You got it." Virgie put an arm around the limp Yvette and began to lead her away. Virgie was amazingly strong.

"And, Virgie, have Carmen call Yvette's mother. Carmen should tell the mother she'll have to take the kids overnight, and Carmen shouldn't listen to any excuses. Got that?" Virgie didn't pause, but raised one hand, thumb and finger in a circle.

Crystal turned to the young woman and said, "Well, Madame . . . ?"

"Racine. Marie Racine."

"Thanks for your help, Madame Racine. I'm Crystal Cole, the head midwife, and I'll bet you're going to need my services pretty soon."

"Comment? Services?"

"For *le bébé . . . le,* um, *naissance*?"

"Ah. *Oui.* Yes." A shy smile.

Just then, one of the other nurses came rushing in. "Crys, you're needed in the Birthing Center. Delia Rodriguez's contractions are three minutes apart."

Crystal shook her head. "Damn, two months early. I just hope she hasn't taken any of those home remedies her grandma is always brewing. You know Delia. She follows our orders until she feels better, and then she figures she better switch to the *real* stuff. She was showing a lot of edema this morning. But she shouldn't be going into labor yet. Well, here we go!" She hurried off, shaking her head.

Crystal should have examined Marie Racine, but obviously that was out of the question now. When a baby decided it was time to get born, there was no arguing with it. Marty knew she could call someone else, but it was so tempting to just do it herself. "Have you seen a doctor before? For the *bébé*?"

Marie Racine shook her head. "No. I am . . . I am well, and Gregory, he . . . he wishes that we wait, and so . . ." She tried to smile, but it quavered and quivered and turned into tears.

Marty whisked her through the waiting room to an examining room, closing the door. She motioned Marie Racine to a chair and sat herself next to the tiny desk, a writing surface hinged into the wall. The examining rooms were all minuscule, just the desk and two chairs and the examining table squeezed in; but in a way, it was good. There was an instant feeling of intimacy when you sat so close.

"Do you want to tell me what makes you so sad?"

The girl shook her head, biting her lips. "*Non. Merci. C'est rien.* I will be . . . I will be *calme.*"

Okay, then. "Why don't you sit up there, on the table." And chatting lightly, Marty took blood pressure and listened to the girl's heartbeat, apologizing for the cold stethoscope. In a combination of halting French and English, she had Marie get undressed, into an angel robe and onto the table. Gently, she palpated the abdomen, her hands moving almost automatically. Working with a patient made her feel so good, so . . . *useful.* The fetal heartbeat was already strong and steady. She gave Marie the stethoscope, to listen, and was rewarded with a broad, delighted smile.

"So, generally speaking, how're you doing, Marie?"

"*Comment?*"

"You are strong? *Forte?*" She made a mock muscle. "Tired?" An elaborate yawn.

Marie giggled. "Ah. *Oui. Et non.*" Apparently, she understood English if it wasn't too slangy; speaking it was more of a problem. Well, Marty thought, wasn't it the same with her French? Voilà! She would speak in English and Marie Racine would answer in French. And so they did. After that it went quite smoothly, and the two of them smiled at each other, delighted with this clever idea. Slowly, the young woman's story began to come out, as Marty took blood for the necessary tests, put Marie on the scale, and put everything down on the chart.

Marie had been working as a cocktail waitress in a Eurotel in the Dominican Republic when she met Gregory Thornwood, a vacationing American who was not only *très charmant*, but handsome beyond all dreams. Marty tried to keep her face devoid of comment but apparently she didn't do too well, because Marie slid off the table, holding the dove-gray sheet around her slender body, and dug into her leather purse. She brought out a photograph—not a snapshot taken on the beach, but a theatrical, posed and lighted portrait. The man *was* good-looking, in a dark and dramatic way. In fact, he was vaguely familiar. Marty was sure she'd seen him somewhere before. Marie tried to explain. At first, Marty got the idea he owned a laundry, but it turned out that he was a soap opera star. An actor. And then she had it: that's where she'd seen him, on television.

He'd come to Marie's hotel not as a tourist, but on location. With plenty of empty hours just waiting to be filled up. Marie had come across the border from Haiti, knowing only enough Spanish to get a job. He hardly spoke French, she barely spoke English; they had no language but sex, but that, it seemed, they spoke well and often. *"Sans un mot"*— without a word, they fell into each other's arms. For the six weeks of his stay, they spent every spare moment with each other, mostly, Marty gathered, in Gregory's room, on Gregory's king-sized bed.

And then—Marie's pretty face saddened—*le shoot, c'etait fini*. The holiday was over. He began to pack to go back to New York. Vows were exchanged, promises were made. He had to go, but she must be patient.

"I wait. I have patient. I love him, and soon we be together," she told Marty. "At first, Gregory, he write to me many letters," she said. "And then . . ." She snapped her fingers. ". . . no again. *Rien. Silence.*"

Most women would have written it off. It had been just a
fling. But not, apparently, Marie Racine. "He love me, he love
me," was a phrase she kept repeating, like a mantra. When he
stopped corresponding, she took every cent she owned and
bought a plane ticket to New York, to look for him. She found
him, all right. He was shocked to hear from her. And when she
said she was here, *mon amour*, right here in New York, she
heard him give a little moan. So she knew something was
wrong. They met that evening, in a dark little bistro on Eigh-
teenth Street, far from his job and far from his apartment on
West Seventy-third Street. Then it was her turn to be shocked.

"He is . . . *marry!*" Marie told Marty, her big, beautiful
brown eyes filling with tears. "But . . ." Her voice dropped to a
whisper. ". . . he still love me. He still love *me*, Marie. He want
me . . . oh, so much! And I give in to him. Oh my *maman*
would be so shamed for me! But I love my Gregory, and now
I have his *bébé*, and *she* . . . she, she cannot. She cannot have *le
bébé*, *jamais*." There was a note of triumph in her voice. "I am
. . . how you say it? . . . I am win!"

Oh, you poor baby, Marty thought. You are *not* win; you are
screw! How did you say "They never leave their wives" in
French? But when she looked into the trusting sloe eyes, she
just couldn't rain on this particular parade. Maybe the baby
would make a difference; maybe it would even make a *miracle*.

She patted Marie's hand and murmured, "Well, in the meantime, Madame Racine, I must ask you to take this cup and
make pee-pee in it for me." That got another giggle. What a
sweet girl. That Gregory should be shot. "Leave the cup on the
shelf, *comprenez?*"

Five minutes later Marty walked the girl back through the
clinic and up front to Carmen. "Carmen, Madame Racine will
come to us in two weeks . . . *deux semaines*. . . ." She held up
two fingers just in case.

"I will ask for *madame le docteur*."

"And then you will go to Mademoiselle Cole, the midwife.
She is a specialist in *les bébés*."

"Oh. *Une specialiste. Bon.*" Both Carmen and Marty
watched Marie Racine leave the clinic area. As erect as if she
were balancing a basket on her head, she went gliding across the

room and out the door. Marty couldn't help but notice how the security guard turned his head to watch her.

Echoing Marty's thoughts, Isabelle's voice came from behind her left shoulder. "Elegant, huh? What is she? Five months?"

"She was very vague about her last period. Well, it was a long time ago. But I'd guess five."

As they talked, a small dark head peered around the doorway to the Conference Room and a little voice piped, "Mommy, can I come out *now*?" It was Sarita, Isabelle's four-year-old. Sarita usually stayed with her grandmother; what was she doing here? Oh no, Isabelle's mama must be sick again.

Isabelle gave a nervous little laugh. "Mama was so tired this morning. She dragged herself out of bed but she looked so awful. I sent her back. And she *went*." Isabelle turned her head away, blinking rapidly. Mrs. Vargas was a tough lady, who had got dressed every day of her life at six A.M., no matter what was going on, and made breakfast for her family.

"Oh, damn," Marty said, with feeling.

"Yeah. I don't need to tell you I'm worried. I wanted to call EMS and bring her right in but she said no chemo, no more chemo. You know Mama, when she says no, that's it. So I got Sarita dressed and brought her with me." She looked a question at Marty.

"Of course she can stay. Don't worry about it. We'll all keep Sarita busy. There should be something wonderfully educational on Public Television, don't you think?" There was a small TV in the Conference Room. Marty watched as Isabelle took her daughter's hand and led her away.

A little over a year ago, Izzy had brought her mama into CCC and asked Marty to give her a thorough examination. "She hates doctors, but I explained to her that you're not a doctor, so she was willing to come in. But not *very* willing. She's been so tired lately, it's not like her, and I'm scared, Marty. So is she, I think. But she doesn't want to know what it is, and I *do*."

Marty had found a lump in Mrs. Vargas's left breast, just under the armpit, a spongy mass. She'd called in Dr. Zee, whereupon Mrs. Vargas learned there was at least one doctor

she could love. Dr. Dimwit himself had done the surgery, and
he had actually behaved like a normal human being, patient
and kind and reassuring. The breast was removed and Isabelle's mama was put on an eight-month course of chemo and
radiation. They got the whole growth out, all of it that they
could see. But in the privacy of his office, Dennis had told
Marty, "You know as well as I that there are no guarantees
with cancer. But there's no reason to say anything to either
Mrs. Vargas or Isabelle," he'd said, his voice putting a question mark on the end of the sentence. And Marty had agreed.
She usually liked to tell patients the whole truth, but there were
times when there was no up side to candor. To suggest it was
the end of the road would only create misery and tension.
Everyone would know soon enough, anyway.

When Isabelle came back after leaving Sarita in the Conference Room, her eyes were still moist. She continued their conversation as if it had never been interrupted. "Oh hell. We all
know what this means, don't we? But when I ask her does she
want me to take a leave and stay with her, she's all insulted!
You can't win!" Abruptly, she changed the subject. "Your
beautiful patient, I don't suppose she's, like, happily married
with a husband who's all excited about the baby and working
double shifts to pay for it?"

"I'm afraid not."

They exchanged wry smiles. When we were girls, Marty
thought, to have a baby out of wedlock was to be ruined. Back
then, abortion was frightening and illegal and unsafe . . .
although it could be done. But if abortion was out of the question, you were whisked away to an aunt or a grandmother—
preferably half a continent away—under some pretext or other,
and only returned when your belly was once again flat. But
now! Girls of thirteen and fourteen were coming in, *proud*
of their pregnancies; and their boyfriends strutted around as if
they'd just invented it. Of course, once the baby was a reality,
the guys disappeared.

"This girl's story is a *little* different," Marty said. "She was
under the impression he was going to marry her. In fact, she
still *is*, although she's mistaken."

"My god, she's gorgeous, who'd dump *her*?"

"Hey. He was already married. Big surprise, right?"

Isabelle sighed, crossed herself and then hurried off. Marty headed for her office, then stopped.

"What's happening with Crystal's unexpected delivery?" she asked Carmen.

Carmen rolled her eyes. "Still there. Last I heard, the contractions slowed down. That baby, he don't want to come out. Every once in a while you can hear Delia cursing her husband. That's when she's not calling either her mother or Jesus." More eye-rolling. "I wish they'd all take Lamaze. The natural childbirth women don't holler and scream, they sit in bed and read and time their contractions. This is so . . . undignified, you know what I mean?"

Marty smiled grimly. "You expect a girl who didn't know about birth control to sign up for Lamaze classes? You *are* a dreamer, Carmen."

"Here's what gets me, Marty. Why *don't* they know about Lamaze and birth control? Jeez, everyone around here *tells* them. And there are all the brochures . . ." She gestured at the rack next to her desk, laden with leaflets on everything you could think of. Every clinic had a complete supply of them, too.

"Why? They don't listen. They don't pay attention. They don't believe in it. Their pastor tells them it's the work of the devil. Their husband is against it. Who the hell knows?" Marty was suddenly very weary. Why was it that the women who needed help the most were the ones who thought they didn't need it? "Anyhow, who am I to give advice?" she said. "At least in the end they all have a baby to love."

Marty had to turn her head away. The sympathy that suddenly softened Carmen's eyes gave her more pain than she would have thought possible.

6

Crystal Cole came bouncing into the small office at the back of Clinic B on the dot of 5:45. She looked gorgeous and glowing, Dr. Zee thought, even after a double shift, not to mention a difficult patient this afternoon. Oh, to be young again. Of course, even the young Julia Zachary had never been what you would call a beauty. But it would be nice to have that endless energy again.

She looked down ruefully at the pile of papers on her desk. Maybe she shouldn't go to Marty's. Maybe she should finish this stuff and go home and get some rest. To hell with it, she decided, scooped up all the papers and put them into her briefcase. She'd get to them later. God knows, she was having enough trouble sleeping. Why not make good use of those empty, haunted hours?

"Did Delia's baby arrive yet, Crystal?"

"No. The strangest thing happened. The contractions were regular, about three minutes apart, but when I looked, there was nothing. It was like a blank wall. And that's exactly what it was. The baby came down the birth canal so fast, it pushed the placental opening out of the way. The cervix was dilating, but no way that baby was coming out."

"Oy," Dr. Zee said.

"Right. We waited to see if it would change. I don't have to tell you that Delia was complaining the whole time. Well, labor slowed down and then it stopped. I explained it to her, how Mother Nature knew what to do, that everything would straighten out in a day or two and then she'd go back into labor again. . . ." There was a pained look on Crystal's face.

"So . . . ?" Dr. Zee prodded.

"So she demanded a C-section. I told her, no way, Delia, you don't want a C-section, that's major surgery. You just need to wait a little while longer. But she didn't *want* to wait. She came into the Birthing Center to have her baby, and by God, she was going to have that baby! Not that I blame her. It's tough, getting all set, psychologically, and then . . . something like this, a one in, what? Ten thousand chance? So I told her she could stay overnight, and as soon as the placenta straightened itself out and labor began again, I'd be there. Hey. We ready? Marty said six and it's nearly that now." Crystal laughed. "I'm *hungry!*"

Dr. Zee was not hungry. She rarely was, these days. She'd love to think it was just another sign of advancing age, but you couldn't blame *everything* on advancing age. "Me, too," she said. "Especially for Proto's pizza." As she pushed herself up out of the chair, she called Crystal's attention to a new study of nurse-midwives versus obstetricians. She'd become quite clever at creating diversions so nobody would notice how stiff her joints had become, how slow her movements.

Crystal glanced at the study. "We won," she chortled. "Again. About time, too. When did you tell me New York City got rid of its last midwife?"

" 'Fifty-seven, I think. Oh, we were so proud to see the last of the bad old ignorant unsterilized days. Little did we know how smart those healing women *were*."

She'd made it to the door without revealing anything. She hoped. Crystal was very sharp; she seemed to have eyes everywhere on her body. She usually knew what everyone in the hospital was up to, long before anyone else had a clue. Dr. Zee had been expecting questions from Crystal about her health for weeks now. But either Crystal was preoccupied or she wasn't looking as old and feeble as she thought. As I feel, she amended. The minute she thought it, she straightened up, pushing her shoulders back.

"Your back bothering you? I'll give you a massage when we get to Marty's."

"Thanks, but no, my back's fine. I think it's the heat."

"Yeah, it's getting to everyone. We've had more fights in the waiting rooms for the past two weeks than in the previous two years. We've also had about twice as many patients coming in as usual. I think they come to sit in the air-conditioning. Not that it works so great . . ."

Crystal talked all the way to Marty's. She was on a tear this afternoon, about how the black community was going to destroy itself if it kept making more fatherless babies with babies for mothers. She was still going on about it when they climbed the stone stairway and rang Marty's bell. Julia did agree with most of it, but Crystal's animation was beginning to make her feel tired.

Once they were buzzed in, Marty's apartment door opened and out came a hand with a twenty dollar bill in it. A minute later Marty peered out."Oh. Sorry. I thought you were the pizza."

"Can we come in anyway?"

"Oh Christ, of course. Come in. Welcome to my humble home."

Crystal eyed their hostess. A shame Marty didn't realize how she spoiled her good looks by frowning that way. And those two little furrows between her eyebrows were going to become permanent if she didn't loosen up. What that girl needs is to go out on the town, Crystal thought. I could teach her how to have a good time! Marty's trouble was she took everything much too seriously. Crystal often wanted to say to her, "Yo, Marty, get a life!"

She was pacing around now like there was something important she'd forgotten to do. The girl was fussed, Crystal realized, and couldn't help wondering if it had anything to do with that new doctor she'd asked about this morning. When anything was bothering a woman, you had to *cherchez* le man, Crystal knew that. Men were almost more trouble than they were worth. Almost.

"What's going on, Marty? You seem agitated," she said.

"The lab in the clinic was messed with today—oh yes, that was the good news I was given on my way out tonight. Nothing missing, but things put in the wrong places. Why? I can't figure it out! And I found my air conditioner turned off. *Again!* In the middle of a heat wave! The office was like an oven!"

Crystal threw her shoulder bag onto a chair and headed for

the couch. "You know those air conditioners are always going on the fritz. As for the lab . . . maybe someone was in a hurry and made some mistakes and doesn't want to say. In any case . . ." She shrugged.

"You think I'm creating problems where they don't exist?" Marty was trying very hard to keep the irritation out of her voice. "You'd be singing a different tune if it happened to you, Crys."

"Oh, nothing ever happens to me, Marty. I'm a witch! Just ask the patients!" She laughed to show she was kidding, and watched as Marty got annoyed again. Marty was grim all the time lately; it was getting to be a bore. "Was anything missing from the lab?" Crystal asked.

"It's hard to tell, when everything's been moved where it doesn't belong."

"See what I mean? Somebody messed up and didn't know how to make it right, that's all. Are you offering wine, by any chance?" Might as well change the subject. If possible.

"None for me tonight," Dr. Zee said.

Marty turned. "Are you okay?"

"You think when someone doesn't want wine, that makes them sick?" Dr. Zee's tone was amused, but her eyes were tired. And her voice was a little hoarse. Maybe she has mono, Crystal thought. She had noted the careful movements.

"No, it's just . . . you always have a glass of wine."

"Okay, then, I'll have one."

"You remind me of my granny tonight, Marty," Crystal said. "Have a drink and chill out." More and more, Crystal was convinced that the new doctor was the pain in Marty's butt. So why didn't the woman *say* so? Big deal! Were they friends, or what?

Come to think of it, the answer was probably "or what." They couldn't be much more opposite. She was a black girl from Bed-Stuy in Brooklyn, whereas Marty was lily-white, and had grown up on the Connecticut shoreline. How different could you get? Yet, they got along. It was always a royal pain in the ass having a woman for your boss. There was no way to get leverage with a woman.

But Marty was pretty cool. She mostly left her head nurses alone. But she didn't know how to let things go, and that could be trouble. Also, she never opened up, the way most women did; you couldn't get anything juicy out of her most of the time. Still, they had become *compadres*, able to trade war stories and opinions over a bottle of red wine. Hey, it was *something*, right? Better than plenty of others she'd worked for. At least Marty wasn't jealous of her.

Marty took a hefty slug from her glass. "Much better," she said and smiled. The timer in the kitchen buzzed and she laughed. "That's the signal. Time for Pierce's newscast. Who knows? One of us may hear from Hollywood."

So they settled in, Marty and Dr. Zee side by side on the couch, while Crys curled herself into the big easy chair. Marty surfed rapidly to Channel 12. And suddenly there it was, in living color: the hospital baking in the hot sun, the Life Saviors waving their fetal pictures, some of them prayerfully on their knees, some making one of their "circles of friendship" around the frightened girl; the crowd of onlookers, the noise, and Clive Moses's unmistakable deep voice. Crystal hated that superior Ivy League sound he was so careful to cultivate.

"Until today," he was saying as the camera zeroed in on him, "these people have always kept the distance mandated by law. They have not interfered with safe passage to the clinic building. What happened today is a different story, and you can be sure that All Souls Hospital will take all necessary legal steps—"

"That jerk!" Crystal said.

"Oh, I don't know," Marty said, "he's always struck me as being pretty reasonable—"

"Excuse me? He's an arrogant pig."

"In the arrogant pig category?" Marty said. "I vote for Ham Pierce, personally. He can edit everything so it comes out the way he wants."

"You just want to blame Pierce because you favor Clive."

The doorbell buzzed twice in an impatient way, and Marty opened the door for the delivery boy from Proto's. He looked puzzled and then a bit hurt when the three women burst into applause, but was mollified by a two-dollar tip, twice his usual. Marty carried the large hot box carefully to the table. It smelled divine. Proto's pizzas were almost twice as large as anyone else's, and were cut by hand into a dozen or so slender slices.

Marty brought out napkins and plunked the wine bottle in

the middle of the circular oak table. They all sat down and ate greedily, not talking. When there was only one lonely slice sitting on the grease-stained box, Crystal said, "I've got the munchies! Anyone else want it?"

"No thanks."

"I'm stuffed," Dr. Zee said, although Crystal had noticed how she'd taken only two slices and kind of pushed them around.

While they sipped at their wine, Marty filled them in on Marie Racine, her Gregory, the pregnancy ... the whole ridiculous story. Crystal shook her head in disgust.

"Don't tell me, let me guess. She thinks she's going to hold him ... no, wait ... she thinks she's going to get him away from the wife? She thinks that once she produces this baby, this half-black baby, he's going to leave everything behind and settle in with her? Oh, denial, thy name is woman!"

"Now, wait, Crystal. He did set Marie up in an apartment on Riverbank Avenue."

"As far from his real life as he could get, right? Keep the little black bitch for fucking, in a place nobody ever heard of!"

"Aren't you being a little harsh, Crys?" Dr. Zee's tone was mild, but she looked taken aback. Well tough, Crystal thought. It happened to be the truth. But they could never understand. They came from a different world.

"Maybe," she said in a mollifying tone. Daddy had taught her early on that you had to be careful when you were with white folks. "They'll let you go just so far," he'd said, "and then, if you cross that invisible line ..." and he'd made a slicing motion across his throat. She knew it was true, and sometimes it made her so damn mad.

Marty leaned forward. "You have to wonder why she wants *him*. He's hardly ever available. Forget weekends! That's for the wife! And he's an actor, on a soap, which means he's working all the time. It's not a deal any of us would go for. But she 'love him.' She says he's excited about her pregnancy. He wants a son."

"Yeah, yeah," Crystal said. "She can believe any goddamn thing she wants. She could have quintuplets—it's not going to bring him flying to her side. She's *black*, Marty. White men don't leave their wives for black women. They just keep them on the side, a tasty little tidbit of dark meat!"

"Crystal!" Marty and Dr. Zee spoke together.

She'd crossed that line. Too fucking bad. "Well, it's true," she said. "Take it from one who knows."

There was a moment of silence. And then, in a very guarded tone, Dr. Zee said, "Would you care to elaborate on that one?"

Another tense silence. She had to do something, so she laughed, like it was all a big joke. "Are you kidding? After I dig myself a grave, you want me to jump into it? It was a joke, just a little black humor, yuk, yuk. Something Marty's getting fonder and fonder of, right?"

"Crystal, what are you talking about?"

"Clive Moses, of course. I always thought he had a secret thing for you, but lately it ain't so secret."

"Don't be ridiculous."

"The way he looks at you . . . !" Crystal leaned forward. This was more like it, this was fun. Look at the girl begin to blush! She hadn't meant it, just said it because she needed something to say, but it looked like maybe she'd hit a nerve. "You know, I'll bet *you* could get him to do something for us. Just cozy up to him, flash him a little leg. He'll start singing the praises of nursing and CCC all *over* the place!"

"Crystal! That's a terrible idea!" But Marty laughed anyway. He *had* been flirting a lot with Marty lately; Crystal had seen him. Of course, he was an arrogant pig who thought he should give every woman a break.

"Look at the girl! Marty, you're all embarrassed!" Crystal teased. "He's after you, Marty, and you like it, admit it."

"I like *him* well enough, why not? But I don't . . . Oh, God, this discussion is absurd. Clive Moses and I aren't sixth graders, Crystal. And I don't screw men to get favors."

"You've got a crush on him! Dr. Zee, you're my witness, she's got a crush on Clive Moses!"

"Crystal," Dr. Zee said. "Come on! Enough is enough!"

Yeah, sure, Crystal thought, pull doctor rank on me. But she only said, "I'm sorry, I grew up with brothers and that's how we always kidded around. Okay, Marty? Forgive?"

"Sure," Marty said. "Forget it. And never mind what I

think of Clive Moses, look at the TV—" And then she stopped. Because the camera was closely following a tall, determined woman, her bright auburn ponytail bouncing on her back as she pushed her way through the crowd toward the teenager, thrusting people aside. The woman's face filled the screen, eyes blazing, talking a blue streak . . . and looking not so awful, actually. Marty stared at this apparition, knowing it was herself but unable to believe it. Was she really that good-looking? How very strange.

"And you are?" Pierce was saying.

It was weird, to have her own eyes boring into her own eyes. "Marta Lamb, Nurse Practitioner, and the director of CCC. I've been very patient about the constant demonstrations in front of the clinics, but if this sort of harassment of children continues, I shall have to consult the hospital attorneys." Cut to Ham Pierce's face as he commented.

Wait a minute! What about everything else she had said? What had happened to all that talk about Jessie's age and the fact that she'd been held without consent?

Crystal bounced up from the couch to refill her glass. "The bastard! He's made you sound so tough and unfeeling."

"I thought he was on *our* side! Christ, I can't believe I was so stupid! I sound like a prime bitch. As if I even know the hospital attorneys, whoever they are. Does the hospital even *have* attorneys?"

"Oh yes," Dr. Zee said. "Samansky, Devlin, Crane and Tortelli. Nice mixed bag, just like in all those old World War Two movies—one from each major ethnic group. Mostly for malpractice suits and complaints from Medicaid patients. Not that I've ever seen any of the guys on the letterhead in person; as a matter of fact, I think at least one of them is dead. They send us the younger associates, and from what I've seen, they all think doctors are too rich, too powerful, and too self-absorbed, and probably deserve to be punished. And maybe they're right."

She heaved a noisy sigh and held out her glass for more wine. Marty got up and obliged, giving herself a refill as well. But her mind was busy trying to figure a way to convince Administration that the Life Saviors had really gone too far this time. She'd love to have them banned from in front of the building.

"Oh boy . . . look who he's got *now*," Crystal called out. On the screen, Marty, her arm around Jessie Trudeau's shoulders, was disappearing into the center of the throng, and then the camera moved in close to Rabbi Zeke Brown, his intense eyes looking directly at the viewer. "All Souls Hospital cannot be allowed to play God," he intoned in his Rabbi Voice. It *did* put a chill down your spine. "There is already the one true Lord God, the Creator of all life. Ms. Lamb may think she is doing the right thing, but she is going against the Almighty's law which tells us that all life is sacred to Him . . ."

Marty eyed the image on the screen, the saturnine face with its perfectly barbered beard, the thick, shining black hair topped always by the *kippah*, and the carefully orchestrated casual clothes. For the cameras, he had put on his satin basketball jacket embroidered with "Rabbi Zeke" to show he was not one of your old-fashioned hidebound rabbis, but a regular guy. He was idolized by his congregation; they all thought he was wonderful. Maybe he was good at religion. Maybe he really believed what he was saying. But he was so sharp and so well-read, it was hard to understand the way he lived. She wondered just what went through his head . . . just how much of what he said he really believed.

"Excuse me while I go pound my head against the wall," she commented.

"He does have that effect sometimes," Dr. Zee agreed. "And he complains the *hospital* likes to play God!" She rolled her eyes expressively.

"Well, he's no worse than a lot of doctors we know." Crystal pushed back her chair and walked away, not quite slamming the door to the bathroom.

Marty and Dr. Zee stared at each other.

"Maybe it's PMS. Or maybe . . ."

"Maybe what?" Marty asked.

"Nothing, really. Just that I've seen her several times in the past couple of weeks, coming out of Joel Mannes's office at very strange times. And she always looks—forgive me, Sigmund—rather guilty."

"As well she might, if she's going to Joel for therapy. Haven't you ever heard her go on about how psychiatry is bullshit? So she wouldn't want anyone to know. It might ruin her image."

"Maybe. It's just that . . ."

"That what, Julia?"

"Nothing. I have too much imagination sometimes. Fate of the generalist. We think we understand everything. Joel is happily married, and in any case, I wouldn't think he was Crystal's type. Never mind . . . and speaking of PMS, which we were, if you'll recall, let me tell you the latest. Shayna Brown spotted this month . . . I think it won't be long before she starts to menstruate. Sixteen's kind of late, but . . ." A meaningful shrug.

"Oh great. I suppose that means her father will marry her off as quickly as possible."

"We all know that's been his agenda right from the beginning." Dr. Zee looked thoughtful. "He didn't care what spina bifida was, or what it meant. All he cared about was how they could cover it up and pretend it wasn't there. Of course, he was relieved when we told him about the shunt to take the water from her brain. Mental retardation was out of the question. But the rest of it? Brushed aside. So she couldn't feel from the waist down. Could she bear children? Yes? Good. But no braces. No special shoes. No corrective surgery. No nothing. They've always kept a quilt or a coverlet over Shayna's legs so that no one would guess she wasn't able to walk.

"Miriam wept plenty of tears, trying to get him to stop and *think*. But he had it all figured out. The spina bifida would never be mentioned. It would be a secret and nobody would ever know. I told him that wasn't possible, but he just said, 'Watch me.' I didn't realize that he was perfectly capable of keeping her imprisoned in that apartment her entire life." The doctor made a face and waved away her irritation.

"I warned Zeke and Miriam that there was a five to ten percent chance with every pregnancy that there would be, if not spina bifida as bad as Shayna's, other kinds of handicaps, up to and including anencephaly. 'Whatever God wills,' he told me. What arrogance! There was no question of abortion, of course. It was forbidden. As was birth control. As we all know," Dr. Zee finished, sliding Marty a look. Marty nodded in agreement. Miriam was often pregnant. Too often.

The Browns had three sons, all born after Shayna, and none with neural tube defects. The rabbi thought it was the will of God. What the rabbi did not know was that it was the will of Miriam, who had come quietly to the hospital for an Alpha-fetoprotein test whenever she thought she was pregnant. Several times, she had chosen abortion. The last three pregnancies, she hadn't even bothered with the test before she aborted. "I'm getting too old to start more babies," she'd told Marty. "Especially with this arthritis of mine." They clucked a lot, in the rabbi's congregation, about the poor little *rebbitzin*, so prone to miscarriage.

"Poor Miriam," Dr. Zee said. "Shayna's her daughter, too—although you'd never know it to listen to *him*. Miriam's pregnant again, by the way."

"Oh dear! What's she going to do this time?"

"She's not sure. She thinks he may have guessed. Oh, it all makes me so mad. To think how self-sufficient Shayna could be if only her father weren't so dishonest. And why? *Because no man will take a wife who is not perfect!* I guess that means that men *are* perfect." She snorted.

"As I remember only too well," Marty said, "It *is* a male-centered religion."

"What religion *isn't*, I'd like to know!"

"Goddess worship," Crystal said, emerging from the bathroom.

Dr. Zee snapped her fingers. "I just remembered, Marty. You were asking me about the new doctor I'm considering. Paul Giordano. He seems perfect."

"New doctor? Is he cute? Would I like him?" Crystal patted her curly hair and posed.

Marty couldn't help laughing. "Probably. To all three questions."

"I'll tell you who *does* think he's cute. Aimee Delano," Dr. Zee said. "She was cooing all over him when I brought him upstairs to meet Dr. Messinger."

"Aimee Delano, the Ice Maiden? Cooing? I thought she saved her honeyed talk for the profit-and-loss statement." Crystal was laughing.

"Did you actually talk to Dr. Messinger? In person? Face-to-face? And did *he* coo?" Marty was aware she was babbling, sort of, but she was desperate to change the subject. The mention of Aimee Delano flirting with Paul had constricted her chest, and she just hoped it didn't show. Still jealous, after all these years. What a fool she was!

Dr. Zee gave her little bark of a laugh. "*Talk* to Dr. Messinger? In the hallway? You've got to be kidding. Of course we didn't. But Aimee said—on Dr. Messinger's behalf—she hoped that Dr. Giordano would be joining the staff. She came up very close to Dr. Giordano and kind of leaned on him. He seemed puzzled but not displeased."

"When was this? Today?"

"This afternoon." Dr. Zee's dark eyes regarded Marty with interest.

Crystal's beeper went off and she ran to the phone in Marty's room, saying she didn't want to bother them. It might be Delia or one of the pregnant women at the HIV night clinic. Five years ago AIDS patients were mostly middle-class gays with good manners. Which suited All Souls just fine, since they were the only male patients in the place. But all that had changed— so many of them had died, for one thing—and now the clinic was crammed with intravenous drug users, not necessarily a rough, tough crowd, but very likely to be. Kenny Rankin and Emilio Chavez were the nurses on duty for the HIV clinic for very good reason. They were often needed to break up fights.

Five years ago a nurse-midwife would have had no business in an HIV clinic; but unfortunately, that was no longer the case. More and more HIV-positive women were appearing at CCC, and lots of them were pregnant.

There was a moment of silence after Crystal had closed the bedroom door. Then Dr. Zee said, very casually, "Did you love him *that* much?"

To her utter astonishment, Marty burst into tears. Dr. Zee stood up and knelt by her, arms awkwardly around her, one hand patting her back while she murmured, "There, there. There, there."

For a few minutes the tears came gushing out of Marty—as if someone had opened a faucet. She had no control over them. Even when she told herself firmly, That's enough now,

what if Crystal walks back in? they didn't stop. And then, suddenly, they did. She sat, numb and exhausted, sniffling like a
child. Dr. Zee handed her a handful of tissues and she blew her
nose, feeling more and more like a stupid child every minute.

"I . . . I don't want to talk about it."

"That's okay, Marty. I think you answered my question.
You should know that Paul Giordano is very likely to be on
staff here. Also, I got the impression somehow that he was here
because he'd found out *you're* here."

"I hope not." She blew her nose again. "He has no right to go
anywhere to be with me. . . ." Her voice began to wobble dangerously so she stopped talking. "Never mind. I'll tell you all
about it another time."

Suddenly appearing from the other room, Crystal picked up
her handbag and headed for the door, talking as she went.
"Emilio. Some guy went ballistic after his pregnant girlfriend
told him the baby isn't his, but his best friend's. . . ." She rolled
her eyes. "He's having a snit fit over there, threatening her. He
knows me. Maybe I can calm him down, keep him from
spending a night in jail."

"Why did she tell him?" Dr. Zee asked.

Crystal gave a bitter laugh. "Oh, it's not *true*! The girl-
friend's positive, too, and so is the fetus, probably. And she's
crazy about him. She just wanted to yank his chain a little.
Stupid girl! But . . . she's my patient and I have to make sure
she stays healthy—at least until the baby is born. Well, so long.
See you tomorrow!" And she was gone; they could hear her
footsteps, muffled by the thick rubber soles of her nursing
shoes, racing down the front steps.

Dr. Zee got up from her chair, stretching and groaning, "God,
old bones! About Paul Giordano: tell me whenever you like, we
have time. Unlike Isabelle's mama." She shook her head sadly.
"I promised I'd go over there tonight and have a look at her. But
I think I know what it is. And I think she knows, too."

"What an idiot I am, sitting here, caterwauling over my
stupid broken heart of ten years ago, while Mrs. Vargas is . . .
well, I think I know, too. When Isabelle has to bring Sarita into
work because Grandma is too tired to baby-sit . . . ! She's
dying, isn't she?"

Somberly: "Yes." She lifted the black doctor's bag that was always with her. "She wants to talk . . . about her options, such as they are. She's a tough lady." Marty could see Dr. Zee's eyes misting over.

"Julia, listen. Do you want me to go with you? I don't want to interfere. But maybe you'd like my company?" Isabelle and Marco lived in Hollis, in Queens.

"No, thanks, though. She's in terrible pain. I'll give her a shot of Dilaudid for the pain, and what's more important, let her see I'm still here for her." The doctor bent for her bag, then straightened and took in a deep breath. "Dying should be everyone's right."

"I know."

A small smile. "There should be a law. I know, I know . . . there already is. But the one we've got is all wrong."

"I know."

Marty got up and gave Dr. Zee a big hug. "Don't let it get to you," she said.

Dr. Zee let herself out, and all of a sudden the apartment felt empty. Marty picked up the pizza box and the rumpled napkins and the dirty glasses and began to clean up. Her mind was on nice Mrs. Vargas, plump and curly-haired—until cancer. Cancer had eaten her alive; the last time Marty had seen her, she was a withered husk. But she was still Isabelle's mama. She pictured Isabelle, sitting by her mother's bed, holding her hand, knowing her mama would soon be gone, weeping and weeping. . . . Marty began to cry.

The phone rang. She let it. She really didn't feel like talking to anyone right now. The answering machine clicked on and Paul's voice filled the room. "Marty? If you're there, please pick up. Marty? Okay, I guess you're *not* there. Listen. We really have to talk. Please don't—" Then his voice cracked and there was a long silence, and she could hear him swallowing hard. She stood there, quivering, wanting so much to run to the phone, to pick it up and talk to him; but she made herself stand right where she was, waiting for him to speak again.

But he didn't speak again. He made a strangled sound and hung up.

7

As soon as their eyes met, she had known: *This is the one.*
She'd seen him around. In July, when she first came to the hospital, with all the other new nurses and the new batch of residents, she kept seeing him, in the halls and the cafeteria. New England Memorial was a huge teaching hospital. You'd think an attractive young nurse like Marty Dauber could get this one particular resident—with whom she'd never even exchanged one word—off her mind and out of her dreams. But there was something about him.

He was dark and compact with sleepy, heavy-lidded eyes and a Roman nose; and whenever she heard laughter from the residents, who always sat in huge groups in the cafeteria, he would be the one talking. He was so alive, she thought, so full of energy and good humor. She found herself longing to meet him. But come on. She wasn't the type to moon over a man she hadn't even met. There were plenty of residents—and doctors, too—who asked her out. And she went with them. Even so, she always looked for him, whenever she walked into the cafeteria.

One day, she spotted him, sitting alone for a change, scowling over some papers. She stopped a few feet away, holding her tray of food tightly, trying to get up the courage to sit down next to him and just say "Hi." Everyone did it. She couldn't. As she walked by his table she thought she felt his eyes on her back; but that was probably her imagination. She contented herself with finding out his name. Paul Giordano, PGY-1. A first-year resident. That meant he'd be around for a few years. She had plenty of time to work herself up to speaking to him.

When he rotated to the Psychiatric service, where she'd been a floor nurse for a month, she finally met him. It was his third day—actually, night. She had the eleven-to-seven shift that week, and he was the intern on call. At three in the morning Frank Cagney, the schizoaffective in 518, woke up and began prowling the halls, looking for a piano so he could continue his composition, "Funeral Mass for Bobby Sands." Bobby Sands was an IRA hero who had starved himself to death in a British prison. Frank had told her the whole story about fifteen times. Of course, there was no piano on the Psychiatric floor of New England Memorial Hospital in Boston, but that didn't make any difference to Frank, not in his present state.

Marty was making her rounds, checking everything very carefully. There was a full moon. She had just come out of 540, where she thought she'd heard whimpering, when she was nearly run over by Frank Cagney. He was so frantic, he could barely talk. He didn't seem to recognize her, and that was bad news, because when he was feeling good, he flirted with her. Now he was angry because "they" had taken his piano away and just as the *Dies Irae* was coming through loud and clear. "Loud! And clear!" he kept repeating as she walked him in the direction of the nursing station.

As they passed the station she said very calmly to the nurse behind the desk, "I think Frank needs some help. Get the resident on call." And continued on her way, holding firmly onto Frank Cagney's arm. He talked very earnestly, explaining how Stelazine interfered with his creativity but the doctors wouldn't listen to him. "They don't care! All they care is they get paid!"

The intern who came running, with rumpled clothes and red-rimmed eyes, was Paul Giordano. He took over right away, walking Frank back into his room, chatting with him and treating Frank's delusions very seriously. Marty was a bit miffed at being left out, but she liked how he dealt with Frank. One thing she hated was the way a lot of the staff treated the psychiatric patients—as if the patients had lost their feelings along with their sanity. She especially hated the way they would talk about the patients, right in front of them, as if they weren't really there. Marty felt keenly that there was a person in there somewhere, no matter how irrational the behavior.

Paul Giordano had to be sleep-deprived—any resident on call usually was—but he was deft and brisk. In two minutes he had Frank sitting in a chair and was giving him a quick physical. "What medication are you taking?"

Frank gave him one of his superior smiles. "You mean, what am I supposed to be taking?"

"Oh, a wise guy." Paul turned to Marty and remarked, "I thought he was decompensating, but if he's stopped taking his meds . . . well, that explains it." So, he did it, too. Marty was disappointed. He turned back to Frank. "What have you been doing with the pills?"

"Down the toilet! Like Bobby told me! Down the toilet, out to sea! They couldn't make him eat, you can't make me swallow poison pills. You're mad at me. Well, I'm mad at *you*, too. I'm sick and tired of being told what to do, what to do, what to do. . . ." He sang the last phrase. "Marty, give me a sleeping pill. I'm so tired." Paul Giordano, busy writing on the chart, snapped to attention. "Your nurse's name is Miss Dauber."

Frank gawked at him and so did she, although for quite different reasons. "We're not so formal here, Doctor," she said, surprised and, yes, pleased, that he knew her name.

"We are when I'm on duty. And when I'm on duty, patients don't prescribe for themselves. I'll let you know," he said, looking straight at Frank, "if I think you should have a sleeping pill."

"Well, excuse *me*!" Frank sniffed. He appealed to Marty, "You see why my creativity is stifled here."

"Tell me about it!" Giordano said, and suddenly yawned. This elicited a smile from Frank. Much better, Marty thought. She would have been so disappointed if Paul had turned out to be just another pompous PGY-1, all full of himself and unwilling to admit he didn't know a damn thing.

"You can't be creative if you're not getting enough sleep, Frank. I know I can't. Just give the pills a try, okay?" Paul stifled another yawn, and actually smiled. "Then we can both get some rest."

As he continued writing on the chart, Paul repeated the instructions out loud, for her benefit. "Yes, Doctor. Right away," she said, with some resentment. He handed her the chart—it was her job to put it back where it belonged—and she checked it over. He had written Thorazine.

"Thorazine, Doctor?" she said.

"Of course not. Stelazine." His tone was impatient.

"Yes, Doctor," Marty said, following him out into the hall. "But you wrote Thorazine," she continued in a low voice and showed him the chart. Now maybe he'd come off the arrogant-doctor routine. "And maybe you'd like him to have Restoril. I know Frank, and when he's like this, he really *can't* sleep."

"Shit!" Paul said, with feeling, burying his forehead in his hand. "Boy, did I goof!" He corrected the mistake, then looked up. Finally, their eyes met. His were bright blue, she noted. There was dark stubble on his jaw, a cleft in his chin, a bump in his nose. He was beautiful, she was a goner, and they were both heading on a perilous course. She knew, because a big dopey grin was spreading all over his face just as she could feel a big dopey grin on her own. She tore her gaze away and turned to go, acutely aware of the pulse hammering in her throat.

"Thanks," he said. "And, Nurse? Miss Dauber? Marty?"

"Yes, Doctor?" To her amazement, her voice sounded perfectly normal. "Is there something else I can do for you?" *Can I kiss you? Can I have you for my very own?*

"When you go off duty . . ."

"Yes?"

"What do you say we have some dinner?"

"At seven in the morning?" Why was she arguing?

"Dinner. Breakfast. Lunch . . . who cares? Do you?"

She shook her head. "No." It was crazy, but at the same time so comfortable.

He took a few steps toward her, his eyes still locked on hers, and she stood, unable to move, thinking, He's going to kiss me, right here in the middle of the hall. And she wasn't going to stop him, either.

But then his beeper went off. He shook his head and grinned. "Rotten timing. I'll meet you in the main lobby in . . ." He looked at his wristwatch. ". . . in just three hours and five minutes." Again, a huge yawn. "And twenty-six seconds."

"How long have you been on duty?" Marty said.

"On call every other night for the past month, in Peds. Then I catch it again, on Psych. But now I'm glad." A big crooked grin.

She could feel the blush rising in her cheeks. "Shouldn't you go home and get some sleep?"

"Probably. But I'd rather see you." His beeper went off again and he was running down the hall, away from her. She missed him already. Absolutely nuts!

Later, she stood in the lobby waiting for him to show, feeling conspicuous and stupid, her heart sinking as five minutes passed, then ten. At last he appeared, running, his hair still wet and with comb marks, looking for her, and her pulse began to race.

"How did you know my name?" That's how she greeted him, like a stupid child, blurting out the first thing she thought of.

"Are you kidding? The first time I spotted you, I asked somebody who you were. I have a terrible weakness for red ponytails." He grinned at her and, in the most natural way, took her hand. She thought she could be perfectly happy just to stand here with him, hand in hand, for the rest of her life.

Eventually, though, they made it to a big cafeteria near Copley Square, sitting across from each other in a booth, a bit bleary-eyed but happy. All around them were people who had just begun their day, full of morning cheer, gobbling their muffins and eggs and swinging on out with their attaché cases, ready for business. They ordered soup and burgers and then forgot all about them. They both hated pomposity, advertising, and the Academy Awards. They both thought "M*A*S*H" was the best thing that had ever happened to television and they were bummed that it was ending. They both liked Italian opera, Woody Allen, and dancing ... "slow dancing," Paul added, "where you don't have to know any steps."

"Yeah, me, too," she agreed, smiling back at him.

He came from a small town in upstate New York, "Millville," he said with such obvious distaste that she laughed.

"Does it look like a Millville?"

"Exactly. Gray and ugly. And small-minded. They don't like Italians in Millville, look down on them." He grinned suddenly. "But I showed 'em. I was class valedictorian. My brothers and sisters, too, we were all top students. I hope you like small towns," he added suddenly.

"I beg your pardon?"

"I hope you like small towns. Do you?"

"No," she said, laughing again. "Not at all. I come from a small town and I haven't been back since I left for nursing school."

"What about your family?"

"No family." Usually, she didn't think about her parents, the ugly little house, any of it. But now, seeing the sympathy in his eyes, she had to blink hard, not to puddle up. She pretended to get interested in her burger so she wouldn't have to look into those eyes. "Nobody."

"You can borrow mine. I have plenty . . . Mom, Dad, three brothers, two sisters, a million cousins. Millville's full of Giordanos. You'll have plenty of family."

She couldn't look at him. He wasn't saying what she thought he was saying, was he? He couldn't be, it was too soon. Christ, they hardly *knew* each other! "I don't know what you mean," she lied.

"I mean you're going to marry me, oh yes, you are, stop shaking your head. . . ."

"Paul, come on."

"I've known since we fought in the hospital, before. I really was going to call you and ask you out, you know, like a gentleman. But work . . . well, you know how it is with residents. But now we've met and the thunderbolt has struck. You know about the thunderbolt? It's Italian, Neapolitan, actually. It means you and I will get married. You'll see." He grinned and took a forkful of french fries from his plate, putting them right back down. "I just hope you won't mind living in Millville."

"Live in a town where you say they hate you? A town you describe as ugly and small-minded? You kidding? What would make you even *want* to? Yeah, I'd mind. *If* I was going to take you seriously."

"Oh, Marty, you can take me seriously. I've never been so serious in my whole life. And Millville *is* a pretty awful place. But I've got to go back there."

"Why?"

"Our plan is that we go back to Millville and become the beloved town professionals. My brother Mark is going to be a dentist, and my brother Gene is at law school, and my brother

Joe . . . well, he can't decide whether to go in for medicine or law. We're all going back there and become beloved leading citizens and run the damn place. The best revenge is living well . . . isn't that the saying?" He leaned back in his chair, smiling broadly and looking kind of dreamy. "Yeah, I'll be Doc Giordano. Everyone will call me Doc. I'll deliver everyone's babies and then I'll give them their shots and talk turkey with them when they're adolescents. I'll know everyone's family and my patients will feel better the minute they come into my office. Maybe I'll run for mayor. So, Marty . . . what do you think?"

"I hope it all happens for you."

"I meant, how does it sound for you?"

"Well, it doesn't appeal to *me*." Although she had to admire the idea. There was something very creative about taking revenge by taking care of your tormentors. "But remember, I hate small towns."

He frowned. "Gee, I'm sorry I gave you the idea it's, like, horrible. It really isn't. But tell you what. We'll go there, the first weekend we both have free, and you can see for yourself."

Marty laughed. "We only met today . . . sorry, last night. Slow down, okay?" But she didn't mean it.

"Besides being beautiful, Marty, you saved my rear end." He smiled at her. "Not to mention my life and possibly my career. And by the way, the patients can call you whatever they like. I was way out of line there. And I shouldn't have yelled at you."

"That's what nurses are for."

"Are you giving me the business? Never mind. I don't care. Do your worst. It can't even come close to what I go through with Dr. Retch. Jesus, what is he doing, heading up a department in a major medical facility?"

Dr. Retch was the staff nickname for Myron Rich, a fussy, plump man with a reputation for stupidity. "They say he can't be fired because he's somebody's nephew or something," she said. "Isn't he only the interim chief?"

Paul groaned. "Yeah, but it's *my* interim. I try to get things done, only everything has to go through the chief resident, and the chief resident does not like me. He thinks I'm a wise-ass." He stopped, thoughtful, and laughed. "Actually, he's right. I am. You know, when I picked this hospital, McDermott was chief of Family Practice. We got along great. Why'd he have to die?" He groaned again. "We're slaves, especially us lowly H.O.-1s. 'House officer!' Sounds good, doesn't it, but we're just overworked peons. Drudgery, drudgery!"

Well, she had to laugh. "It sounds like nursing! Only you're an M.D., and sooner or later you'll get all the prestige and all the power and all the big bucks."

"Oh, you think so? So how come you chose nursing? Why not go to medical school?"

"No money, for one thing. And it never occurred to me. But now I wouldn't change it. It seems to me that medical training teaches you guys to stay at a distance—to see diseases, rather than people."

"Oh, and I suppose nurses are better?"

"Damn straight! We don't just walk in, look at the chart, and prescribe more drugs. We talk to the patients."

"You try being up for over thirty-six hours! You'll find you're not exactly talkative."

"Oh, really?" Marty said, leaning back and giving him a humorous look. "I hadn't noticed *you* running out of words, not while you were giving orders."

There was a very long moment of silence while she regretted her big mouth. Then he said: "Do you know you have the most astonishing eyes? Sometimes they're green and sometimes they're gray, and sometimes they're golden. Actually *golden*." He reached across the table to take her hand. She was almost unable to breathe. "When I look into your eyes," he went on, "I forget how totally wrongheaded you are."

It took a few seconds and then she began to laugh. What a nerve! What a guy! He yawned, loudly.

"I'm sorry," Marty said. "I've been shooting off my mouth and you're exhausted. Why don't you ask the waiter for the bill? Then you can go home and get some sleep."

"Oh, no! I want to be with you."

"Well, then I guess I'll have to go home with you." It just came out of her mouth.

For a moment he just stared blankly at her, and she felt like an idiot. And then that grin spread across his face and his eyes lit up and he leaned right across the table and kissed her, saying against her mouth, "Let's go."

They went to his bed-sitter, three long flights up in an old brick house with very high ceilings. Paul stopped at every landing and kissed her. Inside, he turned on one dim lamp and kissed her again. She got a quick impression of the large cluttered room with a bed shoved against one wall. They headed straight for it, kissing each other, undressing each other. The shock of his naked body against hers was electric. He pulled her down onto the bed, into his embrace, whereupon he fell instantly asleep. And, after a while, she slept, too.

The afternoon sun woke her. They were still wound around each other, and one of her arms was numb from his weight. She pulled herself carefully away and sat up in bed, studying him. He had thick black eyebrows and a definite Roman nose, high-bridged and bold. Thick black hair on his chest and his legs and his arms . . . everywhere. This was so weird, sitting on a strange bed in a strange room with a strange man, looking at him and loving him, feeling totally at home, as if she'd been here forever.

His eyes opened. He looked at her without surprise and smiled. "Good," he said. "You really *are* here. I was afraid it was just a beautiful dream."

They made love for the first time in the daylight with their eyes open, looking at each other. It was perfect, and it didn't matter if they hardly knew each other. Nothing mattered except that they had found each other. She moved her things in the next week. Not that they saw a whole lot of each other. But they knew they were together, and that's all that mattered. Or so she thought.

They had lived together six months when she came home from work one day and all his things were gone. Paul was gone. He was gone from the hospital. From Boston. He'd just disappeared. People asked her in hushed whispers what had happened, and all she could do was shake her head. For weeks she walked around in a haze of pain, doing her job like a robot, trying not to think about Paul and unable to think of anything else. There was no street in Boston, no restaurant, no corner in the hospital, where she could escape her memories of him. She was slowly suffocating from her misery. Finally, she left. She took the first job offered, at Middletown Mental Hospital. It was awfully close to Madison, and she really didn't want to be near her old hometown, but she was desperate to get away.

She'd learned a couple of things, that was for sure. Love at first sight was a crock. Love of any description was dangerous. And loving someone could damn near kill you. After a while she had it all figured out. In every relationship there was one who loved and one who was loved. It was never even. Well, never again, she promised herself, would she be the one who loved, the one who came out losing. Never again, never.

8

Thursday morning, about quarter to seven, the city was still hellishly hot. But Marty Lamb was up and running, and Shayna Brown, sitting in her window on the world, was dressed and resplendent in some gorgeous Israeli jewelry Marty had been told was about two thousand years old.

"Marty, do you have a minute?" Shayna called.

Marty walked over. "I always have a minute for you."

"Not for me. For Mama. Can you come in and talk with her?"

"What's the trouble?" The request was unusual. It had to be serious. Miriam came to the center for her medical care. As the *rebbitzin*, the rabbi's wife, she'd set the example for the rest of the Survivor women, so now they all came to the center. Since they paid, and since so many of CCC's other patients did not, they were greatly appreciated.

"Just her old arthritis."

Her old arthritis? Marty doubted it. For Miriam to call her in, at this hour of the morning, something else must be bothering her. Maybe something about the pregnancy. Oh dear, and

Miriam had wanted to reassure Zeke with a new baby, didn't want him guessing, *ever*, about all her abortions. But what could it be? Maybe this time she was going to have a genuine miscarriage. Maybe—Marty stopped herself. It was stupid, to try to guess before she'd even talked to the woman.

She was buzzed into the large, ornately furnished foyer. The Survivors seemed to go in for heavy, dark furniture, deep colors, and Oriental rugs. No pictures on the walls, no paintings, no sculpture. But sconces and beaded curtains and crystal chandeliers and vases? Loads of *them*. And filigreed screens and Chinese figurines and velvet draperies. And smoked mirrors. Nothing modern; at least Marty had not seen anything that looked as if it dated later than the nineteenth century.

Once in, she hesitated. Outsiders were not often invited into a Survivor's home, and she wasn't sure of the rules, even after all this time. Then she heard her name being called, very softly, and turned. Miriam was standing in the door to the kitchen, motioning to her.

Miriam was a good-looking woman, too thin, Marty thought, but beautifully turned out, even at this early hour, and wearing a designer dress. Marty recognized it because she'd seen a sketch of it in *The New York Times* a few months ago. Although the Survivor Orthodox women did not wear wigs, like the Hasidic women, they did keep their bodies covered. Marty had never seen any of them in shorts, or even long pants. Which she found strange, since trousers covered more than even a longish skirt. But it was their rule and their life, and she didn't have to follow any of it.

The kitchen was a *big* surprise. It was huge, with doubles of everything. Two Zero-King refrigerators. Two large Aga cookers from England, shiny and black. Large double sinks, microwaves, toasters, broilers, mixers, choppers, food processors, coffee makers, bread makers . . . her head began to swim. And it was all modern—shiny with stainless steel and ceramic tile and high-gloss enamel. Everything gleamed and glittered.

Marty's face must have been a study because Miriam began to laugh at her. "Didn't Zeke tell you we're up-to-date in some ways, Marty?"

"Zeke didn't tell me you had kitchens like this . . . my God,

Miriam, it's like a showroom . . . like a spread in *Architectural Digest*!"

"Survivors like to eat. It's a defense mechanism of some sort."

"But . . . two of everything?"

"Oh, that. We keep kosher. You can't mix meat and dairy. So . . . yes, two of everything." She laughed again. "Never mind the lesson. Can I give you coffee?"

Marty had smelled it when she came in, and she was longing for a cup. "Yes. Please."

Miriam poured them each a mug, brought out cream and sugar and sweetener and motioned toward a butcher-block counter lined with stools. They sat side by side, and for a moment said nothing, just sipped the fragrant brew.

"Good," Marty said.

"Zeke gets a special blend at the coffee store. I'm glad you like it."

"So." Marty turned and looked straight at her hostess. "Your arthritis is bothering you, Shayna says."

"You know about the pain in my fingers and wrists . . . it's there, I ignore it, and sometimes I even forget about it. . . ."

"I hear a 'but.' "

"You're right. But. I don't know, maybe I'm imagining things. I know that rheumatic diseases run in the family. I remember how surprised I was when Dr. Zee told me that my arthritis and my father's gout were first cousins, so to speak. Oh, my father, of blessed memory, and his gout! When he had an attack, he gave everybody hell!" She laughed. "He gave us hell all through my childhood. Now that he's not here, yelling and grouching, and now that *I'm* hurting, I understand a little better. He must have suffered horribly. To move an inch in his chair made him scream with the pain."

"I remember. Dr. Zee told me the story of how she finally figured out that it was his homemade wine."

Miriam laughed. "That really annoyed him, you know? He was so proud of his wine, he had inherited the recipe from *his* father, who had it from *his* father of sainted memory. . . ."

"And he made that wine every year down in the basement of

the building. But there were old lead pipes down there, and lead was seeping into the vats of wine."

"He just wouldn't believe that his good wine, that he made with his own hands, could be giving him a disease. Someone else's wine? Maybe. But not his."

They both laughed. It occurred to Marty that Miriam had managed to avoid talking about whatever was really bothering her. Well, enough of these family tales.

"You don't think you have gout, do you?" Virtually all gout patients were men, so she knew the answer.

"No, no. My feet are fine."

"What's the trouble, Miriam? It's not your pregnancy, is it?"

"How do you know I'm pregnant? Even Zeke doesn't know yet." She gave Marty a sly smile.

"Dr. Zee mentioned it. She says you're due in this week, for your Alpha-fetoprotein test."

"Yes. Maybe this time the poor little *rebbitzin* won't miscarry." She smiled, but her eyes were sad. "No, it's not the pregnancy that's bothering me. It's my arthritis. I think." There was a long pause and then she blurted out: "My hands are so much worse, suddenly. And then there are the other things . . ."

"Other things? Like what?"

"My hair is falling out, all of a sudden."

Marty looked at her more carefully. She'd thought there was something different about Miriam. Her hair had been cut so short, it was only a curly cap. The long braid was gone.

"Yes, I had it cut. I was hoping that might make the hair loss stop. I thought . . . maybe all the brushing, all the pulling when I braid it . . . I don't know *what* I thought. But it hasn't helped. It still falls out."

Marty took one of her hands to examine. "Anything else?" she asked, frowning because she couldn't help noticing the inflammation around the edge of the nails.

"I'm very tired. Of course, that could be the pregnancy. The first three months, I want only to sleep, sleep, sleep. But . . . somehow this is different. Sometimes I feel that I'm running a fever. Like today."

"Fever . . ." Marty repeated. "Did you take your temperature?"

"No." A little laugh. "I think I didn't want to know. I can't afford to stay in bed; too much to do."

Marty put her hand on the other woman's forehead. Definitely feverish. "Maybe you have a flu. Your stomach bothering you?"

"Well . . . I've been feeling queasy, nothing big, just enough to kill my appetite."

Her fingers were an odd bluish-white color, quite unlike the rest of her olive skin. Fatigue, fever, hair loss, nausea. Years of arthritis-type symptoms. *Lupus?* Marty had wondered, several times in the past. *Please, no.*

"Are you making a lot of cold food for your family, lately?"

"Don't ask! I'm in and out of the Zero-King all day getting cold drinks and ice cubes! But what does that have to do with my hands?"

Lupus. She was almost certain. But not a word, not until Miriam had come in for a workup with Dr. Zee.

"You'd better start wearing cotton gloves when you go into the refrigerator and freezer, Miriam."

"Gloves? You're kidding me."

"No, Miriam, I'm not."

"So. What is it?"

"I have a notion, but I don't tell people my notions. Why don't you make an appointment with Dr. Zee and—"

"I love Dr. Zee. I respect her. But you're as good as a doctor. Maybe better."

Marty slid her an amused look. "You shouldn't believe everything Zeke says, Miriam."

Stubbornly: "You're as good as any doctor. Wasn't it you who discovered what was wrong with his sister when to every doctor it was a mystery?"

"It just happened that my own father had been accused of being drunk during the day because people saw him staggering down the street. We had a smart doctor. He made a guess—that it was an inner-ear thing—and he was right. That's how I recognized it so quickly when Rachel came into the center. I'm not a miracle worker . . . and I'm not a doctor."

"No, just a brilliant nurse-practitioner who's a great diagnostician." Miriam smiled at her winsomely. "I don't want to be a pest, but since you began to take care of us, it's the first time I ever felt I had something to say about what happened to me. You know what most doctors are like: they give orders, we follow, no? But it's different with you. You get . . . involved. I feel that, if I needed a friend, I could call on you. Even though you're not a Survivor. So. Tell me? Please?"

Marty took one of Miriam's cold little hands in hers and said, "It wouldn't be right, Miriam. It wouldn't be professional." But she was pleased at the kind words. She had a good eye and she did diagnose better than some of the M.D.'s at the hospital—she suspected it was a talent you were either born with or not. She was forever reminding her staff that every single patient, even a stinking alcoholic sleeping in doorways, even a crazed crack addict, deserved respect as a human being. It was nice to have her philosophy appreciated.

"Look, Miriam," she continued, "I could be way off base. Even if I was a doctor, I'd tell you the same. Please. Make an appointment to see Dr. Zee right away, okay?"

"Zeke would rather you took care of me."

"The hospital would rather Dr. Zee saw you. Don't worry, I'll always take care of you. But I'm not sure of anything, Miriam, really," she said. If it was lupus, Zeke would have to be told. And he'd also have to be told that a pregnancy was contraindicated. What, she wondered, would the rabbi do about *that*? Would he insist that an abortion was out of the question, even if Miriam's life were at stake? Oh, Christ, what a mess *that* could be. "I want you to see Dr. Zee. Let's find out what's going on, okay? I don't like you being anorectic."

"Anorectic?"

"Not eating. It's not good for you and it's not good for the baby, either." Marty paused. "Sometimes—" she began; but Miriam pulled her hands away, shaking her head, tears slipping down her cheeks. "Miriam, what is it? Is there something you haven't told me?"

"No, no. It's just . . . I've been so terribly tired lately. And worried. About the pregnancy. And now . . . something *else* is going wrong! I feel terrible, you know, that I can't give him a nice big family of healthy children. That's my job, to bear him healthy children."

"Miriam, Shayna's spina bifida is not your fault. And you have three healthy sons."

"I know, I really do. Never mind my tears. I'm feeling sorry for myself. Thank you for coming in this morning. I know how busy you are."

"Maybe you should have talked to me sooner. I'm not *that* busy."

"Please. I'm a strong woman. I will handle this, whatever it is. Only . . . don't tell *him*. Don't tell him I'm pregnant and don't tell him I'm not feeling well. I will, all in good time. He . . . he isn't very good with sickness, as you know. I think it scares him because he doesn't know what to do. So . . . not a word. Deal?" She managed a shaky smile.

"Deal." Interesting, Marty thought, how Zeke Brown's women almost never referred to him by anything other than the lordly "he," as if there were no other male in their world. Before she left, she elicited a promise from Miriam to make an appointment with Dr. Zee.

The rest of Marty's walk to the hospital was thoughtful. What did Miriam mean by "handling" it? Maybe I should have told her, she thought, prepared her a little, let her know that she might have an illness she won't be able to keep a secret from her husband. Maybe I should have explained that her pregnancy could be dangerous to her. But why scare her? Maybe it wasn't lupus. You could never be *too* damn sure of yourself.

When she got into the hospital lobby, there was a little knot of people on their way out, too intent on their conversation to notice anybody else. When they saw her, everyone nodded but nobody bothered to introduce her. Although she didn't need an introduction to recognize Dr. Eliot Wolfe of Harmony Hill Hospital.

She watched them exit, thinking hard. Dr. Wolfe *again*? Twice in one week? And with Stuart Wanamaker, the chief financial officer of the hospital, very interesting. Ah, and Clive Moses, too, head bent to the visitor to catch every golden medical word. Eliot Wolfe must know some great jokes, because as they stopped a moment, Clive put his head back and laughed heartily. Then they pushed out the revolving door and left. Except for Clive, who came right back in on the next turn of the doors.

"Marty!" he called. "Just the person I wanted to see."

She stopped. "And why does that make me immediately hang onto everything I own?"

He laughed. He did have a great laugh. Clive Moses, Mr. Charm, Mr. P.R. Clive was charming and intelligent, a master of the sound bite, and loyal to *his* master, Dr. Messinger. Marty just knew she was right—All Souls must be up for sale, because Clive was so busy making it look mainstream and important. For the past two years he'd concentrated on pulling in donations from all the doctors who had ever worked at All Souls, printing their pictures in the slick, shiny newsletters he put out, and making lists of donors, patrons, and grand patrons, so everyone could see how much each doctor had given. Marty hated that, but when she said so to Clive, he'd shrugged and grinned and said, "Hey. It works." He was also great at planning huge formal parties in someone-or-other's honor; he was glib with visitors and gracious with Administration.

But lately, all of a sudden, he was interested in the clinics. He came out regularly to monitor the Life Saviors, and he was sending stories about interesting medical innovations to the media. Suddenly he was painting the hospital as a place of health and healing. Interesting switch.

For Clive, Marty made an effort and smiled. He could be a formidable pain in the rear, but his heart was in the right place, and anyway, you never knew when you might need him. Not to mention that he was a great-looking guy, if you liked them tall and brown and muscular. Which she did. Sometimes. She and Clive had a kind of love/hate thing going.

"I wanted to apologize. For butting in on your speech the other day."

"Don't worry about it," she told him. "But don't do it again."

"Don't hate me. I thought Pierce was gunning for you, and I was only trying to head him off at the pass."

"Cowboy metaphors? From you?"

He did have an engaging grin. "Haven't you heard? There were tons of black cowboys back when the West was won."

"I was referring to your urbanness. And I suppose I should be grateful to be saved from the tender mercies of Hamilton Pierce. But I can handle him."

"You're a nurse, not a P.R. person, Ms. Lamb. A very good nurse, a very experienced nurse, and, if I may say so, a very attractive nurse—"

"Whoa." But she couldn't help a little smile. The man was shameless. "I accept your apology, okay?" She turned to go.

"Then there's a chance for me?"

"Clive, Clive." He really was appealing; too bad he was so aware of it. "I'm not the girl for you. Why don't you use your considerable magnetism on Crystal? Don't let her incredible beauty fool you; she's also very smart."

For just a moment the pleasant expression on Clive's handsome face disappeared. Marty was startled. She couldn't remember ever seeing him rattled; but he sure was rattled now. He couldn't even look at her! "Not my type," he said tightly. "Well . . ." And he left, pushing back out through the revolving door.

Very interesting. Mention Clive, and Crystal snaps at you; mention Crystal, and *he* comes all unglued. She'd like to find out what *that* was all about . . . and who had dumped who—*whom*. But not now. Now she really *had* to get to her office and get going on her paperwork.

She hustled through the lobby, went through the swinging doors, stopping just long enough to get herself a candy bar out of the machine, in case there wasn't time for lunch. When she let herself into her office, she swore at the thick, stuffy heat. Somebody had come in again and turned off the air conditioner? What the hell was going on? But when she tried to snap it back on, it didn't cough and wheeze and finally begin to clank, which meant it was working. Shit. It hadn't been turned off; it was broken. Muttering vague curses under her breath, she huffed and puffed and finally forced the other window open—not that there was much in the way of fresh air, anyway. She'd have to call Maintenance, always an exercise in futility, but the damn machine had to be fixed. She sat down, prepared to call, and there, still sitting on the desk, was yesterday's lunch, unwrapped and unappetizing. No wonder she felt so empty and tired lately! She kept forgetting to eat.

The phone rang. She picked up, saying "Yes?" in a voice that sounded much more out of sorts than she felt.

"Is this Mrs. Lamb, Marta Lamb?" asked a male voice she'd never heard before.

"Yes. How can I help you?"

"You could help me, Mrs. Lamb, first by explaining why you haven't had the courtesy to return my calls."

What an attitude! "Excuse me? Who *is* this?"

"Dr. Armand Chen."

She waited a few seconds. "Dr. Chen?" It didn't sound familiar. "I'm sorry, I don't think I know you."

"You don't *know* me, Mrs. Lamb . . . except for the fact that I've left three messages on your machine in the past few days and you haven't had—"

"I received no messages, Doctor."

"Oh really, Mrs. Lamb, do you expect me to believe that?"

She almost hung up on him. "As a matter of fact, Doctor, yes."

"Three messages got lost? *Three?* I find that incredible."

Now she had to laugh. "Dr. Chen, if you worked here, you wouldn't find it incredible at all!" But there was no answering laughter. Okay, then. "Why don't we start from the beginning, Dr. Chen. You may have left three messages, but I didn't get them. My machine wasn't even blinking when I walked in a few minutes ago. Of course, my air conditioner wasn't working, either. In any case, how can I help you?"

"I am Armand Chen, director of the Mansion. You're familiar with the name, I presume?"

Her heart began to race uncomfortably. "I am familiar with the Mansion, yes. Is Owen back with you? Has something happened to him?"

"Ah. Then I *do* have the right person. What has happened to your husband, Mrs. Lamb, is nothing short of a modern-day miracle. He is asking for you, and I am calling to suggest you come here to see him at your earliest convenience." The plummy voice had changed from annoyed to enthusiastic. But what was he talking about? Go up there? What for?

"Why should I do that, Dr. Chen?"

The voice became etched in acid. "You *are* his wife?"

Marty, drawing in a deep breath, massaged the back of her neck with one hand. "Technically. But the last time I saw Owen, Dr. Chen, he had made his way to New York and ended up in Bellevue. They were calling all the Lambs in the Manhattan phone book looking for me because he'd been raving about his wife the devil nurse who made him sick. They thought they could get me to pay the bills, you see. They finally found my name in the nursing register, and bingo!

"When I walked into his room at the hospital, Doctor, he shrank back on his bed and screamed. He held his fingers up in a cross, Dr. Chen, and yelled, 'Get thee behind me, Satan.' It took them a long time to get him calmed down, I understand. They suggested I not attempt to see him again. And I was only too happy to oblige."

"You don't understand—"

"No, Doctor, it's *you* who don't understand. You're calling the wrong Mrs. Lamb. The one you want is Beatrice. His mother."

She thought she heard a smirk—how could you *hear* a smirk?—as he said, "I know Mrs. Beatrice Lamb. She brought her son in to us eight weeks ago. We put him on Clozapine and it has worked wonders with him, Mrs. Lamb. I promise you, he is much improved, *much* improved. In fact, he is asking for you. 'My wife,' he says. 'Marty.' That *is* you?"

You know fucking-A that's me, Marty thought, but did not say. "Look, Dr. Chen, are you new at the Mansion?"

"A year. I have been in charge for a year."

"Well, perhaps you don't know the whole history of Owen Lamb and our marriage."

She paused, then decided. No, not the whole history, not in ten minutes, over the phone.

"We should have been divorced long ago. When he wasn't out of touch completely, he refused to sign the papers. Most of the time he wasn't competent to sign *anything*. And then I became very involved in my career. I went back to school. I have both a master's and a Ph.D." Let him put that in his pipe and smoke it! "However, I now have divorce papers and I—"

She stopped. She was beginning to quiver with tension. "Do you understand what I'm saying, Doctor?"

Stubbornly: "He has been asking for you. By name. And he is, I promise you, a changed person. Could you not find it in your heart to just *see* him for a few minutes, over the weekend?"

Oh shit. "I'll see him. But that doesn't mean—"

"That's all we ask, Mrs. Lamb. I think you'll find him *greatly* improved. I think you'll be pleased."

In a pig's eye, she thought. She had stopped having any feelings for Owen a long time ago. Well . . . pity, yes, sure. Compassion, she hoped. But nothing you could call *wifely*. Just the thought of having him touch her . . . !

After she hung up, she sat at her desk, mad at herself. Why did she still let certain people push her around? Certain *men*? Oh, hell! She was tired, she was hungry—she eyed the salad from yesterday and politely declined—and she was melting because of the broken air conditioner. There were two clinics this morning, and that's where she should be. She was leaving.

As she was closing the door, the realization came like a kick in the stomach. Her messages had been erased. On purpose. By the same devil who was leaving all the hate mail. She pictured this person, sneaking into her office, her private space, listening quietly to her phone messages, stealthily erasing them, tiptoeing out, carefully closing the door. For how long? How many weeks or months of watching and waiting and listening? *Who*, for God's sake? Who hated her so much? Who would go to so much trouble to make her afraid?

She left the office in full tilt, as if something were after her. It was stupid; she knew she could not run away from it. She wasn't the only target; it seemed to be all of them at the Community Care Clinics. Someone had a crazed agenda, and she had to confront it. It was either that or submit to the craziness, and submission, she decided, was *not* her style. Sooner or later she was going to have to find out who it was and face her . . . him . . . it . . . whoever, and put an end to the harassment.

9

As soon as I-95 turned into the Connecticut Turnpike, everything looked greener, cleaner, serener. Marty had the stereo on as loud as she could stand it, playing one of her James Taylor tapes, singing along at the top of her lungs. Not that her voice was so wonderful, but making a lot of noise was one way not to think about where she was heading—which was the Mansion, the expensive psychiatric hospital half hidden in a fold of gentle hills not far from the ferry slip at Cold River.

She was on her way to visit Owen—not her idea of a great way to spend a Saturday afternoon. She hadn't laid eyes on him since that time in Bellevue. As a medical professional, she had to believe Dr. Chen when he told her that Clozapine had rendered her husband healthy and human. But in her mind's eye she still saw that sweating, stick-thin figure cowering into a corner of the bed, shrieking at her. Her lawfully wedded husband, once a beloved Wesleyan University associate professor of English Literature of the Nineteenth Century, now lost in schizophrenia.

Most of the time for the past eight years, Owen might just as well have been on the planet Mars. Only now, apparently, he was getting better, *much* better. That meant she had to tell him she'd stopped loving him long ago. He had to realize that she'd gone on with her life, had changed. So much had changed. It was stupid to have put off getting the divorce. The separation agreement sat crisp and unfolded in her briefcase on the seat next to her. Today was the day. It had to be. Otherwise, she had a sinking feeling, she might find Owen dumped into her lap. Into her life. What in hell would she do *then*? She *was* still his wife, and he was, however improved, a sick man with a fragile

ego. Well, she didn't want to think about it; she was not going
to think about it!

She turned the sound up on the tape player and decided she
would not think about her marriage at all. She'd think about
something else, *anything* else. But what she ended up thinking
about, of course, was last night.

She and Clive Moses happened to be together yesterday, at
a long, boring meeting with Dr. Messinger and Stu Wanamaker, discussing how many ways she was going to have to
cut back in the clinics. As they left, Clive asked if she'd like to
grab some dinner at Protozoa. She started to decline and then
changed her mind. What was wrong with her? Why shouldn't
she go out with a good-looking, charming man? All right, so he
was a public relations hack, but he was a fairly nice guy, not to
mention a hunk. She deserved it!

"Will you take me the way I am, in my nurse clothes?"

He grinned at her and said, "I'll take you dressed any way at
all." And she felt herself blush. It was his voice, she decided;
his voice made the most innocent things sound suggestive.

They sat in one of the quieter corners of the room, sharing a
bottle of wine and talking about this and that. Marty was
enjoying herself, and then she spotted Aimee Delano, all shim-
mery in a silver-gray silk suit. She was perched on a bar stool,
a cocktail glass next to one hand. And the other hand . . . the
other hand, by God, was caressing Paul Giordano's arm. Well,
resting lightly on his arm, but still . . . ! And he wasn't exactly
pulling away in disgust.

Marty turned her head away quickly and smiled at Clive, but
her mind was racing and her good feeling, draining away. She
didn't look toward the bar again but she could *feel* the two of
them, their heads getting closer and closer together. When the
homemade Portobello ravioli was set down in front of her, it
smelled lovely and tasted even better; but she only picked at it.

She was sick with jealousy. She, a thirty-four-year-old professional woman who certainly ought to know better. Poor
Clive, he tried hard, he even made her laugh several times; but
she was not great company. Finally, she said, "Clive. I'm so
sorry. I—"

"Forget about it."

"No, I won't forget about it. I've been enjoying myself so much, but ... I've just got a lot on my mind. I have an unpleasant task coming up this weekend, I guess that's it. Can we do this next week one night?"

"*I'd* like to, very much. But I don't want to be anybody's charity case, Marty. It just so happens I like you. You're a straight shooter and you laugh at my jokes. Both rarities."

She reached out, placing her hand over his. "I swear. This is just a bad time for me. I can't talk about it, I can't answer questions. Maybe next week. It all depends. . . . There. You see? Too complicated."

So they left Proto's early. He walked her to her building and didn't even suggest he might come up for coffee, just lifted her hand to his lips briefly and said good night. Then she recalled Aimee's long, slender hand and her mood instantly changed. Maybe it wasn't fair; but who cared? She was sick and tired of always being dumped. It was never a good idea to get too friendly with the other hired hands, but everyone did it anyway. And who would know? She watched his broad back, fast disappearing up the block.

"Clive! Wait!"

He stopped instantly and turned, waiting while she ran up to him. He was grinning.

"You look like the wolf preparing to eat Little Red Riding Hood," she said.

"I'm willing to try," he murmured, reaching out one hand and putting it on the back of her neck. A chill ran right down her spine, and suddenly she was short of breath.

"You're on," she said, and they began to walk back to her brownstone. They did not hold hands, and they both kept a fairly sedate pace—until she unlocked her apartment door and they were both inside. Then, with one move, Clive kicked the door shut behind him and scooped her into his arms, bending his head to her and pulling her into a long sweet kiss that kept heating up until she thought she would melt into the floor. It had been such a long time!

When he left the apartment, sometime in the middle of the night, he had reached out a finger with a tender touch to the tip of her nose. "To be continued, Marty Lamb, to be continued."

* * *

But that was crazy! The whole idea was nuts. It had been foolish to go to bed with him. They both held positions of responsibility at All Souls. She couldn't *do* this! No matter how much fun it had been . . . and it *had* been. And anyway, why was she thinking about Clive Moses as she drove to see poor Owen! The night with Clive was a momentary glitch, it would never happen again, and nobody would ever know, right? Right, she told herself, giving her car more gas, pleased when it responded instantly.

She loved her car. The little red Honda Civic was ten years old and didn't have air-conditioning. She really ought to sell it. Today, the sun roof was wide open, as were all the windows. Fortunately, traffic kept moving on the turnpike. Otherwise she would be broiled alive. She promised herself she would trade it in on a new Civic, a civilized car with air-conditioning, if she ever found enough free time. If she still had a job.

Automatically, she turned off at Exit 61. Madison. Her hometown. But she didn't drive toward the shore, which would bring her into the beautiful and charming little main street that looked for all the world like a stage set for a play about the simple joys of New England life.

She turned the other way. Her childhood in Madison, Connecticut, had not been joyful. Since she had been forbidden to have visitors in the house, the young Marty had concentrated on schoolwork. She had been an excellent student. In ninth grade she met Gerald Kelly, head of the high school English department, who had a little coterie of teenage girls he called the Group. It was several years before she realized he'd stolen the name from Mary McCarthy.

Jerry Kelly taught "Women in Literature," a course he had advocated and for which he'd written the syllabus. He was also advisor of *Fireworks*, the school's brand-new feminist newspaper. In traditional Connecticut he was considered something of a rebel, but interesting, and he certainly kept the kids busy and off the streets.

She was chosen to be one of the Group—"I'm taking you under my wing," he told her, laughing and bringing her close to him in a mock embrace that both thrilled and scared her. "I want every single member of the Group to realize her full potential. You women have been held down too long!"

Prof, as Gerald Kelly was called by all the students, was very popular. He was full of energy, always on the kids' side in any issue. He was willing to hold *Fireworks* meetings at his own house, after school; and there were many evenings when eight or nine girls would be gathered around his dining room table with layout sheets and rubber cement, pasting up the pages.

The rumor was that Prof had been almost married. According to the story, his bride-to-be had been killed in a terrible automobile accident on her way to the wedding; so there was an aura about him of the tragic hero. Marty had a terrible crush on him; all the girls did, but hers had a special edge to it. Before him, no adult in her life had ever paid attention to her. Prof paid attention. She was a star student, but they didn't talk only about school. They talked about all kinds of things.

He took her for long rides in his old Chevy, up the shoreline, stopping to walk on a deserted beach, chucking stones into the Long Island Sound, talking about . . . oh, everything. About the Indians who once lived here. About life in the sea. About people. He knew all about this part of Connecticut; he said he was the unofficial historian of the Connecticut shoreline. She thought he must be the most brilliant man in the world, maybe in the universe.

One gusty, bright October afternoon they were gathering shells on a beach with no name, a tiny curve of sand and rock hidden from the road by a copse of blazing scarlet maples. It was a beautiful day, smelling of the ocean and the clean, sharp wind, and she found herself telling him a little of what it was like at home. She was sixteen and it was the first time she'd ever talked about it to anyone. When she began to cry, he pulled her into a tight comforting embrace, patting her back with one hand. After a while the tears stopped, but he kept holding her and the hand slipped down her back and the pats turned slowly into caresses and then she became suddenly, thrillingly, scarily, aware of the big hard bulge on his belly.

She'd heard about this, heard jokes and snickers and slang words, but she didn't know what she was supposed to do about it. Prof began to kiss her neck, very sweetly, and then he pushed her away and said, "Oh Christ. I'm sorry. But you're so lovely, so special. Oh, little Marty, can you forgive me?"

"I . . . guess so. Sure."

He pulled her back into him. It was so good to be *close* to someone, to hear someone else's heartbeat, to be cuddled and loved. He said, "Don't be afraid, Marty, let me show you how I can love you." And she was happy to do it. She loved him so much; she needed his love so much.

She'd never told anyone about Prof—Jerry, as she learned to call him. Not even Dr. Zee; and she had bared her soul to Dr. Zee. But not about him. It had seemed so good at the time, and it seemed so bad in retrospect. They had been lovers until she went away to college. It was wrong of him, very wrong of him, but on the other hand, he had probably saved her sanity. She certainly would have gone crazy, living in that house filled with her father's anger.

It wasn't fear of seeing Jerry that kept her from visiting the old hometown; he had died of cancer when she was in her first year of nursing school. She just hated the very thought of driving down there. It wasn't Madison's fault, it wasn't even her father's fault. Especially, it wasn't her mother's fault. Then who *was* to blame? Her mother's family, still living somewhere in Trieste, she supposed? Oh, to hell with it. She had no reason to go to Madison, no reason at all.

She was so lost in her thoughts, she almost missed the Mansion's half-hidden driveway. She drove slowly up the twisting road until the hospital materialized, in all its gabled glory, like some lord's Stately Home, in a clearing bordered by huge rhododendron bushes. Marty pulled around the side and into the discreet parking lot in back. Everything at the Mansion was terribly circumspect. If you wanted to deny to yourself that your loved one was as nutty as a fruitcake, this was a place you certainly could give it a shot. She got out of the car and locked it, even though there was nothing of value in it. But she had been told by the manager, that it was . . . er, um, wisest not to put temptation in anyone's way. What did that mean? she wondered. That the patients here were in good enough shape to hot-wire her Honda and escape? Or simply that someone feeling particularly hostile might get into the car and slice the uphol-stery to ribbons?

Her heartbeat sped up as she approached the baronial front entrance. What if the doctor was wrong? What if she found Owen all wild-eyed, talking in disjointed fragments of thoughts, accusing her of being the enemy or an impostor?

"You're not my wife! Get out of here! Get this strange woman out of here!" That used to happen, the first few months he was sick, back when she thought he might get better. Unless he was curled in a corner, lips moving silently, eyes squeezed shut, acknowledging no one. Or distant and dis-tracted and unconnected to this world. Or none of the above.

Once, six years ago, before Bellevue, he was at the Mansion and they had been able to stabilize him—enough so that he wanted to see her. Beatrice had called to tell her.

"My dear, he's been bothering everybody night and day, *insisting* you come see him. I know he wasn't a good boy the last time, but he asks for you so *piteously*."

Marty, still half hoping a miracle might happen, had come for a visit, joining him in the cafeteria. He had looked up and said, "Hello, Marty. Coffee?" It wasn't the old, charming, eru-dite Owen, but it was a human being, even though the voice was flat. This Owen would answer direct questions, with one or two words, and then the eyes would slide away and go blank. She hadn't stayed long and he didn't even say good-bye. He had lost interest completely. The *idea* of her was the thing. Once she was there, he had nothing to say to her, nothing he wanted to hear from her, either. She hardly existed in the real world, only in his own. She knew all about flat affect, from psychiatric nursing, but being faced with it in Owen . . . that was different. It hurt; and it reminded her painfully of her childhood. But that visit was light-years ago . . . well, a few. A lot had happened in the field of psychotropic medicine in those few years. A miracle might occur, she supposed.

Taking a deep breath, she let herself into the main reception area, a huge open space with a vaulted ceiling and twin carved staircases curling down from a balcony, one on either side of the reception desk. The floors were marble. The volunteer behind the huge, carved admissions desk in the entrance hall was a beautifully groomed older woman with pink hair. Bright pink. Marty tried hard not to stare at it.

"Mr. Lamb? Let's see now. Ah, here we are. Yes, he's out in the rose garden, waiting for you, Mrs. Lamb."

You never visited a mental patient in his room. It was always in a public place: the gardens, the coffee shop, one of the three-sided lounges. The lounges were arranged like miniature living rooms, pretending to be part of somebody's home—except for the fact that hospital workers patrolled regularly, walking back and forth, checking casually on each of the stage sets.

"I wonder . . . before I go to see him, do you suppose Dr. Chen could spare a minute for me?"

She was in luck. The doctor was in, he was free, and yes, he'd be delighted to see Mrs. Lamb.

And he *was* delighted, giving her a big toothy smile and actually patting her hand after he shook it. "Owen has been thrilled over your visit. I'm so glad you reconsidered."

"I didn't reconsider, Doctor. I told you I would come on Saturday and here I am."

The doctor nodded, smiling. "You'll be wanting to take him home very very soon, and I think we'll be able to accommodate you, Mrs. Lamb."

She sat, staring at him in disbelief. *Take Owen home?* Had he not heard a single word she'd said to him over the phone?

"Dr. Chen, perhaps you don't realize that Owen has been in and out of hospitals since 1985."

"Yes . . . ?" Puzzled.

"That's eight years . . . eight and a half, really. We don't have a marriage. We don't even have a friendship. I don't want to take Owen home with me, not ever! I believe he's always gone home to his parents."

"He has been asking for you. He's been very definite."

She knew what Chen would say if she told him how Owen blew hot and cold about her, sometimes loving her and sometimes convinced she was the enemy. He'd say yes, but this is different. Maybe it was and maybe it wasn't. She didn't care. She wasn't going to take Owen home with her!

"I think you'll find his mother's signature on every single paper having to do with any of his stays here. In any case,

Owen and I were married such a very short time before he . . ." Her voice faded; she could see by the set of his face that he did not want to hear her and was not *going* to hear her. "In fact"—brandishing the briefcase—"I've brought a separation agreement with me. I'm hoping he'll sign it before his release. I don't want to give him any false hopes . . . if indeed he's hoping anything."

The doctor pushed his thin lips in and out several times, steepling his fingers thoughtfully. "It seems unfortunate timing, now that he's so much improved. . . ." His eyes were unreadable behind the glinting spectacles.

"Yes, Doctor, but I'm not responsible for his illness. And it's been a very long time."

"Well, yes, I *must* agree with that. And you've gone on with your life. As is right, of course, as is right."

"Well?"

"Well, what?"

"Is there any objection to my going ahead with this today? I mean, I can wait a week or two . . . even longer, if necessary, I suppose. I wouldn't want to do anything that might interfere with his recovery." Why did she feel as if she were prattling?

"What you do is entirely up to you, Mrs. Lamb."

Oh, right, make whatever happened *her* fault! No more cordial smiles now. His entire posture said, *I have completed my experience with you.*

"*Ms.* Lamb, if you don't mind," she snapped, and then felt like an idiot for losing her temper.

She marched out, trying to shake off her resentment. Owen would be sure to pick up any emotional overtones. The mentally ill were always tuned in to all feelings, real and imagined. If you weren't perfectly calm, they knew it instantly. And reacted instantly, too. She didn't want to agitate him. It occurred to her that, in spite of her years of training, in spite of her doctorate and all the published articles, she was *scared* of him.

Owen was sitting on one of the ornate wrought-iron benches that dotted the rose garden, a tall man, slender almost to wispiness, his sandy hair thinning, his shoulders bent inward. He looked so frail and sad, sitting there among the rosebushes, all ablaze with red and pink and white blooms. He was smoking a cigarette. Most mental patients smoked a lot, she remembered.

"Hello, Owen." How tentative her voice sounded.

He looked up and actually smiled. "Hello, Marty, long time no see."

"Yes, a long time."

"I'm sorry . . ."

"Sorry? What for?"

"Sorry that I'm back here."

She tried to smile. "Yes, Owen, so am I."

After a long moment he said, "I feel much better now, Marty. I think I'll be leaving soon. I hope I haven't forgotten how to drive." Another pause. "Do you still have our car? The Volvo?" His beloved '73 Volvo had been sold for scrap as soon as she realized that he wasn't going to get better.

"No, of course not." She tried to keep her voice light. "It was a 'seventy-three, Owen, ten years old and on its last legs when we had it. Like the one-hoss shay, it just suddenly gave up."

"We said we'd keep it forever." His lips twitched into a half smile. So he remembered. They had loved that car, and yes, they had made a pact one night over a bottle of wine, only half joking, to keep that car maintained so that it would never die. Like their love. In any case, he'd just managed to touch her. It was going to be very hard to say, *I'm glad you're coming along so well and so long, we're getting divorced.* But she had to.

"Why don't we take a walk, Owen. There's something we need to talk about."

"Walk? All right." When he stood, she could see a little potbelly. The medication often caused patients to put on weight. That's why so many female psychiatric patients took themselves off their meds; they wanted to stay slim. They weren't *that* far out of reality! But Owen had always been skinny. A few extra pounds wouldn't do him a bit of harm. She remarked that he seemed a bit heavier.

"Yes. I don't know why, but I seem to be putting on some weight."

Marty paused. In the beginning, Owen had denied, no *insisted*, that he wasn't schizophrenic. His enemies had made up the lie in order to keep him prisoner here, in this terrible place where they spied on you—through the television, through the radio, through the electrical wires. There had been a time when the mere mention of his medication would send him into a fury. But she might as well give it a shot.

"You're putting on weight because you're on a new medication, Owen. You're aware of that, aren't you?"

He stopped, scowling. Uh-oh, she thought, now I've done it. But he said only, "Oh. Right. I forgot." And then lapsed into silence.

She kept chattering to him as they walked. As long as she asked him about himself—what he'd been doing, whether he'd tried to write poetry again, stuff like that—she would get answers. Sometimes he managed several sentences. He wasn't what she would call normal yet, but he was on the verge.

By the time they had walked to the building and had taken seats at a table in the cafeteria, she wished she hadn't come. Owen was convinced they were still a couple, and she found herself becoming angry with his mother. Beatrice had been in charge of him all these years; why hadn't she ever talked to him about it? They picked a table by one of the many large windows, overlooking the manicured lawns. Small tables were scattered around the room, set at angles for a feeling of privacy. But there was no real privacy. The attendants who stood or sat at attention had a good view of the entire room from anywhere. She was feeling terribly conflicted. It wasn't fair to disappoint him. But it would be even more unfair, she told herself firmly, to let him think something that just wasn't so.

"There's something I want to discuss with you, Owen. . . ."

"Marty, I never explained to you, why I sometimes had to yell at you. You know how it is . . . when you're told something, you just have to check up, find out if it's true or not. You understand, don't you?"

"Who tells you bad things, Owen? That's what I don't understand."

His eyes slid away from hers, then back. He gave her a tiny secretive smile. "I have my sources."

"Sources?"

"I can't say more than that."

Her heart sank. It was the same old story. He was still

unwilling to believe that his "sources," his voices, came from his own head. How recovered *was* he? Just how miraculous was this miracle medication, anyway? She sat, silent, for a moment, then decided what the hell, she'd just jump in with all four feet.

"Owen, do you realize? We've been apart over eight years."

"I had to leave, Marty. They made me."

"What I'm trying to say is . . . Look, our marriage has been over for a long time and——"

"Who told you that? They lie! They lie all the time! We're still married!"

"I know, Owen, but——"

He leaned closer to her, his eyes narrowed in a way she remembered only too well. "Who told you? Who? I'll make them take it back!" His voice was rising and it had that old edge to it. Without thinking, she leaned back, away from him. From the corner of her eyes she saw one of the attendants, lounging against the doorway, stand a bit straighter, suddenly alert.

"Owen, please. Don't upset yourself."

"I want to know who is telling you lies!" His voice was very loud now.

Marty stood, holding tightly to the briefcase. "Owen, I'm sorry. I can't stay if you yell at me."

"I'm not yelling!"

The aide was at Owen's side in a second, holding his arm firmly, murmuring into his ear. For a moment Marty watched, trying to catch Owen's eye, maybe give him a smile before she left. But he had gone back into some private hell. He had seemed so good at first; but he had probably cheated on his medication. In the early years he'd only take half of what the doctor prescribed—if he took it at all. Or so Beatrice had told her.

Marty did say good-bye, but Owen was too busy arguing with the aide to hear her. She watched as he was gently but firmly marched out of the cafeteria.

Outdoors, the bright sunlight made her blink. Fumbling in her bag for dark glasses, she walked toward the parking lot, chiding herself. She must have handled it wrong, to upset him like that. She needed some professional advice. She should talk to Joel Mannes . . . he was a good shrink. Not only that, but he knew the whole story.

Years ago she had gone to Joel when she could no longer deny Owen's strange behavior. She was scared to death to say anything at all—for fear it might be true. But at least Joel was a friend—and a friend of Owen's, too. The two couples had seen each other socially. She knew Joel would understand and be kind, and wouldn't immediately jump to the worst conclusion. And he wouldn't tell anyone.

Joel had listened intently, looked at her and said, very seriously, "I think Owen is sick, Marty."

Panic squeezed her chest. "He's always been a nervous wreck. And he has a tendency to get . . . overwrought. It must be the Irish poet in him." She laughed, but Joel would not play.

"I'm not talking neurotic, Marty," he said.

She sat very still—they had gone into an empty room in the hospital where, at least, neither of them was likely to be noticed and needed. A thousand thoughts raced through her head, a thousand arguments, a thousand reactions. But she said nothing because she knew, with sinking heart, that Joel was right. Owen was sick and it wasn't just neurotic.

"What should I do?" she finally said.

"Get him admitted."

"Not to Middlesex!" The State Hospital for the Criminally Insane in Middlesex County. The whole idea of gentle, poetic Owen being criminally insane was ludicrous.

"Shhhh. Not so loud. I meant here, at Middletown Mental. That way, we can do a workup. *I* can do a workup, see what's going on. Although . . ."

"Although?"

"Nothing. Really, nothing."

"You were about to say that you're pretty sure you know what it is."

He pulled in a noisy breath. "Yes, that's what I was going to say. But how can I be sure without observing and testing?"

"What do you *think* it is?" She was panicked, sure he would say the same thing she was thinking. The unthinkable. But he refused to say the dreadful word "schizophrenia," because that was the same as saying "incurable."

Strange, how vivid the memories were; it had all happened so long ago. She unlocked the car door and stood outside a minute, letting the heat out, thinking, What next? Her first move should be to report this visit to Joel. Joel would know what to do—and then, with a start, she realized suddenly that he was *another* person who knew she was married to a psychotic who had tried to kill her. That made three, Dr. Zee, the poison pen, and Joel.

Or how about only two, if Joel were the poison pen writer. She was immediately ashamed of herself. Joel? Sweet funny Joel? Her friend of long standing? Still, hadn't she thought Owen—even during his odd, overwrought wooing—totally incapable of violence? Never mind that . . . hadn't she thought that Paul Giordano would love her forever? And what about Prof, what had *that* been about? Love . . . or sexual abuse? And her cold, distant father, how about *him*? Had she *ever* been right about a man?

She slid into the driver's seat and, gripping the steering wheel tightly, wept frustrated tears. Was there a single man she could count on? Who in the world could she trust?

10

Marty stood alone in the Conference Room. Alone and shaking and scolding herself for being such a wimp. She'd found another one of those gray hospital envelopes in the middle of her desk this morning. Her heart had started thumping heavily the minute she spotted it. Damn it, she should be able to handle this. She was trained to deal with *anything*. And what was it, anyway? Just a pamphlet for Clozapine, the kind that was included in every shipment of drugs, extolling the virtues of the medication and giving warnings about possible side effects. All very medical and impersonal. There had been nothing scribbled on the margins, no note attached, no horrid picture or pasted-together message saying something odious . . . nothing like that. She just hated knowing that somebody nameless and faceless and nasty knew so much about her.

Furthermore, it was Wednesday and she still hadn't gotten up the courage to call the Mansion and arrange another meeting with Owen so she could tell him she wanted a divorce. Every time she even thought about doing it, she got a stomach-ache. So here she was, still as married as ever.

"I don't know who you're thinking about right now, but I hope to God it isn't me." Joel Mannes came into the room, eyeing her with some trepidation. Joel looked like the Mad Scientist, his springy hair rumpled, his tie askew, the pockets in his white coat stuffed with . . . *stuff* that kept falling out. Everyone said you could always find Dr. Mannes by following the trail he left behind him.

"Don't mind me. And no, it wasn't you. You're a good guy. You *are* a good guy, aren't you, Joel?"

"Of course. See my white hat? Oops, pardon me, white *coat*?"

"Make me laugh, Joel, please! I'm losing it!"

"Not you, Marty! You're too young to lose it. But why don't you tell the kindly old shrink what's putting those grooves between your beautiful green-not-hazel-*green* eyes."

She laughed at him. He really *did* know her. Too bad he was shorter than she was and already taken; otherwise, she might marry him. She eyed him with a mixture of affection and shame. He was such a dear old friend. How could she think for a moment he might be the poison pen? And yet, who knew? She hated not being able to trust people. Pretty soon the room would start filling up with her nurses. She'd *hired them*, she'd chosen them from dozens of applicants—but in spite of herself, she would be studying them, watching for the odd expression, the strange question, the weird smile, wondering all the time who was hiding madness—or maybe just meanness—behind a mask of normalcy. In any case, this was no time to fill

Joel in on Owen's "miracle cure" and Dr. Chen's insistence that she play wife. Later.

"It's the curse of the executive, Joel. Grooves between the eyes. I'm worried about accreditation," she fudged. "The hospital made all those big promises, three years ago, and *nothing's* been done. Except," she couldn't resist adding, "new goodies for all the *attendings*, if I remember correctly. Including a humongous television set in the doctors' lounge?"

At least he had the good grace to look sheepish. "We *are* cads. We know it. But when we were in medical school, staying awake for thirty-six hours at a time, on call, having to make instant decisions while totally sleep-deprived, they swore we would all be rich one day. They *promised*."

Marty repeated slowly, ticking the points off on her fingers. "Staying awake for two days . . . uh-huh . . . on call all the time, yup . . . making decisions without enough sleep . . . yes, that sounds exactly like a typical day in nursing. So how come they never promised *us* a rose garden?"

Joel threw his hands up in mock surrender. "Give me a break! In a few minutes I'm going to be outnumbered! And they're your people, to boot! Please don't let them start in on me!" He poured himself a mug of coffee and plopped into one of the chairs drawn up around the large wooden table.

"Never mind casting yourself upon my mercy, Joel Mannes. Now that I'm on the Executive Committee, all this doctors-are-better-than-nurses shit is going to stop!"

Laughing with him, looking at his sweet, slightly dopey face, she decided she *had* to trust him. She had to trust *someone*, and who else if not the man who was there right at the beginning. Hell, he already knew the worst.

"Joel, listen . . ."

He rubbed his hands, still joking around. "Tell Dr. Mannes everything. . . . You say you are sexually frustrated? Come closer and show me exactly where it bothers you." He leered.

"No, Joel, seriously. Owen thinks he's coming back."

The expression on his face changed instantly. "Owen? As in Owen Lamb, the man you used to be married to?"

"Still am, Joel."

"You never got divorced?"

"Please. Don't start. The thing is, it's not only him—although that's bad enough—it's these letters—"

"Wait. Here they come," he warned.

Even with rubber-soled shoes, the tread of half a dozen people all heading in the same direction made plenty of noise. They trooped in, chatting, laughing, helping themselves to coffee from the party percolator. The room was large but crowded. Banks of file cabinets filled one wall. The other walls held bookshelves and corkboard with notices: bulletins, jobs available, community services, support groups, volunteers wanted, research projects, hot lines. And the drug cabinet, where they kept all the medication samples. No controlled substances, of course. Just cold pills, antacids, tubes of salve for vaginal infections, and the like. Still, the cabinet was locked.

Soon the room was filled with her people. And incredibly, coming in the door right behind the nurses, was Aimee Delano. Marty stared, dumbfounded. She couldn't remember the last time she'd seen Aimee in the clinics. Had she *ever* been here?

"Ms. Delano, what a nice surprise," she said. "Look, everybody, it's the boss." She smiled warmly, and—amazing!—got a smile back. "What brings you to CCC, Aimee? Can I get you a cup of coffee?"

"I'll get my own, thanks. I haven't completely forgotten what it's like to be a working nurse." Aimee turned to the percolator, but Isabelle, quick as always, had a steaming cup all ready for her. "I'm looking in at all the units. Consider this a well-baby visit."

Would wonders never cease? Marty thought. The Ice Maiden was actually trying to joke with her underlings.

"You're in luck, Aimee. We're having grand rounds this morning, not just a regular meeting. So instead of listening to everybody's gripes and complaints, you get to hear Dr. Mannes."

"Lucky me." Aimee turned a dazzling smile on Joel, who blinked and quickly glanced at Marty, his eyebrows shooting up. The Director of Nursing took a seat right next to him and crossed her legs. Since she was wearing a severely tailored suit with a short skirt, her long slim legs were very much on view. Joel waggled his eyebrows at Marty and she shook her head at him warningly. She didn't know what Aimee was doing here, but it must be compelling.

At a few seconds past eight Marty cast a glance around, mentally counting. Everyone was here. Now that the space had become crowded with camaraderie and conversation, her suspicions began to fade. She knew these people, knew them all well. How could she suspect any of them? It was ridiculous! Must be someone from elsewhere in the hospital . . . or maybe an angry patient? Whatever she thought of seemed equally preposterous.

She gave everyone a minute or two to settle down and then said, "Okay, people, the discussion today will be run by our own beloved Dr. Joel Mannes, of Psychiatry, who will talk about mourning the dead infant with us."

"Huh!" Emilio snorted. "No dead babies! Not around here! We don't *get* stillbirths."

There was an outburst of arguing and agreeing which Marty cut off by banging on the desk. "As a matter of fact," she said, "Even though there is the occasional problem, Community Care Clinics has every reason to be proud of our record. Crystal? Will you do the honors? We should hear the good news before we start discussing sad things."

"As you all know, for the past year we've been part of a statewide study of one thousand poor pregnant women. Half were cared for by first-year residents, half by nurse-midwives." Crystal grinned. "Well, the patients cared for by nurse-midwives—you can block your ears, Dr. Mannes, if this is too awful for you to hear—did twice as well as the ones taken care of by the docs. Nurse patients had no stillbirths, no low-birth-weight babies, one C-section, and all our teenage mothers went right back to school! Whereas—" She was interrupted by loud cheering. She tried to speak again but they wouldn't let her so she gave up, saying, "Okay, okay, we're wonderful."

"That *is* wonderful," Marty said, clapping and smiling. "But things still happen."

Joel said, "Think about it, people. We do abortions here." There was a murmur of assent. "Right. Even women who choose abortion may need to mourn and grieve. The days of saying, 'Well, but it wasn't really a child yet,' are over. And the same goes for miscarriages. Many women suffer needlessly because their families—and their nurses, too, I'm afraid, as well as their doctors—won't acknowledge that a miscarriage is a child lost."

"Or they blame it on the mothers," Crystal put in.

"What you're saying is meat for those Life Saviors, Dr. Mannes. Do you really believe that we're aborting little people?" That was Linda, one of Dr. Zee's nurses. "I think of them as fetuses, barely formed, and certainly unable to live on their own."

"I hope you all know I don't agree with the Life Saviors. I only meant there's a real loss—even when the abortion is wanted." He looked around quickly and added: "A miscarriage is an unwanted abortion, people, a natural abortion."

Isabelle had been shifting on her chair, and now she piped up. "You know what I hate? I hate those TV commercials they're showing now, the ones with the adorable little girl who grows up in front of you and then you find out it's a quote *ghost* unquote. It's a child the woman aborted a long time ago and it continues to haunt her. What a terrible thing to do to young people who might be watching . . . who might be trying to make a decision! I'm Catholic and I know the Church agrees with that, but I don't care! I say it's baloney!"

Several voices agreed with her, several others didn't, and pretty soon there was quite an argument going, with Joel putting in his two cents and Aimee taking notes. Marty decided to let them all have their say—if any of the nurses were anti-abortion, she'd like it to come out where she could hear it. She'd heard about nurses who sabotaged abortion clinics . . . oh, not physically, but by spreading horror stories amongst the patients when nobody else was around. She didn't want that here.

"What do you all think about the baby in the Neonatal nursery?" Marty asked.

"You mean the one with water on the brain? Whose parents won't let the doctors put in a shunt? The Christian Scientists?"

"Yes. What do you think?" There was such a long silence that Marty added: "I'll tell you what *I* think. I think the parents need counseling, a lot of it. And I also think the hospital needs the same."

"Why can't we *make* them do it?" Emilio wanted to know. "Aren't we the experts?"

"Right," Isabelle agreed. "Why should they have the right to sentence their child to death, or a life as a retarded freak, just because their religion says so? Aren't we supposed to have separation of Church and State in this country?" She looked around for affirmation and apparently found it, because she gave a brisk little nod and settled back.

Joel hunched forward in his chair. "We may consider ourselves the experts, Izzy, but they *are* the parents and the baby *is* their baby. It must be a nightmare for them. And I think we ought to give them our sympathy and not our disdain."

"What would *you* do, Dr. Mannes, if it was your case?"

"Me? I don't know. I'd counsel everyone in sight . . . well, actually, I'd probably send the baby home, since they're the parents. But of course, I could be overruled. Hospitals have to watch out for malpractice suits and—"

"That's the damn trouble, isn't it!" Crystal flared. "The hospital won't take a stand because it might leave them open for a lawsuit and that might cost *money*!"

"Well, it has to be taken into consideration."

"I'll tell you what gets *me*," Virgie said. "Dr. Fassbinder pats the woman's head and says, 'Now, now, Mother, let's get ahold of ourselves.' And then he says, 'Nurse will explain what's going to happen.' And away he goes. Three guesses whose shoulder the mother cries on?"

"So what else is new?" That was Kenny, and brought forth a ripple of laughter.

"Maybe God is punishing them," Emilio burst out, glowering at all of them. "Don't look at me like that. Maybe you don't believe in God, but I do. And I believe in heaven and hell, too. Maybe they're sinners!"

Joel waved down the murmur of objections. "And if it *is* God's punishment, Emilio, don't they deserve our sympathy for *that*?"

"You're making fun of me!" Emilio sprang to his feet.

"No, of course not. Please hear—"

But Emilio pushed back his chair, tipping it over, and ran out of the Conference Room, slamming the door behind him.

"What's *with* him?" Virgie said.

Marty said, "Kenny? Got any clues?"

Emilio's partner shook his head and shrugged. "He's always had a short fuse."

"Do you think it's gotten worse?" Marty asked, wondering about all that self-righteous anger . . . the talk about God and punishment. Was he the poison pen? But from what she knew of Emilio, who dashed from one place to another and seemed unable to keep still even when relaxing, she didn't think he'd have the kind of patience it took to cut out words and letters and paste them down. Today, for instance, she'd noticed his foot tapping and his fingers drumming as soon as he sat down.

"Worse? Maybe. I learned a long time ago to tune him out a lot. He likes to explode, you know what I mean? It relaxes him, or something."

"I don't like it when someone thinks he's got God on his side," Isabelle said. "What does that mean for the rest of us? Kenny, is he, like, a born-again? Some of my cousins became Holy Rollers." She rolled her eyes expressively. "You can't talk to them."

"Maybe he is. I don't really know." They all looked at each other, somewhat surprised to discover how little they knew of this man, even though they worked side by side with him every day. Well, his temper tantrums had gone on far too long, Marty thought. She'd be having one of her famous little chats with him today.

"Perhaps, Marty, you should talk to him—" Aimee began, when Virgie burst out with, "Maybe it's him!" and burst into tears. For a moment nobody could do a thing but stare at her in astonishment. Marty got up from her seat and went to Virgie, putting her hands on the shaking shoulders.

"Virgie, what is it?" she asked. But she knew. Virgie had found one of those plain gray envelopes in her mailbox, too. It was strange to have to comfort her. Virgie was usually so composed, so imperturbable, so above it all, that she had long ago been labeled the Virgin Queen. Of course, All Souls was the kind of hospital where everything and every-body got a nickname sooner or later. "You don't have to tell us, if you don't want to," Marty said, still absentmindedly rubbing Virgie's back.

The blond head came up. Tears were streaking down the nurse's face and her lashes glittered with droplets but, oddly, the elaborate eye makeup was unsmeared. "No, no. I *have* to figure out what to do about—about this."

"What the hell *is* it?" Crystal said. "Let us in on the secret."

"Maybe you'll be next," Virgie warned her.

"Next at *what*?"

"I'd like to know what's going on, too," Aimee said. She was back to using her executive tone of voice.

Marty went back to sit behind the desk. To barricade herself from what was coming? she wondered.

"I've been keeping it quiet, and I hope all of you will keep this just amongst ourselves for the moment, okay?" She paused, thinking, well, here goes nothing. "We have a poison pen writer." Feeling guilty, she swiftly looked from one face to another, hoping to get a clue.

"A what?"

"An extremely angry person," Dr. Mannes explained, "with an agenda of revenge. Who sends nasty messages to people."

"Revenge on what people? And why?"

"It all depends," Joel said. "Sometimes it's revenge for an imagined wrong. Sometimes it's grandiosity, feeling like God, being able to reach down and punish or just make someone uncomfortable. It's meant to make the recipient suffer. And suffer where the poison pen writer can see it and feel superior."

"Well, it worked! I'm suffering!" Virgie said in a shaky voice, dabbing carefully at her eyes with a lace-edged hankie.

"But why revenge on so many of us?" Kenny asked. "I got one. Angie Buonanotte got one, and it was so horrible she quit. Now that I think about it, maybe Emilio got one and that's why he's so jumpy. Anyone else?"

There was silence. Marty was sure they'd all turn to stare at her and she'd be forced to admit that she had received one, no, *two*, as of today. But no one even glanced her way.

When the door opened suddenly, everyone jumped. But it was only Norma McClure, explaining her lateness as she came in, clutching a stuffed plastic bag. ". . . got a problem over there. What's wrong with getting a doughnut and a cup of coffee, that's what I'd like to know. I only took one!"

Everyone howled. Maybe it wasn't really that funny, Marty thought, but it was a relief to have the subject changed so naturally.

Aimee primly asked, "What were you supposed to be doing, Norma?"

"Why, leaving notes, of course. That's always the first thing I do, Miss Delano. But I'd finished and I heard that there was a breakfast in OB/GYN—"

The nurses all exchanged quick glances.

"Did you have business there, Ms. McClure?" Aimee again, looking very grim and directorial. "Didn't Dr. Dinowitz request that—"

"I said I'd finished my notes," Norma put in quickly, looking aggrieved. "I always do my job." She was Family Practice's Quality Control nurse. Every unit had one, and of course, it had to be the best—or maybe worst—nitpicker they could find for the job. That was Norma; but she often went beyond the bounds, suggesting that a patient was malingering, or questioning the specialists' orders.

A few weeks back she'd questioned the doctor's choice of medication for a patient transferred to Family Practice for recuperation from a hysterectomy. Unfortunately, the woman was Dr. Dinowitz's patient. Dinowitz sat on every committee in the hospital. Some said he sat on the right hand of God, meaning Dr. Fassbinder, who was Dr. Messinger's man. It was the usual convoluted hospital politics. In any case, Dennis Dinowitz had not taken Norma's notes kindly. The word was, he'd said if he ever caught sight of her on his service, he'd fire her himself.

Aimee regarded Norma as if eyeing a lower form of life. "I suggest, Ms. McClure," she said coldly, "that you stay where you belong, in Family Practice. In any case, you have no business horning in on some other unit's breakfast . . . which I understand you do quite often."

Norma sniffed loudly. "What a bunch of jealous, vindictive people!" she declared, helping herself to coffee and a Danish. "Well, I could tell everyone a thing or two about . . ." Her voice trailed off as she turned to find everyone in the room looking intently at her. "What's going on? Why are you all looking at me like that?"

"We were just talking about the poison pen letters," Crystal said, in dulcet tones.

"The what?"

"Come on, Norma, surely you know about them. You usually know everything that goes on around here."

She flushed. "I don't know what you're talking about. What poison pen letters?"

Marty was sure that everyone was thinking what she was thinking: how convenient if it turned out to be Norma. What a good candidate. Everyone found her a little bit loony. Everyone knew she was always taking free samples of everything. Not just food, but a new antibiotic here or a different antacid there, anything she could get her hands on. Maybe she'd finally gone around the bend. But Norma was not devious. Quite the opposite.

"If you haven't received one," Marty said in her best head-nurse voice, "then we needn't discuss this any further. In any case . . ." She consulted her watch. ". . . clinic hours will be starting soon, so . . ."

As everyone started to leave, the office door opened, admitting Dr. Zee and, right behind her, Dr. Paul Giordano, both somewhat short of breath.

"Are we late?" Dr. Zee stopped and laughed, watching the exodus. "Never mind. I see we are. But before everyone leaves, I'd like you all to welcome Dr. Paul Giordano, who has joined the Family Practice service." Everyone smiled and said hello as they were introduced. At Aimee, Dr. Zee stopped, did a brief double take, and then said, "I think you and Dr. Giordano are already acquainted, Aimee."

"Indeed we are." Aimee colored slightly, gave Paul a big smile, and got to her feet. "I'm due upstairs for Pediatrics grand rounds. The head nurse from Mt. Sinai is lecturing. It was nice seeing everyone. Twelve-thirty, Paul." She left, followed by all the nurses.

Dr. Zee helped herself to coffee, gulped some and said, "Sorry we missed the discussion, Marty," to which Marty answered, "No, you aren't. We got completely off the subject."

She avoided looking at Paul, but she could see him anyway. *Twelve-thirty, Paul.* So cool and self-assured. Aimee might just as well have stuck out her tongue at the rest of the women and said, "First dibs on the new doctor, everyone!"

"Tell me about it over lunch?" Dr. Zee suggested. "Right now, I have an elderly patient who neglected to tell her surgeon what drugs she was already taking for her depression and her insomnia and her heartburn. So when he put her on Percodan, after the operation, the mixture made her hallucinate. And now she's damned if she'll ever put another medication into her mouth! When will doctors learn that you must begin by getting a history!" Shaking her head, she hurried out, with Joel racing after her, yelling, "Wait, let me talk to her. Maybe I can help!"

Quite suddenly she and Paul were alone in the Conference Room. And quite suddenly Marty didn't know what to do with her hands or her eyes. He looked so familiar . . . so different. The touches of gray in his hair still looked unreal to her, and there were lines around his eyes and grooves on either side of his mouth that hadn't been there before. His mouth . . . She shifted her eyes nervously.

"Marty," he said softly. "Why won't you look at me?"

She laughed, her eyes shifting. "I *am* looking at you, Paul. Your hair has some gray, but you haven't lost any, congratulations. I'm sure you—"

"Stop it. You won't *really* look at me."

"I don't want to."

"Why not?"

"For obvious reasons."

"Not obvious to me."

"I wish you'd leave, Paul. I have work to do and this . . . this is stupid."

There was a long silence. She kept her eyes firmly on a corner of the table, waiting for him to turn around and walk out.

He didn't. He stood there, one hand shoved into his pants pocket, jingling his keys. He'd always done that when he was agitated.

Finally, he said, "You're behaving just like a schoolgirl with a crush."

That brought her eyes up. "And you are obviously still just as vain as—" And then she saw his grin.

"Gotcha!" he said.

"Paul, that's not funny." But she was laughing. "No, really, none of this is funny. I want . . . I don't want . . . I want you to stop. It's over. It's a long time over—as you should know, better than anyone."

"I know I deserve whatever you think of me. All I want is the chance to explain."

"We can't be friends, Paul. It's impossible."

"Who said I wanted to be only *friends*, Marty?"

Why wouldn't he go away and leave her alone? "Stop it, just stop it. I mean it."

"And so do I." He came closer and she drew back. He made a little sound in his throat and said, "Oh God, I never wanted to see you *cringe* from me. Did it hurt that much?"

Now, blazing with anger, she looked him straight in the eyes. "You can ask me that? 'Did it hurt that much?' How in hell did you *think* it made me feel? One day you were my lover, we were living together, and the next day you were gone! Yes, Paul, it hurt *that* much, and no, Paul, I will never—"

"Oh Jesus, Marty, I am so sorry! I *had* to leave. I was going to send you a note . . . but it was so complicated and . . . and ugly. . . ." His voice suddenly dropped to a whisper. "Someone else was involved and I wanted to keep that quiet. And I was ashamed."

"I should think you would have been. Nobody knew *what* happened to you. In fact, we all thought for a while that you had just dropped out . . . or had snapped—" Her voice broke; so talking about that time could still make her cry. How fascinating. "Look, Paul, I thought I would never get over it, for a long time I didn't get over it. Now, finally, I've made my peace with what happened. So do me a favor, will you? Leave me alone. Just keep your distance and leave . . . me . . . alone." She couldn't help it, tears were leaking out of her eyes.

In a second his arms were tight around her. He still smelled the same. And when he bent his head to kiss her, he tasted the same. It felt so right, like coming home. Then she caught herself and pulled away from him.

"Marty, don't. Please. Maybe you'll hate me after I tell you what happened. But at least you'll know why I . . . disappeared. Please. You have to give me a chance to explain."

"I'd rather not know." Her heart was hammering in her chest and the tears kept falling.

"Dammit!" He pounded the table with his fist. "What I did was not . . . subtle, but it *was* kind. Trust me on this one, it *was*. I didn't want you getting involved in something . . . sordid. So I disappeared. But only for a while. When I was fin—when I felt I could go back to medicine, I looked for you. But they told me . . ." His voice wavered and stopped.

". . . I was married. Well, I couldn't wait forever for a ghost, could I, Paul?" To her horror, she was softening, she was beginning to feel sorry for him.

"But you're not married anymore?"

She gave him a level stare. "Oh, but I am."

"But . . . they said you live alone. . . . They said—"

"Nobody around here knows. He . . . he's not . . . we don't live together. It's . . . complicated."

"It seems to me we have a lot of complications to explain to each other."

"That's assuming we want to, Paul."

"Marty, I'm going to be around from now on. You can't go on punishing me forever."

"I don't owe you any explanations," she said, carefully not looking at him. "You're not part of my life."

She waited to see what he would do. Would he beg and grovel, thereby making one of her favorite fantasies come true? No, he would not. He turned on his heel and left, closing the office door quietly behind him, leaving her filled with a nameless emotion she thought might be relief. Unless of course, it was remorse, and if that were the case, she was in big trouble. *Big* trouble.

11

Impatiently, Marty paced back and forth near the door to the Genetics clinic waiting room, looking at the entrance every few seconds for Ham Pierce. Clive Moses had been after him for a long time to do a positive story on the hospital, and now Ham was ready to oblige. The Birth Defects clinic seemed ideal, Clive thought. There could be a little education thrown in for free, explaining that many of these problems could now be helped and here's the phone number ... that sort of thing. Marty was surprised but grateful. With New York City's large immigrant population, too many people fell through the cracks, simply because they didn't know help existed.

Finally, twenty minutes late, Pierce came strolling in, scouting the territory. "What a zoo!" he muttered to Marty. "Excuse me, Ms. Lamb, but how can I do a sympathetic story on *this* crowd?"

"Excuse me, Mr. Pierce," she said tartly, "but our patients aren't professional models. I know it's maybe a bit bleak and, okay, a little depressing at first glance, but you don't have to bring your cameras into the waiting room. You can come straight back to the examining room. I've arranged for you to talk to a couple of the patients and their parents. It's very important that this gets covered. You know how many kids in this room have inherited sickle cell disease? And there's a family that's had four boys, all with muscular dystrophy—no cure, in spite of Jerry Lewis—"

"Okay, okay. Can I have a look at them?"

"Let me introduce you to Georgie Heller. Georgie's the genetic counselor for the hospital. She's the expert."

"Could she see me now?"

"I'll see how quickly she can be free." Marty had a sudden thought. "How come you're willing to come here with your camera, to a small private hospital that serves mainly women, *poor* women at that, all of a sudden?"

"Hey, Ms. Lamb, didn't you hear? It's the Year of the Woman."

"Give me a break!"

"There's a trend growing and I'm going to be the first one to cover it. Big hospitals are buying little hospitals with a neighborhood feel. Haven't you noticed how you're being courted? First Harmony Hill, and now I hear Cadman Memorial is quote looking into the possibilities. That makes you medical news, and as you know, I specialize in medical news." He grinned.

So, a sale really *was* in the works: it *was* going to happen. She had learned a long time ago that word of mouth was a helluva lot faster—and more accurate—than a lot of official memos. As uncomfortable as it was to contemplate being swallowed alive by a big, tertiary care hospital, it was a lot better than simply closing down. She'd have to get busy figuring out how to sell the virtues and wonders of CCC to the new owners. But first things first. She called to arrange for Pierce to see Georgie, and then began to fill him in on the kind of patients they had.

"Over there, see? The little boy in the wheelchair? Next to the older boy in the wheelchair? They're brothers."

"Oh, Jesus. What a nightmare."

"Yes, you might say that." She told him the family's story.

Roberto Colon was the fourth son with muscular dystrophy in his family. The firstborn, a girl, Irma, was free of the dreadful disease, which struck only males. The parents had been warned about it after their eldest son, Jorge Jr., was diagnosed at about age four; but by that time a second son had been born, and Cruz, the mother, was once again pregnant—with another afflicted boy, as it turned out. As for Roberto, the baby, he was "an accident." Roberto was now six years old and in a wheelchair, and, of course, had no hope of ever getting better. The first boy had died recently.

"Didn't they hear? Abortions are legal," Pierce remarked.

"Out of the question for Cruz Colon. She's a devout

Catholic. And yes, that means that birth control was also out of the question."

Jorge, the father, had disappeared when Roberto was three, leaving Cruz—and her mother, and poor little Irma, too—to cope with this family of doomed boys, all of them needing constant care. Every time Marty saw the Colons she was struck again by how crushed Irma looked, as if she were being slowly compressed—as indeed her brothers really *were*. She felt sorry for the boys—who wouldn't?—but long after they were gone, poor babies, the damaged girl would be left to make what she could of her blighted life.

"And there's Irma," Marty concluded. Both of them regarded the girl, who stood, her shoulders slumped, waiting to push Roberto's chair while her mother got instructions from Virgie. Suddenly, like a bad dream, a man appeared, wild-eyed, needing a shave, and very drunk—you could smell stale booze all the way across the room as he came lurching in. He was shouting in loud, slurred, incomprehensible Spanish. Oh Christ, it was the father, Jorge!

A couple of weeks ago, Marty recalled, there had been some talk that he was back in the neighborhood, out of work, looking for a handout from his wife. Cruz probably would have helped him, too, except that her mother had kicked him out, cursing him, his sperm, and his entire line all the way back to the beginning of time.

What in hell was he doing here today? He headed for Cruz and Virgie, his arms flailing wildly. And then Marty saw the flash of light. Oh my God, the idiot was holding a knife! And he looked as if he intended to use it, too!

"Guard! Guard!" Marty bellowed, and began to run toward the demented man. When she got close enough, she grabbed at Jorge's arm, but he tore away from her, leaving her with only a handful of filthy rags. He headed for Roberto, trapped in the wheelchair, yelling "monster" in Spanish, over and over. Jorge was going to kill his own child, in front of his other children!

Marty reached for him again, but the other patients were in her way, trying to get away. She couldn't just push and shove through the handicapped. Damn! Damn! It was like being in a nightmare where you run and run and run but never move at all.

Then Virgie went sailing through the air, landing next to Roberto's wheelchair. With a mighty push, she sent it careening down the side of the room at top speed. There were screams of "No! No!" as it tilted and threatened to tip over, but it finally righted itself and came to a halt against the admissions window. Roberto wasn't even crying. Julio, the older boy, sent his own chair hurtling after his brother's.

Virgie and Marty reached Jorge at the same moment and grabbed him. He thrashed around wildly, finally throwing Marty off; but Virgie clung to him like a limpet, hanging on, her teeth bared with the effort. Slowly, Jorge began to topple. At the same moment, Marty became aware of a great blinding light, and when she turned, she was looking right into the eye of a television camera. Ham Pierce was approaching, mike close to his lips, talking a mile a minute.

Happily, two security guards appeared right behind him. By the time they got to Jorge, Virgie had forced him down. The two guards managed to handcuff him, and the knife clattered to the floor. Abruptly, he stopped shrieking curses and began to cry in great gulping sobs.

Marty took advantage of Pierce's interest in the action to crawl out of camera range before he thought to interview her. She did not want to see herself on television again; she had been told by Aimee, in the sweetest possible way, of course, that Dr. Messinger did not like seeing directors of programs in his hospital on TV—except in well-planned interviews.

The waiting patients and parents had been stirred up by all the excitement, and it took a good hour and all of her energies to get everyone calmed down again. By the time she had a minute to herself, Pierce and his camera were gone.

At six that evening, in Protozoa, they were standing eight deep at the big mahogany bar, every head aimed toward the huge television set that was bolted into the corner. On the screen, Hamilton Pierce was telling his audience that there had been "some excitement at the Community Care Clinics in uptown Manhattan this afternoon—a knife-wielding madman, two threatened children in wheelchairs, and—most important of all, a *heroine*, a nurse whose swift actions saved who knows how many lives . . ."

"He's talking about *you*, Virgie!" Crystal chortled, knocking back her glass of wine and gesturing for another. The six of them: Crystal, Emilio, Virgie, Kenny, Isabelle, and Marty had the best seats in the house, at the bar, with the huge color TV looming directly over them.

"You're a fuckin' heroine!" Kenny added, and then, laughing, threw his hands in the air and said, "Oooh, I said a naughty word. Sorry, Virgie."

"Well, you may joke, but I don't think it necessary to hear that word every two seconds!" She tossed her head as if to say "so there!"

And then they all concentrated on the big screen again, watching as the camera panned across the building, focused on the entrance to CCC with its make-do sign, then entered. Pierce's voice intoned: "It's two in the afternoon and the Genetics clinic at the Family Care Center is packed with mothers and children . . ."

There was the scene, familiar to most of them. The women sat, listless and exhausted for the most part, while children whined and whimpered and wriggled and squirmed and fought with each other, even the ones in wheelchairs or braces. Marty watched it all happening again: the staggering man, the flashes of light glinting from the big knife. And there was Virgie, looking like a ballet dancer as she launched herself into the air and got to the wheelchair a split second before the maddened father did.

The crowd around the bar murmured approval. Someone shouted, "Yo, Superwoman!" as they watched the wheelchair hurtling past startled, frightened faces, tipping, almost falling, not falling, righting itself. A cheer went up.

Next came a close-up of Virgie, her nurse's cap looking like gull's wings. She was the only nurse that Marty knew of who still wore a uniform and cap. "Cherry Ames always wore her cap," she would say, smiling mischievously. "And so shall I. Cherry Ames was my role model."

"Where did you learn to jump like that?" Pierce was asking her, on-screen. "Girl's basketball?"

"In a manner of speaking. What I mean is, I always *loved* basketball, but they wouldn't let me on the team. Couldn't make baskets."

"Well, you are the hero of the day . . . or should I say heroine?"

"Heroine is just fine. Although I don't think I'm really a heroine. I'm a nurse. My job is to keep my patients from harm."

"What you did was very brave, Ms. Nesbit."

"But you see, Mr. Pierce, nurses are *trained* to be selfless, to put other people's needs well before their own . . ."

A groan went up from the watching crowd. Nurses hated being told that they were always sacrificing their own needs. What else were they supposed to do? There were several cries of "Right on!" and "You tell 'em, Virgie!" But none of them from other nurses.

Then it was back to shots of Jorge Colon being taken away, a close-up of the knife, a really heartbreaking close-up of Roberto strapped into the chair, and poor little Irma with her sad, pinched features standing behind him, as Pierce's smooth voice wrapped up the story.

Whistles and cheers filled the bar. Someone wanted to know if any of the papers had got the story. When Virgie began to answer, a male voice yelled, "Can't hear you!" So, preening just a little, she hoisted herself up and perched on the bar, taking questions with great aplomb and, Marty thought, loving her fifteen minutes of fame. Well, she deserved it; she worked harder than lots of the other nurses. She often took people's holiday shifts and substituted for sick nurses, never complaining or whining. Marty had to wonder sometimes if Virgie had any personal life at all.

Dr. Zee, who was sitting on the next stool, took another sip of her drink. "Where'd Jorge *come* from, in the name of heaven? I thought he left the neighborhood for good."

"Carmen told me, a week or so ago, that he was around and not in good shape, hoping to get Cruz to take him back."

"The bastard. Leaves her with all the problems and then wants her to take care of him, too—agh, never mind," Crystal grumped. "But I must say I'm getting sick and tired of these grown-up babies who can't cope when life deals them a bad hand. Speaking of which," she added, now with a twinkle, "I saw Emilio heading for your office around lunchtime. How did your 'little chat' go?"

"You see me sitting here."

"Meaning?"

None of your business, Marty thought, but did not say. "Problems at home. Did you know that he's raising his two younger brothers? His father is dead and his mother is in a wheelchair. Rheumatoid arthritis."

"No. Really? Emilio of the hair-trigger temper, taking care of a household?"

"When he finishes work, he goes home and makes dinner, takes care of his mother . . . He's exhausted."

"Yeah, yeah, poor guy. How about all the women who do that, all the time? Finish work, go home and make dinner, take care of the kids and the mother in the wheelchair, *and* the old man, if they're lucky enough to have a man living at home."

"Whoa, Crys, who are you yelling at? I'm not sympathetic to women who do it all?"

"Sorry, sorry. It's just that men are such babies."

"I gave Emilio a prescription for Valium. He needs it." What she didn't mention to Crystal was the younger brother on drugs stealing from the household.

"Me, too," Crystal said. "Give *me* some Valium. No, Marty, not really. I'm fine. I'm in control."

Marty smiled at her. "Me, too. I'm fine. I'm in control."

They laughed, but the laughter was rueful.

When the phone rang at ten-thirty, Marty was just about to put her book down and try to get some sleep. Her poor, beleaguered brain was going around in circles and she had read the same page about four times without seeing a single word. Paul was going to be in the same hospital with her, every day. She wished he would go away; she desperately wanted him not to go away. Clive had called her this afternoon with an invitation to "dinner and," and she'd been so tempted. Not that she was either very hungry or very horny; but if she kept herself busy with Clive Moses, she wouldn't have time to think about Paul Giordano. Right.

Plus, all day, she had meant to call Miriam Brown to see what was going on, since Miriam hadn't yet called Dr. Zee for an appointment. That worried Marty considerably. She'd thought about picking up the phone four or five times, but things kept coming up, and in the end she'd left the hospital without talking to Miriam. Obviously, she was losing her mind.

And just to add to her misery, Owen had left a message on her machine. It hadn't happened in years. When he was first hospitalized, he'd call her twenty times a day, never with anything to say, really; but his messages would become more and more agitated with each call. And she'd feel her heartbeat speeding up with each rise in his decibel level. She had come to loathe the sound of his voice, loathe and fear it.

Tonight he had sounded almost normal, just slightly slurred, and he put his words together with extra care, so there was a tiny little pause between each one. He sounded mechanical.

"Dr. Chen says we should talk," Owen's voice said. So that's where he'd gotten her number. "There's something we need to discuss. Call me at . . ." And he left a number. No salutation, no good-bye, no please, no thank-you. His meds really did make him sound like a robot; a superior robot, but a robot nonetheless.

Oh Christ, what did he want? What did Dr. Chen want? But she knew. She knew.

When the phone rang, she picked up, hoping it wasn't Owen again. She didn't want to talk to him, but she knew from experience that if she didn't talk to him now and get it over with, he'd only call again and again. He never noticed what time it was, and he didn't really care. He had no idea that other people had an existence separate from his.

So she was somewhat abrupt. "Yes!" she said.

"Sorry to wake you, Marty." His voice sounded tight.

"You didn't wake me, Clive." At least she wouldn't have to deal with Owen. "What's wrong?"

He gave a brief laugh. "Just what I always wanted—to be thought of as the bearer of bad news."

"Are you? The bearer of bad news?"

"As a matter of fact . . . I don't know what to call it. I think we should get together right now. It's business, don't worry. Hospital business."

"So talk. I'm awake. I'm even alert."

"Well, throw some clothes on, because I don't think this is something we should discuss over the phone."

"You're absolutely sure we have to talk right now?" Now she was really curious. "What's it about? One of the patients?"

"Absolutely sure," he answered. "And no, not one of the patients. And, to answer your next question, nobody is dead. But it's serious and I think you'd better be filled in before morning, okay?"

"Okay. Come over." As she hung up, she was already pulling on a pair of shorts and a T-shirt she'd left on a chair.

"Where'd you call from?" she asked him when he got upstairs, barely five minutes later. "The corner?"

"Almost."

"Soft drink? Seltzer?"

"Anything, just so long as it's cold and wet." He was wearing chinos, T-shirt, and a worried frown. "Jesus, it's hot. It doesn't even cool off at night."

"Tell me about it." She turned away and fussed with bottles and glasses and ice. "The wiring in this building is too old to take air-conditioning."

"It's comfortable."

"Many fans." She handed out the frosted glasses. "And an engineer friend who told me how it's done."

"Will you tell *me*?" He was standing very close to her, and she was aware that she hadn't bothered putting on a bra. Although he wasn't looking. In fact, he looked grim.

"Whenever you say, Clive. But you're stalling. This is real bad news, isn't it? Well, let's have it."

"Like I said, I don't even know *what* the hell kind of news it is. Here. Have a look." He produced a manila envelope from which he drew a snapshot. She took it and looked at it. Like most snapshots, it was a bit blurry. Somebody's birthday, she thought, some kind of party. Three men, heads close together, sitting at the table, drinks in front of them, balloons behind, grinning, obviously posing for someone they knew well.

"Yes, and . . . ?"

"Look at it, Marty. Really look at it."

She studied the small, slightly out-of-focus images. The three faces were very much alike, familiar in an odd way, and one of them had strange, pale gray eyes. . . .

"Aha!" she said. "These guys are related to Virgie, aren't they? One of them has the same eyes. What's this, a picture of her brothers? And why are you showing me this now?"

"The guy in the middle? That's not Virgie's brother, Marty. That's Virgie."

"What? Wait a minute. This is Virgie, dressed up to look like a man? And . . . ?"

"This is Virgie before she was Virginia. When he was Virgil."

"What are you saying, Clive? That Virgie is a . . . a . . . transvestite? That she's really a man?" She stared again at the snapshot as if it could tell her something.

"No. Not exactly. Virgie's really a woman. *Now*. Three years ago, she was a man. She's a transsexual."

"That's impossible!"

"Think about it, Marty. You must have noticed how coy she can get. Shit, *I've* noticed. That's a guy's *idea* of a woman. She's pretending, she's playing a role. And because she's new at it, she overacts."

All the times she'd wondered about Virgie came galloping through her head. The nurse's cap. The disdain of women who wore pants—"trousers," she called them, like someone out of a British novel. The patting of her hair, the exaggerated swing of her hips, which was not quite sexy.

"Oh Christ," she said at last. And then repeated it, with a moan. "How did you find this out?" she asked, thinking to herself, the poison pen strikes again. "Does Virgie know you have this? And what are we going to *do* about it? We have to do something . . . but what?"

"Whoa! That's about seventeen questions. Someone called Ham Pierce, someone who's holding a grudge. Ham said the voice on the other end of the phone—female, by the way—sounded positively gleeful."

"Ham Pierce! Well, that ties it! It'll be all over the news in about ten seconds flat!"

"Nope. He's holding it. He's not going to do anything about the story until he checks the source."

"How about checking to see if it's *true*? Christ, it's so sur-real! Oh, poor Virgie! She's ... I guess I say 'she'? She's going to be devastated. And she's such a good nurse, sweet yet strong, terrific in an emergency. Oh Christ, why do I think now that all these are masculine traits?"

"It's true, all right. Ham got the call right after the program this afternoon and, give the guy credit, he called *me* instead of a television crew. He thought it was a dirty trick for someone to snitch. So he asked if I could check on it. I called Dick Shat-tuck at Harmony Hill ... the urologist. He does a lot of those operations. He had a patient named Virgil Nesbit, who had gone through all the stuff they have to go through—apparently it's a rigorous procedure before they'll cut the guy's ... Anyway, yes, Virgil Nesbit assumed the identity of a woman about seven years ago, just about the time Virginia Nesbit entered nursing school."

Marty remembered the newly minted nurse, so much more confident and competent than any other they'd ever seen.

Dr. Zee had remarked on it. "She knows too much to be a new nurse. And at the same time, she gives practically nothing away about herself. Take it from me, she's hiding something."

Marty had agreed. "I wish I could figure out what. But I don't care! She's a terrific nurse. She can handle anything without so much as a murmur. I figure, some people are just born with the talent."

Now, Marty asked Clive, "So, what did Virgil do, before he ... I'm sorry, *she* went to college for nursing?"

Clive gave her a crooked smile. "Big surprise. He was a paramedic, on a hospital ambulance. St. Francis Assisi, I think. Or, no, maybe St. Vincent's. One of those saints. Sorry, I'd need to look it up."

"A paramedic. Of course. No wonder she's so competent." If it was St. Francis Assisi, could Crys have been there at the same time? Even if she had been, that didn't mean she'd known one particular paramedic. Well, she'd ask Crystal anyway.

Tomorrow morning, first thing, she'd get Virgie into her office, listen to her story and . . . her head was beginning to hurt.

"You're going to get back to Pierce?"

"I told you. He's not going to deal in rumor. But if this woman on the phone called him, doesn't it stand to reason that she's mouthing off all over the place? If she wants to get back at Virgie for something, it's a great way to do it."

They lifted their glasses silently and drank. "Oh Christ," Marty said, putting her glass down, putting her head into her hands. "What now?" She looked up, meeting Clive's warm brown eyes. He really was a good guy, in spite of his job. He didn't have to warn her. He could have just reported what he'd been told to Dr. Messinger. But he hadn't; instead here he was, protecting a nurse. For one mad moment she thought she would tell him about the poison pen letters, but she stopped herself.

"I'm very grateful you came to me, Clive."

Very carefully, he put his glass down and pushed himself up from the table. "I'll tell you what I'd like to do. I'd like to come over there and take you in my arms and . . . do whatever comes naturally." He grinned. "But I'm such a Boy Scout that I'm not going to do it unless you say go. I'm going to get myself the hell out of here and not take advantage of a lady when she's in a weakened condition."

She regarded him. "Clive, listen, the other night . . . it was lovely. I know I'm behaving badly. It's not you. It's my life. Suddenly, my simple, boring life has become horribly complicated. Oh Christ, can you possibly believe that? But it's true!"

He came over to her and put one finger, very gently, on the tip of her nose, which for some reason brought tears to her eyes.

"Marty, I remember that other night, I remember it well and often. But I'm a man who always waits to be invited."

"Oh, Clive. I'm probably going to hate myself in the morning for saying not tonight. But . . ."

"Not tonight," he finished. When he left a moment later, he kissed her on the tip of her nose, right where he had put his finger. And then he was gone and she *was* sorry. He was turning out to be unexpectedly sweet. But, come on, there was

Virgie to think about. What a strange and unexpected twist! She was going to have to be very careful not to *stare* when she talked to Virgie. What in hell was she going to *say*? What was she going to do about Miriam? And what about Owen? And what about Paul? She poured herself some wine and got up to pace. It was nearly midnight, time to go to bed, but she was now wide-awake. It looked like there'd be very little sleep for her tonight.

12

Virgie sat as straight as she could in the chair opposite Marty Lamb, trying not to cry. But she couldn't help it, the tears just kept coming.

"Why couldn't they just leave me alone?" she finally managed to say. "I was doing fine! They never leave you alone, Marty, never! What's the matter with people, that they want to destroy anything they don't understand?"

"That's called human nature, Virgie. People are scared of anything . . . unusual. Maybe you should have stayed away from Ham Pierce and his television cameras?" She spoke gently, but it made Virgie mad anyway.

"One minute I'm a heroine, and the next minute I'm a piece of shit! Excuse my French. They're jealous! I got on TV and they didn't!"

"Virgie, who is 'they'?"

"You think I'm a nutcase! Well, I'm not. I'm a transsexual, that's all. I'm a woman who had the bad luck to be born into a male body. Don't ask me why, or how it happens. I don't know! I've been to thirteen shrinks and *they* don't know!" She took in a deep breath. "Look, Marty, I realize that someone—

one person—who doesn't like me did this. So, okay, I'm out of the closet. Why is it such a problem? Why does anyone *care*?"

Marty looked unhappy and clueless. "Virgie, I'm sorry you're being tormented. I'm not happy about it. But right now, what I need from you is some information. Okay? I know you're hurting, but can you try to concentrate for a minute? And then I'll concentrate on trying to help you, to keep this off the evening news until we figure out what we should say—if anything. So, Virgie . . . please?"

"I suppose I *am* being rather difficult," Virgie admitted. "I can't expect even someone as intelligent as you to just accept me the way I am. You've got to have questions, of course you do. And I suppose—" A horrible thought came to her. "Wait a minute, this isn't going to cost me my job? My *career*?" She reached for her hankie with its tatted edge of rose-colored lace and dabbed carefully at her wet eyes.

"Okay," Marty began. "Let me say, first of all, that I don't think any of this is anyone's business." Virgie couldn't agree more and opened her mouth to say so, but Marty held up a warning hand. "Unfortunately, I am in the minority. Now that the story's been given to Ham Pierce, it's safe to say that soon everyone will have it—and have a good time with it. So let us be prepared."

Virgie nodded, wiped her cheeks, and sat straight in her chair, legs crossed at the ankles. "Stupid of me, crying like that, acting like a baby. I knew this would happen at some point. And you're right, Marty, I should have known better than to go on television. Stefan—he was my driver when I was a paramedic—Stefan's probably the one who got in touch with Pierce. We were a team. We were good, too. We got so we could read each other's minds, almost, you know what I mean? I'd start a thought and he'd finish it . . . and vice versa.

"But I was afraid to tell him . . . about the cross-dressing. Two or three times a week, I'd get all dolled up as a woman and go out. Not to pick up men or anything, it didn't have anything to do with sex. But I felt so strongly that some terrible mistake had been made, and I just *knew* I was really a woman, inside. It was always such a shock to look into the mirror and see a man. So it was important for me to see if I could walk around as a woman, to see if I could pass. . . ." She paused, remembering, then took in a deep breath and said, "I don't want to bore you, Marty. I saw a shrink who specializes in gender confusion. And I went to an endocrinologist for female hormones. I did everything you're supposed to do. I had electrolysis—for the beard—and I saw two different urologists. . . .

"When Stefan began to notice the changes in my body, I knew it was time to leave, so I could live as a woman. He would have *hated* the whole idea; God, I don't know *what* he'd have done. Well . . ." Little laugh to show she was under control. ". . . actually, now I *do* know what he'd have done. I mean, he's done it, hasn't he? Taken my story to the TV people. I don't know how he found out, but—"

Marty held up a hand. "Two things. First, it isn't too hard to trace you, Virgie. You have practically the same name and you stayed in the same profession. Someone was *bound* to find out, sooner or later."

"Yeah, I guess I wasn't thinking."

"And second . . ." Marty hesitated. ". . . I'm told that it was a woman who called Ham Pierce."

"A woman?" Oh Jesus, Virgie thought. She knew who, she knew damned well. She'd thought the message in her mailbox was all the punishment she'd get. She should have known better. Oh Jesus, what *else* was that bitch going to—"What woman?" Virgie asked.

"She didn't give her name," Marty said. "But think. Do you know of a woman who might want to hurt you?"

"No, no." Virgie felt her throat begin to close up. She mustn't panic. Besides, now that it was out, what else could hurt her? Not a damn thing! "It could have been Stefan making his voice high," she improvised, talking very fast. "He liked to do that. Stefan got a charge out of making fun of gays . . . *fags.*"

"Well, that's a possibility," Marty agreed. She scribbled something on a piece of paper. "Nobody else? A woman who loved you?"

"No, no one. I'm sorry, Marty, I've led such a quiet life. The only unusual thing that ever happened to me was my surgery. I don't know why anyone should want to hurt me!"

Marty sighed and said, "I don't know why, either, Virgie. Especially since . . . the surgery—your surgery—it must have taken a lot of guts to take such a final step."

"It wasn't so brave, Marty, honestly. See, Virgil had died— that's how we say it—Virgil was dead. I had changed my name legally, on everything. Only I couldn't put 'female' on my driver's license, or anything. And anyway, the penis was discordant with my female identity. Dr. Mannes agreed that—"

"Joel? Joel Mannes was your psychiatrist?"

Virgie had to smile at the astonishment. "Not since the beginning. But you have to get several opinions, and he was recommended."

"No, no, you don't have to explain anything to me."

There was a loud knock on Marty's door and it opened. Sharon, Clive Moses's assistant, came in. She was a secretary, really, but all the secretaries wanted to be called assistants. Especially this one, Virgie thought, Sharon Graves. She was a pusher. She used too much makeup, though, and her skirts were too tight. You can take the girl out of Brooklyn, Virgie wanted to say to her, but you can't take the Brooklyn out of the girl.

"Sorry to interrupt. They told me I'd find Virgie here. You're Virgie, right? Well, you've got to come with me. Our phones are ringing off the hook, Geraldo is on his way, and there's a reporter from the *Post* sitting outside my office right this minute, refusing to move until she can talk to you. I'm not sure if I got the story straight, and I don't even know if you *want* to talk to the press. But you've got to come with me. Now."

"I told Clive this would happen!" Marty said. You can't trust a newsman. Once Ham Pierce knew, it was bound to spread everywhere. "Damn it!"

"Maybe it was the same woman who called Channel 12, Marty," Virgie said.

Marty studied her. "Do you want to face the media, Virgie? If not, just tell us what you'd like us to say."

Virgie got to her feet, her mind made up. There would be no more tears, no more hiding, no more fear. "You know what?

It's my life. It's my story. And it's my fault that the hospital is being bothered. *I'll* talk to the press and they can be damned!"

13

Marty felt like a child on her first day of school. Did she have enough sharpened No. 2 pencils? Was her hair okay? Would she get along with the other kids?

After all her anxiety, however, there was nobody else from the Executive Committee in the conference room when she got there . . . well, except for Max. Max Beardsly. Aimee's secretary and, some said, her sex partner. Rumor had them involved in some very outré scenes involving a whip and a dog; but Marty didn't believe it . . . well, maybe just a little bit. Max was a very slim, very elegant young man with slicked-back, patent-leather hair. He spoke in the bored drawl and italicized words of an upper-class Englishman—which evidently he *was*. Marty liked Max. He might be affected in his mannerisms and his dress, but he was sharp and imperturbable, two attributes she admired.

"Yo, Max. Am I early?"

"No, dear Marty, *they* are always *late*, you see. I must admit to the tiniest little bit of disappointment. I thought you were lunch."

"If you wait till the lions get here . . . I might be."

One perfect black eyebrow went shooting up. "You think you have been invited to sit on this committee to take the heat?"

"Don't you?"

"If you want to know what I think . . . Yes . . . ? I think you are tougher than they imagine." He arose from his chair and began gliding around the table, setting out tablets of dove-gray

paper and dove-gray ballpoint pens. "You are a strong woman, Marty Lamb. Haven't you discovered yet that strength in a woman inspires fear in most people?"

"Unfortunately, in spite of my title, I have no real power. I'm just one of the peons, following orders."

"The mere fact that you don't back down easily is enough." He laughed. "Your face is a study, my dear. A warning—don't show anything on your face. *Appear* to care about anything and you *will* be eaten alive. Just keep in mind that you do have friends here.

"You know who all the committee members are? Dr. Fassbinder, Dr. Mannes, Dr. Dinowitz . . . Dr. Carlton, who is on vacation right now, and rumor has it that it may well be a permanent vacation, but you never heard that here . . . Where was I? Oh yes, Ms. Delano, Dr. Messinger, Dr. Zee, and now, your own sweet self. Ah, our leader arrives. . . ."

Marty was struck again by how ordinary-looking Dr. Messinger was—an average-sized man in a plain blue suit. Not dove-gray? she thought. His hair was receding a bit in typical male-pattern baldness. He nodded to her, sort of, although he didn't meet her eyes, and sat himself at the head of the table. During the next few minutes the others came in and greeted her so casually, she might have been part of this group forever. Dr. Zee took what was apparently her usual seat, next to Messinger, and patting the place next to her, motioned to Marty to come over.

"Dr. Dinowitz always sits there, Dr. Zee." That was Aimee. Little buttinsky, always looking for infringements of the rules. It was a mystery to Marty why this woman with an accountant's soul had ever chosen nursing. She'd been so different, sitting in on their meeting, that Marty had dared to hope that Aimee had had an epiphany and would join the human race.

"He isn't here, and Marty is a newcomer and a friend of mine. I'm sure Dennis won't mind taking a seat next to *you*, Ms. Delano, since we all know he is a great admirer of good-looking women."

Aimee colored, but there was no retort to that, except to nod graciously and wave Marty on.

"Where *is* Dr. Dinowitz?" Dr. Messinger sounded grumpy. "He knows how I feel about promptness."

"Indeed he does, Dr. M," said the intrepid Max. "And I'll call his office to see what has held him up, shall I?" A grunt was apparently a yes, because Max reached for the phone and punched out an extension, murmuring into the mouthpiece briefly. "On his way," he announced. "Difficult case." There was another grunt from Dr. Messinger.

A moment later Dennis Dinowitz came hurrying in, rather breathless, Marty thought, and slightly disheveled. That was a new one. He was a bit of a fop, always impeccably put together, as if he called in a stylist from *GQ* to do him every morning.

"Sorry. Sorry. Something came up ... terribly sorry. And then, when I went to lock up ... no key! Well, I couldn't— Well, it doesn't matter." Really, wasn't he a bit too flustered for a man who was only a couple of minutes tardy? Was the dear doctor perhaps feeling guilty about something? Marty wondered. Or was it only fear of what Messinger might think of him?

Max handed out the agenda and Marty read it rapidly. Number one was Virginia Nesbit, R.N. She could just guess what *that* discussion was going to be about.

Clearing his throat a little, Dr. Messinger said, "Let us discuss Nurse Nesbit. Ms. Lamb, perhaps you could tell us—"

But Dr. Zee, a smile on her face, interrupted. "Perhaps Ms. Lamb should be introduced, as the newest member of the committee." Another grunt gave assent; and Dr. Zee went on: "I'm sure Marty Lamb needs no introduction. Nevertheless ..."

Everyone smiled and said hello; there was even a smattering of applause—if you could call two people a smattering. And then Milton Messinger glared at her and said: "Well?"

"Well what, Doctor?"

"I think you owe this committee an explanation."

"About Ms. Nesbit's transsexuality? I *can't* explain it. I didn't do it. I didn't know about it. Perhaps you'd like me to have her come in and explain? She does a very good job."

"I don't like hostility, Ms. Lamb."

"I assure you, Dr. Messinger, I am not being hostile. I am

completely sincere. If anyone here is confused about Ms. Nesbit's gender, I'm sure she'd be glad to discuss it."

"You hired her." Messinger said belligerently. Was this how he ran his meetings all the time? She certainly hoped not.

"Yes, I did. But I did not know that she had once been a male. How could I? She fooled everybody. I'm sorry . . . I shouldn't say 'fooled.' Virgie—Ms. Nesbit—honestly feels she was meant to be female. She's a wonderful nurse, you know. She's extremely competent and extremely cool in emergencies. . . . I've rarely worked with a nurse who can stay so on top of an emergency situation . . . and I hope nobody is going to suggest that I fire her, because I won't. We don't have enough nurses on staff as it is." Marty's heart was pounding but she felt very sure of herself.

"I agree," Dr. Zee said firmly. Joel Mannes added, "Psychologically speaking, Marty's right. Ms. Nesbit isn't hurting anyone." From the others, silence.

"It could reflect badly on the hospital," Messinger said.

Len Fassbinder, Chief of Neonatology, snorted and said, "A nurse who's peculiar? God knows we always have enough of *those*! If she's doing her job—and I see here that the patients in her care are dismissed from the hospital in timely fashion—then why are we even talking about this?"

Marty turned to give Fassbinder a hard stare. She did have to admire his style. He'd just insulted all of nursedom *and* Virgie while managing to be the good guy. He was a big and bulky man with a broad fleshy face that once might have been pleasant but now looked like a petulant baby's, with its round cheeks, pouting lips, and heavy jowls. He looked, in fact, more like a baby than most of the newborns in his charge; because most of them were preemies, puny and skinny, with wrinkled little faces like dried apples.

"I don't know," Messinger said. "Am I the only one here who sees a possible P.R. problem?"

Into a ringing silence, Marty spoke up again. It occurred to her that she was doing more talking than anyone else around the table. "I understand this hospital has been entertaining the presidents of Harmony Hill Hospital and Cadman Memorial, as well," she said boldly, waiting for the thunderbolt to come down and zap her. But nobody fainted and Dr. Messinger only kept looking at her, waiting to see what she'd say next. "Well, I'm perfectly willing to ask Dr. Wolfe of Harmony Hill how he feels about Virgie—Ms. Nesbit. Maybe he doesn't care. In fact, I'd bet my job he doesn't care." What bravado! She was clueless as to *how* Eliot Wolfe might feel about anything.

Messinger stared at her. Then, to her surprise, he said, "Ask him. Report to me. And be grateful I'm not a betting man, Ms. Lamb. And now, to the next item." So now she had to do it. Well, and why not? She was in charge of CCC, and Dr. Wolfe was looking to buy it. She had a right to talk to him. And she would.

The next item on the agenda put a few extra wrinkles in her brow. "Clinic Cost-Effectiveness," it said. Now she was in for it.

"I have before me," Messinger announced, "figures for the past six months for the outpatient clinics in Community Care. Max? Would you hand out the copies?"

Max did so, and even though Marty knew the numbers, she looked the page over carefully. General Peds was doing okay, as was Genetics and the Birthing Center and General Ob/Gyn. Of course, the big losers were High Risk Pregnancy and the HIV clinic.

"Now then, Ms. Lamb, the chief financial officer and I have been discussing these figures and we would like you to improve them."

"Improve profits in High Risk Pregnancy and HIV? But we're cut to the bone as it is. These are the people who have no money, Dr. Messinger. Most of them have no insurance, especially the IV drug users. They *can't* pay us."

Very patiently: "Then perhaps we ought not to be treating them."

"Dr. Messinger. If these people aren't treated, they will just spread the plague further. And how, in all good conscience, can we turn away people who need us so badly? We *are* a hospital, the only one for miles."

He stared at her, thinking, his lips moving in and out. "We are a hospital, not a mission house," he said finally. "And saying that we're badly needed does not help with the P and L statement. A cut in staff, perhaps."

She opened her mouth to protest once again; but finally the Director of Nursing felt moved to speak. "The clinics are very short-staffed, Dr. Messinger. Many of the nurses have been taking double shifts. It's all on the report I sent you. To cut staff would be to—"

"All right, Aimee, all right. But we need some new ideas here. And a moratorium on hiring." He looked around the table, as if daring anyone to differ with him.

"For how long?" Marty said, aghast.

"For the duration." *For the duration* meant "until we've made a deal with one of those hospitals." She'd bet any amount of money on it.

"*I* have an idea," she said. Len Fassbinder's lips tightened in irritation. She guessed that on her first day she was supposed to kick back and stay quiet. But this was too good an opportunity to miss. She looked directly at Dr. Messinger and said, "Store-front drop-in clinics. I've sent you two, no three, memos outlining my plan."

There was a funny little quirking around Messinger's mouth and he dropped his eyes. Could he be hiding a smile? Was it possible? "Ms. Lamb, I have an entire drawer in my file cabinet dedicated to your memos. Refresh my memory."

"Milt, is this really the time?" Fassbinder said, sounding annoyed.

"I said we needed new ideas, and Ms. Lamb seems to be the only one in the room with any." He paused and turned back to Marty. "Go ahead."

"Outreach is the most desperately needed aspect of medical care today," she said. "Patients, particularly those who are addicted, poor, elderly, overburdened—in other words, most of our clinic patients—miss appointments. Why? Because they can't afford a baby-sitter. Because they can't afford the subway or the bus. Because they don't have a phone to call and say they're sick. Because they're depressed. Because their husband or boyfriend beat them up last night and they're ashamed to be seen. Whatever the reason, we don't have the personnel to go chasing after them. And anyway, chasing them down is very expensive." She stopped, taking in a deep breath, waiting for someone to stop her. But they were all looking at her; they were all *listening*.

"Storefront clinics bring patients in because they can drop in. They can come in when they need care, not when they're scheduled to appear. They don't forget because the place is right there. Not only do patients use these small clinics, but the clinics make money. You only need two nurses and a receptionist."

Fassbinder took a theatrical look at his wristwatch. "Milt, is this really—" he began.

"Send me a cost analysis," Messinger said to Marty. "No memos." Again she thought she saw the ghost of a smile.

"Yes, sir," she said meekly. She knew she ought to take her winnings and run, while she was ahead. However, now that she had Dimwit right across the table, why not confront him? What she wanted to say wasn't on the agenda, but what the hell.

"While we're on the subject of profits," she said sweetly, "I have here in front of me statistics for the past four months, showing that voluntary D and Cs for our patients—the women who come to Community Care Clinics—went up by thirty-five percent." *Voluntary,* of course, meant that the patients weren't showing any pathology. But if a woman came in complaining of heavy periods or bad cramps or a strange discharge, a doctor looking for ways to make money might very well schedule a D and C—"just to make sure." Looking as innocent as she possibly could, she went on: "Now I do understand, I understand totally, that D and Cs are highly profitable and the department that does them seems to be making a lot of—"

She was interrupted by Dr. Dinowitz, Dr. Fassbinder, and Aimee, too, all squawking at once, sounding quite a lot like a gaggle of geese. Only a baleful glare from the head of the table brought silence.

Equally guileless, Dr. Messinger asked: "Is this matter on the agenda, Ms. Lamb? No? Max, please add it to the list for our next meeting. Next?"

Marty raised her hand again. "I'm sorry. But I didn't realize I would have to put my concerns on the list beforehand. So may I add something else to the list for our next

meeting?" Grunt. "Well, it's that new ruling sent down by the Medical Staff, that my patients must be examined and okayed by M.D.'s before they're allowed into the hospital for surgery or tests, and that we will be charged for those examinations. I'd like to remind the committee that I am a licensed nurse-practitioner, and by state law I am qualified to—"

Dennis Dinowitz, very irritated, called out, "You aren't qualified to be a *doctor*, Marty! And that's what you N.P.'s think you are! Doctors! Just because you can write prescriptions, that doesn't mean you *know* anything!"

"Nurses nowadays don't know their place!" That, of course, had to be Fassbinder. He was the kind of doctor who called women patients "Mother," as if they didn't have names of their own. As if they didn't *deserve* names of their own. "Perhaps that's why," he added, "once again, the nurse-run programs have failed to produce a profit!" And he sat back in his chair, a pleased smile on his broad face.

Sweetly, Marty responded, "But if you'll look at the statistics, *we* lose many fewer babies to incompetence."

Dr. Fassbinder's lips tightened. "*Those* babies, who will grow up to go on Welfare just like their mothers, we don't need!"

Marty's eyes widened as she stared at him. Did he just say what she thought he said? But she knew damn well she'd heard right. The sanctimonious, conservative bastard! Well, if he could change the subject, so could she. She pushed her anger down. "I know there's a moratorium on hiring, but we really need a Crisis Intervention Officer—a nurse with her master's in Psych—and we badly need another nurse-midwife in the Birthing Center. Which *does* show a profit," she added, looking directly at Fassbinder.

"I almost forgot. You're going to have another nurse-midwife," Dr. Dimwit said. "She'll be starting in another week or two. Check with me later."

"Excuse me," Marty said. "Since when does OB/GYN hire nurses for me?"

"Well, you needn't get all huffy, Marty. I'm only trying to be . . . collegial . . . to help out. She came to us and we can't use

her. So I just naturally thought—since you're always bitching about how shorthanded you are . . ."

Only Dr. Zee's elbow in her arm stopped Marty from saying something she might be sorry for. So she concentrated on the speed with which Max's pencil flew over the shorthand pad. Did all this squabbling get neatly typed in minutes form and sent out in the interoffice mail? Finally, the urge to kill passed.

"Oh, and that reminds me," Dinowitz said, shuffling some papers. "I understand your clinics are being plagued . . . by, ah, *poltergeists*, I believe is the phrase." He looked so damn pleased with himself!

"Really? Why do you say that?"

He smirked; there was no other word for it. "The word is out. Bloods mixed up, missing drugs, patients complaining. I'm surprised you haven't come to us for help, Ms. Lamb."

She gave him a level look and said, "I'm surprised that a physician of your stature pays attention to cafeteria gossip." Where in hell had he found out? Shit. Well, she shouldn't be surprised. Rumors and half rumors spread like the plague around here. "Yes, someone in the clinics has a very strange sense of humor. No real damage has been done. No patient has suffered. It's a nuisance, that's all. Which I can handle."

"Be sure that you do," Dr. Messinger said, fixing her with one of his unreadable stares. "And now. Violations. The entire New Wing is an offender. If these items are not cleared up by the time the accreditation people get here—"

"May I see a list of the violations?" Dr. Zee said. A sheet was handed over. She scanned it and looked up, frowning. " 'Stairways too narrow'?" she read. " 'Dead-end corridors'? 'Improper ventilation'? 'Lack of air-conditioning'? Good God, Dr. Messinger, that building was put up in 1920 as a temporary quarantine space! Of course the stairs weren't built to take gurneys. Of course there are narrow corridors and a lack of proper ventilation. I'm sure they had no idea it would still be part of the hospital seventy-five years later."

"We must fix the most obvious violations," Messinger said.

"Would you like to tell us all *how*?"

"Call in builders . . . plumbers . . . air-conditioning experts.

Surely, Dr. Zee, a woman of your age shouldn't need to be told how one goes about fixing violations."

Marty was breathless. *A woman of your age?* Had he really said that? Yes, he had. If she couldn't believe her ears, she had only to see Dr. Zee's heightened color and the look of stupefaction on Joel Mannes's face.

Dr. Zee rose from her chair and very carefully pushed it in, under the table. "I hope you will excuse me, Dr. Messinger. I have patients to see—before I get too old."

He had the grace to flush deeply. Well, there was nothing else to do but follow her out, Marty figured. So she stood. "I'll call in maintenance to start fixing what they can," she said, keeping her voice very businesslike. "You *will* tell them we get first priority, Dr. Messinger?" It took a minute, but he grunted, and Max said, "The proper calls will be made, Ms. Lamb." Was that a little wink? She thought so.

"Now, Marty, there's no need for *you* to leave." Dr. Dimwit, being nice to her. Now *there* was a mystery. "We've ordered a really nice lunch from Protozoa, in your honor. And . . . and I must apologize for yelling, before. I . . . I'm upset and it's something I'd like to discuss with this committee. . . . Please. Sit down."

She was curious. She sat. And then, to her amazement, Dimwit pushed a sheet of paper into the middle of the table. She knew instantly what it was: hate mail. Aimee was the first one to pick it up. She scanned it and made a little noise, then pushed it away from her, so that it slid up the table to Marty. Marty grabbed it. The usual Xerox copy. This one was a hodgepodge of newspaper headlines, all about doctors, bad doctors, doctors being sued, doctors botching operations, doctors heading sex rings, doctors on drugs, doctors raping women under sedation. There was no message, no comment, just the headlines, cut out of the paper and pasted any old way over each other.

"When did you get this?" Marty asked Dennis, passing it to Dr. Messinger.

"It's not a *this*—it's a *them*. This particular one I found this morning when I came into my office." Dinowitz's voice was high-pitched with tension.

"Where are the others?"

"I threw them out, of course. I didn't realize it was going to be a *campaign*. But today was the last straw. It's gotten so that every time I come into my office, I'm afraid I'll find another one." Tell me about it, Marty wanted to say.

Fassbinder, who now had it in his hand, snorted. "Afraid! What for? It's the work of an infantile mind. It's nothing, Dinowitz, nothing at all. It's not as if it's about *you*." He gave a hearty laugh. "Unless, of course, there's something you'd like to tell us."

Dinowitz colored. "It's the knowledge that someone is watching me to see when I'm out, and creeping into my office."

"Yes, that's the worst part," Marty said, before she thought. Then, quickly, she added, "In cases of this kind, it's always the invasion of privacy that drives people crazy." She had been so sure these things were aimed at the clinics. But if Dinowitz was getting them—and maybe others, too—then who knew?

"Are they always more or less the same?"

Dinowitz flushed an even darker pink. "More or less," he said. There was something he wasn't telling. Everyone else's "letters" had been very personal, and that meant his were, too. All but this one. This one was safe to show others.

"I don't see what can be done about this," Dr. Messinger said. "Unless we call in Security."

"Oh, for God's sake!" Dinowitz snapped. "No, I'll take care of this. I just thought maybe someone else was getting them, too." He looked around the table, but only silence greeted him. He shrugged elaborately.

Joel glanced over at Marty. His look asked permission to say that others had gotten them, but she shook her head ever so slightly. So he said something soothing, about poison pens not being violent, just malicious. "If you have nothing to hide," he said, "you have nothing to fear. It's as simple as that." Marty noticed that Aimee looked strange, almost frozen. But then lunch came and everyone began to talk about the food, the latest film, generalists versus specialists—anything but Dennis Dinowitz's hate mail.

Marty ate little and said less. She wondered whether she would find another gray envelope sitting on *her* desk when

she got back. It drove you nuts, even if it didn't really hurt you, she thought. It felt as if someone was invading your brain.

When she left, they were still digging into the impressive spread of Aldo's best antipastos, hot and cold, and several loaves of fresh semolina bread. She was sorry she had no appetite. As she hurried down the corridor of executive offices she heard her name being called. She turned. Aimee was standing by her office door and sounding out of breath, as if she had been running, although her office was only three doors away from Messinger's.

"Marty. Please. Just a minute of your time." Aimee beckoned her in and closed the door, locking it.

"Aimee, what's the problem?"

"Look, Marty, I heard about Angela's letter . . . the baby in the bath. You knew about that, of course. It was horrible. You never said anything. I must admit I was peeved because I wasn't told. I *am* head of Nursing in this hospital. But that's in the past. Here's what I need to know. Have there been other messages? Besides hers and Dennis's, I mean."

Marty thought, then nodded.

Aimee heaved a sigh. "Then I'm not—never mind. Look. Can you stand something really disgusting?"

"I think so. What—"

"I just wanted to warn you. This . . ." She proffered one of the dove-gray envelopes. ". . . I found last week. Thursday, I think." She shuddered.

This one must be something, Marty thought. She opened it and gasped. "Oh my God!" Some man had stood over the Xerox machine, laid his erect penis across it—it was most definitely erect—and made a copy. The contrast was strong, so that every little wrinkle and hair stood out clearly. It looked *larger* than life, actually.

"Who could have done this?" Marty said, not really expecting an answer. There was a message made of letters cut from magazines: MISS ME?

"Marty, swear on your mother you'll never repeat this to a living soul! I have reason to—oh hell, it's Dennis!"

Marty stood very still. She was *not* going to say, "Are you

sure?" She was *not* going to say, "How do you know?" She
was not, she decided, going to say *anything*.

"This is Dennis's—" Aimee made a strangled sound. "And
now he's getting poison pen stuff in the mail and he's going to
think it's from me. I know he thinks it's me, and it isn't, Marty,
I swear to God, it isn't me. I wouldn't do anything like that, not
even if—well, I wouldn't, that's all. You have to believe that it
isn't."

"I believe you." And she did. What she found hard to
believe is that Dr. Dimwit was that stupid. Or that he was the
poison pen. He didn't care enough about other people's lives,
for one thing. "I believe you, Aimee. And I'll tell you something else. Virgie got one—before her story came out." That's
all she was giving away. But Aimee deserved something. It
had been an act of bravery to confess to her when they had
always regarded each other with suspicion. And it was rather
nice to find that the cold, aloof Aimee Delano had actually carried on with one of the doctors. It made her much more human.
Although . . . *Dimwit?*

"Dennis and I had a little fling, but it was a while—"

"Aimee, listen. You don't have to explain anything. You
didn't do anything terrible. You and Dennis are both divorced.
We're all human. And you know—" She laughed a little.
"Probably everyone in the hospital knew all about it. You
know how everyone knows everything about everybody's sex
life around here."

Aimee laughed, too. "You're right, of course you're right. I
don't know why it upset me so much. It was just . . . I mean
it looks so horribly *big*, doesn't it? It's disgusting. Not
the . . . actual thing—the picture. To think he'd go to all that
trouble, just to disgust me. I don't get it. We didn't fight, or
anything. He just . . . he went on to someone else."

"Tell you what I think," Marty said, gathering her things
together, preparing to leave. "It wasn't Dennis. It was someone
else. Someone else who knows him pretty damn intimately.
Christ, someone who talked him into putting it onto the Xerox
machine!"

"But that means . . . someone was with him, you mean . . .
but that means it had to be . . ."

"A woman. Yes. Exactly. I've always thought so and now I'm sure. Our poison pen writer is a woman."

14

What a week! Marty thought. Just one damn thing after another—beginning every morning with workmen coming into her office, shaking their heads sadly. The wiring was too outdated for central air-conditioning . . . the plumbing was rotting and should be ripped out . . . the walls were all bearing walls and *couldn't* be ripped out. In the meantime, all their work gear had to stay in the middle of the clinics, while they figured out how to do some of the repairs. Patients were forced to pick their way around ladders and piles of tarps and sit amidst the sounds of hammering and sawing. Not to mention that the number of Life Saviors marching outside had doubled since the heat wave had abated in the beginning of August. So anyone trying to visit one of the clinics had to run the gauntlet of men and women brandishing their placards and Bibles like weapons.

Right in the middle of everything, Miriam Brown had developed a terribly high fever. She'd been in bed for three days, hardly able to open her eyes, just moaning. Zeke was so frightened, he'd actually asked for a medical visit from Dr. Zee. As soon as Marty heard about it, she told Julia about her visit to Miriam.

"Lupus," Dr. Zee said. "Of course. Now, why didn't *I* think of that?"

"Because she doesn't tell anyone what's going on, that's why. Anyway, the real question is why she never made a date to see *you*." Marty made a face. "I know, I know. She doesn't

want *him* to guess there's anything wrong with her. Well, in my opinion, there's something wrong with *him*."

Dr. Zee waved that off. "What's worse is that she was going to carry this baby to term. I'll have to tell her . . . I really ought to tell him—Oh hell."

"Yes," Marty agreed. "Oh hell. But what's the difference? He'll never allow an abortion."

"That never stopped her before. No, the real problem is whether she'll let me tell him about the lupus."

"*If* she has lupus. You only have my guess, Julia."

"Your guesses are usually better than most people's sure thing."

Later, Dr. Zee told her that when Miriam was asked to let the doctor tell her husband what was happening, she shook her head fiercely, weak as she was. Zeke was to know nothing. This troubled Marty, who saw secret piling upon half-truth piling upon lie, creating a highly combustible mixture. One of these days, she thought, it was all going to blow up in their faces. She had to talk some sense into Miriam. She had stopped by a couple of evenings on her way home, thinking to have a nice little chat. But she always found two or three Survivor women there, cooking and cleaning; taking care of the three little boys, home from their ten hours of schooling; or bustling around Miriam's room, giving her alcohol rubs to bring down the fever, or just sitting there, holding her hand. There was no privacy.

Marty even considered talking to Zeke Brown herself, but the rabbi was usually in his study whenever she came in, standing with his back to the door, swaying, his eyes closed, his lips moving in prayer. For some reason, this sight made Marty furious. Not that she didn't believe in the power of prayer, but she *did* believe that Zeke would be doing everyone a whole lot more good if he'd spend that time with his daughter, stuck away in her room, unable to do anything except become more and more anxious. Shayna was a nervous wreck.

"Marty . . . Marty, I know they're saying that Mama has the flu, but I don't believe it. It's something really awful, isn't it?" Shayna had asked yesterday. And Marty decided, on the spot,

that *someone* in the family had to know. So she told the girl, trying to make lupus sound less dire than it was.

"She's not going to die, is she, Marty?" And then, fists clenched: "She *can't* die! She's my only ally in this house, my only friend."

With much more confidence than she felt, Marty said, "She's not going to die. Lupus never goes away, really, but it can go into remission. Many women live with it for years and years."

This morning, while walking to work, she heard Shayna calling to her; when she went over, the girl asked her to come in. Miriam's friend Selma opened the door, saying, "Thanks be to the Almighty, Miriam woke up this morning, her old self, no fever, just terribly weak. And now she's sleeping like a baby. Our prayers have been answered."

When Marty let herself into Shayna's room, she expected the girl to be all smiles. But Shayna said, without preamble, "Marty, do *you* think we're cursed? Our whole family?"

"Who told you that?" Marty asked, horrified.

"Who do you think? He's said it before, many times. Not today, not about Mama. He doesn't know what she has. He has no idea."

"I know."

"She doesn't want him to know. She let him think it's a flu. And now that she's feeling better, he thinks that God made her well, 'specially for Rabbi Ezekiel Brown."

"Shayna, I know this is very hard for you. But maybe this *is* an answer to all the prayers. At first, Dr. Zee thought we might have to send your mother to the hospital, but now the crisis is over." For the moment, she added silently. Except for the pregnancy. "Look. Your mother didn't want you to know, either. She didn't want to worry you."

"I'm already worried, Marty. She keeps everything to herself, Mama. But I've seen her, doubling over with pain. She'll stay like that for many minutes, and I can hear her struggling to breathe. She tells me it's heartburn." Shayna gave Marty a steady look. "And that's not true, either, is it? It wasn't the flu and it's not heartburn, either."

"No, it's not," Marty said, after a moment of considering her

answer. "It's probably part of the lupus. But like I told you before, it can all go into remission. It can be helped. But it's a serious disease, very serious. I've never lied to you, Shayna, and I don't intend to start now."

"I know you always tell me the truth. Marty, I love the truth, I worship the truth. The truth is *my* God. Oh, he would slap me if he heard me say that, but I wouldn't cry. I wouldn't let one tear out of my eyes and I would say it again. The truth is my God. Do you have any idea what it's like to live a lie, to have your whole *life* a lie?"

Marty hesitated. Suddenly she was back in the dark kitchen of the little house on the wrong side of town in Madison, with the old green and cream tiled floor, the old-fashioned refrigerator, the scarred table covered with cheap oilcloth in yellow and white checks. A chill winter light was trying to come through the grimy windows. School had been closed early, and she was making a peanut butter sandwich when her mother wandered in, that sweet vacant smile on her face. "They killed him," she told Marty, speaking in Italian. "*E morto.* I forget his name." In English, Marty had said, "It was President Kennedy. Our President," she repeated more loudly, hoping by sheer volume to penetrate the fog in her mother's brain. "*Presidente,*" her mother repeated in Italian, smiled, and drifted out of the room.

"Yes. I know what it's like," Marty had answered Shayna. Living a lie in a life that was a lie. Oh, how she knew.

"You always understand, Marty, and I'm so grateful to you."

Marty had to leave—she didn't want Shayna to see any tears. By the time she got to work, she'd be okay.

As she got close to the hospital, she saw a large crowd of protesters and decided to detour around them. But then she saw the big placards hoisted by those in the front of the pack, and she felt a little jolt, like an electric shock. They read: WANTED FOR MURDER: DR. RICHARD LIONHEART. Rich Lionheart, a *killer*? What insanity! But there was his picture, a big poster-size blowup of him, his glasses a bit askew, a drink in his hand, a silly grin on his face. She thought it might have been taken at a party. But where in the world had they gotten it? He looked . . . well, not drunk, but . . . *degenerate*, somehow.

It was a cheap shot, but obviously these people would stop

at nothing. Hell, why should they, since they had God on their side? She believed in the right of all Americans to congregate and speak their piece, but sometimes the Life Saviors made her very tired. And today they were making her mad.

Annoyed, she turned and headed for the CCC entrance—and nearly bumped into someone. Stammering her apologies, she looked up and was surprised to see that very neat, very scrubbed young man who had joined the Life Saviors earlier in the summer. He was a devoted protester, here every day, rain, shine, storm, or steamy heat. Dr. Zee had told her that the Life Saviors considered him a gift from heaven. Nobody knew anything about him. Nobody knew where he'd come from. He didn't make friends, was the report. But he was always *there* and willing to do anything to help the cause; and everyone had their little quirks, didn't they?

He gave a brisk nod in answer to Marty's "Sorry" and continued on his way. He looked like a preppy in his white shirt and chinos and blue backpack.

From the corner of her eye she saw someone waving at her. Clive Moses. She waved back and kept going—but not before she noticed the stretch limo parked by the curb, around the corner on Hamilton Place, in front of the clinics. It looked familiar. The license plate was a simple HHH. Harmony Hill Hospital. Dr. Eliot Wolfe was back once more to see if All Souls was the bargain hospital to buy. She lengthened her stride. Dammit, he couldn't just come charging into the CCC and look around without a word of warning! Christ, it wasn't even eight o'clock in the morning!

She strode past Carmen's desk, barely answering her greeting, and went racing down the hall, past the clinics. Nothing. Empty. Quiet. Two nurses and three mothers in the Birthing Center. So he wasn't there. As she turned and walked toward her office, she saw two suits and Aimee Delano, strolling past the food machines, heading for the main lobby. One of the men was Dr. Messinger, and, with a little shock, she saw that the other was not Eliot Wolfe, but Paul, minus his white coat. So the gossip was accurate, that Aimee was dragging Dr. Giordano with her wherever she went. They were often seen at lunch in the cafeteria, not to mention at the bar in

Protozoa. Well, it showed improvement in Aimee's taste, at least. And if it made Marty Lamb heartsore, tough. She didn't own Paul. In fact, she'd asked him to stay away from her, so she deserved whatever she got.

From behind her a pleasant voice asked "Marta Lamb?"

She turned to find herself facing Dr. Eliot Wolfe. A good-looking man in his fifties, maybe early sixties. Tall, much taller than she was, and that made him well over six feet.

"Eliot Wolfe?" she asked back.

He shook her hand. "I was hoping to see you this morning. Since you're in charge of the clinics."

"If anyone had informed me you were visiting today, I would have been here earlier and given you the welcome you deserve."

So quickly that she wondered if she'd really seen it, a puzzled frown creased his brow, and then disappeared.

"That's probably my fault," he said. "We had a visit scheduled for next Monday, but I found I'll have to be out of town. I called very late yesterday. I'm sorry. Do you have a few minutes, now that we've met so felicitously?"

Dammit, he had no right to be *nice*. "Certainly. How can I help you?"

"I like your idea for spotting storefront drop-in clinics all over the catchment area, and I wonder if you've worked up any figures yet?"

So. Her memos did not all go into memo purgatory. "Yes I have. I picked twelve places I know are vacant at the present time." She shook her head. "In some of the outer neighborhoods, there's nothing *but* vacant stores. I don't know how people live that way! I don't know why this city keeps ignoring it!" She stopped. "Sorry. But I feel very strongly about our rapidly expanding subculture."

He nodded. "As do I, Ms. Lamb, as do I." His lips curled in a wry smile. "My ex-wife would be amazed to hear me say that. She's a doctor, and she and I . . . well, we used to differ a lot, often and loudly, on the subject of neighborhood clinics. But I've changed my mind. It's an idea whose time has come. And my ex-wife would *faint* at that admission. But I'm willing

to admit when I'm wrong. Small-scale neighborhood health care is the wave of the future."

"If there is a future," Marty said daringly. "Here, I mean. At this hospital."

"Let's see if any of us can survive what's going on in Washington. Whatever new health plan gets through Congress and past the President, I'm afraid it's going to make a lot of dinosaur hospitals extinct."

"Not All Souls. We're already family-oriented. We'd be a great asset to a general hospital looking for more outreach."

He looked at her thoughtfully. "Are you selling All Souls? Or maybe Community Care Clinics?"

"Neither," she answered promptly, grinning up at him. "Both. You must know what you think of All Souls. I'm just letting you know that our nurse-run clinics get good results . . . very good results."

"Yes, well, I already know that. If we doctors aren't careful, nurses are going to take over our jobs completely."

"Not to worry, Dr. Wolfe. There'll always be a place in medicine for doctors."

He laughed and said, "I sure hope so. Well, I'd be very interested in seeing a cost breakdown for those storefronts."

"I'd have to check it through Dr. Messinger, of course."

"He's already said it's okay. But of course."

"Speaking of Dr. Messinger . . . the other day, at an Executive Committee meeting, your name came up and I volunteered to ask you a question." She paused, and he said nothing, just looked expectant. "You've undoubtedly seen the stories about our transsexual nurse. . . ."

"Oh yes, the heroine." He smiled. "It's the talk of Harmony Hill. Apparently, one of our people did the . . . ah, final surgery."

"Do you think she ought to be fired?"

He looked stupefied. "Fired? The nurse, you mean? What for?"

"Thank you. That's what I wanted to know."

"You weren't planning to fire her, were you?"

"No, but some of the doctors thought Virgie would give All Souls a bad image." When he gave a dismissive gesture to that

idea, she was emboldened to say, "Can I ask what you plan to do with All Souls? If you buy it."

"There are no specific plans at present. We're looking at it. We're looking at a lot of smaller hospitals. Now that I've seen the light, I've become a believer in neighborhood clinics and going back to general care. Well, I'm glad we bumped into each other this way." He put out his hand. "It's been a pleasure to meet you. We may well be speaking again."

"I hope so." Much to her surprise, she meant it. Working under Dr. Wolfe might not be half bad. And then Aimee appeared through the swinging doors and caroled, "Oh, *there* you are, Eliot. We're waiting for you! Hi, Marty!" Wolfe hurried off to rejoin his tour, and Marty went to her office.

The plain gray envelope sitting in the middle of her desk might just as well have been lit up with neon. The sight of it made her heart begin to thump. She'd actually been waiting for the next one, and here it was. She picked it up gingerly, as if it were hot, and considered tossing it, unread, into the wastebasket. But her curiosity got the better of her. She ripped it open.

And felt like a fool. It was just a note from Crystal, hastily scrawled, saying, "Add me to your list. I got one of those poison pen things this morning. Odious thing! I flushed it down the toilet."

She flushed it down the toilet? Well, wasn't that where it belonged? That was the idea: get *rid* of it. Get it out of your sight and out of your memory. That's what Marty Lamb ought to do, she thought. Why were a few words pasted on paper so threatening? How could a couple of messages about Owen possibly hurt her? The days of hiding your personal schizophrenic in the attic were long over. In fact, she didn't have a clue why she'd kept it a secret in the first place. In fact, why didn't she start telling people today? Well, maybe not today. But she would definitely drive up to see Owen on Saturday and get those divorce papers signed.

That decided, she felt much better. Before the lunch-hour meeting, she'd go over her list. First things first. Those dreadful "Wanted for Murder" signs. Someone would have to tell the Life Saviors they had to get rid of them. There was no excuse for something so inflammatory, so . . . libelous. Hell, it

must be libel to call someone a murderer who wasn't. Serve them right if they got slapped with a lawsuit! She punched out Clive Moses's extension. It was *his* job; let him do it. But she only got his assistant. Of course. He had probably joined the Eliot Wolfe All-Hospital Tour Group. She'd get him later.

Next, she headed for Dr. Zee's office at the back of Clinic B; nobody there. That's right, Julia was making rounds upstairs. Too bad. They needed to discuss Miriam's case. Knowing Miriam, the woman might have skipped telling Dr. Zee about those bad chest pains. And maybe she'd get the doctor's opinion on some other things, Marty thought. She was always able to sort things out when she talked to Julia. If the hospital were sold, they might very well end up in different places. How would she ever manage without Dr. Zee to talk to?

When Marty went back into the corridor, Marie Racine went walking by. It was hard to miss her, with her brightly colored turban, large hoop earrings, and even larger pregnancy.

"Madame Racine. Can I help you?"

Marty could see that she was pale and sweating. She quickly went to the pregnant woman and, holding her arm, urged her into a seat in the hall. "You don't look well," she said. "Are you in pain?"

"Non. Mais . . . sangre. How you say? Blood. *Un petite peu."*

Uh-oh. She was only in the sixth month, as far as they knew. "You're spotting. Okay. Have you broken your water? Did water come out . . . suddenly . . . whoosh!"

"Non. C'est mal?" Marie's voice was panicked.

"No, no, I don't think so," Marty soothed. "Let's get you to Mademoiselle Cole."

"Ah, oui, I come to see her."

"Did you call first? *Téléfoner?"* No, she hadn't called first. At least Crys was in; it couldn't be more than half an hour since she'd left that note on Marty's desk.

But Crystal was nowhere to be found. When Marty asked Carmen, who usually knew everything, Carmen wrinkled her nose and said, "Actually? I don't know. I could send a search party."

"No, no. She didn't tell you where she was going?"

"Tell you the truth, I never saw her leave. Maybe she went out the back."

So, once again, Marty examined Marie. She was dilated, but barely, so it might not be early labor. She had developed hemorrhoids, but that was to be expected—she was a small, lightweight woman and this was a large baby. That, she felt when she palpated Marie's abdomen. The fetus was also pretty low; Marie might be closer to her due date than they had figured. But who knew? Predicting a date for birth was a game, not a science. For the hemorrhoids, Marty suggested an ointment—she was able to find a sample—and they discussed constipation and how to cope with it. When Marie finally understood what a "prune" was, she made such a funny face that Marty had to laugh. She told Marie—in her best pidgin French—to watch the spotting and to call Crystal if it became heavy.

Even though both of them stayed away from the subject of Gregory, his presence seemed to hover. Secretly, Marty thought a lot of Marie's discomfort might be caused by anxiety. She told her to go home and rest and not to worry. Stupid, of course the girl was going to worry. She was very young and she was having her first baby far from home, all alone, without benefit of marriage.

Marty had scheduled a meeting for noon, for her own staff plus several of Dr. Zee's nurses. Lunch—thanks to Doug Lavoro—included. At ten to, she pushed the calculator away, got up and headed for the Conference Room, her head buzzing with cost projections, patient load guesses, and all the other fantasies that made working up a budget for a new project so much fun. She only hoped she would be able to concentrate on today's agenda—helping patients fill out the ever-increasing numbers of health insurance forms and explaining to them why Medicare was no longer paying for anemia tests or for HDL/LDL percentages of their cholesterol or for so many other things. She also hoped her nurses would find the topic fascinating, but she doubted it, not with Virgie there.

It had been over a week, but the entire hospital was still buzzing about the sex change revelation. Virgie had been on the Maury Povich show, all the local news programs, featured with Ham Pierce on "Voice of the City," and was going to

appear with Geraldo. There was even a rumor that "60 Minutes" was interested in her story. It wasn't quite clear whether people were cheering Virgie on against all odds, or just wanted to know all the gory details.

Sure enough, when the meeting got going, she saw that everyone was sneaking looks at their celebrity. Maybe it was just the topic, Marty thought; God knows insurance forms bored *her* to death.

Virgie sat quietly, her hands folded in her lap in ladylike fashion, occasionally patting her hair. Doug Lavoro, the drug rep, dropped into the conference room, bringing hero sandwiches and Italian cookies, as promised, as well as various samples. When he spotted Virgie, he did a dramatic double take, a big stupid grin on his face. Virgie simply gave him a royal inclination of her head.

Suddenly, Emilio stood up, pushing his chair back so hard it fell with a crash.

"I won't stay here!" he burst out. "I won't stay here and look at that fairy!"

Virgie kept her cool. Sweetly, she said, "I'm not a fairy, Emilio, I'm a woman."

"A *woman*! *Dios*! A *woman*! You sick sonofabitch, you're nothin' but a fuckin' *freak*!" He slammed out of the bubble, leaving an uneasy silence behind.

Marty and Crystal exchanged looks. Virgie tightened her lips, and nodded gravely when Kenny said, "Give him some time, Virgie, he's a really conservative guy. But he'll be okay."

Emilio had better get himself up to Joel real soon, Marty thought, or she was going to have trouble keeping him here. Ever since their little chat, she realized that poor Emilio was suffering from responsibility overload. Of course, that didn't mean he could continue to take it out on everyone else. She scribbled a reminder to herself to find a home health aide for his mother. The druggie brother could wait. One thing at a time. And Emilio's pride was at stake, so helping him was not going to be a walk in the country.

"All right, people," she said. "Let's get back to insurance. I know, I know, it's just about as exciting a topic as the correct way to make hospital corners . . ." At least she got a little ripple

of laughter; memories of nursing school. ". . . but it has to be done. So, let's go."

When the meeting was breaking up, Crys came over and began speaking in a low voice. Marty expected her to talk about the poison pen letter she'd received, but that wasn't it at all. "Did you hear? Because of those terrible signs the Life Saviors are carrying, Rich Lionheart is going to be quietly replaced."

"Good idea," Marty said, wondering why the hushed tones.

"And guess who's going to do the abortions instead?"

"Obviously I don't know, Crys, or you wouldn't be taking such evident pleasure in telling me."

"Well, excuse *me*. I just thought you might like to know your old friend Giordano has offered to take over. The idea is, they won't shoot at *him*." She laughed and hurried away.

"Wait, Crys, when—" Marty began, but Crystal was out the door and gone. Maybe she *was* having secret therapy sessions with Joel Mannes. Well, Marty thought, she couldn't very well chase Crystal into a psychiatrist's office. So she went looking for Dr. Zee—they really had to talk about Miriam and how to tell Zeke. And maybe while she was at that end of the clinic, she'd look in on the operating room. But Julia had been waylaid by a new patient who thought every little twinge signaled some horrible disease; and Marty knew that the doctor would spend plenty of reassurance time with her. And she changed her mind about checking up on Paul.

So, back to her office. She was trying very hard to get interested in a long-winded manuscript the *American Journal of Nursing* had asked her to edit when her office door opened and Paul came in. "Knock, knock," he said. "Sorry to barge in like this, but I don't see how else I'm going to get you to talk to me. Have you had lunch?"

"No," she lied. Now why did she do *that*? But she knew damn well why. Because she wanted to hear him invite her to lunch. Because she didn't want to end the conversation because she didn't want him to leave.

"Good. Come to lunch with me. Come on, Marty. Give me a break, let me explain, let me *try*. . . ."

"Well . . . I just heard what you're doing for Rich, and I *am*

grateful. And maybe I've been a little stubborn. But I can't have lunch with you." With pleasure, she watched as his face fell. "How about dinner?"

"You mean it?"

"I mean it. I'll listen to you. But no promises."

"No promises. I promise."

He backed out of the doorway, grinning like a schoolboy, so obviously and openly pleased that she just couldn't help smiling back. It didn't mean a thing, she told herself, not a goddamn thing.

15

Eyes followed them as they walked to a table in the back corner of Protozoa, and Marty, careful to seat herself with her back to everyone, could nonetheless still feel those eyes boring into her. As if she weren't already supremely uncomfortable!

"You still drink Chablis?" Paul's tone said, *Hey, so a doctor and a nurse are having dinner, no big deal.*

So she kept her voice on the same cool level. "No, actually, I've switched to red wine. It's healthier."

One eyebrow went up questioningly. "Which red is healthiest?"

"Cabernet sauvignon." She didn't care *what* he thought about the health benefits of red wine.

He ordered a bottle and an antipasto from Aldo's brother, Ray, who was waiting tables tonight. Ray nodded—he never wrote your order down—and asked if they'd like to try the shrimp marinara. He kissed his fingers and said, "Maddalena made a sauce, you wouldn't believe it unless you ate it, in person, I'm telling you."

"Then how can we say no?" Paul laughed.

Marty regarded Paul across the table. He still looked rather forbidding—it must be the heavy dark eyebrows that almost grew together, she thought—until he smiled. When he smiled, he looked like an angel. She had to stop thinking like that. It was over, and he was going to have to talk mighty fast and be awfully convincing for her to even *think* that they might start up again.

Giving him her best professional smile, she said, "How did it go today? With the abortions? How did you find it?"

"Exhausting."

"I didn't think there were so many this morning."

"It's not the number. Marty, it's the emotional atmosphere. I had women of forty and girls of fifteen, and they all looked like they were facing death."

"Well," she said carefully, "in a way, you know, they *were*."

"What do you—oh. The death of the fetus. Okay, yes. But you *do* counsel them, don't you? I mean, this isn't a spur-of-the-moment decision?" She nodded. "Then I don't get it. Why all the tears? We spent more time holding hands and so forth than we did on the procedure. We got *way* behind on our schedule."

Aha. In some ways he hadn't changed. Patients were still not quite real people. That was too bad. "So? How important is a schedule?"

He grinned at her. "You haven't changed a bit, have you, my dear bleeding heart? A schedule, allow me to remind you, is important in a hospital that's trying to improve its profit margin. And—before you haul off and hit me—to the patients who are waiting for *their* turn. Don't you have a little pity for *them*?"

Marty took a deep breath. She was not going to lose her temper. "Paul, when you're doing abortions, holding hands and so forth is *part* of the procedure."

"I know that. It's just that—ah, here's the wine." He sounded like a man who'd just been reprieved.

"Here's the wine," she said, grateful to agree about anything.

They raised their glasses in a silent toast—to what? she wondered—and drank. "Something this morning puzzled me,"

Paul said. "I think one of the women was a Survivor. But I thought they didn't allow abortion."

Miriam, Marty thought. Oh no. "What made you think she was a Survivor?"

"The way she was dressed. Long sleeves, long skirt, scarf wrapped tightly around her head."

But the Survivor women didn't cover their hair. "Was she pretty?"

"Honestly, Marty, I didn't notice. I was focused on—uh, other things."

"Do you remember her name?"

"Silverman? Silverstein? You could get it from the nurse who assisted."

"No, it isn't who— It's not important."

The big platter of antipasto arrived and they began to eat. "Those clinics of yours are really popular. You're doing a great job, Marty. I'm very proud of you."

"Thank you. I think I'm doing a great job, too. I'm not so sure Administration agrees, though."

"Of course they do! The clinics serve the neighborhood, they're well-run, and not incidentally, I'm told the two big hospitals love them. Outreach, you see. Flavor of the month."

"Who told you that? Aimee?" Shut up, Marty, she told herself.

"Aimee, for one, and also Dr. Wolfe and Dr. Winter."

"Two of our clinics never show a profit, and the others just squeak by. So many people don't have any insurance at all. At the Executive Committee meeting, I was told to make money. And I thought I heard the echo, 'or else.' Christ, Messinger is more like an accountant than a medical man!"

Paul laughed. "He *is* an accountant, for Christ's sake! Didn't you know that? He went to medical school when he was in his thirties . . . but we all know the first love is the real one." Abruptly, Paul stopped himself and took in an audible breath.

Yes, yes, the first love really is, she thought. But she wasn't, in spite of her rapid pulse, ready to say it aloud. "I knew it," she babbled. "Dr. Messinger is also Dr. Scrooge."

Gently, Paul said, "Marty, you *know* a lot of the services we have for the poor people in this neighborhood are going to be

considered 'frills.' And they'll be the first to go. But they'll keep *you*—"

"If they close up CCC, I won't stay," she said, with some heat. "Maybe I'll take it to Mt. Sinai. Or Beth Israel. Or to Harmony Hill, if they don't buy All Souls. Now that I've had a little chat with Eliot Wolfe and we're buddies."

"You've had a little chat? You mean an interview?"

"No, it wasn't an interview, just a casual meeting. We're not really buddies, that was a joke. Don't repeat it to Aimee, all right?"

"Aw, Marty." He put his fork down. "I don't . . . Aimee isn't . . . oh, shit. I thought we came here to talk about *us*."

"There isn't an *us*. Not anymore." She had to lower her eyes.

"I refuse to believe that. I wouldn't have spent all this time tracking you down if I didn't think there was an *us*." He reached out and put his hand over hers.

Marty blinked back sudden tears and gently extricated her hand. "Then maybe you'd like to tell me what became of you on February sixth, 1983." Now she lifted her eyes and looked into his.

"Yes, I'd like to tell you what happened to me. That's why I've been looking for you . . . and, you should know, I left a perfectly good job to be where you are. I was always so ashamed of what I'd done . . . of everything. My original plan was to forget you and get *on* with my life. Only I couldn't. Forget you." He stared over the rim of his glass. His eyes, fringed with thick, straight, black lashes, looked at her tenderly, and she was drowning.

"And then," he continued, "I couldn't find you; I mean, I couldn't find Marty Dauber. You'd gotten married and changed your name. You didn't even do the simple thing and use your maiden name as a middle name, either. And you had left Boston. I managed to track you to Middletown, Connecticut, but by the time I got there, you'd left *there*, too. Then—"

She was suddenly alert. "Have you mentioned to anyone here that I was married?"

"I don't know, I might have. Why?"

"Ah . . . I haven't told anybody . . . well, almost nobody."

"Why keep it a secret? They let nurses get married these days—or hadn't you heard? Is he a criminal or something?"

She was damned if she'd tell him everything; he didn't deserve it. "So you disappeared on me . . . on all of us. You say you were ashamed. What'd you do, go get shrunk?" She smiled to show it was no big deal.

"In a manner of speaking."

She waited, but that was it. He wasn't going to offer anything else yet. "So why did you come looking for me, after so long?"

His eyes bored into hers. "I never stopped loving you, Marty. You've got to believe that. I—It couldn't be helped, what happened. It was the only way. To tell you the truth, I was kind of scared to find you. But then I had a seizure . . . blacked out for a minute or two—"

"Oh, Paul! Have you seen a doctor about it?"

He laughed, putting a hand on her cheek. She didn't pull away. "Hello, Marty. *I'm* a doctor, remember? But yes, I saw a specialist, got an EEG, the works. I'm okay. It was apparently an anomaly. But I suddenly realized that I could *go* . . ." He snapped his fingers. ". . . just like that! I didn't *have* forever to make up my mind whether or not I could ever face you again. I had to find you. Aw, Marty—"

Tears were sliding out of her eyes. She felt like a complete idiot. This time when he reached for her hand, she didn't fight it. Why was she wasting so much time fighting him off, pretending she didn't care, acting so cold and unforgiving? One touch from him had created total meltdown. That hadn't changed, either.

Signaling for the bill, he said, "Let's blow this joint."

"Which door, and how fast?" It was a signal of theirs, that they both felt the need to be private. They'd taken the lines from an old Mae West–W. C. Fields movie. He hadn't forgotten; nor had she. She realized now that she hadn't forgotten a damn *thing*.

They practically ran to her place, holding hands, and began to undress each other the moment the door was locked behind them. Not a word was spoken. It was all silence except for the

harsh sounds of their excited breathing, the small sounds of rapture as hands, lips, tongues, touched and probed.

The first time, they made love right there in the entryway, on the thick Oriental rug. The second time they headed for the bedroom but never made it past the couch in the living room. Then they had decided to be sensible, make themselves something to eat. When they made love again, standing up, her back pressing uncomfortably against the wall, she began to giggle uncontrollably. He tried to kiss her into submission but then it struck him funny, too, and they ended up laughing hysterically.

In her bed, she said, "We're too old for fancy gymnastics," and he answered, "You're never too old." And closed his eyes and fell asleep instantly! But that wasn't quite all. Sometime during the night, she had awakened to his caresses. This time, their lovemaking was long and languorous and lovely.

She came awake again, to a big warm hand stroking her back and then her hip and an arm encircling her, pulling her in tight. And pressing into her back and buttocks, a huge, hard erection. Her loins flooded and she moaned happily.

She opened her eyes to the pallid light of dawn edging the shutters. Paul was spooned around her. Wide-awake, she turned to him, and he slid into her, grunting with pleasure. This time they were urgent, avid, eager, frantic, and it was over in minutes. Paul held her close, looked into her eyes, and with feeling said, "Shit!" And they laughed again.

A few minutes later she rolled out of bed, groaning. She was more than a little stiff and sore; screwing all over the apartment was work for kids in their twenties, not out-of-shape women who should know better. Nonetheless, she felt happier than she had been in years. Looking into the bathroom mirror, she saw a face glowing with . . . with what? Love? Or just the expert scratching of a sexual itch? Whatever it was, it had pushed all her anxious questions, all her doubts about him, far far back into the recesses of her mind. To hell with her questions and her doubts!

Bringing them coffee on a wooden tray a bit later, she gazed down on him, curled up on his side, the sheet over his head, just the top of his thick hair showing. A wave of tenderness swept over her.

"I had forgotten what a wonderful lover you are," she remarked.

He turned over onto his back instantly, sheet pushed down to his waist, grinning like a schoolboy. "Really?"

"No. I'm a liar," she admitted, holding a steaming cup out to him. "I did remember . . . only too well, sometimes."

Paul laughed and sat up. He took the cup and sipped at it. "And you still make the best coffee in the universe. Marty, let's call in sick and just stay here in bed all day."

"You're kidding."

He groaned. "Unfortunately, yes." He pushed back the sheet and swung his legs over the side of the bed. She could see his naked body reflected in the window. He stretched out one arm and picked up a pair of Jockey shorts from the floor, where they had been flung at some point last night. Why shouldn't they play hooky? It was only one day. But of course, they couldn't. He was a doctor, she was a nurse. Period.

"You seem to be in the loop," she remarked, watching him get dressed. "So tell me. We're going to Harmony Hill, aren't we?"

"You think I know *that*? Hey, I'm wonderful, but I'm not *that* wonderful. And what loop am I supposed to be in?"

"Nothing. Forget I said it, okay?" She really had to stop this dumb jealousy thing. After all, it wasn't Aimee he'd had his way with all these hours. Not this time. Her heart stopped for a beat. "If you want something to eat for breakfast, you won't find it here. I usually grab a Danish or whatever, in the hospital."

"You're kicking me out."

"You're getting dressed."

"I can always change *that*. In fact . . . take a look at what's happening here! Don't you want to take advantage of a man in an aroused state? Never mind, I'll get you later."

It was so much like the old days, the straight-faced banter, the thread of sexuality that ran through everything. When he passed her, he ran his hand across the back of her neck, sending a chill all the way down her spine. He put on his T-shirt and raked his fingers through his hair to "comb" it. He had always done that; she had always scolded him about it. She opened her

mouth to do so and shut it. You're still a married woman, she told herself. But not for long. She really *would* get Owen to sign this time.

"Paul . . ."

"Yes?" He came over, tipped her head up with a finger under her chin and gave her a light kiss. "Name it, it's yours."

"Are you in any danger, doing the abortions?"

"You worried about those placards? They don't mean anything. These people like to look tough. . . . No, I'm not in any danger. Besides, I wear a bulletproof vest."

"You *do*?"

"Sure, everyone does, since the crazies started killing doctors. So you see, I'm perfectly safe. Don't think I'm changing the subject or anything," he said, moving away from her to get his shirt, "but Rich thinks that Dr. Dinowitz is under disciplinary review. I thought he was a young medic on his way up."

"So did I," Marty said. "But I'm not surprised. There's something . . . I don't know . . . slimy about him." She opened her mouth to say something about Dimwit's habit of making passes, but thought better of it.

"Of course, that's a deep dark secret."

"Naturally," Marty countered. She began to dress. "Of course it's a secret. What if he should turn out be guilty? We don't want patients losing faith in our doctors, do we?"

"You know how doctors stick together, Marty!" He said it lightly; but there was something in his voice. She lifted her head and turned to look at him. "But you were going to tell me why you were separated from your . . . husband, ex-husband, whatever," he said.

"Husband," she said tersely. "Still my husband. It's a complicated story."

"You already told me that."

"That's right, I did." Quickly, she went to her closet, pretending to be choosing an outfit. She grabbed slacks and a shirt and busily moved hangers around on the rod.

"I'll bet I could understand something complicated," Paul said.

Why in hell should I tell you *anything*? she asked him silently. You've managed to talk about everything but the one

thing I really need to know. *What happened on February 6, 1983 that sent you away from me without a word?*

"Marty?" he prodded.

Saved by the bell. Well, actually, saved by the strange chirping sound that phones made these days. She ran for it.

"Marty?" a familiar male voice demanded. She said yes. "This is Max. A meeting of the Executive Committee has been called for eight-thirty A.M. . . . Yes, today. You will be there on time?" She said she would, he said, "Smashing" and hung up. She put the receiver down, wondering what was up. And the phone chirped again.

"You always get calls this early in the morning? Because if you do, I'm not so sure I'm moving in," Paul said.

The riposte died on her lips as she heard the stilted, too-loud tones of a man on medication yelling, "Hello? Hello? Hello, Marty? Marty? Are you there?" She was sure Owen's strident voice could be heard down the block, never mind across the room.

She turned so she was facing away from Paul and said quietly into the phone: "Do you know what time it is?"

"No. What time is it?"

"Never mind! It's very early in the morning. What do you want?"

"Dr. Chen thinks we should talk."

"Dr. Chen should do something with his thoughts," she muttered; and was instantly sorry when Owen hollered: "I can't hear you, Marty! Speak louder!"

In a more normal tone she said, "But *I* can hear *you*, so you can stop yelling."

"What?"

Oh Christ. She couldn't talk to him with Paul standing there, waiting and listening. Maybe trying not to listen, but how could he help it? She turned and made a gesture and a face, hoping to indicate she was tied up with this call, that it was a pain in the butt, but she had to do it and she'd see him later.

He got it. He looked hurt. So she held up five fingers and he disappeared into the kitchen.

"Look, Owen, you tell Dr. Chen for me . . ." Why was she wasting her anger on poor Owen? ". . . tell him that I plan to

come up this weekend. There's something very important I have to discuss with you."

"I want to come home, Marty."

"Owen, now is not the time to discuss this."

"I want to come home."

"Owen, for God's sake, it's been eight years since anywhere with me has been your home!"

"I miss you, Marty. I want to come home."

She gritted her teeth. "We will talk about this on Sunday, all right?"

"Sunday?" The medicine must have made him a little dopey; his responses were none too swift. Or maybe it was just the disease, she thought. Schizophrenia interfered with all the thought processes. The young professor who had been considered a bit eccentric but brilliant was long gone. Once he began concentrating on his voices, she remembered, he would be totally unable to concentrate on anything else: reading, music, hobbies, even the television. He could have gone almost nine years without a new thought or a new idea entering his brain!

"Sunday. I'll come up on Sunday and we'll talk, okay, Owen?" Silence. "Okay, Owen?"

He didn't answer her, just hung up. Good manners were something else that got destroyed by psychosis. How could that doctor even *think* it was a good idea for them to live together? The man had to be an idiot!

Paul, hearing no conversation, wandered back in. "We ready?" he asked casually; but there was a question all over his face.

She said, "I'm wanted, it seems. Meeting of the Executive Committee."

Nice Paul, he did not say, What about your other call? He smiled and said, "Oh, the new spending guidelines."

"What new spending guidelines?"

"The ones Dr. Messinger is going to announce at this meeting."

"I've noticed you're privy to a great many things. Part of the Ice Maiden's pillow talk, no doubt." What a dumb thing to say; why was she doing this?

"The Ice Maiden? Oh . . . you mean Aimee?" At least he had the grace to blush!

"So. You *did* take her to bed."

"Marty, come on!"

"But you did. Didn't you? Was it good?" Stop it, she ordered herself. Stop it this instant. This is crazy; he doesn't belong to you. And it doesn't matter if he did. But her mouth would not shut. "Did you enjoy it? Enough to do it four times, like we just did?"

"Marty, please. You wouldn't even look at me a few days ago, remember? And, anyway, I'm not saying we did."

"You don't have to! I can read it on your face!"

His voice got icy. "Who I sleep with is my business. And I never kiss and tell."

"How thoughtful." She fastened the buckle of her belt, her heart racing, regretting her outburst but damned if she would take it back, any of it. "I hope you'll do the same for me."

"Just what is *that* supposed to mean?"

"You haven't yet managed to tell me why you left me. You keep talking around it. Since you apparently don't intend to tell me, I don't intend to start up with you again."

"You mean, the way you haven't yet managed to tell me why you're separated but still married?"

She took a deep breath. She could agree, *You're right, Paul, we've both changed the subject, over and over again.* Or . . . "Are you ready?" she said coolly.

"To leave? Indeed I am."

He waited politely while she double-locked both her locks. They went out into the muggy day together, then he turned to her. "I'm not coming to the hospital with you; I'd like to go home and shower. . . ."

"Get rid of any traces of me?"

"Marty, for God's sake. Don't do this." They stared at each other for a moment. "I see you're not going to stop," he said after a moment. "You're quite right, you have no reason to trust me; no reason at all. Except faith, and you don't seem to have any of that. I have a great deal to think about." He touched her hand. "I'll talk to you." Quickly, he trotted down the steps.

"When?" It just came bursting out of her.

Paul turned, squinting up at her. "I don't know, Marty, I just don't know." He strode away. She watched him march toward the river, her heart sinking with each step he took. What had she done, what had she *done*? She stood, blinking back tears, hating her big mouth.

Then she shook herself. There was no taking back what had already been said. And Paul Giordano was *not* going to make her a basket case, not this time.

16

Thursday turned out to be a typical New York August day— damp, muggy, hot, sweaty. But a good day nevertheless, Marty thought, yes, even in spite of the fact that Paul had avoided her for the past two days. To hell with him. Wasn't today the day the new nurse-midwife, Angie's replacement, was slated to arrive? Yes, it was. Marty hoped she was half as good as Angela had been. Of course, the woman had come through Dimwit's auspices, but that didn't mean she wasn't competent. Marty had called all her references. They all loved . . . oh, Christ. What was her name? Gone, gone with the wind.

She hoped the new nurse was big and tough, because she was going to throw her into the High Risk Pregnancy clinic, to deal with all the dope addicts, alcoholics, whores, raped teen-agers, and the hyper, unreachable crackheads. They were always the biggest problem. They thought they were just fine, drugs were just fine, the problem was you, and *you* were obviously—

She interrupted her thoughts as she realized she'd walked right by Shayna's window. It bothered her when Shayna wasn't there. It usually meant something was amiss. Could it be Miriam again? Marty added another note to her mental list:

call Shayna. If she tried often enough, she was bound to get her sooner or later. Then, at least, she could find out if Miriam needed help.

When she reached the front entrance to All Souls, Gilbert said, "There's someone waiting for you, Ms. Lamb. I asked her to sit down."

There was indeed someone: a very large someone wearing a pale blue nylon pantsuit and a broad smile that flashed very white teeth against smooth brown skin. She stood up as Marty approached. Wow. The woman was nearly six feet tall. Marty had hoped for a big strong nurse; well, she had gotten one. Sonya Washington. The name came back to her in a flash, as she pictured the woman's résumé. Nurse Midwife Sonya Washington, lately of Baltimore, Maryland.

Marty put out her hand. It was instantly engulfed by Sonya Washington's big broad one. "Am I glad you're here, Ms. Washington! Today's one of our toughest clinics, and you look as if you could handle anything."

The nurse's chuckle was rich. "Don't worry, Ms. Lamb, I can. Who've we got coming today? Crackheads? Back in Baltimore, I worked with a lot of them. AIDS patients out of their heads, too. Nobody gets wise with me, I can promise you that."

"I believe you," Marty said with a laugh. "Come with me. We'll go to my office and have coffee and get acquainted. I'll call Crystal Cole, who'll be your, um . . . boss."

"Ms. Cole and I will get along just fine. I don't have a problem with anyone being my boss. Just so long as I don't have to take orders from a doctor."

"Do you have a problem with doctors?"

Another chuckle. "It's *their* problem. You know how they love assertive nurses! Not! Well, I'm assertive. Hell, in my opinion, nurses could run the whole medical establishment without a single M.D. Who'd miss them? The patients? They hardly get to *see* them. Who do they see? Us! Anyone who reads history knows that before the middle of the nineteenth century nobody even trusted a doctor. Doctors killed you, and everyone knew it. But now they're glamorous. Right. They get the glamor and we get the burnout." They pushed through the

swinging doors and strode past the machines, down the hall, into Marty's office.

"Here's what I wish," Sonya continued. "I wish all doctors would be turned into nurses for just one day. Then maybe they'd see what it's like on the front lines. The doctors, they get to be like the generals in the army, sitting well back from the fire, moving troops around on a map—and acting like they know it all." She laughed again. "Sorry, Ms. Lamb. I tend to be pretty mouthy."

"That's okay with me. Just be nice to the patients." But something Sonya had said stuck in her brain. *I wish all doctors would spend just one day as a nurse.* Yes! What a concept! Just do it with all the new doctors and let them see what it was *really* like . . . what happened *after* they casually ordered more tests and more bloods. She scribbled a little note to herself. Next Executive Committee meeting, she'd mention it. But first she'd send a memo. Of course.

"I love my patients," Sonya Washington was saying. "They're my babies. They have to be, seeing as I'm forty-two and single and not a prospect in sight."

As they entered, Marty's eyes had flown to the desktop. Nothing. Good. She started to breathe again. That's why they called them poison, she thought.

As she plugged in the coffeepot, which started to burble and bubble immediately, she asked, "While we wait for the coffee, do you have any questions about your job, Sonya?"

"You covered just about everything the times we talked on the phone, so no, I don't think so. I'm eager to get to work."

"I'm not sure if I mentioned we do abortions here. I hope you don't have a problem with that?"

"I was brought up Baptist, Ms. Lamb, *strict* Baptist, as in Mississippi. But my job is taking care of people, and I never let religion get in the way of my job."

"You just gave me the answer I wanted to hear."

There was a flurry of activity out in the hallway and Crystal came in, obviously agitated. "Marty, your poltergeist has struck again!"

"What is it this time?"

"Kenny went into the lab for our bloods for our regular

patients this afternoon, and when I looked at Harriet Gold's sample—on account of the Rh thing—it wasn't hers. She's A negative and this one was O positive. Then we began checking. Marty, someone went into the lab and switched the vials around."

"Damn! But why?"

"Search me. A prank?"

"That's not a prank, Crystal, that's nasty!"

Kenny's round face with its halo of curly sand-colored hair appeared around the doorjamb. "Crys! Two of the IVs have been tampered with."

Crystal went pale. "Tampered with! How?"

"No, no, take it easy, nothing was substituted. They're still just Percodan and Demerol, but they weren't put back right. I mean, you could see right away that someone had messed with them."

"This is horrible!" Crystal cried. She looked ready to burst into tears. Then, in one of her rapid changes, she smiled and said, "I know. Dr. Dinowitz is a vampire and goes to the lab at night to get his breakfast. And then—"

"Excuse me, Crystal," Marty said. "Let me introduce you to our new nurse-midwife, Sonya Washington—"

"Who is ready to begin work right this minute," Sonya added, rising to her feet and offering her hand.

Now Crystal really grinned. "Welcome, Sonya. This is Kenny Rankin, he's a nurse here, too. He's been filling in at the Birthing Center, so he's going to love you for setting him free. We have two in labor right now. Boy, do I need you!"

"Glad to be of service."

The three of them disappeared down the hall, chatter trailing behind them. Marty looked down at the folder on her desk containing Sonya's papers. She didn't really care what they said. She'd spoken to the woman at length, and then there was her gut reaction. And her gut told her Sonya Washington was just fine.

She put in a call to Shayna's private number, without much hope. To her surprise, the phone was picked up after the second ring.

"There you are. Are you all right?"

"Good morning, Marty. Yes, I am fine." There was a question in her voice.

"You weren't in the window this morning. I worry when I don't see you."

Shayna laughed. "You're wonderful, you know that? But it was nothing. Mama had me in the bathroom, washing my hair. It takes forever."

"I've also been worried about your mother. How's she doing?"

"Mama? She's perfect." The voice was, perhaps, a bit over-bright. "In fact, she's right here, next to me. Would you like to speak with her?"

Miriam said, "Hello, Marty, so good of you to keep track of Shayna, it's like having a guardian angel." She sounded very up, very lighthearted.

Marty made her voice the same. "Well, your guardian angel is wondering why you weren't in on Monday, to see Dr. Zee again."

"Oh, Marty, I haven't had a *minute*. Anyway, I'm feeling so good . . . I don't want to go in when I have nothing to show her. And Rosh Hashanah comes early this year, so I've been cooking and baking and freezing. Don't worry," she laughed. "I wear my gloves, just like you told me."

"So, you were cooking and baking all day Monday?"

"All day. I never got out at all. Shayna knows, she wanted me to pick up books at the library for her and I couldn't."

So Paul's patient had been someone else. That was a relief. A moment later Miriam said good-bye. Marty could hear her footsteps leaving Shayna's room, and then the girl whispered into the phone.

"Marty, just a few minutes ago she stopped brushing my hair and she put a fist to her chest, it was just for a minute. Not like the other times. But it isn't good, I know that."

"You are absolutely right, Shayna. Listen, it's very important that she tell Dr. Zee everything that's happening to her. The lupus is in remission right now, but that doesn't mean it's *gone*. I'm worried about her."

"Me, too, Marty."

"I'm going to tell Dr. Zee what's going on. Your mother has

to get a complete workup. I know she thinks she already had one. But lying in her bed, she can't be checked the way she should be. She really has to come in to the hospital."

"I'll *make* her go to Dr. Zee," Shayna promised, and hung up.

For a change Dr. Zee was in her office, between patients, looking through her desk for something. She was unaware that anyone was nearby, and when she straightened up, she groaned aloud. Marty ducked back, behind the doorjamb, not wanting to catch her friend off guard.

When she popped her head around the edge of the doorway again, she called the doctor's name. Dr. Zee looked up, and Marty was shocked to see how worn her friend looked. For a split second Dr. Zee looked like an old woman. She *never* looked like an old woman; she couldn't; she was ageless.

"I'm not going to keep you. Just want to tell you I spoke to Shayna just now. And Miriam, too. Miriam *says* she's as good as new, and she sounds very chipper. But Shayna says she's still getting those chest pains and taking care to hide them. I wondered . . ."

"If I thought I should make a call to Miriam. Yes. I even have an excuse. Her Alpha-fetoprotein test says the baby is probably normal." Dr. Zee made a little face. "That makes it a very tough choice."

"If you need me for any reason . . ." Marty said.

"Right. I'll talk to you later anyway. Maybe we can grab lunch tomorrow?" She was looking perfectly normal now.

"You're on."

Back in her office, there was a message from Dr. Chen. One from Joel. One from Crystal, rather breathless, saying that Sonya Washington was a dream. Nothing from Paul. She supposed she'd better see what Chen wanted *this* time. Had Owen had an episode?

When his mother had first put him into the Mansion, he'd insisted that Marty was making threats to him through the electric outlets; they had to cover them all with tape. All Marty could think of, when they told her this, was the old James Thurber piece about his elderly and eccentric aunt who was positive that electricity leaked out of open outlets. She had laughed. Very inappropriate.

Might as well get it over with. After she punched the number on her phone, she poured herself another cup of coffee. She had a feeling she'd be needing it. The doctor must have been sitting at his desk waiting for her call because he picked up on the first ring.

"I'm calling you because now it's time."

"Time?"

"Yes. Time to discuss just when your husband will be coming home."

"Coming home," she repeated, like an automaton. "You mean . . . my home? You think Owen will be coming back to live with me, is that what you're saying?"

"Why, yes, of course."

"Dr. Chen, we have already discussed this and I told you that I'm about to divorce him. The marriage is long over. I don't want Owen to live with me. I *refuse* to have Owen live with me."

After a tiny but significant silence, Dr. Chen said, "That's an . . . unfortunate attitude. You *are* still married to Owen and he is still counting on coming home. He's looking *forward* to it."

"Doctor, do you realize he became violent with me, more than once . . . that once he nearly *killed* me?"

"Oh, surely we exaggerate."

She could hardly believe that oily, condescending voice. "I assure you, Dr. Chen," she said acidly, "we do not exaggerate. And, quite frankly, we take exception to your tone."

Chen went right on, as if she hadn't even spoken. "If he stays on his medication, in the proper dosages, you should have no trouble with him."

Exasperated, she snapped, "Dr. Chen. I'm a nurse-practitioner with a Ph.D. in psychology, not the village idiot."

"What *I* hear is a very angry woman. Perhaps you'd like to come in to discuss your feelings. I can fit you in—"

Fury, hot and bilious, rose up in her throat. Why was it that men, when they were at a loss, fell back on the angry-woman thing? Tightly, she said, "Excuse me, Doctor, but you are clue-less." And hung up, breathing hard, her fists clenched. What made him think he could run her life for her? But she knew the answer to that, because nurses did it, too. Do enough healing,

save enough lives, alleviate enough suffering, and you think you're pretty goddamn hot shit.

Anyway, why waste energy being mad at a man she barely knew and would never see again? The real problem wasn't Chen, it was Owen. Christ, Owen. She knew she should call Beatrice and tell her what was going on. After taking a hefty swig of coffee, which was now cold and disgusting, she started to dial the Colorado number, where Owen's parents would doubtless be, in the middle of the summer. And then she thought, To hell with it, and put the receiver back down, checking her watch. She had a luncheon meeting downtown, where she was reading her paper on "Management of a Birthing Center." If she hurried, she'd actually be on time.

When Marty walked into her office at three-thirty in the afternoon, she was astonished to find Aimee Delano sitting behind her desk. Aimee rarely left her own elegant rosewood table with its onyx accoutrements, unless, of course, she was in the company of Very Important People. And what the hell did she think she was doing, sitting in someone else's chair? Marty felt like one of the three bears—although, she couldn't help thinking, Aimee Delano made a poor Goldilocks. She was too tall, for one thing.

Marty cleared her throat. Aimee looked up, a bit surprised, but not at all embarrassed to be caught swinging back and forth in someone else's executive chair. She must think that their little conversation after the meeting gave her property rights, Marty thought. Aimee might have been snooping; yet, nothing on the desk looked as if it had been touched.

"Can I do something for you, Aimee?"

"I'm so glad you put it that way, because that's exactly why I'm here. To tell you how you can do something for All Souls." Marty made a questioning noise, wondering how she was going to make this woman move. She decided on the direct approach and walked around the desk, saying, "Would you mind?"

"Oh. Oh!" Light little laugh. "It was naughty of me. But I've been thinking of ordering a chair like this one and I wanted to try it out. Sorry." She sprang up, moved to the other side of the

desk and stood there. Did Aimee think that was going to make her taller than her, Marty wondered, once she sat down? So Marty stood, too. Apparently their little truce had already come to an end.

"It's just one of the office chairs they order for us. Nothing special, I assure you. In fact, now that I have you, I wonder if we could talk about the budget for—"

Another tinkly laugh. "Please, Marty, I came here for a specific purpose, and much as I'd like to talk money matters with you, my visit is for something much more important."

"Really? I thought money matters were number one with management."

A tiny pout appeared on the perfectly made-up face and the blue eyes grew hard. But just for an instant. Then Aimee smiled, saying, "Oh, I see. That's a joke. Yes, you do have a wonderful sense of humor. No, what I'm about to tell you is one of *your* top priorities. And when Dr. Messinger said that now was the time to do something about it, I was pleased, and I knew you would be, too, so I just had to tell you personally."

Into the long and expectant pause, Marty finally said, "Oh, that's very nice of you."

Apparently, that's what Aimee had been waiting for. She leaned forward and said, in conspiratorial tones, "Dr. Messinger has been very impressed by the way you handle difficult situations. For instance, when the Life Saviors were harassing that young woman last month . . ."

Again the dramatic pause. Could we just cut to the chase, here? Marty thought, but she only said, "Yes, and . . . ?"

A little frown. "The announcement will be made formally this week. But I'm here to tell you that Dr. Messinger has appointed you Crisis Intervention Officer for Community Care Clinics." She stopped, smiling broadly. "Congratulations."

"You're kidding."

"Why, no. Of course not. I never kid."

Oh, I'm sure of *that*, Marty thought. "I *have* a job; several jobs, if the truth be told. Look, Aimee . . . I'm already over-extended. I can't take on yet more responsibility."

"But you *must*. Dr. Messinger has already sent out the memo."

"Well, Dr. Messinger shouldn't send out memos until he's sure of his facts."

"There will be a great deal more money in your paycheck, Marty. And let's face it . . ." She leaned forward, a tiny little frown between her eyes. ". . . it might be wise for you to get on Dr. Messinger's good side."

Marty took in air, let it out slowly. "You're right, of course. But there will be paperwork. I can't handle any more paperwork. I'm drowning in paper as it is. I appreciate your . . . advice, I really do, but if I take on another job, I'm likely to have a breakdown." And maybe, she couldn't help thinking, that's exactly what they want. Maybe that's what this is all about: getting rid of me for cause. Well, fuck them, they can't.

Abruptly, she sat down. "You know what, Aimee? You're right. I've changed my mind. I could use the extra money. I accept."

Later on, while she crunched numbers—gummed them to death was closer to the truth—she wondered why in hell she'd ever done such a stupid thing. The nerve of them, anyway! She asked and asked for a Crisis Intervention Officer, so they made *her* one? It was like the old joke about the Jewish genie who appeared to someone, and the lucky person said, "Make me a malted," and the genie said, "Poof! You're a malted!"

She was an idiot to have accepted. Well, it was never too late. She hoped. Grabbing her handbag, she trotted down her hallway, through the swinging doors, and into the executive corridor, nearly skidding on the newly polished travertine floor. Nothing substantive was being done, no new beds, no new bathrooms; but there was a general smartening up around the place.

She went steaming into Aimee Delano's office but was stopped in her tracks by Max.

"Ms. Delano? Not here, I fear."

"Well, where *is* she? This is important."

Max shrugged eloquently. "Everything is important, in a hospital." She was thinking of reaching across the desk and grabbing his ear, very hard, when he suddenly softened. "Look, I don't know where she is because she didn't tell me. But if you want an educated guess, I'd say the ladies' room. She spends

half her life in there—doing what, I cannot even begin to imagine." He rolled his rather protuberant brown eyes.

"She's probably putting on fresh makeup," Marty mused.

"I don't know *what* she does. . . ." Max paused and gave a little giggle. "Maybe she dances. She always takes her little portable radio with her."

"Well, when she dances back in, would you please have her call me?"

His lips twitched in an appreciative smile. "Will do!"

But will didn't, apparently, because by five-thirty she still hadn't heard. And when she punched out Aimee's extension, there was no answer. Damn, damn, damn! And there was the budget in front of her, stubbornly refusing to expand itself, to make room for a few more nurses . . . hell, for a Crisis Intervention Officer. She was tired and cranky and wanted her mommy. She folded her arms on the desk and put her head down.

A deep voice at the doorway said, "Are you awake? Because if you're asleep, I'll come back later."

She raised her head. "Clive. You have no idea how glad I am to see you." Strangely enough, she meant it. There was no harm in finding him charming. It didn't mean she had to fall into bed with him. And she hadn't had a single word from Paul, of a personal nature. When they happened upon each other in the course of the day, he gave her a polite hello and that was it. Well, let him sulk. Did that mean she had to sit around, doing nothing but wait?

"You'll be gladder when you see what Aldo's cooking for us, special."

"Well, I—"

"No, no, don't thank me. Just shut up and come to dinner. You'll be a better person for it, trust me."

"I wasn't going to say no. I was going to say yes. I accept your invitation. That makes two so far today and it's by far the better one."

"Meaning?"

"I'll explain on the way. But first, I'll go fix up the eyeliner."

"You look gorgeous just the way you are."

Funny, how much better she felt all of a sudden. Must be the promise of a good Italian meal and a glass of red wine.

17

Marty straightened up and stretched. Ouch! Her back was killing her. She looked down at her desk, littered with masses of paper, and cursed Dr. Messinger for ruining everyone's weekend. She should have been up at the Mansion, finishing her business with Owen. She would have been, too, if at four P.M. on Friday the word had not gone out from Messinger's office that the accreditation people would be around in five weeks. He wanted a complete review of what had been promised plus complete reports on what had been done or was being done—that included every program, department, and unit in All Souls Hospital—and he wanted it first thing Monday morning. The shrieks and squeals of outrage carried all the way to New Jersey, she was sure.

But Dr. Messinger was the boss, so she'd been here at her desk all day Saturday and Sunday, and here she was again, on Monday, since a little after five A.M. He wanted it "first thing"—well, he'd get it first thing. Melissa and Joan, the clinic secretary/bookkeepers, would proof it and run it through the computer, printing pages just as fast as they could. They were coming in at seven-thirty because they were angels. It was now—she checked her watch—almost seven. What a pain! It had to be done, but over a weekend? The man was a sadist!

And there was another problem. When she'd come in earlier, the light on the answering machine had been blinking. She punched the replay button while she sifted through papers. One, two, three messages from Clive Moses, wanting "a reprise on the dinner scene." Oh dear. She knew it had been a mistake to go out with him the other night. They had ended up

in bed, as she knew damn well they would. But it had been nothing more than revenge on her part: revenge on Paul. What a dreadful thing to do to Clive, who was a very attractive, sexy man. But he was not Paul; it was as simple as that.

She needed a break . . . a treat . . . say a Danish and hot coffee from the cafeteria instead of stale cookies and warm brown water in a Styrofoam cup from the machines. A knock came on the door frame, since her door was wide open. She turned to see Sonya Washington standing there.

"Hi, Sonya. What's doing?" Sonya had taken the last shift and she looked tired. Five of their beds were filled with women who had come in with complaints and were staying here until all tests were completed. Two were battered women who needed a safe place to stay even more than they needed medical help. Two were HIV-positive pregnancies, and one a sixth-month pregnancy with spotting and bleeding, whom they were keeping under observation.

"Problems?" Marty went on.

"Problems? Let me put it this way. Not with the patients."

It was unlike Sonya to be coy. "Whatever it is, I'd better know."

"It's Crystal, actually. She just came in, and already she's snapping everyone's head off, even the patients. I know she's hassled with all that paperwork the Lord God over there in his big fancy office wants done all of a sudden. But hey, everyone's in the same boat."

"Crystal does erupt every once in a while. I've found if you just ignore it—"

"Well, Marty, when she takes the bloods I just collected and throws them—the whole rack—across the room and breaks every vial, and splatters blood everywhere, it's a mite hard to ignore."

"Christ!"

"And then she busted into tears and ran out. I know you two are friends, so I thought—"

"Oh, absolutely. Absolutely. I'm on my way. Where is she?"

"In her office." It wasn't really an office. Crystal had been assigned a real office, a biggish one near Marty's, as head nurse-midwife. But she said she liked being close to her

patients, so she had cleared out a corner of the storage room behind the lab in the Birthing Center, where she kept a desk, a battered metal file cabinet, and a small lamp. No pictures, no plants, no bits and pieces of nostalgia. Interesting, Marty thought . . . she and Crystal were the only people in the program, male or female, who did not have at least one photograph of a loved one on display in the office. So far as anyone could tell, they both might be without a family or a past—or a life, come to that.

Marty ran the whole way to the O.R. with Sonya, past the birthing rooms and through the lab to the storage room.

"This is where she threw it," Sonya said, a little out of breath. Someone had swept the broken glass into a neat pile but there were splotches and dribbles of blood all over the wall. "I didn't want to take the time to clean it up, but I called Maintenance."

The door was firmly closed to the storage room where Crystal had created her space. Marty did not bother to knock. She yelled, "Crystal!" and getting no answer, barged in. The room was empty. Where the hell *was* she? Crystal's handbag was in its usual "hiding place," which everyone knew about: middle drawer, file cabinet. That meant she hadn't left the building.

"Where do you think—" Marty started to ask, when Crystal's familiar voice caroled, "Good. You're here. I'm starving and I was about to call you and see if you wanted to get something to eat."

"Crystal! Where were you? *How* are you?"

"Me? I'm fine. Why?" Then she caught sight of Sonya and threw up her hands. "Oh God, Sonya, I'm so sorry! I had a temper tantrum, Marty. I just lost it. I've been buried in my files all weekend, and when I got in, I couldn't find *anything* I needed for the report to Messinger. It just got to me, I guess. Forgive, Sonya? I'll take those bloods again for you."

"The bloods aren't what's bothering me, Crystal. I gotta tell you, I'm not crazy about having you scream at me in front of the patients, you hear what I'm saying?"

"Hey, I said I'm sorry and I mean it. Come on, Sonya, cut me some slack here."

"Well . . ." Sonya studied the other woman for a moment

and then gave a little nod. "But you were scary, you know that? Man, you had *blood* in your *eye*."

"I hate paperwork more than I hate Mondays, and this weekend, that's all I've been doing. Not only that—I can't find some of the most important files. I don't know where they are. I know I had them, but I'm clueless." She didn't sound in the least bit perturbed.

Dryly, Marty said, "I think it might be wise to find them."

"Don't worry, I'll find them. Maybe if I get some food into me, I'll be able to concentrate better." Crystal bent to get her handbag. "Listen, Sonya, what can I bring you? I owe you big. I wasn't aiming at you, but, God, what if some flying glass had hit you? I'd never be able to forgive myself."

"Just don't let it happen again, if you don't mind. I better get back to the patients before they think they've been deserted. Anyway, I'm glad you're feeling better." Sonya's voice was mild as milk but her sharp eyes were alert. So she had noticed it, too, Marty thought: Crystal's slight slurring of words, her slightly loopy smile.

"Oh yes, I'm certainly feeling better. In fact, I'm feeling just great." Crystal gave a giggle. "Maybe losing your temper cleans out the poisons."

She certainly did not walk over to the cafeteria like someone who had been bent over a hot file cabinet for days, Marty thought, trying to keep up with Crystal's pace. "It must be great to be able to bounce back like that," she remarked, and got more giggles for an answer.

At the entrance to the cafeteria, they both stopped in surprise. The large garishly lit space, usually empty and echoing early in the morning, was buzzing, its shiny turquoise and orange tables all filled. Apparently, *everyone* wanted a break from the paperwork. Marty wondered if any patients were being taken care of while the staff went through memos, invoices, bills, itemized lists. Norma McClure steamed right by them with a loaded tray.

"How does that woman eat so much and never gain a pound?" Crystal said. "It's a mystery."

"She must burn it all up. She strikes me as someone whose motor is always revving."

At the food counters, they found that everything had been picked over, leaving not much of a choice. Canned peaches with dollops of cottage cheese and a wriggling square of red jello offered on a bed of limp lettuce. Mystery sandwiches, wrapped in plastic. Glutinous piles of macaroni salad and potato salad. There was even a steaming metal caldron of soup—in the middle of the summer.

"Wait! I see two sliced chicken plates hidden in the back," Crystal said.

"Quick, grab 'em before they get away!"

Carrying their plates and glasses of iced tea, they headed for a table where four doctors in scrubs had just finished their meal. One of the cafeteria workers was clearing off the debris. Everybody matched—the scrubs and even the busboy's jacket were in the obligatory dove-gray. But where were the ramps for wheelchair patients? Where were the grips in the toilets for the elderly? Where were the badly needed beds and new nurses? Where were *all* the things this hospital needed? Not to be found, but in the meantime, everything had been color-coordinated!

As soon as they settled down, Crystal said, out of the blue, "I get the feeling there's something between you and that new doctor, Paul Giordano. Am I right?"

Marty kept her eyes on her plate, trying not to be annoyed. "Something between us?" She had been trying like hell to keep any thoughts of Paul Giordano out of her mind—and failing miserably. His aloofness hurt . . . even if it *was* her fault. "Well . . . we used to . . . go out. Years ago. We worked at the same hospital." She lifted her eyes and looked straight into Crystal's. Crystal's amber eyes were bright and amused. Maybe *too* bright and *too* amused.

"Really? You went out?"

"Crys, why does it matter? It was years and years ago. It wasn't important. He was a resident, a PGY-1. He left the hospital very . . . precipitously. It was a big mystery. We all wondered what had happened to him. Now, suddenly, he's here . . ." She was surprised to find how easy it was, to tell half of the truth and even begin to believe it. "It was a shock to see

him, especially since he looks the same. His disappearance was a ten-day wonder."

"Disappearance!" Food forgotten, Crystal leaned forward. "You mean literally? He actually just disappeared?"

"I thought you were starving, Crys. You haven't even touched your food. Not that I blame you. It's not terribly good. But at this point, anything will do." The longer they sat here, the more Marty was convinced that something was amiss with Crystal.

Like an obedient child, Crystal picked up her fork and took a bite. "Do you know, once I was very fat?" she said.

"You? When? When you were an infant?" Marty laughed.

"I was fifteen. I was a model. I made a small fortune. I began when I was eleven. Not a child model. I wasn't allowed to look my age. No, they made me up and dressed me up to look like a grown woman, only like no real grown woman could ever look, with a girl's skin, not a line anywhere, not a blemish, and pert little tits. . . ." Her voice sounded sad and her eyes were focused far away. "They posed me seductively and had me pout my pretty lips and lower my pretty eyelids, they painted on shadow and contour and highlight." She caught herself, smiled, and looked directly at Marty. "I'll bring in my old portfolio one day. You'll recognize me. My face was on every other page of the fashion magazines for a while."

"It must have been . . . exciting."

"It sucked." The crude phrase was spit out. "*I* didn't want it. My father did. And what Daddy wanted, Daddy got. Until Daddy got more than he bargained for."

Chilled by Crystal's tone, Marty asked carefully, "What do you mean?"

An unreadable expression passed over Crystal's face, like a shadow across the moon. Then it was gone. "We all showed him, my brothers and I. We had to do what he wanted when we were kids. But each one of us managed to escape, one way or another. And my way was to get fat. I ate and ate and ate and ate. And pretty soon, nobody wanted me for their ads anymore. Nobody loves a fat girl, Marty. But I loved her. She saved my life. And then I didn't have to pose anymore. I could just go to high school and be a *girl*. Although it was a little late for inno-

cence, I'd already been laid by three different photographers, my business manager, and, one time, by every man in the room. Equal Opportunity Night." Her laugh was ugly.

"Crys, are you sure you want to tell me all this?"

"Aren't we friends? Isn't that what friends are for? To tell things to?"

Marty gazed at the beautiful, unreadable face. Are we friends? she wondered; and then answered herself, Of course we are. Crystal was right. Friends talked to each other. "I . . . I had a difficult father, too. . . ." she said, forcing the words out.

Difficult was not quite the correct word. Depressed. Her father had been a depressive. And mean. Angry. More than angry. Raging. He had hated them both, his poor unfortunate wife and the daughter she had borne him.

Anton Dauber had already lost one wife and one child. He had been taking them to a doctor's appointment in a snowstorm and drove the car into a telephone pole. He hadn't been scratched, but the right side of the car was stove in completely. His wife and the baby, a three-month-old boy named Andrei, were both crushed against the pole, their bodies pierced by pieces of the car.

He was never the same again, or so Marty had been told by her aunt Rose. Her father never spoke of his first family. He hardly spoke of anything at all. She knew him mostly as a large, silent shadow, always with a burning cigarette in the corner of his mouth. She looked like him, Aunt Rose always said. Marty had hated that as a child. To her, he was a dark giant, silent and smoldering. But she could see now that her auburn hair and green eyes, her lanky height, came from him.

Two years after the accident, he was still grieving. Because he gave no sign of ever getting back to normal, his sisters, Rose and Esther, took matters into their own hands. They had friends who had friends who had a cousin just in from Trieste with a daughter who they swore was a raving beauty. The only difficulty was that she spoke no English, couldn't seem to get the hang of it. But it wasn't right for a young man to be without a wife, without a family. Perhaps no one could ever take the place of the woman he had adored, the child he had loved so

much; but they persuaded him to meet her, look at her. A young man, still in his prime . . . he needed a woman.

And so they brought Lydia to him and she really *was* lovely, although very shy and quiet. Either he was starved for love or was genuinely smitten by the girl with the cloud of curly black hair and the round black eyes. She was tiny, with little hands and feet and large breasts. In any case, he wanted her. He hadn't had a woman in two years, he had been buried in his grief. It was time. It was time to begin living again and to start another family. The sisters smiled at each other and were satisfied. Within a month of first seeing her, Anton had married Lydia.

It had been good—for a short time. For a very short time. Soon, even without a language in common, he discovered what Lydia's family hadn't bothered to tell him. Lydia was . . . well, they weren't sure just *when* it had happened. Either she had had "brain fever" as a baby or she had fallen from a tree at the age of four. Who knew what had really happened?

"She was a child, mentally. I suppose she was retarded." Marty was surprised she could say it so easily—she had said the word only once before, to Dr. Zee. It had been drummed into her for years that it was *never* to be spoken of, *never*. Once—she couldn't have been more than three or four—she had innocently asked her father if Mama was dumb. He had slapped her across the face, hard. She never asked anything about her mother again. It was Aunt Rose who, bit by bit, fed her information, always furtively, always looking over her shoulder to make sure her brother didn't know. Everyone was afraid of him. He was like a volcano that could erupt at any moment.

"My mother was sweet and loving, but otherwise . . . there was nothing. She had no idea how to take care of me or of the house or of anything. She spoke a little Italian, but she never could learn English. Just a few words . . ."

"Your father. He was disappointed."

Marty gave a brief unhappy laugh. "When my mother's family finally admitted there was something wrong with her, he nearly killed her *and* himself. My aunt Rose told me. He was in a rage like nobody had ever seen. Nothing in that house was left

undamaged. Aunt Rose said she always thought the only thing that stopped him was the fact that my mother was pregnant. Aunt Rose said she was surprised the neighbors didn't call the police. But back then, people minded their own business. Especially in Connecticut, in a sedate New England town.

"After that he . . . I don't know how to describe this . . . he *dismissed* us from his life. He barely spoke to me. He *never* acknowledged her, never looked at her. And I soon learned that nobody outside was to know about her. She was our secret."

Marty paused to take a sip of iced tea. It actually felt good, talking about it. "I never had friends over to play. He wouldn't allow it. And then, when I got old enough to realize what she was like . . . well, to my eternal shame, I didn't *want* to bring anyone into the house."

"How did *you* escape?"

Marty paused, flooded with memory. She shook it off. "A teacher," she said. "He helped me apply to colleges, and made sure I got scholarships."

"You must have loved *him*."

"I suppose so. I thought so at the time." She looked down at her plate, concentrating on her food. She didn't want to think about Jerry Kelly. She wasn't sure what might show on her face if she let herself remember.

"Do you ever see him? Or your parents?"

"They're all dead." Marty didn't mean it to come out like that, so flat and final. But if she said any more, she knew she'd burst into tears. So she managed to smile and said, "It was all a very long time ago."

"No wonder you have such feelings for that poor Shayna!"

Marty was so grateful to have the subject changed. "You *are* a witch, aren't you? I always think of myself whenever I see her. Even though it's not at all the same."

"So what's *with* her, anyway? How come she's never allowed out of that apartment? I hear she's gorgeous."

Marty regarded the face across the table, the avid eyes, the Mona Lisa smile.

"She *is* gorgeous," she said, ignoring the other questions. "And very bright, too. Listen, Crys, we need to talk about something else."

"I'm all ears."

"I hope so. Look—"

"There you are!" It was Emilio, sweating, out of breath, and not at all happy. They both looked up at him in surprise. "Crystal! Where the hell's your beeper? We've been trying to get you now for fifteen minutes!"

"Oops! Forgot it!"

Emilio's scowl echoed Marty's thought that this was not the appropriate response. "Never mind that. What's up?" Marty said, getting up, ready to deal.

"One of Crystal's patients. Teenager."

"Pretty little girl?"

Emilio stared at Crystal. "Right now, she don't look so good. Spotting, staining, abdominal pain—"

"That's what she gets for coming in to us so late in the pregnancy," Crystal said.

"Crystal!" Marty and Emilio both spoke together.

"Emilio," Marty said, "get back and do what's necessary. Get Lydia down from Family Practice. She can take over today."

"Hey!" Crystal objected.

"Go on, Emilio."

He turned, then said, "I think you oughta know. The Life Saviors are marching again, twice as many as usual."

"With those dreadful pictures of Dr. Lionheart?"

"Yeah. And he's such a nice guy, too."

As soon as Emilio left, trotting out of the cafeteria, she turned to Crystal, reaching across the table to grab both her arms. "You're high, Crys. What the hell are you on?"

"Nothing! Well . . . okay. Every once in a while, when it gets to me, I take a Valium." She reached into her bag, came up with a vial of the familiar capsules, rattling it. Marty held her hand out and, with a pout, Crystal handed over the bottle. "I can still function. I could deliver a baby right now, no problem."

"You don't know *what* you could do right now, Crys. Your eyes are glazed. You sure all you took was a Valium?"

"Maybe two. Look, Marty, I swear to you, I won't do it again, okay? I promise. I've been having a rough time . . . a

romance that's ending . . . but that's done with now. I think I've found someone new. I'm going to be fine. If you ever catch me like this again, you can report me, okay? I'll *want* you to report me. But give me a chance, okay?"

"I swear to *you*, Crys, friend or no friend, the very next time I see or even hear about you getting high, you'll be reported to the nursing board. And you'll sure as hell be outta here. Is that understood?"

Instead of answering her, Crystal put a great big smile on her face and caroled, "Look who's here!" Marty looked up. For some reason, she expected to see Paul; but it was Joel Mannes, loaded tray in hand.

"May I join you ladies . . . excuse me, women . . . excuse me, nurses."

Crystal gave a tinkling laugh and patted the chair next to hers. "We can *always* use the company of a charming and funny man, Dr. Mannes." Christ, Crystal was *flirting* with Joel. She really was flying. Well, it wouldn't do to have Joel sit down with them; he'd spot the problem in a New York minute, and Marty wanted to keep it in the family for now.

"Sorry, Joel," Marty said, right over Crystal's words. "We're just finishing, and Crystal has paperwork to finish for Dr. Messinger." She hustled Crys out of there, giving Joel an apologetic look. She'd talk to him later because, promises and vows from Crystal notwithstanding, she definitely was going to discuss the problem with him.

On their way back to the clinics, Crystal prattled and chattered like a child. She didn't seem one bit worried about her job. It could be, Marty thought, that Crys had already forgotten their conversation; drugs did really strange things to the brain.

"Can't we do anything about those nuts with their Bibles and their nasty signs?" Crys said. "With all the lawyers this hospital keeps on retainer, you'd think they'd have hauled them all off to jail."

"There's a thing called the First Amendment," Marty said. "Although I thought Clive Moses was going to read them the riot act."

"Clive Moses is all mouth, Marty, haven't you realized that

yet? Anyway, he's a right-to-lifer, didn't you know? I guess not, or you'd never have gone out with him."

Marty thought of several sharp retorts and decided against all of them. "Please go and come down off whatever you took. I don't want to see you near a patient until you're straight, you got that?"

Crystal muttered something under her breath and broke away, walking rapidly down the hall and out the door. Marty watched her, thinking, Christ, a few minutes ago we were sitting in the cafeteria, exchanging confidences, and now . . . ? Well, drugs did terrible things to people. She really *would* talk to Joel. Today. Right after she looked in at the abortion clinic. She had to know which doctor was doing the operations today. It was getting too damn personal for comfort.

By the time she got to the Family Planning clinic, it was well past nine o'clock, opening hour for those who were scheduled for abortions, as well as women just needing a refill on the pill or wanting to know if douching with Coca-Cola was really a good way to avoid getting pregnant. The waiting room was filling up and there were lights on in the O.R.

She walked back there.

"Hi, Marty." She turned to find herself looking right into Paul Giordano's eyes. He had come up behind her so quietly, she hadn't heard a thing, and now here he was, so close to her. She heard a strange little sound and realized it was coming from her own throat. Quickly, she changed it to a cough and backed away.

"What are *you* doing here?" she said. He looked as if he was getting ready for patients.

He smiled wryly. "Not that I expected a warm welcome, but . . ." He shrugged.

"I'm sorry. But I thought for sure Rich would be back." She thought of adding, *And I figured you were busy tagging along after Aimee.* But of course she didn't.

"Did you see the new signs those people are carrying?" Paul asked.

"New? Besides the ones with his picture?"

Paul grimaced. "Now they've got his face blown up so big, you'd know him in a minute. Yeah, they really don't know any

limits. But their spy system isn't *too* good, since none of the Life Saviors knows I did the abortions last week. Since they don't know me, they can't pick on me. So I'm back for a return engagement."

"You could be putting yourself in terrible danger. If you think nobody will know you're doing abortions, you don't know this place. Soon *everyone* will know . . . and we—" She stopped; she had been about to tell him about the poison pen writer.

"Don't worry," Paul said. "We may be foolhardy but we're not reckless." He opened his white coat so she could see the bulletproof vest wrapped around his chest. More softly, he said, "It's nice that you care."

She could feel the heat climbing in her face. She ignored it, saying, "Do you realize that we're standing here, in the middle of the twentieth century, in one of the world's greatest cities, in a modern medical facility . . . and you're putting on armor against the fanatics! We might as well be in sixteenth-century Spain!"

"In sixteenth-century Spain you'd already have been burned at the stake, you and all the nurses. They thought women healers were all witches." In a more serious tone, he added: "Well, in spite of my macho posture, I must admit it's getting scary."

"But we can't stop giving abortions! The anti-choice people may be utterly sincere, but they have no right to force their beliefs on anyone else. It's really sad, that good guys like you and Rich are the only doctors in this neighborhood willing to take the chance anymore. There used to be half a dozen!"

He buttoned his coat. "Look, I don't blame the others for closing up shop. Doctors giving abortions are in danger these days. But someone has to do this procedure. First of all, it's legal, which is a point all the anti-abortion people keep forgetting. Anyway, I don't consider it a moral issue." He shook his head. "I grew up knowing I was an unwanted child. They didn't even say I was a 'surprise,' which is at least *kind*. I was an 'accident' . . . like a broken bone or a concussion." He made a little face.

"How awful for you." So he hadn't told her quite *everything*.

"Yeah, well, it used to bother me. But not anymore," he said bravely. "They were both sixteen years old, my parents. Who could blame them? But it makes me very determined that every child should be a wanted child. Not that I wish I'd never been born . . . but dammit, the pregnant woman ought to be the one to say what happens inside her body . . . not a bunch of zealots with their own personal ax to grind!"

Marty stared at him. "Wow!" she said.

"Didn't think I could make a speech, did you? Oh, hi, Rich. Couldn't stay away?"

Dr. Lionheart ambled in. "Just came by to say thanks. Again. There's an empty office back there and I'm going to catch up on my paperwork."

"The dreaded word," Marty said. "Speaking of which, I've got to go crunch some numbers."

As she turned and began to walk away, Paul asked casually, "Marty, how about a drink or something later?"

She turned with what she hoped was a pleasant expression on her face. "Sorry. Meetings up the gazoo, and I've been asked to work up some figures on an idea I had, and you know how I am with numbers—" *Whoops*. Rich gave her a look full of interest. "Female fear of math," she added quickly, and hurried away, hoping he wouldn't ask Paul too many questions.

She hadn't gone far when she heard the shots and stopped in her tracks. One. Two. Three. Somehow unable to move, she found herself counting them. And then she ran toward the back. It felt like plowing through water. Her heart was beating thickly, and when she saw that Paul wasn't there, there was a sudden sour taste of panic in her mouth. Oh God, gunshots! Paul! Rich was going out the door, yelling, "What have those idiots *done*?" She followed him.

Outside, it was chaos and confusion multiplied by ten. People were milling around and everyone was shouting at once. Paul was on the ground, curled up strangely. A shrill wail came from someone. It took a moment to realize it was her own voice. She broke out in a sweat, running, yelling, "Paul! Oh Christ, no! Paul!"

To her surprise, he turned his head instantly, raising himself up on one arm. "I'm fine. But I need you! Hurry!"

As she knelt beside him, she saw the small, slight body he had been protecting with his own. The woman sprawled limply, like a rag doll, was wearing a dress that went almost to the ankles, with long sleeves and high neck. Marty knew that dress, knew the woman who wore it. A crisp pink and white scarf had been fastened around her head but it had come off in her fall, revealing the thick, curly close-cropped hair. And the neat little hole in the back of the skull. Miriam. Oh, my God, no, not Miriam!

"She's dead," Marty said. Her voice echoed in her head.

"Yes. He meant to shoot *me*, but she got in front of me. I heard him yell, 'M.D., Murdering Doctor!' "

"Oh Christ, this is horrible, horrible." Marty began to shiver violently.

Paul grabbed her arm tightly. "Are you going to be all right? Marty, answer me!"

As suddenly as the shaking had started, it ceased. "I'm going to be fine. I'm not going to fall apart. I'm going to be fine." But she wasn't at all sure. She focused on what was happening around her. She could hear Rich Lionheart, exhorting the growing crowd—where did mobs of people always come from, within moments of a tragedy?—pleading with them to move on, please, we have work to do here, leave room for the medics, for the ambulance. Knowing that Rich was doing something, anything, steadied her somewhat.

"How about you, Paul? Are you okay?"

"Who, me? Yeah, I'm fine. Not a scratch on me."

A young policeman appeared and knelt beside them. "Is she . . . ?"

"Dead, I'm afraid," Paul said. "Did you get him?"

"You bet. He didn't even put up a fight. He wanted to be caught. He did say he was sorry . . . sorry he didn't get *you*, Doc."

"Oh, swell. Well, he did get this innocent woman. . . ."

"He was using an old Army .45." The cop pushed himself up. "We gotta get handguns out of the hands of the crazies. Too many people getting shot in this town!" He shook his head. "Poor lady. You think she was here to get an abortion?"

Marty didn't answer him. She stared at Miriam's limp body. It was all still so unreal.

"You know her?"

Grimly: "I know her. Her name is Miriam Brown. She's the wife of Rabbi Ezekiel Brown." She mustn't cry. She musn't cry.

"Get outta here! But I thought the Orthodox, they don't allow abortions. Like the Catholics."

"You're right. They don't." After the cop left to make his report, still shaking his head, Marty put her face into her hands and breathed in deeply. Somebody was going to have to tell the rabbi. Somebody was going to have to tell Shayna.

"Wait," Paul was saying. "This woman is Rabbi Brown's *wife*? And she was coming for an *abortion*? I didn't see her name on the list."

Marty spoke very slowly and carefully. "She always uses a false name. This wasn't the first time. It was always a secret. She always came early, so she wouldn't be seen. Poor Miriam! Oh, Christ, poor Shayna! And those little boys! Zeke will be insane, he'll go bananas! Dear God—" And then it overtook her and she began to shake again.

Paul put his arms around her, holding her tightly. She knew she had to stop this; she had work to do. She had to tell the family. She had to talk to Shayna. She had to face Zeke Brown. With great effort, she willed her muscles to stay still, and they obeyed. Paul let her go immediately.

"Dr. Zee," she said. "We have to find Dr. Zee. We have to tell her."

"I'm here, Marty." Dr. Zee was standing next to them.

"Why? Why was Miriam here today? She just got out of a sickbed! Couldn't she wait a week or two? What was she *thinking*?"

"It's a nightmare. She never discussed this with me. They've gone to get the rabbi. Nobody seems to know exactly where he is. But we'll find him and, don't worry, I'll handle him. I know he's going to be inconsolable and impossible, and I know he's going to blame us—why not?—but I've faced worse. You get yourself to a chair somewhere, or maybe a bed. You look

awful." She turned, to eye Paul. "You look a bit pale, too, Dr. Gee. How are you doing?"

"I'm fine. Really. What did they do with the shooter?" Paul said, once again all business.

"Took him away in handcuffs, and I must say, the Life Saviors are plenty shaken. Nobody knows very much about him, but he *is* a member in good standing. The ones I saw looked scared to death over this. Better than the idiots after Gunn was shot, when they were tripping all over themselves to say it was too bad, but after all, he *had* killed all those babies."

"He must be a sick bastard. The gunman."

"Perhaps. Although he looks like a college boy."

"White shirt, chinos, and a blue backpack?" Marty asked.

Dr. Zee frowned. "Yes. Why?"

"I . . . I've seen him around. Just the other day . . . Who would have thought—Oh Christ!" Again Marty fought off the tears. She had to get ahold of herself. "What's going to happen to Shayna? What will *he* do?" She did not have to say who she was referring to. They both knew she meant the rabbi.

"God knows," Dr. Zee answered bleakly. "God knows."

18

Marty would never, as long as she lived, forget the sound of Shayna's grief when they came from the hospital to tell her her mother had died. Had been killed by a bullet meant for someone else. The howls of despair sounded as if they were being torn from her throat.

Both of them, Marty and Dr. Zee, sat on Shayna's bed, one on either side. Each of them held one of Shayna's hands and she clung to them for dear life. Selma had hustled the three little boys away—where, Marty wasn't quite sure. She knew

she ought to care—those poor children, they seemed always to be pushed here and there by forces they couldn't possibly understand—but she was too exhausted to feel anything but relief. Someone was looking after them and she didn't have to worry about it.

"Why? Why? Why did he do it?" Shayna burst out. "She was so good, so wonderful! Why did this have to happen to *her*?" At least she was talking; it was better than the wild, wordless weeping. The girl's face was as white as the sheets on her bed and her eyes were swollen shut. "Not my mama! It's a mistake! She can't leave me! She promised! She *promised*!"

Shayna turned blind eyes to Marty and fell into her embrace, where she continued to sob and wail. Marty exchanged a look with Dr. Zee; perhaps a sedative? Apparently, the doctor thought so, too. She bent to her bag and came up with a syringe and a vial, but made no move to do anything at the moment.

"Shayna, Shayna, you'll make yourself sick."

"I don't care! I want to die! Let *me* die! She promised me! She said she would always be here, to take care of me! She promised!" Another bout of body-wracking sobs. Marty tightened her arms around the girl and rocked her.

When the sobs had turned to hiccups, Marty said, "Shayna, let us give you something to help you sleep."

"No!" That roused her. She pushed herself upright, sniffling and wiping her nose with the sheet. "No, I don't want to sleep. I want to know what happened—" Her voice cracked and more tears poured from her eyes.

"It was a fanatic, Shayna. . . ."

The girl leaned forward and beat her fists on Marty's arm. "But why *her*? Why should he shoot my mama?"

"No reason, Shayna. I know. It's even more horrible when there's no sane explanation. He was aiming at a doctor and he missed. Oh, don't, please don't, you'll make yourself sick! Shayna, please. Your mother shouldn't have gone for an abortion. She did so without consulting either Dr. Zee or me . . . without telling anyone what she was going to do." Marty took in a deep breath. She was in danger of breaking down herself.

Shayna burst into tears again. "I should have known! I

should have stopped her. When she left the house, I should have called you! It's all my fault!"

"Of course it's not your fault," Marty said. She grasped Shayna's shoulders. "No way!"

"If I could walk . . . oh my God, if he had even let me have a wheelchair! I would know what's going on around here!" She stopped her weeping and said, in a very different tone, "He's with her now, rocking back and forth, isn't he? Tearing his clothes? Crying to God? Here is what I say to him!" She spat, her hands fisted.

"Shayna, let me give you a shot that will help you sleep."

"If I go to sleep, will my mother come back? If I go to sleep, will I be able to walk? If I go to sleep, will I wake up and find that he is no longer my jailer? I will *not* go to sleep, I will—"

"You women, you cursed Gentiles, you will leave my home. *Now!*"

All three of them turned to the doorway, startled. Zeke stood there, swaying a little, his eyes red-rimmed, his shirt in tatters. Marty had been at the hospital when he started to rip his clothing, his head back, his eyes closed, his voice terrible in its desolation as he cried out his grief—or prayed to his god, she couldn't tell which. He had fallen to his knees, banging his head on the floor over and over. Nobody tried to stop him. It was clear, Marty thought, that he might do something awful if he were touched.

And now, here he was, still looking crazed with grief. "Get out of my home!" he thundered again. "I never again want to look upon the face of evil. Evil!"

"Papa! Stop that! They didn't kill her! She had a disease. She didn't want you to know. It was dangerous to have a ba—"

"She had a disease? *She went for an abortion, Shayna!* She wanted to kill our child!"

"She had to go for abortions, Papa!" Shayna was yelling. "She didn't want to have another monster like me for you to hide!"

"Ingrate! I will deal with *you* later! But now . . . these witches will *leave my house!*"

Defiant, Shayna held her arm out for Dr. Zee. "Give me the needle, Dr. Zee," she said, her eyes fastened on her father.

"Now I want to sleep. Give me the sedative, please." It was amazing how like her father she sounded, metallic, hard, implacable.

Dr. Zee slid the needle in, even as the rabbi made a lunge toward the bed. He stopped himself, his whole body quivering with tension, his eyes blazing.

"We're leaving, Rabbi," Marty said, her tone even. "You need some sleep yourself. Later, after your period of mourning, we will tell you everything. Miriam was suffering from a chronic disease called systemic lupus erythematosus . . ." As she spoke she slowly stood up, her eyes on him. He was in such a state, he might do any goddamn thing. She hoped to lull him a bit with a lot of medical words. ". . . one of the rheumatic diseases, like her father's gout, like arthritis. Her arthritis . . . it wasn't arthritis, it was a symptom of lupus. Women with lupus are in terrible danger if they carry a preg—"

"You allowed her to have an abortion! The Lord God alone may take life. Abortion is forbidden. You knew that. You betrayed my trust . . . her trust . . . the trust of all my people. Leave us. Leave us now. My daughter and I need to be alone."

As the two women left the apartment, they could hear Shayna's voice, rigid with rage. "Get out of my room. I don't want you here. Get out, get out!"

Protozoa was mostly empty when Marty wandered in later that afternoon. She sat in a booth at the back, feeling numb. Miriam was dead and Zeke was ballistic and Shayna . . . she was so frightened for Shayna. What was left for her, without her mother's protection? It was appalling—and so depressing! Shayna *needed* her mother! Everyone needed their mother. Tears started at the backs of her eyes. But she had to think, not weep. Shayna needed *her* now. Zeke had gone berserk, and who knew how long it would take him to straighten out? In the meantime . . . poor Shayna, really all alone in this world. Again tears threatened. I've just got to get some sleep, Marty told herself. But she was too damned tired to sleep. Did that make sense? Never mind, it was true.

She had ordered a martini for herself, and it sat on the table right in front of her, but she hadn't yet summoned the energy

to pick it up and take a sip. She wasn't even quite sure why she'd ordered one. She hadn't drunk martinis in years. Paul used to make martinis for her, his own "special version," back in the good old days when they were young.

She couldn't get Shayna out of her mind, the beautiful face so ravaged by grief, the rock-hard voice. With her father's appearance in the doorway, Marty thought, Shayna had turned to stone. Oh Christ, what was going to happen to the girl?

"I don't know if you should drink that, Marty. You look like death." Paul slid into the booth opposite her.

She tried to smile at him. *He* could have been killed, she reminded herself. But the reality was, Paul was fine and Shayna was motherless. Her eyes filled.

"I know you have a special relationship with the daughter. . . ." Paul said, reaching across the table to take her hand.

"Shayna. Her name is Shayna."

"Hey, I'm sorry. Look, if you really need to be alone, I'll leave."

"No, *I'm* sorry. I'm glad you're here. It's just . . . I feel anesthetized." She tried again for a smile and took a sip of the martini. It hit her stomach like a blow. She had forgotten to eat again. And then the alcohol came sweeping up into her chest and her head like a warm puffy cloud. She took another sip and pushed the glass away. "If I'm not careful, I'll just chugalug the whole thing and then you'll have to carry me home," she said.

"I wouldn't mind."

"Quit it. I can't deal with that right now."

"I'm only trying to help—Oh, hi, Dr. Zee. Take a seat, what'll you have? I'm your waiter today."

"That thing on the table looks pretty good to me at this point," Dr. Zee said, sliding into the booth next to Marty.

"Then finish it," Marty said. "One more sip will finish *me*."

"You're still worried about Shayna."

"I am," she agreed. "I've tried calling."

"No response?"

"Nobody's answering the phone. But that could mean anything. I don't like it. She's right on the edge. If she weren't stuck in that chair, I'd say she could be dangerous. Well, I'll try

to check on her later. If he'll let me." Marty shook her head and sighed. "I think she blames her father."

"For Miriam's death? Maybe," Dr. Zee said, giving her a shrewd look. "Unless . . . there's something you know?"

"No, no." It was nothing she *knew*, only something she recognized. The feeling of being helpless, held prisoner inside someone else's secret. Zeke Brown had done it to his daughter, just as Marty's father had done it to her. She could imagine the rage and pain that Shayna was feeling, the desire to hurt *him*, to let him see how it felt—which always dissolved into powerless dependence because that man was, after all, her father. Marty had been trapped in that bleak little house, isolated from everyone, sworn silently to silence, kept friendless by the nasty little family secret, a captive until she went away to college. At least she got to leave. Shayna did not have that option. People without options often did desperate things.

"No, there's nothing I *know*," Marty finished. "It's just a feeling."

Dr. Zee took a hefty gulp of the martini and shuddered a little, adding, "I needed that. Poor Miriam. Poor Miriam."

There was a moment or two of sad silence. Marty thought about the pretty, tired face with large round eyes so pale a blue that they often looked blank. She wondered if Miriam had felt trapped in her life with a charismatic man, beloved by his public, warm and giving with strangers, but a tyrant at home. She wondered if Miriam had loved him; could you love a tyrant?

"I wish I knew what was in his mind," Dr. Zee said, as if reading Marty's thoughts. "He's not a man to accept this philosophically."

There was another thoughtful silence.

"I didn't do it right! Dammit, I didn't talk to her enough!" The words burst out of Marty.

Both Paul and Dr. Zee stared at her and said, "What?"

"I fucked up, that's all." She stopped talking and put her face in her hands.

"Marty, that's crazy and you know it. Miriam was a bright woman with plenty of spirit and courage, and it's *not* your fault that she wanted an abortion. It's not your fault she went

to *get* one. And it's not your fault she couldn't confide in her husband."

Dr. Zee's voice was so matter-of-fact, it acted like cold water. She struggled out of her hysteria, feeling terribly tired.

"You're right," she said. "You're right. I'm indulging myself. And you know what?" she asked, taking her glass back and tilting it to get a few last drops out, "I'm going back to my office and bury myself in papers."

Neither of them said anything. Dr. Zee slid aside and Marty left, walking out of Protozoa into the fading day. It felt as if a year had passed since she had stumbled in there. She had actually forgotten what day or what time it was.

Van Dam Avenue was strangely quiet. Even the traffic had slowed to a trickle. As she turned uptown, the sun in her eyes, she saw a silhouetted figure heading right for her.

"God will punish you!" It was Rabbi Brown, his face as pale as chalk and his eyes glittering darkly. "You turned her against her God and her religion."

"I never said a word—" Marty objected; but the rabbi was not listening.

"I trusted you, Marty. I trusted you with my daughter, my treasure. I allowed you into my home."

"Rabbi, I swear to you, none of us ever urged Miriam to . . . to do anything. Whatever she did, she decided herself."

"Impossible!" He spat out the word. "Miriam was a good and obedient wife. Somebody at your godless clinics whispered evil thoughts in her ears."

"Nobody whispered anything. Rabbi, you *know* us. You know we would never interfere—"

"Excuse me, I must prepare to bury my wife." He swept past her, but not before she saw the tracks of wetness on his cheeks.

"It wasn't our fault," she said to his retreating back. "Please. We grieve with you!" He held his shoulders rigid and defiant. "Forgive us!" She watched him for a moment. He stopped and he turned and now the sun was in his eyes. She knew he couldn't see her. "I will try, for the sake of all you have done for Shayna. But I promise nothing." His voice cracked, and he whirled around and strode away.

Back in her office, she immediately picked up the phone and

pounded out the Browns' phone number. She listened to it ring at the other end. No answer. There was a thick pile of mail in her box. She shuffled through it. Bills. Requests for money. A couple of personal things. She had sent out job feelers to a couple of hospitals, just in case. She'd look at those later. And on the bottom, a plain gray envelope. Putting the phone down, she opened it and pulled out the folded paper. Oh Christ. It was just like the one Aimee had showed her, only the pasted-on letters said LOVE, PAUL. She started to rip it in two, thought better of it, folded it again and slid it into her bag.

That was the last straw. She was outta here! Striding down the hall, she nearly dashed past Paul. The sight of him, right after looking at that note, was a bit disorienting.

"Hey! Wait!" he called as she tried to run right by him. "Where are you going? You said you were going to do paperwork!"

"I can't concentrate, Paul. I can't do anything. I never slept last night. I'm going to fall over if I don't get out of here."

"I know this has been one helluva day for you." His voice was soft with concern, and she felt tears sting at the backs of her eyes.

"Paul—" she began, and stopped. Should she say anything about the nasty thing in the mail? Wasn't it wisest to tell as few people as possible?

"Yes? What *is* it, Marty? For God's sake, you can trust *me*!"

Can I? She looked into his eyes, bright blue, deep-set, enigmatic. They told her nothing new. "Well . . ." she ventured. "Just . . . what could make somebody act out in weird ways?"

"You're talking about something specific, Marty. What?"

"Poisonous messages, anonymous nasty notes."

"Jesus! You've seen those ugly things?"

Instantly alert, Marty said sharply, "How do you know what I'm talking about?"

He reached into his pants pocket, came out with a crumpled dove-gray envelope.

"Oh Christ!" Marty breathed. "You, too?"

"This came a couple of days ago. In my mailbox." He handed it to her.

Swiftly, she unfolded it. She'd seen this one before. It was

looked as if she were carved from stone. "There will be no more children," she had said then.

Of course, her father would not leave her mother alone. Shayna could hear them fighting in the nighttime, her mother's voice rising higher and higher and her father yelling, and then the sounds of her mother sobbing his name. He was a stubborn, selfish man who knew nothing but what *he* wanted; and he had made her pregnant, so many times. She had sworn to have no more children, but like God, he did not listen. *He* was the guilty one. *He* had killed her mother. He had taken her mother from her the same way he had taken the life she might have had; and he would pay. She, Shayna Razel Brown, would make sure of that. This was her solemn vow to God. Her father was a murderer just as if he had held that gun and aimed it and pulled the trigger, and she would make sure he was punished.

If it was the last thing she ever did.

20

His name was William Blenheim, and his bland, handsome face stared out from the front page of the *Times* with pale blank eyes. ACCUSED KILLER REFUSES TO TALK, said the headline. William Blenheim had grown up in Pennsylvania, had dropped out of junior college, held only part-time jobs, had no close friends. His backpack had contained the handgun that killed Miriam Brown, a Bible, and a collection of mailings from Rescue America. He had told police that he was following the word of God and that he was sure he would go to heaven for his act. He then refused to utter another word.

"The guy is a nutcase," Emilio pronounced. "You watch. His lawyers'll get him off on an insanity defense."

"He killed a woman and he admits it. He planned it. That's premeditated murder," Kenny said.

The Wednesday morning meeting in the Conference Room was going to be disrupted. Marty had hoped for a regular, normal meeting. Fat chance. The shooting was the topic of the hour. Well, of course it had to be. It was horrible and frightening. It said, This could happen to *you*.

The worst part, she thought, was walking past the line of Life Saviors in front of the hospital, holding up placards that said *God Bless William Blenheim* and *Woe to the Bloody City* and other quotations, equally self-congratulatory—quite a change from their bewilderment and fright yesterday. They were all smiling. She wanted to smack them all, each one, one at a time. *Smiling*, when a lovely innocent woman, a wife and mother, had been murdered. She had actually tried to talk to one of the women, a patient of hers. "Lydia," she'd said, "this was *murder*. How can you be glad?" And the woman had answered, without a blink, "Thirty million dead babies, Marty. Thirty million against one." And she had shrugged. It was the shrug that did it. The urge to hit was so sudden and so strong, Marty had to get herself out of there in a hurry.

"They gotta pass a law," Emilio said. "No more crazies hanging out in front of hospitals and clinics."

"There *is* a law," Kenny argued. "They're supposed to stay a certain distance away and they can't grab the patients."

"Huh! Didn't they grab one anyway, just a few weeks ago? And now someone is dead! Nobody's safe!"

"The First Amendment to the Constitution," Virgie put in primly, "gives all citizens the right to express their opinion."

"Well, they should make an amendment to the amendment and say all citizens except nutcases and crazies!"

"All right, all right," Marty interrupted, clinking a spoon on her coffee cup. "We do have business to discuss this morning, and, Emilio, if they do change the First Amendment, it won't be today. So let's talk about the here and now. Carmen has ordered a platter of food from a kosher deli, to be sent to the Browns'—"

"Wait a minute," Crystal said. "Food? Not flowers?"

"Flowers are forbidden," Marty told her. "I'm not sure why,

so don't ask. The family sits *shiva* . . . that is, they stay home
for a week after the funeral and receive visitors. They aren't
allowed to do any cooking during that period, so gifts of food
are correct. Anyway, Carmen has a condolence card and I'd
like everyone to sign it, please, right after the meeting.

"Also, a memo came around this morning, saying there will
be two security guards posted around the clock at both the
main entrance and the CCC entrance . . ." There was a small
cheer at this. ". . . and we are all advised to keep our eyes
open." Much groaning. "Even Dr. Messinger must feel helpless in the face of this kind of random violence. I know I do.
And poor Miriam Brown . . . her family . . . her children . . ."

She stopped talking and nobody asked why. They figured
she was close to tears. She was, but not just because Miriam
had died so senselessly. She had been forbidden to go to the
funeral. *Forbidden.* By him, of course.

The rabbi had opened the door to her knock this morning,
much to her surprise. As soon as he saw who it was, he
slammed the door shut, without a word. They did that little
dance three times. On her fourth try he said, "Don't come here
again. As far as I am concerned, you are dead." It had given her
cold chills. He was the one who looked dead, no color in his
skin, no expression on his face, the skin pulled taut over his
cheekbones.

"Please—" she began.

"You are dead, to me and to my daughter. You killed
Miriam, just as surely as if you had pulled the trigger. And
now, leave. I must bury my wife, my wife and my unborn child
as well."

"Rabbi, we all love your fam—" Bang! The door had rever-
berated in its frame from the force of the slam, a split second
after he had hissed, "And don't you *dare* show your face at her
funeral."

Thinking about it made her feel slightly sick, so she clinked
the cup again and said, "Yes, Emilio?"

"Three pages from the drug sign-out book are missing. I
looked every goddamn where. And I couldn't find half the
HIV-positive patient records, either. I know you're going to
need them, Marty, for your report, but, my right hand to God,

me and Kenny searched through every cabinet twelve times. How we going to prove our patient load? And how am I going to account for the drug orders if I can't find the sign-out sheets?"

He turned to Crystal. "You're the big expert on pain management around here. Your signature's on those sheets more than anyone else's. You sure you didn't keep them, like, by accident?"

"What are you implying, Emilio? That I don't want those sign-out sheets found?"

"If the shoe fits—"

"Somebody probably put them in someone else's files by mistake," Marty said quickly, not at all sure she believed it. "As soon as this meeting is over, we'll *all*—and that includes me—look through our file cabinets. I'm sure they'll be found." She did not look at Crystal. But just in case Crys was trying to cover up something, let her get the message and produce those pages.

"Not only that," Sonya put in, "but that Dr. Dinowitz . . . he's been ordering a whole lot of amnios and ultrasounds that I don't think are needed."

"That's just a doctor covering his ass and making bucks for the hospital, you know that, Sonya," Isabelle said.

"That doesn't mean I gotta like it."

"Yeah, and you know he's one of the doctors that won't touch HIV-positive patients." That was Kenny. "If he sees one on the list, he says, 'Send her to Dr. Sanders' . . . or one of the other residents."

"And look at this!" Emilio was waving a chart. "This is a mess, with half the dates missing!"

Virgie spoke up now. "We all do our best, Emilio, you know that. It was probably one of the new residents. They seem to think they can leave all the details to the nurses."

"Maybe yes, maybe no. But who cares how it happens? Nurses can't put doctors on report. Doctors can do whatever the hell they want! And then, when we get sued for malpractice, who they gonna blame? The doctors? Hell, no, it'll be us!"

Crystal waved this idea away. "Nobody's going to sue us for

malpractice, Emilio. Only doctors get sued; everyone knows they're the only ones who have any *money*."

Emilio talked right over the little ripple of laughter. "Yeah? Well all the patients *call* us Doctor. They'd blame us. They'd sue us, take my word for it."

"That would be a frivolous lawsuit," Virgie said.

"That's the only kind of lawsuit *you'd* know about!" Emilio burst out. "Frivolous! Yeah, that's something that suits the likes of you!"

"Honestly—" Virgie began, the color climbing in her face.

"Who are *you* to talk about *honest*?" Emilio had bright spots of color high on his cheeks, as if he had a fever.

"Emilio," Marty said, as evenly as she could, "would you please check on the patients. We have an elderly primapara and she's terribly nervous." She gave him a look to remind him of their little chat, and how he had promised not to bring his problems into work. He had the grace to look ashamed, and even mumbled something in Virgie's direction that might have been an apology.

"You should keep your prejudices to yourself, Emilio!" Everyone turned, surprised. That mild-mannered, sweet-natured Kenny would raise his voice even that much . . . ! Besides, he and Emilio were a team; if they had differences, they usually took care of them privately.

"Just who're you lecturing, you with your—?"

"Yo, motormouth," said Sonya, standing up. When Sonya stood up, she was a *presence*. Emilio shrank back. "You finished badmouthing everyone in the place? Then scoot! Marty asked you to do something." As he left the room, she added, "And you might think about washing that mouth out with soap, before someone else does it *for* you." There was some uneasy laughter as Emilio slammed the door behind him.

"Virgie, there's no excuse for his behavior to you," Marty said by way of apology. "Or you, either, Kenny. He's going through a rough time at home, but he can't keep doing this. I'm going to have another chat with him."

"He needs more than one of your famous little chats," Crystal snapped. "He needs a frontal lobotomy."

There was more uneasy laughter, which quickly died.

"You okay, Crystal?" Virgie said sweetly. "Is it your time of the month?"

Uh-oh. Crystal flushed and threw her papers down on the floor. "For Christ's sake, Virgie, give the feminine shit a rest, would you? Excuse me, everybody, but I have a patient who needs me." And she followed Emilio's example, slamming out of the bubble, steaming down the hall and out of sight.

Maybe it *was* PMS, Marty thought. This time. But it wasn't PMS in Emilio's case, was it? It was a shame about his temper. He was a good nurse and he worked well with Kenny. Well— he *used* to. She wouldn't put him on report and she wouldn't fire him, not yet. But she was going to get him upstairs to see Joel Mannes. And if that didn't work, she'd have to find him a job elsewhere in the hospital.

Oh Christ, if that happened, she'd have to look for another nurse to take his place. Just the thought of the search, the résumés, the interviews, the training, the fears, the doubts, the disappointments . . . it all made her very weary. She needed a vacation. Or something. And so of course, Paul Giordano's face popped right up. And Paul Giordano's lips and Paul Giordano's body and Paul Giordano's— Quit that, she scolded herself. There would be plenty of time to have thoughts of sex tonight, when he was with her. And wasn't it nice to have him to look forward to!

"I suggest," Marty said, "that we all go on a hunt for those missing files. Since the meeting seems to be over."

"Aw, Marty, there are already patients waiting. . . ."

"Can't help it, Kenny. Search every file drawer. Sonya, you take Crystal's office, since she seems to be tied up. We can't have patient records just go missing."

The door burst open and Dennis Dinowitz came striding in, talking as he came. "Oh. Sorry, Marty. I thought the meeting was—I saw Crystal and—I thought you were alone," he stammered. "I'll come back later. Sorry."

Dr. Dimwit—*sorry*? It must be something very unusual. "No, Dennis. No need. We were just finishing. Okay, people, on with the search for the patient records. If they don't show up within the hour, everyone's lunch is on me."

Marty and Dennis headed for her office. She closed the door

and motioned Dennis to a chair, but he shook his head, biting his lips and frowning.

"Now we're alone," she said. "You seem agitated. Is it the shooting? Or one of my nurses?"

He began to laugh. It sounded almost hysterical. And then he cut it off. "That's funny, Marty, if you only knew it."

"I'll know if you'll *tell* me, Dennis."

"This is difficult."

"I'm sure it is." She was now certain it had nothing to do with Miriam's death. Dr. Dimwit did not normally bother his head with details about patients, not even if the detail was murder.

"Well, as a matter of fact, it's about—" And then he clamped his mouth shut, his face reddening, as Crystal let herself in.

"Is this a private conversation?" She was as sweet and smooth as honey.

Marty opened her mouth to say yes, when Dennis said, "No. Of course not. It's about—It's about—It's about Mrs. Cuevas."

"Oh. Did Mrs. Cuevas become infected? And wasn't she one of your famous elective D and Cs, Dr. Dinowitz?" Crystal's voice was a pleasant purr but there was steel underneath—sharp steel. "It's getting to look like more than coincidence, Dr. Dinowitz."

"I thought you had a patient," Marty said sternly, noting the rising color in Dennis's handsome face. Mrs. Cuevas, in fact, was *not* an elective D and C, but had been showing symptoms of possible cancer. Crystal was aware of that; well, okay, maybe not. But in any case, there was no need to take that tone—not even with Dr. Dimwit, the man they all loved to hate. How come he didn't fight back? He was not a shy guy.

"Do you feel it wise to leave your patient?" Marty asked meaningfully.

"Oh, it's just Marie Racine. She's fine, just nervous. She's such a baby, Marty."

"Well, she *is* a baby. She's not even twenty years old and very far from her home and mother. And Sonya told me she thinks Marie is in labor."

"I'm aware of what Sonya thinks."

"Well, I'll be going." Dennis was definitely uncomfortable. "I have patients to see." In a moment he was gone.

"What did *he* want?" Crystal tried to sound uninterested, but failed. Her curiosity was beginning to be tiresome.

"Like he said," Marty answered casually. "Mrs. Cuevas."

"All the way downstairs, just to talk to you about Mrs. Cuevas? I find that hard to believe."

Marty's voice hardened. "Well, believe it," she said, in a tone that brooked no argument. Friend or not, she was the boss around here, and Crystal could damn well watch her tongue.

"Sorry, sorry." Crystal slid Marty an amused glance. "I'll bet he was here because he's after you again," she purred. "Some guys just never learn."

"Oh Christ, Crystal, give it a rest, will you? He isn't after me! Life isn't *all* sex, you know."

"It *isn't?*" The tension broke and they both laughed.

"Come on, I'll walk you. I thought I'd have a word with Marie Racine." Marty almost added, "If you don't mind." But she didn't care if Crystal minded.

Marie's color was not good and she was clammy with sweat. *"Madame le docteur,"* she said, managing a shaky smile. *"Merci bien."*

Automatically, Marty took a damp towel and wiped the girl's face, her hand laid gently on the extended abdomen. She felt a heavy contraction, and Marie winced and tensed up against the pain. "Marie, try to take in a deep breath, like this. . . ." She demonstrated. *"Oui. Bon. Et encore et encore . . .* uh . . ." She searched for the French word but couldn't find it. "Slowly."

"How far is she dilated, Crys?"

"The last time I checked, about one centimeter. I told you, I don't think—"

"I know you're the expert here, but do me a favor. Look again. Sonya thinks she's in labor, and now, so do I."

"It's much too early."

"Yes. I know. All the more reason to check."

A moment later Crystal said, "Maybe three centimeters. I'll keep an eye on her."

"Effaced?"

Crystal's voice mirrored her irritation. "Only twenty percent. I'm telling you—"

"Okay. I'll leave you to it, then."

Marty was almost out into the hallway when she heard Crystal muttering, "It would be nice to be trusted." She paused, then turned and said, mildly, "I wasn't trying to undermine your authority, Crys, you know that."

Crystal looked up, eyes wide. "Of course I know that. Thanks for your help."

Had she imagined the comment? No, of course she hadn't. Marty headed back to her office. She heard her name being called and saw Isabelle bearing down on her, waving file folders. A thick stack of file folders bound together with heavy rubber bands.

"What's that?"

"Sign-out sheets for drugs. Patient files. Whatever." Isabelle handed them over, shaking her head. "I found them in the bottom drawer of my desk. . . ."

"Your own desk? But—"

"Yeah. I know. Someone tried to hide them, and maybe that same someone thought they could get me into trouble, too. This particular drawer is usually empty. If you hadn't told everyone to search everywhere . . ."

Marty glanced through the pile quickly. It was the drug sign-out sheets, about six days' worth. "Why would someone want to get you into trouble, Izzy?"

"Marty, why have *all* these weird things been happening? It's probably the same person who's been shifting the blood samples around and mislabeling urine specimens and writing poison pen letters."

"I hate to say this," Marty said, "but it looks more and more like it has to be one of us on the staff."

"Norma, maybe? She's always grabbing stuff and squirreling it away. And you never see any of it again, so why's she doing it? I mean, she's weird enough."

"I don't know, Izzy, I just don't know." She didn't say what was in her head. She had no proof, just a feeling.

"You going to the funeral this afternoon?"

"Miriam Brown's? No, I'm sorry to say. I'm persona non grata."

"He *can't* be blaming you, not you. You've taken care of them for so long!"

"He blames me. He blames *us*, the hospital. And why not, Izzy? It *did* happen on our property. And if it's our fault, then he doesn't have to look at . . . at anything else."

"I feel sorry for the daughter," Isabelle said, with passion. "She's the one who isn't going to have her mother—" Her voice cracked and she stopped. "Sorry."

"Oh, Izzy. Don't apologize, for Christ's sake. It's awful . . . to lose your mother, it's the worst."

The two women looked at each other, both of them on the verge of tears. But they both blinked and parted. They couldn't let the patients see the women who took care of them break down.

When Marty went out for lunch, she didn't stop at Protozoa; instead, she kept going, pulled toward the big brick building on Van Dam. Little groups of Survivors gathered on the street near the rabbi's building; and when they saw her, the buzz of talk seemed to escalate. At the Brown apartment, every window was cloaked in heavy draperies. Marty knew that, inside, all the mirrors had been covered and clothes were being rent, black cloth being tied around upper arms. The funeral, by Jewish law, had to be within twenty-four hours; and doubtless, the police would rush the obligatory autopsy.

She had planned to knock again on Zeke's door; but standing here in the glaring sunlight, with all those eyes on her, she realized how stupid that was. She wheeled around and marched back to the hospital. As she headed back, she realized with a shock that she would never see Miriam Brown again. Miriam, with her wry sense of humor and her endless patience. Miriam had been a wonderful help whenever she had gone in to take care of Shayna, listening carefully, writing everything down. Miriam had made sure everything was done, done correctly and quickly and—often, Marty was convinced—done in spite of her husband.

She would miss Miriam—not the way Shayna would, of course, but she would miss her. Too bad the rabbi was so

furious. She'd like to be able to go to the cemetery and honor poor Miriam.

She fought back tears all the rest of the way, hurrying her steps and putting a busy frown between her eyes, so that none of the press people roaming the neighborhood for human interest would dare to stop her. She ducked up the Hamilton Place side of the hospital, avoiding the clump of parked TV vans.

Shortly after three, there was a knock on her office door, and Crystal let herself in.

"Crys. Good. I'm glad you're here. We're overdue for one of my famous little chats, I think."

"I came to get you, actually. They're marching to the cemetery, and I thought you might want to watch, since you weren't invited to the funeral. I'm surprised you didn't hear all the car horns. They're tying up traffic something awful."

Okay, Marty thought, we can put off our talk for now. She put on a smile and said, "Lead me to it," and walked out of the front entrance with Crys, out into the heat and glare.

Marty was a smart woman, but not as smart as you-know-who, Crystal thought. She'd managed to change the subject every time Marty wanted to talk. She didn't remember much about last night, but she was pretty sure Marty had been mad as hell about something. She'd have to try to find out what happened, so she'd know what lie to say.

Anyway, she was fascinated by this funeral procession. She was fascinated by the Survivors. They were so strange. The entire congregation, it looked like, was walking slowly and mournfully down the middle of the street, ignoring the traffic, the bleating horns, the television cameras, making their way to the tiny cemetery two miles away, where all their members got buried. It might be rather moving—if you were into this sort of thing, Crystal thought. She wasn't. And she'd bet half of those mourners shuffling down the middle of the road weren't into it, either. She figured most people were acting a part to impress other people.

Still, this strange parade sent chills down her spine. They all wore black armbands, and the men were wrapped in big silk prayer shawls. It was totally silent; every once in a while you

could hear a woman crying, but that was it. Bringing up the rear were the rabbi and his sons, even the littlest boy being brave, not crying, holding himself straight and proud and looking neither to the left nor to the right.

"I have to admit, it kind of gives me a lump in my throat," Crystal said. "But, Jesus, do they have to take up the whole avenue? And look who's here," she added quickly. She could feel Marty getting ready to give her a lecture on tolerance, which she really didn't need at this point in time. "It's Dr. Zee."

Crystal noticed right away that Dr. Zee had lost more weight. But otherwise, she looked okay. And she was striding along, the way she always did, always in a hurry.

"Afternoon, ladies. What do you think of this, Marty? It's not a typical Jewish funeral, is it?"

"No. This is a Survivor idea," Marty said. "As far as I know. I'm no expert on Judaism. What upsets me is there's no sign of Shayna. She's not even allowed to grieve for her mother! What lie is he telling *this* time, I wonder?"

"Prostrate with grief, I hear," Dr. Zee said.

"I feel for him, I really do, Julia. But come on, the man is a tyrant where his daughter is concerned. He's unforgivable."

Weren't they all? Crystal thought. Men! She couldn't help but notice that all the Survivor women were covered up to the neck, down to the wrist, and almost down to the ankle, even though it was the worst part of summer. Expensive outfits, though; she recognized a couple of Donna Karans and a Giorgio Armani.

At least they didn't have to wear wigs, like some. Crystal didn't get the wig thing. Oh, she understood shaving a woman's head so she wouldn't be attractive to other men. That was a typical man's trick: to mutilate or make a prisoner of any woman he thought he owned. All you had to do was look at history. Corsets. Bound feet. The veil. Clitorectomy. Hell, a shaved head was *minor* compared to what some men did to their women. But you had to wonder why these women put up with it. Maybe that's why they loved their rabbi so much; he made all their decisions for them. People were sheep.

She knew all about Shayna's spina bifida. She wasn't supposed to, but could she help it if people talked without thinking

who might be listening? It was too damn bad. The girl was stunning, with her thickly lashed eyes and bee-stung lips. Everyone had seen her sitting in her window. She was something! Any guy would want to jump on her bones, and maybe that was why Daddy didn't let her out. He didn't want a riot on his hands.

Crystal Cole knew all about how men just wanted to grab, grab, grab. It wasn't easy, being beautiful, even though you could never *say* it. People thought you were putting them on, giving yourself a little pat on the back while pretending to suffer. But it could be awful. Boys were always sniffing around you, from the minute you got out of kindergarten, and not just boys your own age, either. Men. Sometimes your uncles. Your cousins, for sure. Your father's friends. Even if they never put a hand on you, you could feel their hot eyes following you, licking at you.

Of course, that hadn't happened to the little Jewish girl. She'd been kept at home, as cloistered as a nun. Hell, her daddy was just another overbearing son of a bitch who thought he owned his women and children.

Didn't she know about *that* kind of man, though! For sure, she did. Her father had been small and skinny, but he ran his family like it was his own private country. His word was law, period, the end. There was no Supreme Court, not in her daddy's house.

"I expect excellence of you!" That's what he always told them: Crystal, Cedric, and Clayton. When all three of them tested out with IQ scores over 160, that was it: the beginning of the end of freedom. They were *his* 160s, *his* geniuses, *his* works of art. Her poor mama never had a chance. Whenever she thought of her mother, Crystal pictured her with that fretful frown, wringing her hands and saying, "Now, Carlton . . ." He never listened to her. He never listened to anybody.

That man had *plans* for them. For the boys, it had to be intellectual: Cedric was to be a doctor and a Nobel Prize winner, Clay a lawyer and eventually Supreme Court judge. For the boys, it was reading three different stories in *The New York Times* every day and giving him a report on all of them. And if they did real well . . . they could graduate to five and then ten

articles. By the time he got finished with them, they were
reading the whole damn paper and *knowing* every damn thing
in it. Or he'd know the reason why.

As for her . . . Crystal remembered how he rubbed that little
spot of a beard he grew on his chin while he looked her over
and pondered her future. She was only a girl; however, she was
a gorgeous girl, no doubt about *that*. In fact . . . She remembered so well how he had circled around her, studying her
while she stood there, hating him.

And then he had it: Crystal Cole would be a supermodel and
earn the money that would send her brothers to Ivy League colleges and professional school. And when she got too old for
modeling—say, the age of twenty-four or so—why, then, *she*
could go to school if that's what pleased her. The way he had it
figured, she'd have made them all rich by then.

It happened, just the way he wanted, though Mama
had protested in her faint voice, "Now, Carlton, do you really
think . . . ?" And he'd turned around to glare at her. "Yes,
Marietta, I really think. Which is more than I can say for you."

Oh yes, Daddy arranged it all. He took her around, got her
photographed, posed her, arranged the clothes just so, didn't
even blink when the photographer suggested she pose in
nothing but a fur coat, left suggestively open here . . . and here.
She was twelve, for God's sake! She was a little girl! But
Carlton Cole saw fame and fortune beckoning. Strip she
would, and pose she would, because he said so, that's why.
And if the photographer's hands kept slipping, sliding over her
budding breasts, pausing when the nipples hardened in alarm,
grinning at her, silently daring her to say anything . . . well,
who was to know unless she told, and who could she tell?

Both Marty and Dr. Zee were puddling up. How easily
most women cried. Crystal believed in tears as a healing
agent. She always encouraged her patients to cry if that's
how they were feeling. She often wished she could follow
her own advice, but no tears ever came, they just sat there
behind her eyes, stubborn and unmoving. Like Daddy
always said *she* was, when he had to whip her with his belt.
Oh, the sound of that leather belt, sliding like a snake out of
the loops on Daddy's pants, cracking on the floor in antici-

pation. She had learned early on not to cry, no matter how much it hurt. It made her feel victorious, superior.

Of course, as soon as she began to get top dollar for modeling, the whippings stopped because he didn't want any marks on her. She caught on to *that* soon enough. She listened and she paid attention. Most people let incidents slide right by them. Well, Crystal Cole noticed everything, heard everything, and ignored nothing. They didn't call her the Witch for no reason! Marty better not mess with her. She liked Marty, but nobody could mess with Mr. Cole's little girl without paying.

Marty was brave but she was getting herself in trouble. She kept telling Messinger off. You couldn't do that forever; sooner or later, you got chopped down.

Marty was always standing up to the doctors. She obviously didn't understand how power worked. Dr. Messinger could fire her. Hell, he could fire them all. Marty shouldn't go making him mad; she could lose her program and maybe her job. Angry doctors had cost many a nurse her license. You had to smile and agree with anything they said and find your own way to get your own way. Like you-know-who.

But hey, it wasn't her job to worry about somebody else, no way. She had enough troubles of her own. And that reminded her . . . she had to make a phone call before her friend left his office. He'd better not mess with her, either. Then she scolded herself. You're smarter than all of them, she told herself. You've got yourself covered every which of a way. You're safe, so stop worrying.

21

Paul rolled over onto his back, arms and legs splayed out, his whole body completely relaxed. Completely. He watched

as Marty lifted herself on her elbow, surveyed him, and giggled.

"Ungrateful wench," he growled, but he reached out to put a tender hand on her face, loving the familiar sight of her, the long, curly red hair loosened out of the ponytail and tumbled every which way, the way she smiled with her lips closed, the freckles on her nose and her shoulders, the neat little breasts. Everything.

"You know damn well I am not ungrateful. In fact, I'm rather sore. Do you realize how many times we've made love?"

"No. Who cares? Who's counting? Though I'm sorry you're sore."

"Actually, I'm not. Sorry. Better sore than sorry."

He reached out and pulled her down, flat against him, and kissed her. Nice—sweet, soft, slow—not like their earlier frantic, fevered kisses. She kissed him back. God, it felt so good. He had his darling back, and there was only one word for what he was feeling: happy, happy, happy!

Marty laughed out loud, and he said, "What?"

"I'm happy, that's all."

"What are you? A mind reader?" He kissed her lightly and sat up, stretching. Without even thinking about it, he sucked in his stomach a little and then, with a laugh, let it go. Okay, so he wasn't quite as tight and lean as he had been ten years ago. Who the hell *was*?

"You're still gorgeous," Marty said. "You really haven't changed a bit. It's almost scary." She paused, running a thoughtful finger down the middle of his chest. Casually, she asked: "So what happened, in eighty-three?"

Ouch. He really had to tell her. It wasn't fair not to; but he was damned if he *wanted* to. "I'll give you the whole life history, in return for something to eat. You have depleted all my reserves, woman."

"If I feed you, do I get to deplete them again?"

"Wait and see. But you don't have to feed *me*. Tonight, I'll feed you, how's that?"

He got up and went into her neat little kitchen, where he prowled around, still buck naked, gathering stuff together for a

salad. She followed and sat on one of the stools, nursing a glass of wine, while he diced and chopped and shredded and tore and threw everything into a big bowl. And waited for her to bring the subject up again. It was going to be a long night. They'd talked for an hour, earlier, about Miriam Brown's murder and the Life Saviors and the rabbi who Paul thought personally was slightly crazy. But Marty was hooked into the whole family, especially the daughter. She was obsessed with what was going to happen to the girl. Nurses tended to do that, he'd found. Doctors learned how to do their thing and go on to the next patient. But nurses got all involved in everyone's *life*. They didn't care how messy that life was, but it scared *him*.

"No wonder men are afraid of women," she said.

"Excuse me?" She wasn't reading his thoughts, was she? That made him laugh. "Is there something about me? Something that speaks of fear?"

"No, no. I was just thinking, I should be exhausted, after all that screwing, but the truth is, I'm ready for more."

"Not this minute." It was about sex; that was a relief.

She smiled a Mona Lisa kind of smile. "Right this minute."

"Jesus, Marty, someone might think you're insatiable."

"I *am*."

"Well, I'm staying tonight, so if all goes as planned, you'll get more. We've got plenty of time."

She saluted him with her wineglass and emptied it. He watched her, luxuriating in agreeable sensations. It was cool in the apartment, he had been well-laid, the wine bottle was full, and he was building one helluva salad here. Also, it looked like she wasn't going to pursue her questions. What more could a guy want?

"Anchovies," Marty said.

"Pardon me?"

"You should have anchovies in a Caesar salad. There's a little can of anchovies somewhere in the cupboard, I think."

He rooted around in one of the cupboards and finally held aloft a small oval can. "Aha," he said.

"Aha," Marty agreed. Then she added, "I wonder when in the world I purchased such a thing. I'm not even sure I *like* the little devils."

"You knew that sooner or later I would be here, making you a Caesar salad."

She refilled both wineglasses and raised hers, smiling. "Okay," she said. "Now let's talk."

"What shall we talk about? How about work? That's safe." He slid her a look, smiling to show her he was kidding.

To his surprise, that's what she wanted to talk about. Work. Well, not precisely. "Things have been . . . happening," she said.

"Things," he said.

"Files disappear. Bloods get mixed up. The IVs in the Birthing Center are tampered with. And then there's—" She stopped.

"Yes. And then there's . . . ?" She stared through him, weighing her options. She'd always done that, kind of spaced out when she was thinking deeply, almost in a trance. "And then there's . . . ?" he prodded.

"Nothing, really. Just more of the same. The poison pen letters, too. I'm sure they're all of a piece. I'm beginning to feel that the clinics are jinxed. Oh, I know that's nuts, there's no jinx, there's just a sick person who finds this fun. But *why*? That's what I can't figure out."

"To get you?"

"Again . . . why? Am I hateful?"

Paul plunked the big bowl of salad onto the counter and turned to get dishes out of the cupboard. "Hey, Marty, you're the boss. To some people, that's enough."

"And then Miriam comes to us for help and how do we help her? We *don't*, that's the answer! We don't even know she's coming in for an abortion, and then this crazed guy with a gun—" Tears filled her eyes. Paul reached over and took her hand, but he felt so goddamn helpless. He never knew what to do about a woman's tears.

"Miriam Brown was a grown woman, Marty. She was in charge of her own destiny, just like the rest of us. She *chose* to do what she did. And the shooter . . . that was a mistake, a horrible mistake, I grant you. But it's *not your fault*, okay?"

She sniffled a little and wiped her eyes and gave him a

watery smile. "I wanted so badly to go to the cemetery . . . say good-bye. Well, at least Julia got to go."

"You didn't hear? No, I guess you didn't. Rabbi Brown had her chased away."

"He didn't! Oh, that bastard! But of course, why am I surprised? If he wouldn't let their own daughter go, why should he let Julia? It's her fault, too. It's everyone's fault but *his*."

To tell the truth, he was relieved to see her getting mad. It was better—and maybe more useful—than becoming depressed.

"Oh Christ, it's all been a bit much," she said. "I guess I'm having angst, so please don't downgrade my angst. It's mine and I love it."

"I'll kiss it and make it all better."

"Kiss what? My angst?"

"Name it, I'll kiss it." They both laughed.

She came around the counter and leaned against him. He stopped slicing the bread and put his arms around her. His woman.

"Oh God, Paul, sometimes life seems so simple. Like right now. Only I know damn well it can't stay that way."

"The eternal pessimist. Sure it can. Life can be beautiful, if you just leave it alone." He kissed the top of her head and let her go. "So let's leave it alone, at least for now, okay?"

"Does that mean that once again you're going to dance away from what happened in 1983?"

"No." He couldn't look at her. He dug around one of the drawers and emerged with a salad fork and spoon and began to toss the contents of the bowl carefully. "It's rather complicated," he said. "Marty, when we lived together . . . when we were first in love . . . when I was a first-year resident . . ."

She waited a minute and then said, "Yes?"

Finally, he blurted it out. "I was a junkie." Now he looked at her. What was she going to think? What was she going to say?

Marty stared at him. A junkie? Paul? The man she had loved and worked with and *lived* with? *Slept* with? She couldn't believe it. It couldn't be true. "How?" she said finally.

"How? What kind of question is that?"

"How did I not know? We were together so *much*."

He kept on tossing the salad, very slowly, very carefully. "Marty, Marty, surely you know how easy it is for doctors—and nurses, too—to get the stuff, and keep on getting it, and get really addicted—and meanwhile, nobody ever catches on. We can always get enough to keep us addicted, too. It's right there, in the hospital, just waiting to be taken by someone who hasn't had enough sleep for months, who's been staying awake sometimes for days at a time, and who is expected to make life and death decisions. When we're straight, we *know* we're making mistakes, but when we're high . . . ah, when we're high . . . we feel intelligent and invincible." He made a disgusted face.

"But . . . I still can't believe I never noticed."

"I'm telling you, I was careful. I took just enough to keep me nice . . . until, of course, 'just enough' got to be more and then even more and then even more than that. And then, I began to lose control of it."

"What in hell did you *take*?"

"Oh, in the beginning it was the occasional dose of Valium, or maybe Xanax or Halcion. Then it was more than the occasional dose. And then, all of a sudden it seemed to me, I *needed* it. Needed, as in desperate."

"So you left me? That was your answer?"

"Sweetie pie, they *caught* me. Remember old Dr. Marcus, Chief of Internal Medicine? *He* caught me, sitting in the linen closet at two A.M., smiling to myself and being goofy. I'd left the door open, you see, because by that time I was getting careless. And who expected Doc Marcus to be wandering the halls at two in the morning? But he was dying of cancer, always in pain, and he came into the hospital when it got to be too much and worked. You didn't catch *him* stealing drugs to ease his pain." He winced.

"Oh Christ, Paul, what did he do? I mean, here you are, a sainted physician, instead of rotting away in a jail cell."

He put down the salad utensils and stopped pretending he was thinking about their dinner. "It was bad enough, being what my mother would certainly have called a dope fiend. It was bad enough, lying to you . . . hell, lying to everybody. But what I did then—Marty, I pushed him. I pushed that sweet old

man when he tried to get me to stand up and walk it off. I pushed him into a wall and his head started to bleed. Oh Jesus—" He stopped. "I managed to hurt so many people. That poor nurse—"

"What poor nurse?" She was totally alert, her jealousy antennae up and quivering.

He saw it and laughed. "Oh, don't worry, I wasn't cheating on you that way. It was a male nurse. He was a nice guy . . . why can't I think of his name? Oh well, it'll come to me. Anyway, you know how the drug cabinet works . . ."

Of course she knew. It was a safeguard many hospitals used. The nurses were in charge of the drug supply. Nobody else could go into the drug cabinet, not even a doctor. However, in a nifty little Catch-22 they dreamed up, no nurse could take a drug out of the cabinet without a doctor's signed slip. The nurse was, however, responsible for all the drugs. So, if a doctor faked a slip and it was discovered, nothing happened to him. The nurses got punished. As usual, the doctors were really in charge.

"Ah. You and this nurse—"

"Yes, he took pity on me. He had a habit, too. And always working in hospitals, well, he had it knocked. So, we got to talking and we worked out a deal."

There was a very long silence. Was that the end of the story?

"He'd push the meds cart from room to room, and if the patient wasn't there, he'd leave the little cup with the meds in it. And a few minutes later I'd just drift in and take, say, the green one, the Valium. And then into the next room and the next and the next. Was a patient going to ask how come there were three pills this time instead of four? Or maybe it would be a patient who wasn't supposed to get Valium. Who was going to check up on every single one?

"Then we got caught. The real shame was that he lost his license. Poor Ed—that was his name, it just came to me— Edward Novogrod. He was out on his ass in about three minutes flat, his livelihood destroyed. Whereas I, the brilliant young physician, was forgiven by the powers that be. Christ! Doc Marcus convinced them I was worth saving, even after I behaved so badly!" He stopped talking and took a big gulp of

wine. She watched him, in a kind of daze. This couldn't be true. But it was. And she thought she knew him so well! Who *was* he, really?

"The whole sordid mess was hushed up. A cover story went on my record, that I'd had some kind of minor breakdown and was taking some time off. Actually, I went into a drug rehab program halfway across the country, in Nevada, to kick the habit. After I was clean, I stayed on, as a counselor, for a year. And then it was as if it had never happened . . . oh, shit." He rubbed his forehead, looking absolutely miserable. "Do you hate me?" he said, in a very different voice.

"I don't know. No. No, of course I don't hate you. But I'm . . . in shock, a little bit."

"Marty, does this change anything? About us?"

She stared at him, at that beloved craggy face, the face that had haunted her dreams all these years. But was it a false face? Was it really a stranger she'd stayed in love with, all this time?

"I don't know, Paul. I told you, it's a shock. I have to rearrange my memories. . . ."

"Oh, God . . ." He put his head down into his hands. "I'm so sorry," he said in a muffled voice.

"I wanted to know," she said.

He lifted his head. "So now you know."

"Now I know. You're clean now, of course."

"Marty!"

"Sorry. Of course you are. I . . . I'm somewhat at a loss, Paul. And I'm ravenous. Could we eat?"

It was a relief to both of them to change the subject, set the table, light the candles, chat about nothing, pretend it hadn't been said at all. The salad was delicious; he had heated some Italian bread in the oven, and found two pears for dessert. They talked a lot about the salad, the dressing, why he had taken to cooking.

"The last *I* knew," Marty said, able to laugh and even feel lighthearted, "your cooking abilities extended to knowing the phone number of Pizzeria Uno in Harvard Square. Period."

He laughed, too. "Self-defense. I hate eating alone in restaurants, and after a while I hated always having to find someone to eat with me. So . . ."

After a pause, she said, "You never got involved with anyone?"

And, after a pause, he answered. "Actually? Yes, I got involved a couple of times. But they always asked the dreaded question. *Where is this relationship going?* I never had the right answer."

"Paul . . . I'm sorry I didn't wait. I'm sorry I wasn't in Boston anymore."

"So was I. Especially when I found out you were *married*. Come on. Now it's your turn." He got up and started clearing away the dishes, maybe to make it easier for her to talk.

"Right. I got married." She paused and then thought, Oh hell. "To a psychotic, who's been in and out of an institution—oh, a very expensive, wonderful, private hospital, not the Snake Pit—for eight years."

"And you never divorced him?"

She couldn't help noting how they both kept their voices very emotionless; and that they didn't look at each other.

"Do you know how stupid I feel about that?" she said. "But sometimes he hated me and wouldn't have signed *anything* I wanted. Sometimes he was over the rainbow and not capable. Then I got very busy, working and going to school at the same time and . . . and, no, I never divorced him. Don't ask me why not."

"Why not?"

"I told you not to ask."

"I know, Marty, but I think it's kind of important. Don't you? Maybe you still love him."

She put her wineglass to her lips, but instead of sipping, she nibbled on the edge, feeling cornered. "I don't love him. I never really did. It's funny," she said, after a pause, "I didn't intend to marry him, either. . . ."

"But . . . ? I *do* hear a but."

"He was good-looking and extremely attentive, but I never thought I'd *marry* him," Marty said again. "He made me nervous. Looking back on it, I can see everything very clearly. Right from the beginning, he tried to get *too* close, tried to be *too* involved in my life. He was by my side at every party. I'd look around, seeing the other guys talking

boy talk, telling dirty jokes, arguing about whose team was better, but Owen . . . Owen would be sticking to me like glue, adoring me with all his might.

"I said something to my friends. You know, about how strange it was, testing the waters, waiting to hear what they'd say. And they thought I was crazy, to find it off-putting. I even broke up with him—or tried to—three or four times. Every day in my mailbox at the hospital there was a card telling me how much he loved me. I began to wonder what in hell was wrong with *me*. Anyway . . . I had loved you so much, and I was sure I'd never again feel that way. So I settled." Her eyes filled, and Paul made a move to come to her side, maybe take her in his arms; but she shook her head, blinking rapidly to keep those tears at bay.

"So you got married. And then . . ."

Why did she hesitate? "Owen was schizophrenic, it turned out. He hid it pretty well, in the beginning, but . . ." She stopped. "After a while, he couldn't hide it anymore. And now . . ." She couldn't go on. Just talking about it made her stomach hurt.

"And now?"

"Paul, I've been so happy, here with you. I don't want to think about him."

"I understand, sweetie pie. But you said 'and now.' What's happening?"

"There's a new medication. He's a lot better. I have to settle things. Next weekend I'll drive up to Connecticut and tell him I'm getting a divorce and that will be the end of it." She got up, restless. Why had Owen picked *now* to come back into her life? Her eyes flooded. Well, she wasn't going to stand here and dissolve into self-pity and have Paul feel all superior and sorry for her.

"Let me clear," she said, getting up, busily stacking their dishes, filling the sink with hot water.

"Changing the subject?" Paul said.

"You bet."

"Okay. Let's talk about your mischief maker. Don't you have a single clue as to who it might be?"

"Nope," she lied.

"The cops always say that crimes of a personal nature are usually committed by someone close, a family member or a staff member. . . . You can't think of anyone?"

Much as she'd like to confide in him, it really wouldn't be fair. "No. I already said no."

"How about your friend, the mystery woman? Crystal Cole."

"Why do you mention her?"

"She seems to have quite an effect on men. There are a couple of my colleagues who get very flustered at the sound of her name."

"Really? Like who?"

"Dinowitz, for one. Rich Lionheart. Joel Mannes."

"Joel Mannes! What do you mean?"

"Nothing. It seems to me I keep seeing them together lately. Now why would she be after someone like Joel?"

"He's a great guy. And he has a great wife, too. It must be a coincidence."

"Maybe. Although your friend Crystal is . . . well, you know, there might be more than one reason she's known as the Witch."

"Paul, you know something."

He laughed. "I hear things, bits and pieces, nothing much. Anyway, could we get back to us? I hope you didn't think you were getting away with changing the subject forever."

As he walked toward her, she realized, God, we never put clothes on! And that made her laugh. He put his arms around her and bent his head to kiss her.

"Not so fast, my fine fellow. Not until you spit out every bit and piece you heard about Crystal!"

"Aw, Marty, I can't remember that kind of stuff. She's just supposed to be what we used to call a hot number. Now let us continue . . . no, no, no use using your feminine wiles on me, my lips are sealed. No, scratch that, my lips are about to get very busy doing something else. . . ."

In a heartbeat she was melting. He scooped her up, and all thoughts of anything but him disappeared like mist in the sun.

* * *

When the doorbell began ringing, she dragged herself awake, totally unwilling to give up that nice sweet sleep, and squinted at the alarm clock. Twelve-ten! What stupid idiot would be ringing her bell at midnight? They must want the girls upstairs, who entertained their friends at all kinds of hours. Should she just go back to sleep and let them ring until they got tired of it; or get up and give them a piece of her mind? Next to her, Paul never stirred, damn his hide. Now the bell was being jabbed viciously, again and again and again. The raucous buzz penetrated her brain, even with the pillow over her head.

She would get up and give them a really *good* piece of her mind. Some people were so totally self-involved, they had no idea that anyone else might need their sleep or have a different schedule or—

She stumped into the front room, grouchy and indignant, and pushed the intercom.

"Whoever you are, you have one helluva nerve! Do you realize what time it is?" she yelled as loudly as she could, her voice rusty with sleep.

"Marty!" Even over the staticky intercom there was no mistaking the voice. Her heart stopped for an instant. "Marty, it's me! I missed the earlier train! Do you hear me? It's Owen! I'm all finished at the Mansion, Marty! I'm home!"

22

Sonya heard the girl crying in her bed and she headed down the hall. When she got there, she heard Crystal trying to teach her how to do Lamaze breathing. It was too late for that. Sonya rushed in. She knew Crystal was going to get all bent out of shape, but Sonya had two mothers trying to nurse, and Marie's crying was driving them up a wall.

"I thought you were so big on pain management," she said to Crystal. "Give her some Demerol, why don't you?"

Crystal was in one of her moods. She gave Sonya a black look and said, "This child doesn't need Demerol. She needs some self-control." Any fool, Sonya thought, could see that "this child" was in labor.

You had to go real careful with Crys. You couldn't cross her when she was in one of her moods. So Sonya explained about how the fussing was bothering the other patients, and she told Crystal she thought Marie's legs were hurting. "How about putting a form under her knees?"

Crystal shrugged, saying, "Suit yourself. You think she needs it, you do it."

So Sonya did it. She went and got the big foam form and propped Marie's legs up, the knees high. And what a smile she got!

But Crystal was on a tear. She kept urging the girl on. "Just hang on, Marie, breathe like this. You don't really want a drug, do you? You're doing just wonderful, honey." Crystal might be her boss, but Sonya did not like her insisting like that. Hey, it was Marie's pain, wasn't it, not Crystal's.

Sonya felt sorry for the girl. Marie was biting her lips and trying not to make too much noise. Not like some of them, shrieking and screaming and cursing their husbands or boyfriends. Well, of course, this one didn't have anyone to yell at, poor little thing. Sonya knew she should get back in to her other patients, but she couldn't help wiping Marie's face, patting the forehead where sweat kept popping out in big round beads. The black monitor cuff looked huge on her slender upper arm.

"That's a good girl, Marie," Crystal was saying, her eyes sharp on the monitors, her hands checking out the strength of the contractions. Usually, Crystal was an outstanding midwife, nice and easy, no temperament in her. Usually. But then she'd get into one of her moods, and God help anyone who got in her way!

She could get real sharp . . . and not only with the patients. With everyone. Sonya Washington took shit from nobody, but she stayed easy with Crystal. She thought she knew what was

wrong with Crystal. Not that she'd tell . . . not unless something real bad happened. But like she told Marty when she first got here, she'd had plenty experience with junkies.

"Breathe in deep, let it out slow . . . breathe in deep, let it out slow . . . *slow*, girl," Crystal coached. "No, not like that. Marie, look at me. Tuck your chin down and hold your breath. No, goddammit . . ." There was that edge to her voice because Marie wasn't able to follow her instructions. Well, there was the language problem, and besides that, Marie was scared to death. Scared and all alone, poor little thing. Sonya took her hand and gave her an encouraging smile.

"She's too scared to understand you," Sonya said. "I don't think she gets three words in ten."

That did it. Crystal looked at Sonya like she'd just said the worst thing in the world. "You're so smart," she snapped, getting up from the stool, "*you* do it." And she started to walk out.

"Crys, you can't just leave like that!"

"Watch me!"

"But Crystal, she's only in her seventh month! And I have other—"

"It's gonna be an easy one." She paused only long enough to give a nasty little laugh. "And you'll have Norma to help!"

Sonya didn't waste any time running after her. She had a baby here, getting ready to be born. She got on the house phone and told Ob/Gyn to send one of their night nurses to fill in with the other patients. They already had Norma McClure coming at eleven. Norma was a bit of a weirdo, but she was fine for night shift, in Sonya's opinion.

And then, of course, everything came to a halt. Labor just stopped. When she listened for the baby's heartbeat, she couldn't get it for a bad few minutes. It was faint, but regular.

Marie dozed on and off but she was restless. Any time now, Sonya told herself. She got up a couple of times, went to check on the other patients, got a terrible cup of coffee from the machine and made herself stay awake and alert.

She thought about Crystal, just walking away from a birth like that. She had to know she could be reported for that. But Crystal had become pretty reckless lately, charging forward with whatever came into her head. Like a bulldozer, sometimes.

Last Friday, for instance, when the Gomez twins were born, Crystal had insisted that Gloria Gomez was torn. She wasn't torn; a beginner could have told you that. But no, Dr. Dinowitz had to look at it, and nothing would do but he had to come running and check it out. He was seeing patients in the OB clinic, which was overcrowded as usual, but that didn't matter to Crystal Cole.

Come to think of it, she was always getting him in to check on her patients lately. Well, maybe that was a *good* sign. Maybe she was beginning to realize that her little problem was getting bigger and bigger. She could lose her license, just like that; so why not cover her ass? Yeah, that was probably it.

Around midnight Sonya was jolted awake by a sudden cry from Marie. Damn, she'd dozed off, sitting in the chair. But she was wide-awake immediately. Marie was holding onto her belly. Sonya slid her down, positioning her legs, and took a peek. Nope, not crowning yet. But you could see the contractions, they were real strong now, and only five seconds apart. And she was eighty percent effaced. It wouldn't be long now.

She put her hand on Marie's shoulder and said, slowly and clearly, "Soon. Very soon. Your baby." Did Marie understand? She gave a little smile, so yeah, maybe.

"Mademoiselle Cole . . ." Marie said, in a weak voice.

"She'll be back," Sonya said, but she didn't believe it. She figured Crystal was either outta here, singing and dancing, or she'd flopped somewhere in the hospital. Crystal was popping pills; Sonya Washington would take bets on it. She'd probably started using them when things got rough, when she did double shifts and had to stay awake and alert. And then it began to feel real good, so she'd take a couple just for nothing, just to stay serene. It happened to a lot of doctors and nurses. The stuff was too available. Used to be mostly doctors because only doctors had access. But now, with nurses becoming more professional, hey, what do you know, more drug addiction! It was a damn shame, especially with a smart woman like Crystal.

How many times lately did Crystal excuse herself, saying she had to pee? Yeah, sure, Sonya always thought, and blow your nose, too, right? You think nobody notices those little sniffles you get every once in a while, when you're starting to

crash? You think nobody notices how one minute you're horrible and you go off to pee-pee and when you come back, you're sweet as pie? But she sometimes thought that Crystal hardly noticed what other people felt or thought. Funny, that she'd chosen nursing as a profession. But, hey, she was good at catching babies.

Marie squirmed on the bed, trying to double up, her face all twisted with pain. Sonya checked between the legs. Now it had started. Marie was well-dilated, nearly eight centimeters, she would bet. Little sounds escaped the girl. Sonya said, "You hurting, Marie? In pain? *Ow, ow?*"

"*Oui.* Yes. Oh . . . oh oh . . ." She grabbed at her abdomen.

Sonya mopped Marie's face, taking her pulse, one hand on the abdomen. You could see how quick the contractions were coming, and the poor kid didn't know how to handle them. Even the best-trained Lamaze patient could have trouble with transition, one contraction after the other. Marie was clutching at Sonya's arm, grabbing so hard there was no blood around her knuckles. I'm going to have some bruises tonight, Sonya thought.

"I'm going to give you a shot . . . a . . . oh hell!" The poor kid didn't understand a lot of English at the best of times. Sonya mimed a needle going into her own arm, then gave up and went for a syringe. She'd seen a premixed dose of Demerol on the table, just before, but now she couldn't find it. And then she realized. Oh. Sure. And went to get another one.

Sonya slid the needle smoothly into a muscle, where it would take hold faster. In less than a minute the girl's grip began to loosen and she managed a tiny smile, licking her lips.

"You want ice?"

"*J'ai soif, oui. Merci.*" Sonya held the ice cube to the girl's lips and she sucked thirstily.

Then the baby's head crowned and Marie began to really yell in French, which Sonya didn't understand one syllable of. The child's pretty face was all screwed up with pain and concentration and she grunted loudly as her muscles squeezed and tightened, trying to push the baby out.

From then on it all went very very fast. Once the head had

crowned, that baby didn't waste a minute. Hold out your hands, Sonya told herself, and catch that baby.

She had just grabbed him when Crystal came back in, real mellow. "Oh wow!" Crystal said, grinning. "Good catch. Sorry I missed it, Sonya, but I thought for sure we'd be here another— What's wrong?"

Sonya couldn't answer her. She was breathing into the baby's tiny mouth, praying for him to pull in a breath and start crying. Crystal just stood there, as if she didn't know what to do.

At last! The scrawny little chest shuddered and, with a high-pitched squawk, the baby began to cry. But he was awfully blue . . . little boy blue. Sonya took the tiny little thing and wiped him down, weighed him, wrapped him tightly.

"For God's sake, Crystal, call the Neonatal ICU. This little guy's not even two pounds and he keeps forgetting to breathe! And look how blue he is. He needs oxygen; we'd better get him up there real fast!"

"I've got to call Marty."

"Marty!" Sonya was still holding Marie's baby boy in her arms, aware that she'd better give him to his mother real soon or Marie was going to go hysterical on them. Marie was calling to her in French; Sonya didn't really understand, but she knew what Marie was saying. Is there something wrong with my baby? What's wrong with my baby?

"Marty?" she repeated. "What for? It's two o'clock in the morning! You're not going to wake Marty up at this hour! He's premature and blue but he's alive. We've got it under control."

"I want her here; she's the director; and she's the Crisis Intervention Officer and . . ." With that, Crystal was out the door at a run.

And you need to cover your ass, Sonya thought. Well, this time it won't do you any good, girlfriend, no good at all. She lifted the house phone and gave a series of orders. "And hurry!" she ended. Taking a deep breath, she turned and forced a smile. "Marie," she said, "listen, let me try to explain to you what's happening here. . . ."

23

Marty stood, frozen, staring at the intercom as if she could wish it away. Damn! Damn! *Damn!* "Owen," she finally said, her voice scratchy, "it's very late."

"I'm home, Marty. I missed my train." She closed her eyes briefly. It sounded so familiar, the robotic repetition of whatever thought he had been able to piece together out of the chaos of voices in his head. What in hell was she going to do? He *couldn't* come up. Her heart was beating so hard, it hurt her chest.

"You can't come up, Owen. It's too late. Call me tomorrow and we'll talk." As she turned to walk away, the insistent buzzing began. He wasn't going to take no for an answer. He would stand there and ring her bell forever, if need be. If he got frustrated enough, he might start ringing all the neighbors. Shit.

"Okay, Owen, okay. Stop that, please." She buzzed the door open, regretting it the moment she did it. What was she going to *do* with him? How was she going to convince him to leave? Why *me*? she thought, and she had to laugh. Why her? Because she'd married him, that's why.

She had the door open before he could make any noise, and she pulled him in. He was carrying a small suitcase. He hardly said hello to her, just brushed past her, saying, "Where's the bedroom? And I need to pee."

"The bathroom's right down the hall," she said tightly. "And just leave your bag here, Owen. Somebody is sleeping in the bedroom."

But somebody was *not* sleeping in the bedroom. Somebody was awake and coming out of the room saying, "What the hell's going on, Marty?"

"Shhh. Owen was released from the hospital and decided to come here."

"Well, undecide him. He has no business here."

Just then, Owen came out of the bathroom. "Excuse me, sir, I don't know what you're doing here, but I think you should know that this woman is my wife."

"What I'm doing here is—"

Marty shook her head fiercely. Surely Paul knew better than to try to argue with a mentally ill person.

"Dammit, Marty, I'm not going to shut up. This man has no business here."

"Excuse me, sir, but this is my home."

"Excuse me, Mr. Lamb, but this is *not* your home. This is Marty's home and I—"

"I know all about *you*. I know what you're after. And let me tell you something, you won't get away with it."

"What are you talking about? You don't know me at all. You've never seen me before."

"I don't have to *see* you to know what I know." Owen nodded his head like a wise old mandarin. "I have my sources," he said, pursing his lips.

"Enough!" Marty said. Soon, Owen would get belligerent. "Owen, go sit down on the couch, please. I'll talk to you in a minute."

He did as he was told. She watched him, torn between compassion and angry tears. That damned doctor! Chen, it had to be Dr. Chen. Damn him, he must have encouraged this "return home." Let's get the patients out of the hospital and back into the world and to hell with whatever havoc it might cause in someone's life! Even in an expensive private institution like the Mansion they didn't give a flying fuck!

She gestured with her eyes to the bedroom and, without a word, she and Paul both headed back, closing the door firmly. They both began speaking in tense whispers.

"Why can't you just tell him he's not welcome, Marty?"

"I already tried that. He's incapable of hearing anything he doesn't want to hear."

"Tell him again. Tell him you're getting a divorce. Tell him you don't want him here."

"I can't just kick him out into the street."

"Why the hell not?"

"Because he's a sick man, that's why not."

"Marty, I'm a doctor. I know he's a sick man, I feel for him. But that doesn't give him the right to interfere in your life."

"The fact that we're still married gives him the right."

"You're kidding. No. You're upset. Why don't you let me take care of it?"

"No, Paul. You'll just send him out into the street."

"Marty, for the love of God, make sense! Okay, okay. I won't send him out into the street. I'll send him to a nice hotel."

"All right. No, wait! Think of him, all alone in a strange place, in the middle of the night. It's inhumane."

"You're crazy, you know that? You've just completely lost your fucking mind!"

"No I haven't. Paul, for Christ's sake, I've had experience with him. He . . . he's capable of violence."

Paul grabbed for his clothes, throwing them on. "All the more reason to get rid of him. I'll call the cops."

"No! Paul, please, not the police. There's no reason to call the police. What in hell would we tell them? He hasn't done anything."

"He forced his way up here, Marty. That's something."

She knew he was right, in a way. But in a way, he was wrong, too. "Look, Paul." She took in a deep breath. "When Owen first broke down, I . . . I got rid of him. I got him out of the apartment as fast as I could. And then I called his mother and informed her that he was *her* problem."

"And now you feel guilty."

"And now I feel guilty. No. Not guilty. Responsible. No, not that, either. I feel . . ." She stopped, searching in her head for something that would allow Paul to understand. "I feel I owe him kindness, at least. You can see that, can't you?"

"I see that you're torn." He walked to her and put his arms around her. "This is very difficult for you. So . . . let *me* handle it, okay? You stay here. I'll go get rid of him."

"Oh, Christ, Paul, it doesn't matter *what* you do, it won't make any difference to Owen. He doesn't listen. Maybe he *can't* listen. He'll just come back and start this all over again.

I've had a lot of experience with mental patients. And . . . well . . . he thinks he loves me. So leave it to me, okay?"

Paul regarded her. "If you really feel . . ." He started to peel his clothes off. "I'll get back into bed. Don't be long, okay? And holler if you need me."

"Paul . . . ?"

"What now?"

"Paul, don't get mad. But maybe . . . well, maybe you shouldn't be here. . . ." The woebegone look on his face made her heart hurt. "Paul!" She stood very close to him, her hands on his shoulders, her eyes fixed on his. "You have to hear me. You . . . this thing of ours . . . it's so important to me. I want it to be right with us, do you hear me? I really want it to work out this time."

He pulled her in to him, holding her close. It felt so good. But she couldn't relax and let herself sink into his solidity, his strength. Not with Owen here. "Let me help with this. Let me be part of your life."

"You *are* part of my life." Gently, she disengaged. "That's why you have to understand that I've got to manage Owen myself. If you're here, he'll probably stay agitated. And believe me, if he gets agitated, he'll *never* leave. I know what . . . I'll call you just as soon as I've gotten rid of him, okay?"

He didn't like it, but finally he gave her a grudging "Okay, but—" And she had to promise she'd call him if anything, anything at all, went wrong. A moment later, from the other room, she heard Owen calling out good-bye to Paul, very much the pleasant host, and she started to cry. Dammit, why couldn't Owen have stayed out of her life? Of course, she turned off the tears immediately; there was no time for self-pity. She had to get Owen out of the apartment before he settled in and became stubborn.

She checked her face in the mirror, making sure it showed absolutely nothing. Then she went back into the living room. He had taken a seat in her favorite chair. She sat in the far corner of the couch. "Owen, I wasn't expecting you. Do you know that?"

He grinned. "It was a surprise."

"Yes, but—Owen, you can't stay here. We don't live together anymore."

"We're married, Marty. I know we're married. I remember that."

"Yes, but—" Her head hurt. Her stomach hurt. She could hardly stand to look at him. He was so thin, so frail, so . . . blank, behind the pale eyes. It was like talking to a paper doll; there was no third dimension. She felt for him; nonetheless, she was repulsed. "Owen, you always go home to your parents. I think you should go to them this time, too."

"I don't know where they are."

"They're in Boulder. You remember the ranch in Boulder, don't you?"

"The moose head on the wall," he said triumphantly.

"That's right. The house with the moose head."

"It was over the fireplace. You know, when I was little, it used to scare me. I was so sure it was always looking at me . . . no matter where I went in the room, its eyes followed me." He paused, and added: "And that was even before. Before I . . . before I got sick and scared of everything."

She studied him. It was so strange, how sometimes he could almost pass for normal. "Does the new medication help you, Owen?"

"Help me what?"

"Help you to not be fearful."

He thought about that for a moment. "I understand now that I'm sick. I have a disease. Like the measles, only *not* the measles. I understand all that. I must take my medication because I have a disease." He was talking very fast. He looked a bit agitated, but he really did seem to have had a breakthrough. "And they told me my voices are in my own head, yes, in my own head." He shook his head. "Well, that's bullshit. I guess I know where my voices come from, and they don't come from my head or anywhere near me. They come from . . ." He looked upward. "You know where they come from."

Marty's heart had already sunk back down to where it had been ever since she heard his voice over the intercom: somewhere in the pit of her stomach.

"Owen, I'm going to call your mother now."

"Oh, it's too late. She'll be asleep, and she gets so mad if you wake her up."

"They're three hours earlier than we are. It will be fine. I'm sure she'll be delighted to hear from you." *I hope. Or even if she's not, tough.*

By a miracle, Beatrice was home. "Beatrice, Owen has arrived on my doorstep tonight," she said tightly. "He's been released from the Mansion, and as we are all aware, he doesn't really belong here."

"Marta dear, Owen is an adult. He can go where he pleases."

"Well, he can't come *here*."

"Now, now, no need for histrionics. I'm sure the poor boy only wants the very best for you. He still loves you, you know."

"Beatrice, he's not capable of that."

"At any rate, he believes he loves you." A light, silvery laugh. "And isn't that the way with all of us?"

Without bothering to answer, Marty thrust the receiver at Owen. He took it and said, "Hi, Mommy!" in a bright childish voice, and then lapsed into silence, frowning. Marty could hear the thin squawk of Beatrice's piercing, rather high-pitched voice, but couldn't make out the words. Owen said no several times, that was all.

Suddenly, he held the phone receiver out to her. She took it. "Yes?"

"It seems Owen doesn't want to come home to his mother and father, Marta. What can we do? We can't force him. And I'm sure that if Dr. Chen released him, he'll be just fine." And she hung up.

Marty stayed by the phone, her back to Owen, who was beginning to pace around the living room, restless. That was *not* a good sign. She longed to call Dr. Zee, who always seemed to be awake and alert and ready to help with whatever. But Dr. Zee had looked wiped these past couple of days. She had developed laryngitis from her rotten summer cold and was talking in a hoarse whisper. What if she were finally getting some badly needed sleep? So . . . Joel was elected. He'd know how to convince Owen to leave.

Alice answered, sleepily. Apparently, she looked at her

clock, because when Marty asked for Joel, she said. "Good God, is it that late? Sorry, Marty, but no, he's not back yet."

"Where is he? Maybe I can get ahold of him."

"Gee, I'm not sure, actually. Some meeting or another, but over dinner, so that means endless brandies and war stories, I suppose."

"Do you know who this meeting is with?"

A giant yawn. "Sorry. I'm clueless."

"And you're sleepy and I've awakened you and *I'm* sorry. Go back to sleep."

A meeting at this hour? Well, it was possible, anything was possible.

The phone rang. Aha. Joel had arrived home mere seconds after her call. "So where were you, at this hour?" she said, her voice teasing. "And kindly skip the 'meeting' bullshit."

"Excuse me?" the hoarse voice said, amused. "Just who were you expecting, at this hour?"

"Julia. I was just wishing for you. Are you a mind reader?"

"No, a nightwalker. Bumped into Paul Giordano on the street. I hear you have a problem. Do you want me to come over?"

"Oh my God, do I ever."

"Be right there."

When Marty hung up, she saw the fright in Owen's eyes. "A doctor is coming over," she said. "A friend of mine."

"A psychiatrist."

"No. A family practitioner."

"Oh that's good, Marty. That's very good. Because, you know . . ." He paused, and when he continued, his voice was tight and angry. ". . . you know, it was a psychiatrist who sent the voices."

"Now, Owen . . ."

"Oh yes. I know. I *know*. It was Joel Mannes. He sent them and he told everyone I'm crazy. But I'm not. I'm not crazy! I have a disease, but I'm not crazy, and if you try to tell me I am, you're my enemy!" He started for her with blood in his eye. Marty shrank back against the kitchen counter, thinking, What possessed me to let him up here? Just who do I think I'm

dealing with? And what's happened with this so-called miracle medication that doesn't seem to be working very well?

"Owen, you know perfectly well I'm not your enemy." She was surprised at how firm her voice sounded. "So just calm down please, and stop talking nonsense."

What do you know? It worked. He kind of blinked and turned around and resumed his pacing. She watched him. It was obvious even from the way he moved that there was something wrong with him. He was not ready to come back into the community and live a quote normal life. Even at his best, he could be set off by anything—a word, an *imagined* word. She looked at him, at the tall, delicately built man who was once considered so cute, the stooped shoulders, the silver threads among the gold. There were lines in his face, deep grooves by the sides of his mouth. Smoking did that, but it didn't matter what the reason was. He looked old and fragile and not of this world.

There was no question about it. She couldn't have him here, not even for another hour. She absolutely couldn't be married to him. Why had she kept on putting it off, telling herself she'd get divorced as soon as she was serious about another man! That was bullshit. So why? But she knew. She'd been afraid to tell Owen anything he didn't want to hear, afraid that he'd get angry in that abrupt fierce way he had, and then throttle her. Well, she was just going to have to get over it. And if he refused to sign the papers, she'd just go somewhere and get a divorce without him. It couldn't be that difficult. Movie stars did it all the time, didn't they?

The buzzer startled her. Dr. Zee must have called from a street phone—which was a minor miracle in itself; most street phones around the neighborhood had been thoroughly vandalized. She buzzed her visitor in.

"You look *terrible!*" It just burst out of her.

"Well, thanks," Dr. Zee said dryly, with a half smile.

"I'm sorry, Julia, but you're actually *haggard.*"

"I know. It's this damn cold. It's really worn me down." Her voice was not as hoarse as it had been. "But it'll go away. Let's have a look at your visitor."

Owen had stopped his nervous walking and was sitting at the table by the bay window, smoking.

"Owen, this is my friend, Julia Zachary-Felsen."

He didn't move, and she knew what that meant. He was deep in conversation with his voices. The voices were much much louder to him than anything in reality. You could scream "Fire!" and he probably wouldn't hear you. How could she just put him out into the world, heartlessly? How would he survive? He wasn't taking his meds, she'd take bets on it. He'd been here less than an hour and already she felt the weight of him like a great, heavy burden, pushing her down.

"*Owen.* We have company."

He turned but it was clear that his thoughts were far far away.

Dr. Zee moved briskly into the living room, her hand outstretched. "Mr. Lamb. I'm glad to meet you." She took his hand and shook it. "May I sit down? Thank you." Although, so far, he hadn't said a word. "Now then. I understand you've just come from a hospital. . . ."

"The Mansion," Owen said grandly. "A mental health facility."

"A mental health facility. Very good. You traveled all the way down here from . . . ?"

"From the Mansion. Connecticut."

"Have you forgotten to take your medication, Mr. Lamb?"

"I don't think that's any of your affair."

"I'm a doctor. It's my job to take care of people."

"Well, you're not *my* doctor and I don't have to do anything you say. I'm released."

"If you don't take your meds, Mr. Lamb, you might have to go back to the hospital."

Owen leaned forward, his face almost in the doctor's, his lips pulled back from his teeth, his eyes narrowed. His voice was a hiss. "That's how much *you* know. They put poison in my meds. They want to get rid of me."

"Who told you that?"

The angry face was gone, wiped away, replaced by that knowing look, that knowing smile. "I have my sources."

Marty couldn't stand it one minute more. "Dammit, Owen, forget your sources. You take the damn pill or you leave."

"You can't make me. And if you try . . ." He picked up a crystal vase she loved, brandishing it.

"Owen, put that down."

"Mr. Lamb. You can't behave this way. Marty, perhaps you should call his hospital. . . ."

"The Mansion. Yes, good idea." And as a matter of fact, she wouldn't mind waking Dr. Chen, not one bit. How could he release Owen in this condition?

"Wait. Wait. Don't call, Marty." Another huge mood shift. "I'll put it down. I'm putting it down. See? I'm putting it down."

"Owen," Marty said, feeling desperate. "Owen, can't you see you're not ready to leave the Mansion yet? You're getting angry and you won't take your meds. You must take your meds, Dr. Chen must have told you *that*."

"They put poison in them."

Oh shit. Well, if you can't fight them, she thought, join them. "Not in all of them, Owen. Six pills are marked—they're the ones with the poison. The rest are fine."

He bought it. He dug into his jacket pocket and came out with a vial. Marty spread all the pills out onto the table and she and Dr. Zee went through the charade of spotting the marked ones, taking them away and putting the rest back. Except for one. That one, Dr. Zee offered to Owen. "This one is good. Take it. You're feeling upset, I can tell. This will make you feel better."

He took the pill, put it on his tongue, then reached up and took it away. Oh Christ, Marty thought, here we go again.

"I need a drink. I can't take pills without water."

"I'll get you a glass of water." She ran to the kitchen and poured him a glass from the bottle in the refrigerator.

When she handed it to him, he smiled at her and said, "I need ice."

"Owen, if you don't stop— Never mind." She went back, put in two cubes, brought it back to him.

At last, he swallowed the pill. As soon as he did, Marty sat in one of the chairs, near him.

"Owen, you really have to leave. You can't stay here."

"Dr. Chen said—"

Briskly, Dr. Zee said, "I'm the doctor here, Mr. Lamb. You will have to go to a hotel."

He folded his arms across his chest, smiling that smug little smile. "And what if I refuse? You can't force a man from his domicile."

"This is not your domicile. It's Marty's."

"My name is on the lease, too."

"No, Owen, it's not." Christ, he couldn't even keep it in his head that the last time they lived together was in Middletown, Connecticut, ages ago.

"Well, what am I supposed to do?"

"I know a small hotel not too far from here," Dr. Zee said. "I'll take you there. I'll make sure you have a place to stay."

"Marty. I'm back. I'm home. You *have* to live with me. You're my wife."

"No, Owen. I told you. You have to leave."

He sat back, folding his arms firmly across his chest, his head thrown back, smirking at the two of them. He knew there was no way they could make him move. Marty looked at him, hating him. He was dangerous and untrustworthy, and she was so tired.

Her beeper began its insistent call. Alarmed and grateful, all at the same time, she leaped up and grabbed it. It was the Birthing Center's number, she saw. Uh-oh. Quickly she jabbed out the phone number. The phone on the other end was picked up quickly and she recognized Crystal's voice.

"Crys! What's going on?"

"Marie's baby decided to get born. A boy, two pounds three, weak pulse, apnea, blue . . ."

"Yes, and . . . ?" Why the hell was Crystal calling about a preemie? They saw dozens of preemies every week. She knew what to do. "You've sent the baby to the Neonatal ICU."

"I—no. I don't know! I—"

"You . . . don't . . . know?" Oh Christ, she was going to have to get over there, and fast. It sounded like Crystal was really flipping out. "Well, hang on, Crys, I'm on my way." She hung up and went for her bag.

And found herself face-to-face with Owen. For a moment,

there, she had almost forgotten about him. What was she going to do? She stared at him and he stared back in that blind way.

"Something's happening at the Birthing Center," she said to Dr. Zee. "I have to get over there."

"Do you need me?"

Marty eyed her friend, taking in the tired eyes, the dark circles. "No, I can handle it."

"And what about . . . ?" She made a small gesture toward Owen, who had already lost interest and had his back turned to them.

"He'll just have to stay the night. I can't deal with him right now, and God knows when I'll get back. Owen can sleep on the couch tonight," she said, more loudly, "and in the morning, he'll leave for that nice hotel. Won't you, Owen?"

No response. To hell with it. "Come on, Julia, he'll be okay." She hoped she was right. "Thanks for coming over. You'd better get some sleep, if you're going to get rid of that cold."

At the door Dr. Zee said in a low voice, "Are you sure, Marty?"

"There's a lock on the bedroom door. I won't be ravaged." She laughed bitterly.

"But . . . are you sure you'll be okay with him? We can always call the cops."

"How can I do that to him? It's not his fault he's sick. I've certainly dealt with worse, at the clinics. No. I won't call the police. I owe him that much. It'll be fine. Let's go."

But a backward glance showed Owen gesticulating at an unseen person. Realizing that his voices were telling him terrible things, she knew she had plenty to worry about.

24

The next morning, in her office, Marty listened impatiently to the messages on her machine. There were two from a popular radio talk show and two from Hamilton Pierce, wanting "a more personal look at the victim of the abortion shooting, from someone who really knew her. And maybe," he ended, "some anti-abortion folks will see that you're a good-looking woman, a health professional, and not a hired killer who hates babies." It was tempting, but not compelling. As much as she'd love to speak her piece, she knew that, for news people, the story was the thing. Pierce could slant her comments any way he wanted—and would. Besides, she had a feeling Dr. Messinger wouldn't want anyone but Clive Moses saying anything to the media.

Ah, Joel at last. "Got your message. I'm ready to take off the horn-rims and nerdy tie and reveal myself as . . . *Supershrink*. Pick me up after work, say six, and I'll buy you a drink and listen to your troubles. Can anyone top that offer? I don't think so."

She smiled. Joel always made her laugh, but this morning, after four hours of trying to sleep on the cot Julia kept in her office for emergencies, laughter was out of the question. She was stiff from not turning over and fuzzy-minded from the lack of rest. She slurped at the very hot, very strong, very black coffee in her mug, hoping the caffeine content would jolt her brain to life.

She had such a bad headache. Well, why not? She swallowed an extra-strength something from a box she kept in a desk drawer and put in a call to Joel's machine. "Hi, Joel, it's me and we have to talk about . . ." She paused. She couldn't

say anything definite, in case someone else was in the room when Joel played it back. "We have to talk about Owen. He appeared on my doorstep last night and he doesn't want to leave. I need your psychiatric input, please."

Her office door banged open and Paul came in. He did not look happy.

"I thought you were going to call me as soon as you got rid of him."

Oh Christ. She'd forgotten. "I was. But I didn't."

"He's still there? In your apartment? How the hell could you let a thing like that happen? Have you taken leave of all your senses? I mean, it's okay for you to have feelings for the man. He's sick and you did marry him. But Jesus, Marty! And not even a call to let me know? What the hell—"

He stopped talking because she had got up, walked around her desk, and was kissing him.

"Shut up. Please," she said, when she let him go. "I apologize profusely. My beeper went off, there was . . . an emergency here, a preemie. I grabbed twenty winks on Dr. Zee's emergency bed. Now I know why she calls it that. Sleep on it and you're an emergency case. I'm sorry I didn't call you, but it was much too late."

"Never too late," Paul growled, but he was no longer really mad. "I mean, there you were, with your ex, no not ex, with your *husband*, a mental case capable of violence, and—not a word. But you're okay, so okay. I guess."

She was tempted to tell him what happened when she got here. It would be such a relief to share some of these problems, at least talk them out. Which got priority, the lover or the colleague? She knew the answer. As long as she was in charge here, the people under her had to come first. So she couldn't talk about it.

When she'd let herself in last night, using her key on the front entrance to the clinics, she could hear Marie Racine sobbing and crying out in French. Her voice was clogged with anxiety and tears. And then Crystal sang out, "Is that you, Marty?" She sounded strangely blithe, as if she were drunk. She wasn't drunk, but she sure was floating, a great big silly smile on her face. What in hell was she on? It wasn't a Valium

now and then. Marty guessed Percodan, which usually produced this kind of goofy euphoria.

"Crys, why aren't you attending to your patient?"

"My patient? Oh you mean Marie? She won't stop. She thinks her baby is dead because he isn't here. I tried to tell her but she won't listen."

"We're going to go in there and calm her down. And then, Crystal, you and I—"

Crystal giggled. "We're going to have one of your little chats, aren't we?" Marty wanted to smack her.

Marty sat on the side of Marie's bed and touched the girl's arm. As soon as Marie focused on her, she flung herself into Marty's arms, weeping wildly, and Marty found herself rocking Marie like a small child, patting her back and saying, "Shhhh now, it'll be fine now," all those meaningless phrases that somehow comforted.

At last the sobbing died into hiccups and Marie was able to hear *"Pas mort"* after twenty or thirty repetitions. *Not dead.* When Marty and Crystal left her bedside, her poor swollen eyes were closed. Maybe she'd be able to sleep. They gave her a shot. Crys wanted to give her a sleeping pill, too, but Marty shook her head. "Not unless she needs it. She should be able to sleep on her own now."

She took Crystal into her office, looked straight into the dazed eyes and said, "Crystal, I'm going to be forced to report you to the Nursing Board."

"What for?"

"You've got to be kidding. You're as high as a kite, Crys, you're flying."

"I only took a little mood elevator."

"The hell you did. I'm sorry I don't have a video camera, but Sonya's a witness. That will be enough. You left your patient, you got yourself high, and you didn't even bother to hide it. That's *more* than enough."

Crystal's voice was still chirpy as she said, "Well, Marty, you do that and I'll ruin your good buddy Mannes."

Marty kept her voice even. "I don't know what you have in mind; but you hurt Joel and I promise you, you will lose your

job, you will lose your license, and I might even do some damage on you for good measure."

Crystal began to laugh. "What happened to your sense of humor, Marty? That was a joke. Just a joke!" She kept on laughing, unable to stop.

"Go home, Crystal. Sleep it off. I can't discuss anything with you until you're straight."

"Right on, sister," More laughter. "When I'm straight!" And she had gone dancing out.

Until she knew all the facts, Marty felt she couldn't confide in Paul about this mess. Anyway, it had nothing to do with him and it might get out. That wouldn't be right. So she gave him a light kiss and said, "Let's hold off this discussion until we're alone."

The eruption of shouting startled both of them. It was one of the nearby clinics, probably Birth Defects. Fights often flared up in that waiting room. "Sorry. Gotta go."

As she ran out, Paul called after her, "I'll pick you up and we can get some dinner and then go home."

She started to say "Great!" and then she remembered. She stopped mid-stride and turned. This was not going to look good. "I'm sorry, Paul, I'll have to call you later. Joel's coming home with me to deal with my little problem. Joel was the doctor who first had Owen admitted to the hospital. You understand."

"Yeah. Sure," he said. The last glimpse she had of him, he was looking rather sad and forlorn. But she just didn't have time to worry about it.

The din coming out of the waiting room of the Birth Defects clinic was unbelievable . . . well, not really. It had been noisier; but not lately. So she screeched to a halt and made a sharp left. It was pandemonium times two. Two chairs had been tipped over, most of the children present were crying, and a circle of strident noncombatants, three deep, surrounded a group consisting of Elaine Berryman—an obese woman of questionable intelligence who kept producing children with problems—and four nurses, including Emilio and Kenny.

Elaine was mad as hell and, as was her habit when annoyed,

she was bellowing at the top of her voice. The nurses were all trying to calm her down but she wasn't having any.

For some reason, Elaine had taken a liking to Marty, so when Marty marched over, pushing through the thicket of onlookers, calling her name, Elaine paused to look at her.

"One minute, Elaine! What's the problem?"

"Get these motherfuckers offa me! Sorry, Miss Lamb, but I been waiting fucking long enough!"

"Now, Elaine, tell me. You've waited a long time to see the doctor?"

"Fuckin' A! Longer than anybody."

"Bullshit," yelled one of the other mothers. "I been here longer than you. You just never learned how to tell time, Elaine, that's your problem."

There was a great deal of laughter over that. Elaine's face began to turn red, so Marty spoke quickly. "Of course Elaine can tell time. She's just in a hurry, right, Elaine?"

"Fuckin' A."

"Who are you bringing today?"

"Melrose." Melrose, named after the television program Elaine loved, was just past two. He had been born with Down's syndrome and was quite retarded. He also had the heart condition that often went hand in hand with Down's, so he was a sedentary little boy, very small for his age, and with a bluish tinge to his pale skin. He had never, to anyone's knowledge, uttered a single word.

"Where are the other kids, Elaine?"

"Uh . . ." The huge woman twisted her head around, her mouth hanging open. Marty knew she would probably forget what she was looking for, halfway around the room. "Dunno . . . around . . ."

"Kenny, you want to hunt them up? They can't have gone far. Try the candy machines." Elaine's kids often wandered away from her, and they usually knew to station themselves near food. They had learned that sooner or later somebody would take pity upon them and feed them. Everyone felt that the children should be taken away from Elaine, everyone including her Welfare social worker. But so far, in spite of everything, nothing really bad had happened to any of the children.

Marty held onto Elaine's hand, thinking fast. The woman's patience had given out; if they didn't want more trouble, Melrose had better be seen right away. But if Elaine was hustled into the doctor ahead of others, there'd be another kind of riot.

Suddenly, like the answer to a prayer, Dr. Zee appeared. She was looking quite a bit better, too. Her cheeks were pink, sort of. When she saw Marty, Dr. Zee stopped and asked a question with her eyes. *Did he leave?* Marty shook her head and gestured for the doctor to come over.

"Okay, Elaine," Marty said, "Let's see if we can get Melrose checked over by Dr. Zee. Melrose loves Dr. Zee, don't you, Melrose?" Marty bent to pick up the child, who smelled even worse than his mother. Oh dear. Well, Dr. Zee had handled worse, she was sure.

"Dr. Zee, could you quickly check over Melrose," she asked politely, meanwhile sending eye messages of desperation. "Elaine's been waiting and waiting and she's about run out of patience."

"Fuckin' A," agreed Elaine.

"I'll see him right now." Dr. Zee held out her arms for the little boy, wrinkling her nose as she took him. "Woo! Melrose needs to be changed, Elaine. Did you bring a fresh diaper?"

"Uh-oh," Elaine said.

"Well, never mind, we'll have a box of Pampers somewhere. Come on."

"Wait a second," Marty said. "How are you feeling? You look better today."

"I got some sleep last night, after all."

"Your color's good."

Dr. Zee gave her a crooked smile. "Is it? I stopped looking in the mirror a few years ago. Well, come along, Elaine, we'll sneak you in ahead of everyone else."

"Fuckin' A," Elaine said, mightily pleased at this special treatment. Dr. Zee grinned and gave Marty a little wink; and that made Marty realize how long it had been since she'd seen her friend a hundred percent, or anywhere close to it.

Marty headed for Crystal's office. The door was open and there was Crys, crisp and beautiful in a chintz jumpsuit, sitting at her desk, bent over some paperwork. Marty dreaded their

first few words. What did you say to a woman who had walked out on her job, who had threatened to blackmail a respected doctor, who was either sick or on drugs, or both? But she didn't have to say anything. Crys sensed her presence and looked up. She smiled. "Good morning . . . or is it a bad one? They said you slept here last night on Dr. Zee's emergency bed." She rolled her eyes and laughed.

Marty's mouth hung open, but she could find nothing to say. Was it possible that Crystal had no memory of last night? A knock on the door frame was followed by Sonya, talking very fast. "Crys, it's Protozone. Contractions every three minutes. She's knitting; she figures she'll finish the sweater in time for the baby to be born." She laughed. "I love it when they've had so many babies they can tell *you* what to do!" Sonya left, but not before she shot Marty a questioning look. *No, I haven't,* Marty answered her silently, *but I will.*

"Well, Loretta Protozone better not try that with *me*," Crystal said with a smile. "This kid's gotta be a boy or I don't know what will happen."

"I know what will happen," Marty said dryly. "Your reputation as a witch will go down the drain. Honestly, Crys! The needle and thread thing? With *Aldo*? You know he still believes in all that stuff."

Crystal looked a bit abashed, but she didn't sound it. "Hey, so do I," she said lightly, and then got up. "Excuse me, there's a baby waiting to be born."

"Before you go . . . how is Marie Racine?"

"Marie? Fine, fine. She finally fell asleep and she's still sleeping now."

Marty checked on that. It was true, the girl was so deeply asleep, she might have been drugged. Oh Christ, no. Crystal wasn't capable of— She stopped. She was no longer sure *what* Crystal was capable of. Joel. Miriam. Shayna. Crystal. Owen. Oh, damn! *Owen.* So many people she felt responsible for. This was not going to be her very best day, that was for sure.

When she got to Carmen's desk and saw the receptionist digging into a carton of Chinese takeout, she realized it was getting close to lunch. Lunch! What a concept! She marched over to the candy machine. Sixty-five cents bought her a

minuscule version of a candy bar she had loved as a child—and had bought, if memory served, in a much bigger size for a nickel.

"I'm on my way up to the Neonatal ICU," Marty said. "In case anyone wants me. I won't be long; I just want to see Marie's baby for myself and make sure everything's okay. Oh, and Carmen. Can you arrange for flowers or something to be delivered to Marie? I'll pay."

"Sure. Speaking of flowers, Marty. Before you go . . ." Carmen's vivid face had such a strange, stiff expression. "A . . . uh, gentleman was here, asking for you. I thought he was from the media . . . on account of the shooting, you know? But he wasn't." She looked embarrassed.

It had to be Owen. Marty's heartbeat accelerated. He was starting up again. "Who was he? When was he here?" She tried like hell to sound casual and calm.

"Around ten o'clock. While you were with Elaine. He had a bouquet of roses . . ." Carmen pronounced it *bo-kay*. ". . . which he would *not* leave with me, even though I told him I'd make sure it got to you."

"Well, thanks, Carmen." Thank God it wasn't anything worse.

"Marty . . . I don't want to be a snoop but . . ."

Shit. "Yes, Carmen, but . . ."

"He said he's your husband! But you're single, right?"

"Oh God, Carmen, I'll explain it all to you later, okay? If he comes back, tell him . . . No, never mind, don't tell him anything. I know he's a little strange, but . . . I'll explain later, I promise." She fled for the elevators.

At the Neonatal ICU she flashed her badge, got admitted, scrubbed and put on a gown—they came in pink and blue here, instead of the ubiquitous gray—and asked to see Baby Boy Racine. She checked the card at the bottom of his bassinet, recognizing all the tests they had scheduled. He was attached to a lot of tiny tubes and he was skinny with a blue tinge to his skin, but he still looked a whole lot better than the crack babies. He didn't quake and quiver, for one thing. While she was standing there, one of his alarms went off. He'd stopped breathing. She tapped the bottoms of his tiny feet and by the time the nurse got

there, which was almost instantly, he was breathing again, although laboriously.

"Thanks, Marty."

"How's he going to be?"

The nurse wrinkled her nose slightly. "Something's wrong with his heart. Dr. Fassbinder ordered an echocardiograph."

"Oh dear," Marty said.

"Don't worry, Marty, most of our babies go home and grow up and are just fine. And you know Dr. Fassbinder is a wonderful pediatric surgeon."

Yeah, maybe he was. But he was also terribly territorial about patients. He was capable of doing a whole number on Marie's baby, without ever informing the CCC director, or the head midwife, either. She left and went to Len Fassbinder's office. She'd get permission for Marie to be admitted to the nursery whenever she wanted. If Baby Boy Racine needed heart surgery, she wanted Marie to have plenty of time with him before he went to the O.R.

The doctor's secretary admitted grudgingly that the doctor was in, then got up and went into his inner sanctum, apparently to see if he would deign to speak with Marty. He would.

Marty took a deep breath, ordered herself not to be intimidated, and walked in. She shook her head when he offered her a seat. "I'll only be a minute, Doctor. It's about Baby Boy Racine. Preemie. Born early this morning. You ordered an echocardiogram?"

Fassbinder tried for a smile, almost making it, and said. "Racine, Racine . . . oh yes. Yes, I have reason to believe he is suffering from transposition of the greater blood vessels to the heart. I can't be sure until we have an echo, and I think we'll give him a cath. But I'm willing to take bets that I'm right. If I'm thinking of the right case."

She smiled tightly. "He's not a case, he's a baby. And his mother is a very sweet, very young woman, all alone in this country. I'd like her to have access to him."

He was already shaking his head. "Wish we could do that, Marty. If we could, we'd have *all* the parents in the nursery all the time. But this infant may have a serious problem, and we'll have to move very fast. . . ."

"Yes, I know. But she's so fearful and she hasn't really seen him. Her English is shaky so it's hard for her to understand what's—"

"I don't know why these people refuse to learn English! It *is* the language of this country they're all so eager to come to!"

"She's learning, she's trying." Why was she standing here in his office, having this stupid argument? "Okay then, Len, just for the first two days ... unlimited visitation. Her baby was taken up here immediately. I don't know if she even remembers seeing him. She was ... knocked out, and while she was asleep, he was spirited away. She's going to be so frightened. ..."

He reddened. "I assure you, the infant was not spirited away, as you so hysterically put it."

"Sorry. I meant only that she'll feel that way. When she wakes up and wants her baby, what are we supposed to tell her? That her baby may need heart surgery and she can't see him and hold him?"

"She'll be fine. I've been in this business for a good many years, and there's one thing I can tell you. All mothers want their babies to live. She may cry now, but when he's ready to go home, you'll see, she'll be on her knees thanking us."

"She really needs to see the baby, see what's happening."

He shrugged. "I'm sorry. I can't have the nursing staff disrupted because this woman doesn't understand English."

"You do realize, Dr. Fassbinder, the power of all of us, all of us *professionals*, all of us *experts*. ... We have the power to frighten people who are vulnerable and ignorant and perhaps panicked."

"I hope you're not suggesting that *I*—"

She gave him the same smile he'd given her a moment ago: brief and false. "I'm suggesting nothing." She waited a beat or two. "Let's be humane about this. I'm only asking for two days."

"That would not be in the best interest of the child." He paused and his lips curled in a very different kind of smile, more like a sneer. "But of course. You've never had a child, have you?"

For a moment she felt very cold, as if all the blood had left her body. The bastard. "No," she said, surprised to hear her

voice emerge sounding quite normal and pleasant, "No, I haven't. But then . . . you've never given birth, either. So we're even."

But she didn't feel even. She held her back very straight as she wheeled around and left his office, but she felt stupid and cornered. And mad as hell. She'd never had a child. He was right. But she had been pregnant.

She'd known right away, as soon as she began the vomiting—more like dry heaves—in the morning. Her jeans had already become uncomfortably snug around the middle. She just felt porky and bloated, though when she checked her image in the mirror in the bathroom, it was the same thin face, chalky from the throwing-up, freckles standing out like dots of rusty paint.

She knew what it was, even though she was scared to name it, even to herself. Panic filled her chest like a heavy gas, weighing her down. What was she going to do? *What was she going to do?* She couldn't tell anyone, not even Jerry. Especially not him. How did it happen? When they began to have sex, he had taken her to a doctor who practiced out of a farmhouse just outside Glastonbury, to get her fitted for a diaphragm. She was wearing a Woolworth's wedding ring. It was so embarrassing. The doctor was very old, and he talked too much and leaned his head too close, so you could smell the peppermint he kept sucking on and hear his false teeth clicking.

She thought she would die, putting her feet in the stirrups, opening her legs so he could put his hand up there and examine her. She held her breath the whole time. But she had to let it out because it wasn't just once. He had to keep getting out these little rubber rings, one after the other, first tiny, then bigger and bigger each time. He would put one in and take it out and mutter to himself and pick another one and then shove *that* in and then feel around. It was horrible. She was so aware of how sexual this all was. Even when he hurt her a little, she didn't dare make a noise or move. Oh God, what if he thought she was *enjoying* it?

Finally, everything finished, she dressed, and sitting behind his desk, he scribbled a prescription for her and said, "Well,

Mrs. King, you're a size seven, pretty big for a girl your age. . . ." Her blood froze; what was he saying about her? Was she large because she was doing it so much? She never met his eyes again, snatching the piece of paper from his fingers and fleeing.

It was horrible. In the car, she had cried and cried and she told Jerry, "I'm never going through anything like that again! It was humiliating!"

"Better humiliated than pregnant," he'd said, reaching over to take her hand. But she jerked it away from him.

"Never again!" she said.

But she was going to have to go through something horrible again because she was . . . come on, Marty, say it, *say it* . . . because she was pregnant. Oh Christ, she was sixteen and a half and she was *pregnant*! Another girl in her class had got pregnant and of course had to leave school. The girl kind of slunk around town for a few weeks while all her so-called friends avoided her. Then she left on a "trip" to "visit relatives," and everybody knew what *that* meant.

The day Marty finally got up the nerve to tell Jerry, she was already two months gone and she was really beginning to get heavy around the waist. He'd driven them out to the big old Presbyterian cemetery out on Route 154, one of his favorite spots because nobody ever came there— "The last person to be buried here was back in the twenties," he'd told her—and they could do it nearly naked because no one was going to come along. So he was whistling all the way, holding her hand, pushing his finger back and forth, imitating what he was going to do in a little while, with Big John. That's what he called his thing, Big John. "You like Big John?" he'd say, every single time he took it out. "Show Big John how much you like him."

He was in a good mood because they were finally going to do it. They hadn't been able to get together for three whole days, and he liked doing it regularly. So he was feeling great because soon he'd have her where she belonged and Big John would be where *he* belonged . . . and he put her hand onto his belly so she could feel how big and stiff it was.

All the time, Marty sat in a sweat of panic, pretending to

listen to him, pretending to smile, pretending, pretending. And the minute he turned off the motor, she blurted it out.

"Are you lying to me?" he demanded, turning to her with an angry face.

She was startled by the question. "Of course I'm not lying."

"Because if you're fibbing, if you're hoping we'll get married and you'll play a little trick on me, I'll throttle you, so help me God, you won't see the sun rise on another day."

"Jerry!" She'd never seen his face look so ugly-angry, never heard his voice so hard. "Prof!"

"Don't 'Prof' *me*, Marty Dauber. Do you realize what you're saying?"

"Yes I realize." Now she was beginning to get mad. "What's with *you*? I'm pregnant, and yes, I'm sure, and I'd say about two months," she said, anticipating his next questions. "And yes, I always use the diaphragm, sometimes I only take it out to wash it and then I put it right back in. In case."

He stared out of the windshield and pounded his fists on the steering wheel, cursing. Finally, he stopped. He sat with his eyes closed and pulled in a lot of very deep breaths. His lips moved silently. The memory was imprinted on her brain, of his profile and, beyond him, a wavery reflection in the car window of her looking at him, and beyond that, the sun beginning to set behind the old lopsided gravestones.

Suddenly, he turned to her, his eyes avid. With one hand he pulled her closer, with the other he unzipped her jeans and the old familiar heat climbed in her. She pushed down her jeans and he pushed down her panties and they weren't even below her knees when he was on top of her, shoving himself into her. She heard her panties ripping as he pulled up her legs. He was frantic, breathing like a steam engine, grunting, gripping her so hard he left the imprints of his fingers on her thighs and rear end. He came in a rush, and then pulled away from her, wiping himself off with a handkerchief. He hadn't even kissed her.

"Okay, little Marty, not to worry. You know that doctor in Glastonbury? The one that fitted you? He does . . . He'll do it."

The next Saturday, after dark so nobody would see, they knocked on the doctor's door and he opened it and said, "Go right into the back."

She undressed and lay under a sheet, her heart pounding, her sweating back sticking to the paper the doctor had laid over the examining table, her feet once again in the stirrups. He washed and everything; it wasn't like in movies she'd seen where it was on a back road and the person wasn't even a doctor and nothing was quite clean. It was a doctor's office and she didn't want a baby and Jerry definitely did not want a baby. She felt the needle slide into her rump and the background noises began to blur and fade. When she opened her eyes again, Jerry was standing there, calling her name, saying they had to get a move on. The doctor handed her some sanitary napkins and said, "You'd better get a really big box. There'll be a bit of bleeding yet."

That was it. Every once in a while she'd try to make herself feel something about that fetus, *something*. But it had never been real to her. She had known from the first morning sickness that she had to get rid of it. So . . . no little "ghost baby" haunted Marty. It had, all of it, been so undramatic—except for Jerry's tantrum in the car—so matter-of-fact. It hadn't made one moment's difference in her life. In fact, she and Jerry Kelly had gone on being lovers until she graduated and went away to nursing school in Boston and just never went back. Later, when he died of cancer, somebody from Madison sent her the obituary from the local paper. So someone in town had known about them all along.

A long, long time ago, not worth thinking about, hardly worth remembering. She took the stairs down to the main lobby, taking a peek outside. The Life Saviors were still there, and so were the media, everyone standing around, waiting. For what? She wondered. Another shooting? She turned away and walked to the back. When she pushed the door to CCC open, she could hear some kind of commotion. The excitement was happiness, for a change. Loretta Protozone had given birth twenty minutes ago, an easy labor, and it was a boy! Aldo was bustling around, congratulating himself, yelling "It's a boy! It's a boy! Aldo Protozone, Jr.!" to anyone who would listen and even to those who wouldn't, handing out chocolate candies and cigars, beaming.

"Marty! I have a son!" He embraced her. "The Witch, she was right!"

"Yes, Aldo, congratulations! I'm very happy for you!" And she was. That little twinge of sadness, or regret, or whatever it was ... that was nothing, just the ticktock of her biological clock. She still had time, plenty of time. But right now she'd better check on Marie Racine. All this happiness about a healthy full-term baby boy couldn't help but make Marie feel even worse, if she was awake.

Marie was awake, and of all the people in the world, Clive Moses was with her, holding her hand tenderly and speaking in rapid French. Marty stayed by the open door, not wanting to interrupt. He was explaining that her baby was fine, just very very small, and was in a special place for very small babies getting special attention. Marie's almond eyes were glued to his face, and with every word she brightened more. Marty decided she wasn't needed at the moment. If ever. So she left.

25

Marty was deep into paperwork at quarter to six, when she looked at her watch and realized she should be picking up Joel in his office. This minute. She punched out his extension but it was busy. What the hell, she'd just go upstairs and get him. He wouldn't leave without her.

When she walked into his office suite, his secretary was gone, so she marched on through. And then pulled back as she heard his voice. "Look," he was saying very earnestly, "I hear what you're saying and I'm not saying you're wrong. But I'm a thirty-six-year-old man who's rapidly losing his hair and maybe his mind, a husband, and the father of three kids. *That's* who I am . . . not a lover, not an adventurer. . . . Please, I don't

like to hear *that* tone. It's just no good and I can't do it." His voice was clear although pitched very low.

Marty felt like an eavesdropper. Hell, that's exactly what she *was*, wasn't she? Now Joel was listening, trying to interrupt but not being allowed. Then he moaned a little, as if he were in pain. Marty was enraged. Nobody could do that to her Joel!

As if she had just got there, she sauntered in, calling out, "Mannes? It's time to play shrink with me. You ready?"

He looked at her, startled and then relieved and then pleased, the emotions chasing each other over his face. He murmured something into the phone and hung up, grinning at her.

"Ready?" he said. "My dear woman, you couldn't have come at a better time!"

Had she heard anything? Joel wondered. He eyed her. She was one sharp woman, his friend Marty Lamb, and very goddamn little escaped her. Nah, she'd arrived too late to catch anything that might make her suspicious. That's what he hated most about this whole business—constantly looking over his shoulder, wondering if he'd been seen or overheard. Well, it was over, finished, kaput, the end, finito, so long baby. It had been a heady ride at first, but—like he told *her* just now—he wasn't a stud like Dinowitz, he was just skinny little Joel Mannes, husband, father, shrink—and a nice guy, for God's sake! At least he'd always *thought* he was a nice guy, but what he'd been doing to Alice lately . . . well, it wasn't nice. It was terrible. He'd gladly grovel to get her back, hell, to get his life back!

Marty said they'd better take the back stairs, "unless, of course, you'd like to be cornered by a pack of hungry reporters." He gave her a hug and walked out with her. He'd liked Marty from Day One, back in Middletown. She'd struck him as a girl with her head screwed on straight, and as a nurse who wasn't going to take the usual bullshit from the doctors. And he'd been right. That's why he'd been so surprised when she married Owen Lamb. When Alice suggested him to Marty, she'd thought he might be fun for an overworked, underpaid nurse. Owen was a character, but he was an associate professor

at Wesleyan, for God's sake! Who knew he was schizophrenic? A bit precious, yes, and a bit overdramatic, yes, and
apt to obsess about something or someone he wanted. But psychotic? Hell, people you socialized with might be neurotic and
notional, but they weren't—they couldn't be—*mentally ill*!
Nobody had recognized just how sick Owen was. Including
Supershrink.

It had occurred to Joel, more than once, that maybe Marty
had realized it but was powerless to prevent herself from being
carried away by Owen's intensity. Once Marty had confided in
Joel about her childhood—the brain-damaged mother, the
silent, angry father—he was able to figure it out. Marty had
grown up in an emotional vacuum, part of a pretend family.
Owen's inner emptiness had probably felt *right* to her, in some
way, had felt comfortable and familiar. And she must have
been so desperate for something that called itself love. Hey,
she wasn't the only needy one, was she? If she were, he'd be
out of business.

They went out the back door. Zigzagging through the
garbage cans with Marty, a wave of nostalgia and affection
swept over him. He realized once again how close he had come
this past month to ruining his whole life. He grabbed Marty
around the shoulders impulsively and gave her another
squeeze.

"Have I told you lately that I love you?"

"What's up, Doc?"

"Nothing." What a liar he was. What did he mean, *nothing*?
He had nearly lost himself a great wife, great kids, a great
job, and great friends. Thank God, he'd put an end to the
lunacy. Never again, he promised himself silently. "Nothing,"
he repeated. "Just grateful for good friends. For you."

"Yeah, me too." She gave him a warm smile. She was such
an appealing woman, he'd always thought, with her clear
green eyes and her clear mind and her sense of humor. The first
time she told him she saw herself as gawky and ugly, too tall,
with kinky orange hair and big feet, he couldn't stop himself,
he howled with laughter. It was so goddamn ludicrous.

"You're like a willow tree with auburn hair, you crazy
woman!" he told her. "Go take a look in the mirror, will you?"

He said now, "We're lucky, you know that, Marty? We know each other so well and *still* we like each other. You have a problem, you know you can call on me for help, and when I—" The words just stuck in his throat. Here he was, babbling about the beauties of friendship, and all the time, he was keeping his big secret all to himself. ". . . and when I have a problem, I'm a shrink so I can talk to myself," he finished, hoping he'd fooled her. But a sideways glance at her face told him that of course he hadn't.

"Sure," she said lightly. "Everyone has noticed how you walk around talking to yourself. Shit. Listen to what I'm saying. Up in my apartment there sits a man who really *does* walk around talking to himself."

They walked to Van Dam Avenue, almost tiptoeing, checking around the corner of the building. Like spies in a Grade B movie, he thought.

As soon as they were sure they'd given the media hounds the slip, he continued the conversation. "Owen openly talks to his voices?"

"You mean his 'sources.' Oh, yes, he's very open about getting the word from them. When I left him, in the middle of the night, he was talking to *something*, waving his hands around." She paused for a moment. "Back when we were first married, he used to wait until the middle of the night. And then if I got up and asked him what was going on, he'd tell me he thought he saw an alien outside the window, or it must have been the typewriter I heard, et cetera, et cetera."

"Besides the voices, what other symptoms have you noticed?"

"Besides repeating himself endlessly and threatening to bop me one with a crystal vase? Nothing much. He had already decompensated when he rang my bell in the middle of the night. Julia came over, and together we managed to get some meds into him. But while we were trying to get him to leave, they beeped me and I had to go. I had no choice," she said, with a pleading note in her voice.

"Of course not," he soothed.

"Joel, you know I started as a psychiatric nurse. I know how to deal with a schizophrenic—it says here. But I'm telling you,

if he doesn't leave my apartment today, you're going to find me hurtling out the window."

"Not necessary, my dear. Put your faith in Supershrink. I will get him out of your apartment."

"You have your work cut out for you, buddy boy."

"Marty, there's a place called Harmony Hill Hospital, with a big psychiatric unit. There's a place called Psychiatric Institute just up the road. And there's always Bellevue."

"If I sent him to Bellevue, I'd feel guilty for the rest of my life."

"*I'll* send him, and believe me, I won't feel a bit guilty."

Marty nudged him, drawing his attention to the three Survivor men heading toward them. The three men, two middle-aged and one just a boy, all stared at Marty and openly muttered at each other, then dropped their eyes as they came abreast. They were not about to move apart, so Joel and Marty did, letting the trio come between them.

"They all hate me," Marty remarked as they continued on. "Zeke Brown has decided I'm to blame."

"To blame? For what?"

"For Miriam. For *everything*." She sounded almost defeated, then added: "Well, I'm not going to let Zeke Brown write my script. No way!"

Then how come, Joel asked silently, you let Owen Lamb do it? You've probably had less intimacy with him than with the rabbi. "Come on," he said as they drew abreast of Protozoa, "Let me buy us a drink. I have a feeling we're both going to need it."

Not such a good idea, Marty thought, as it turned out. Protozoa was jammed. Half the hospital was at the bar, because drinks were all half price in honor of the birth of Aldo Jr. Marty recognized several reporters hanging out. Still, the place was filled with babble and laughter, good smells from the kitchen and the good sounds of Frank Sinatra singing a duet with Barbra Streisand on the jukebox. They were able to push their way to a far corner of the bar, practically in the kitchen, where Joel ordered two extra-dry martinis, no cranberries please, just old-fashioned olives.

"Cranberries!" Marty said and laughed.

"The very latest thing."

"I'm sure." She shook her head. Well, at least she was amused instead of down at the mouth. That was an improvement. "I thought I was the only person in the world who still drank martinis."

"Supershrink knows all, sees all. And remembers quite well what you always drank when we were at Middletown Mental. It wasn't *that* long ago." He waited a few moments and then said, "So. What's Owen doing in your apartment?"

"Doing? Rearranging the furniture! I'm sorry, I'm sorry, but I don't *know* what he's doing. I'm not so sure I even want to go home and find out." She took a sip of her drink, shuddered a little, and then turned to him. "Just what the nurse ordered," she pronounced, draining the glass. "And I'll have another."

"Did you know," Joel said wryly, "that nurses are prone to alcoholism, addictions, sexual liaisons, and other madnesses?"

"Of course I know it. The only reason I'm still sane—oh yes I am, and don't give me that look, I only *seem* a nervous wreck—is because I'm in Administration and no longer have to deal with illness, despair, and death. Not!"

"Tell me all about Owen," Joel said. "Leave nothing out. He came back. Suddenly. Just like that."

"Well, not quite just like that. I had three thousand phone calls from the director of the plush funny farm where he was being treated, strongly hinting that it was my job and my responsibility and my duty to resume my marriage. And now, here he is—Owen, I mean—thinking we're going to live as man and wife. . . . How could that doctor allow him to act out like this? And in the middle of the goddamn night! Which reminds me, what were *you* doing, taking a meeting in the wee hours of the morning when I needed you?"

"Oh . . . it ran late." His voice was so vague, she knew she'd hit on something, and she was sorry.

"I called you at home. I didn't want to, but I was desperate. Didn't Alice tell you?"

"Alice had to leave early this morning . . . she went to her mother's. It was quite sudden. In the rush, she must have forgotten." But Marty noticed that Joel wasn't quite looking at

her. "I humbly beg your pardon for not being home when you needed me. But here I am now, and plying you with strong drink, to boot. How do you think I can help?"

"I don't want Owen around! And he won't go! I don't care how miraculous his medication is supposed to be, he's still talking to his voices."

Joel had on his psychiatrist face, thoughtful and serious. "You know that sometimes they decompensate anyway. Sometimes the voices just break through. But is he taking his medication at *all*, that's the question. What's he supposed to be on? Risperdal?"

"Clozapine."

"It's good but it doesn't work miracles on everyone. So you got him to take his meds?"

"Yes. But I don't *want* that job! I don't want to be in charge of his mental health. I don't want to have any kind of relationship with him. I want him to go away! I need your opinion about . . . your input on . . ."

"Two sentences ending with a preposition. One more and I'll be forced to call the grammar police." He turned and waggled two fingers. "Over our last drink, let us put our heads together and devise a plan."

Aldo himself brought the two glasses this time, plus a little basket stuffed with pretzels and salted nuts, presenting it all with a flourish. He was beaming with goodwill. As well he might, Marty thought; the place was overflowing, as usual, and already a line had formed at the door, waiting for tables.

"For my two favorite doctors, these are on the house," Aldo announced, adding, "You know I got a son. A *son*!" His eyes went dreamy. "Don't get me wrong, I love my girls. But who could play ball with a girl, you know what I mean? A man needs a son. I already went out last week and bought him everything—baseball glove, football helmet, soccer knee guards, balls for every sport!"

"Last week you bought this stuff? How could you be so sure it was a boy?" Joel said. "Amnio?"

Aldo crossed himself rapidly. "Jesus, Mary, and Joseph, no, Doc. No, we don't want no . . . waddaya call 'em . . . ?"

"Invasive procedures," Marty supplied.

"Yeah. Them."

"Then how . . . ?" Joel said with a laugh. "Mother Nature doesn't always play fair."

Aldo bent closer and said in conspiratorial tones, "You know how they call Mrs. Cole the Witch? No offense, they say she has the second sight. My brother told me she . . . well, anyway, the last time Loretta went for her checkup, Mrs. Cole, she gave her the needle and thread test."

Joel looked puzzled, so Marty explained. "You thread a needle, Dr. Mannes, and you hold it over the pregnant woman's belly. You hold it very still, you mustn't move."

"Yeah! And if the needle moves around in a circle," Aldo continued, "it's a girl. But if there's a boy cookin' in there, the needle goes back and forth, back and forth." He demonstrated.

"Then I gather that the needle over Loretta's belly went back and forth, back and forth," Joel said, very solemn.

"You bet! So for sure, it had to be a boy! Yo, they're yelling for me. Enjoy your drinks!"

"Obstetrics goes high-tech," Joel remarked.

Marty made a face. Maybe now, she thought, while they were both drinking in a public place, at ease, feeling not too much pain. "I'm surprised at Crystal, encouraging that sort of nonsense," she said, studying him for a reaction.

There was none. "Let's get back to your problem, Marty. Do you suppose Owen will remember me?"

"I'm afraid so. He says you brought the voices and made him sick."

"They *all* say that. Let's go. I told you I'd help and I'm going to help."

"And while you're at it, I have a separation agreement I want him to sign."

Joel frowned. "How long has it been? Eight years?"

"Abandonment, you mean? Well, maybe. I'm not sure."

"I don't suppose you've consulted a lawyer lately?"

"Joel, if you knew how busy I've been . . ." And then she realized how ridiculous that sounded. They both began to laugh.

Joel leaned across the table and said, in a low voice, "I promise never to tell anyone you said that, if you'll—"

He stopped speaking so suddenly, his eyes fixed on something in back of her, that Marty turned to see what. Crystal was standing at the doorway, her eyes searching the room.

". . . leave with me by the back door, right this minute," he finished. "Come on."

They went out through the alley to Van Dam Avenue. Joel's face looked tight and tense; at least she *thought* it did. There was no doubt he'd wanted to avoid Crys. But she could be his patient and going through transference. Why, Marty asked herself, was she guessing, when all she had to do was ask?

"Joel, are you seeing Crystal Cole?" She was alarmed to see the blood drain from his face and just as suddenly flood back in a flush of color. Oh Christ. "I meant . . . as a patient."

"As a patient? Once or twice. She didn't take to therapy." He tried for a laugh, not quite making it. Marty wanted to say something more, but what was she going to say? *Have you been having an affair with Crystal, Joel? Is she blackmailing you?* It sounded so overdramatic, just thinking it. So she said nothing.

They raced up the street without speaking, while Joel waited for his heart rate to get back to normal. He hoped nothing of his total panic had showed on his face. Apparently not, because Marty didn't pursue it. When they got to her corner, she suddenly stopped walking and moaned, looking up. He looked up, too. Oh, great. Owen had thrown the windows wide open and was yelling something at the top of his voice. He could doubtless be heard clear up to Westchester. Not just random shouting, it had a rhythm to it. And then Joel had it. Owen was reciting. Reciting *what* was another question. Poetry, probably. He'd taught English poetry at Wesleyan, hadn't he?

"He's getting worse and worse by the *minute*," Marty said, her voice tight.

"Of course he's getting worse, Marty. If you're right—and I'm sure you are—and he's decided he doesn't need his medication, he's bound to. The paranoia just makes it that much more— Don't mind me, pontificating comes with the M.D."

She couldn't laugh. She couldn't even smile. "I hate this! I hate it!"

"Of course you do. But now I'm here, and didn't I say not to worry?"

As they mounted the stairs it became clear what the toneless chant was. "Thorazine. Stelazine. Mellaril. Loxitane. Trilafon. Prolixin. Haldol. Moban. Clozapine." The same names, in the same order, repeated over and over again in a chant. An incantation to all the antipsychotics Owen had doubtless been given over the years. All the drugs they had tried on him, all the drugs he had stopped taking as soon as he felt a little better. Or maybe they didn't make him feel better and that's why he always stopped.

All antipsychotics had side effects, some more unpleasant than others. But you'd think that a little weight gain, a little tremor in the hands, a little dryness of the mouth would be much more agreeable than the terrifying voices with their awful messages. Joel would always remember how the child of one of his schizophrenic patients had asked wistfully: "How come Dad's voices never give him any *good* news?" He didn't know; no doctor knew. They just stumbled along, guessing.

"It has a certain swing," Joel said as they climbed up the steps and Marty let them into the hallway. "Excuse the levity, but it actually does sound like poetry."

"He's a very clever and creative man . . . when he's in his right mind."

"And even when he isn't, Marty. Don't worry, I'll get him to take his meds, and to leave, too."

Marty unlocked her door, holding her breath as she did so. Joel could see how her back stiffened in apprehension. She was quite right: if she didn't get rid of Owen, she'd be heading for a nervous breakdown.

As she opened the door the combined smell of unwashed body, stale air, and burned food hit them.

"Owen!" Marty shouted, over his chant. "What the hell is going on?"

He whirled around, the refrain dying mid-word. "Joel Mannes!" he said with a big grin. "Haven't seen you in years!" If Joel hadn't heard the chanting with his own ears, he'd have had trouble believing Owen could shift mental gears so quickly.

"Hello, Owen. You were shouting pretty loudly, you know. We could hear you from the street."

"Oops. Shame on me. But Random House has asked for an epic poem, something suitable for the President, you know, and I thought since the White House is a mansion and I have spent some time at the Mansion, I would do a song about illness, my particular illness, the name of which shall remain nameless. But I can't find a rhyme for 'mansion.' Can you think of one, Joel? I've been searching and searching. I'd love a cigarette. I must be sick because when I'm well the very smell of tobacco makes me ill, but when I'm sick I just want to smoke and smoke. . . ."

"Owen, we have to talk," Joel began, but was interrupted by a loud cry from Marty, who was facing the open kitchen. Joel turned to look. The wall was splattered with what looked like red grease; two pots, burned black, sat on the stove, and others were piled helter-skelter in the sink.

"Oh, Marty, I wanted to make spaghetti for dinner, a surprise. But I forgot how . . ."

"And you had to throw the pot against the wall? Do you see the mess, Owen? *Where do you think you are?*"

"With my wife, of course. Look, I brought you roses, only you weren't there." In an aggrieved tone: "Where *were* you, Marty?"

"Never mind where I was! You've destroyed my kitchen, Owen! You've ruined my pots! You've made a huge mess! You can't just come barging back into my life and—" She stopped, breathing very hard, her hands balled tightly into fists.

"I brought you flowers, Marty. I brought you *flowers*."

"Fuck the flowers!" Marty screamed. Her face was bright red. Joel put a hand on her shoulder and gave it a little squeeze. She took in a deep shuddering breath. "Owen came to the hospital looking for me today," she said, in a completely different tone, very clipped, very angry. Owen seemed absolutely oblivious. "And when he couldn't find me to give me flowers," Marty continued, "he brought them back here."

She picked up a very weary-looking bunch of flowers from a table where they had been thrown. Obviously, they'd never been put into water.

Joel used his best tough-doctor voice. "Where are your meds, Owen? I know they gave you some. And a prescription, right? Where are the pills?"

"Won't tell you."

"You really have to take your medication, Owen. You've made a terrible mess here, and it's Marty's home, you know. You can't mess up someone else's home. She's been extremely patient, but now you must show me where the pills are and you must take them."

"I know I'm behaving badly. I do it to match the mess in my head. They tell me to do so many things, so many different things, I can't find *me* in the mess." Mournfully, Owen added, "I don't even know if I can find my meds." Amazingly, tears leaked out of his eyes and he began to pace back and forth, back and forth, biting his lip hard.

"I'd call the director of the Mansion," Marty said. "But I already went *that* route. He keeps on assuring me that I must be doing something wrong or Owen wouldn't be behaving this way. And Owen's mother is no better. Everyone just wants to dump him. Including me! But Christ, I can't be expected to put up with this!" For the first time, Joel thought, she sounded as desperate as she must feel.

"Marty, I have two words for you. Divorce him."

"What makes you think it's so easy?"

"Where have you *been*, dear girl? You live in New York, and in New York I'm sure he's been gone long enough for it to be considered abandonment or something like that. Call a lawyer and get the proper papers and boom, you're divorced. With or without his agreement."

"Why did I think he had to sign the papers?"

"I don't know. Why did Owen think he ought to come *here*, after all these years?"

"I blame Chen. I'm sure he told Owen to come here."

"No, Marty," Owen interrupted. He'd bitten his lip until it was bleeding. "It was Barbara Walters. She told me I should try again. Second chances are available to all, she told me, even to lost souls. And I am either lost or misplaced . . . a misplaced, displaced, two-faced, one-raced bad taste. . . ." His voice faded and he turned around, to begin packing his suitcase, just

stuffing everything he could get his hands on into it. Pillows from the couch, silverware, a couple of books.

"Owen," Joel said, walking up to him, putting a gentle hand on his shoulder. Owen turned suddenly and gave him a mighty push. "Don't you touch me!" he shrieked. "I am 144 pounds of lethal chemicals!" Joel stumbled backward and was only able to stay upright by bumping into an easy chair.

"That does it!" Joel said. He grabbed Owen's seersucker jacket, half hidden beneath a quilt, and digging into one of the pockets, came up with a plastic vial.

"Water, please, Nurse," he said.

Marty caught on. "Yes, Doctor," she answered, as if they were in a medical setting.

"Here you go, Mr. Lamb." Joel proffered the pill on the palm of his hand. "Either you take this or I call Bellevue. You're right, you're behaving badly, very badly. But you must have been doing well, because they did let you out, and gave you the meds to take. They did their job, now you have to do yours."

Marty held out a glass of water, and Owen knocked it out of her hand.

"Okay, that's it." Joel went to the phone and began punching out numbers.

"No, wait. I don't want to go to Bellevue, I'll take it, I'll take my meds." Owen swallowed the pill. Joel and Marty exchanged glances of relief. Owen looked around wildly, and started to clean up, which consisted mostly of picking up piles of junk and putting them down somewhere else. Finally, Marty told him to go sit down and she began folding and sorting and throwing away garbage. She stripped the sheets from the sofa bed, holding them as if they carried the plague.

Damn! Joel thought. Do we know anything? We can't figure out how to cure this perfectly intelligent, maybe brilliant, man. Shit, we hardly know how to help him. A few years ago we were giving electric shocks; a few centuries ago, we were drilling holes in their heads to let the demons out. Now we have Clozapine, hooray, and Risperdal; and have we come any closer to really understanding what the hell is going on in that brain?

"Come on, Owen," Joel said. "Let's get you a shower and pack you a bag and find you a place to stay."

Sadly: "I can't live with Marty anymore?"

"No, you can't live with Marty anymore. You and Marty are being divorced."

"I'm not leaving. You can't fucking tell me what to do! I'm sick and tired of all you shrinks thinking I'm some fucking baby! I'm staying and you fucking well can stuff it and—" His voice faltered as Joel picked up the telephone receiver again. "Okay, okay. But I'm warning you, I'm having you fired for practicing medicine without a license!" His face was red with agitation.

Joel took in a deep breath. God, how they could wear you down.

"Okay, Owen," he said in the most soothing, bland tone he could summon. "You see about having me fired. But until you do it, I'm still in charge. And you want to know something, Owen? I'm getting you out of here. You're leaving, and what's more, you're going to leave Marty alone."

Of course, they had to call the cops in the end, she and Joel. It was a farce. Joel would talk and talk and patiently get Owen all set to go, and suddenly he'd dig in his heels and refuse to leave. Once, he cried, brokenhearted and totally unselfconscious. She felt terrible, but he *had* to leave. She wasn't a psychiatric hospital, she was just one lone woman.

She felt even worse when the two overweight cops, puffing and grunting, half walked, half dragged him down the front steps. Owen kept turning, calling her name, sounding so helpless, so hopeless. Then he switched to a string of obscene curses and she didn't have to feel remorse anymore.

Joel, bless him, went with the police; he found a rooming house that asked nothing except payment in advance. He called to tell her that he'd given Owen a sedative so he'd sleep, and that when he woke up, the medication would have started to take effect. "I hope," he added. "We're never sure. But I've been on the horn to dear Dr. Chen, and apparently Clozapine kept him pretty damn steady, as long as he stayed on the right dosage."

"Well, I can attest to that. I went up there to see him. He was no bargain, but he was much better than he's been here."

"He's going to be okay," he told her. "As okay as someone like him can be. And you, my dear Marty, are going to get a divorce and get on with your life." He gave her a lawyer's name and phone number. Sarah Fortgang, with an office in midtown. "Call her, do you hear me? Call her. Promise."

And you promise to stay away from Crystal Cole, she answered him silently. She'd call the lawyer. Not tonight, of course. First things first. Owen was gone. Owen was really gone. She was really alone, in her own apartment, in her own life! She picked up the phone to call Paul—Christ, if ever a woman needed her man, the time was right *now*! She was dying to see him. But she didn't want to be semihysterical and fall into his arms weeping. She needed time to prepare herself. The first thing she did was scrub the apartment from stem to stern. Then she showered slowly and carefully, took out some unworn, fancy lingerie saved for a special occasion, and belted a silk robe around her waist. She changed the sheets on her bed, sprayed the room with perfume, and put Mozart on the CD player. The man wouldn't know what hit him.

His answering machine picked up. Damn. Softly, she said into the mouthpiece, smiling, "You said to call you when I was ready. I am readier than you can even imagine." She hung up, still smiling. She hoped it drove him crazy. No, better, she hoped it brought him running.

26

"Everybody's going crazy, you know that?" Isabelle said.

"Who in particular?" Marty asked, glancing through the pile of file folders Isabelle had stacked on the table in the Confer-

ence Room. "This time, I mean?" The folders had grown to quite a mound, but who had the time? "Is going crazy?" she finished.

"Well, for openers, those lawyers for Blenheim. Did you see the papers this morning?"

She had seen the papers this morning, with the now-familiar photo of the killer, the same one every time. Why that particular photo? Marty wondered. In it, Blenheim looked like an all-American boy posing for his yearbook picture, instead of a killer. "Oh. His defense. Yes, I read it."

"It doesn't matter, what he did? What matters is *why* he did it?"

"Izzy, don't let it upset you. It's lawyer talk, that's all. They're going to try to say that his . . . what did they call it? Oh yes, his 'deep religious convictions' . . . made him think of us all as murderers. He meant no evil, it seemed okay to him in the context of his beliefs, blah blah blah. . . ."

"And that means it's okay for him to shoot whoever. Marty, he's not even *sorry*!"

"Izzy, they're going to *try* that defense. Which doesn't mean it's going to work. I doubt any jury would buy such a far-out idea."

"Oh yeah? Then you don't know people very well. What about the rabbi? Instead of being on our side, instead of hating that cuckoo, the rabbi goes and sets everyone against us. I thought he was a smart man. But you have to wonder about him, the way he's going on!" She continued making notes on patient records as she talked, putting them into a pile for filing.

Marty picked up a bunch of file folders, opened the wide drawer of the records cabinet, and started to put them where they belonged. Might as well get something done while they schmoozed.

"You must be the only person in this hospital who didn't hear him last night. On TV, Marty. Channel 87. They call it the nut channel. It's public access, so anyone can get on and talk about anything. I tried to call you," she added. "But your line kept being busy. Who were you talking to for so long?"

"Must have been Dr. Zee," Marty lied. She turned her head away a little, so Isabelle wouldn't see the smile that was

spreading all over her face. Paul had taken the phone off the hook so they wouldn't be disturbed while they were making love. She'd started to object, but he'd said, in a pretty good imitation of a New York accent, "Yo, Marty, waddaya think ya beepa is faw?" And then he began to undress her, kissing each favorite spot as it was revealed, and pretty soon she had no objections whatsoever. "What time was he on?" she asked Isabelle. "The rabbi?"

"A little after ten. When I saw him, I couldn't believe my eyes. But it was him, all right. I said, 'Marco, look at this, it's that crazy rabbi I've been telling you about, the one near the hospital!' And Marco said, 'What's he doing on television?' Well, all you had to do was listen to him for a few minutes . . . you knew what he was doing! Giving this hospital a bad name! How could he say we killed his wife and unborn child? I mean, all right, she was coming for an abortion, but that's legal, nobody can say it's not, and we didn't know there was a crazy guy with a gun . . . and that he'd miss whoever he was aiming at! We didn't have anything to do with that. I mean, everyone feels *awful* about it, of course we do. But she gave a false name, so how could anyone have stopped her . . . I mean, even if he *ordered* us to!"

Marty stuffed BERRYMAN, ELAINE into the B's. "He's grieving and he's very angry. Not that I blame him, but he's pointing the finger in the wrong direction. How about the Life Saviors he's so fond of? He kept bringing them drinks and snacks, so they wouldn't faint in the heat. *They're* what attracts crazoids like that guy!" Marty stopped, realizing she was yelling. Hollering at Isabelle certainly wasn't going to solve anything. "I wish I'd caught it. How did you happen to be watching Channel 87, of all the damn things?"

"Oh, one of his parishioners was in for a checkup and mentioned it to Virgie. Said he told all his people to watch him, he had important things to say. *Important!*" A world of disdain was packed into that one word. "Lies, that's what he had to say!"

"He's into such deep denial, he doesn't know he's lying," Marty said. "It doesn't occur to him that allowing fanatic views free rein can lead to fanatic behavior. Hell, he doesn't even

think it was odd, keeping his daughter from her mother's funeral. I used to think he was intelligent, just a bit of a zealot. But now . . . I don't know *what* he is." Marty angrily pushed another file into the drawer.

"Well, I know what he is! He's a control freak! Men!" Isabelle hefted another huge pile and put it in front of Marty. "They're in alphabetical order. As long as you're already doing it." She gave Marty a sly smile.

"Go ahead, take advantage of me. I'm in a very good mood." Very good mood didn't even begin to describe it. She now knew what it meant to have a song in your heart. Owen was gone and she felt pounds lighter—144 pounds lighter to be exact. She didn't know where he was staying and she didn't *want* to know. He was gone, and Paul was back in her life, that's all that mattered right now.

"But what really got me steamed, Marty . . . about Rabbi Brown? . . . is he said he's going to sit in the middle of the side-walk in front of All Souls . . . he's going to go on a hunger strike if the hospital doesn't admit it did wrong. And when he dies, we'll have three lives on our conscience!" Isabelle's voice rose and wobbled, and Marty looked up from the file drawer, alarmed. "This is a *hospital*! We don't let people die here, not by their own will." Izzy burst into tears.

"Isabelle!" Marty dropped the pile she'd just picked up and put an arm around Isabelle's shoulders. "What's wrong?"

"That poor woman has to have an abortion, and then she's shot by a crazy and then her crazy husband threatens to kill *himself*. And there's my poor mama, praying only for God to release her from her pain, to let her die! But does God listen to her? It's so awful to see how she suffers!" She wept silently, her shoulders shaking.

"Izzy, Izzy, I know it's awful."

"And there's nothing I can do!"

Marty led the other nurse over to a corner and sat them both down. She took Isabelle's hands in hers. "Remember grand rounds last month? Weren't we all discussing pain manage-ment? Isabelle . . . remember?"

Sniffling, she nodded.

" 'We must rely on the patients' own feelings of pain, about

pain, and what they would like done about it,' " she quoted. "Does your mama *say* what she wants? To die? Or . . . ?"

"Yes, she says it. Last night, she grabbed my hand. . . . Marty, her hands are like claws, she's so skinny, she's so . . . wasted. She whispered to me, because she didn't want anyone else to hear. 'Get Dr. Zee,' she said. 'Get Dr. Zee. I want to go to God and see your papa.' Oh, God!" Isabelle dissolved again into tears. "Yes. She wants to die. I'm the one . . . I'm the problem! She's my mama! I don't want her to go and leave me all alone!" Isabelle began to sob with great gulps, like a child.

Marty hugged her, patting the shaking back. She thought of saying, "But you're not alone, you have your husband and your children." But she kept quiet, her own eyes filling. Without your mother, you were all by yourself in the world, a tiny, helpless little creature. Poor Isabelle. Poor Shayna. And, maybe even poor Marty. A few tears slid down her cheeks and she blinked rapidly.

"Of course you don't want to lose your mother, Izzy. Of course you don't. Nobody does."

"Do you still have yours?"

"She's long dead."

"I'm so sorry. I'm being such a baby. I'm a nurse, I'm not supposed to cry."

"You're allowed," Marty said, still fighting tears and mostly losing. She let go of Isabelle and searched for a tissue to wipe her eyes and face. "I'm giving you permission. God knows we don't give *ourselves* permission to be human often enough."

"Waaa!" Isabelle said, but she smiled a little. "Give me one of those tissues, too, would you?" They both blew their noses. "That's enough," pronounced Isabelle. "I'll talk to Dr. Zee before I go home today. It's the least I can do for poor Mama. I just hope she's feeling better, that's all . . . Dr. Zee, I mean."

"That damn cold—or whatever the hell it is—*has* hung on and on. Although I thought she looked better recently. She probably doesn't eat right, doesn't get enough sleep—just like the rest of us. As a matter of fact, I need to see her . . ." Marty consulted her watch. ". . . and she should be around now. Gotta run. I'll tell her you want to talk to her. And Isabelle . . ." She

couldn't go on, she was going to cry again, so she reached out and gave Isabelle a hug.

Marty fairly flew up the stairs to the Family Practice unit and strode down the maze of corridors toward the bubble, passing electricians and painters in their dove-gray coveralls. They were all over the place lately; God forbid you had an emergency, you could trip on a dropcloth or get bopped by a ladder. Anyway, a coat of paint wasn't going to fool the JCAHO. Or maybe All Souls was being prettied up to fool potential buyers, not the accreditation people.

She ducked under a ladder, remembering only after she'd done it that it was bad luck. Well, she didn't remember what you had to do to break the bad spell, so to hell with it.

Messinger had called a meeting of the Executive Committee for four o'clock today. She'd found the memo in her box when she got in and had wondered why another meeting, so soon after the last one. She'd decided to ask Julia if she knew. They hadn't seen each other at leisure for days.

She spotted the white hair from the far end of the hall. Dr. Zee was leaning over the counter at the nursing station, checking charts, scribbling notes, giving orders, and chatting with one of the residents. All at the same time. She'd always been good at that, and she hadn't lost her touch. She *was* thin, but they said some people just shrank as they got older.

"Now, what this patient needs is that powerful medicine, TLC," Dr. Zee was saying as Marty walked up.

"There's nothing really *wrong* with her!" the resident complained.

"She's old and alone and depressed, Dr. Gallant. That may not be a disease, but it's real, all right. I know she's difficult and demanding. But do me a favor. Hold her hand and call her sweetie or honey and sit on her bed and chat her up. You'll see . . . she'll perk right up. . . . Ah, there you are," she said, spotting Marty. "Okay, Dr. Gallant, that's all I wanted to say. You're doing fine. Elderly patients can be a trial, but we youngsters have to be patient with them." That elicited a laugh from Dr. Gallant, who actually looked even younger than her twenty-three years.

In answer to Marty's question, Dr. Zee said, "I have a pretty

good idea what this special meeting is about. The rabbi's excursion into show biz . . . his television show."

"How did *you* find out about it?"

"From the nurses, how else?" It was an old joke between them. "I hear that the rabbi plans to do it pretty regularly."

"Do what? Bash the hospital?"

"Well . . . yes. But what I meant was, he's going to talk on television two or three times a week." Dr. Zee looked heavenward. "I hear that, when he speaks, you can hardly take your eyes off him. I only repeat what I'm told."

"That's all we need—Zeke Brown, the Orthodox William Jennings Bryan."

Dr. Zee began to laugh; but the laughter changed to coughing and the coughing became choking. Marty prepared herself for the Heimlich. Finally, the doctor stopped gasping for air.

"Julia!" Marty was alarmed. "Take it easy! What is it? What's wrong?"

"That cold has dropped into my chest and it's interfering with my breathing, that's all. Nothing to worry about."

" 'Nothing to worry about,' she says! You need to see a doctor, Julia."

Dr. Zee smiled wryly. "Yes, well, I've got to be on my way. Talk to you later? There's something I want to discuss with you."

"After the special meeting? Good, see you there. I'm going to the NICU and see if they've finished checking Marie's baby. Crys is releasing her tomorrow."

Marty took the stairs up to Pediatrics and headed for the Neonatal ICU. She'd just look in at the baby, so she could reassure Marie—she hoped. She hated to send the girl home all by herself, scared to death.

She went to the nursery, scrubbed, and put on a smock. When she walked toward Baby Boy Racine, she saw the tall, elegant figure of Clive Moses bending over the bassinet.

"Clive! How debonair you look in pink!" Her tone was light.

He whirled around, blushing. "Oh. Hi, Marty. I just thought . . . well, everyone deserves a name, don't they, even

a little scrawny fellow like this one." He gazed down into the bassinet, a tender smile on his lips.

He had just taped up a hand-lettered sign, *Edouard Martin Racine* it said, *bébé extraordinaire*, surrounded by happy faces, hearts, and balloons, all colored brightly with Magic Markers.

"How sweet, Clive! No, I really mean it, I'm not teasing you. Did you do it yourself?" She slid him an amused look.

"Who, me? I can't draw. My assistant."

"Well, Marie will love it. And maybe it will show her that this hospital cares about her baby."

"I hope so. That's the idea. She's afraid we're going to mess with him. That's why she doesn't want to go home. And she's right—we *are* going to mess with him."

" 'Mess with' meaning . . . ?"

"Balloon atrial septostomy," Clive intoned. "Don't I have a way with words?"

"So," Marty mused, half to herself. "Len was right. When does the baby go in?"

Clive looked at his watch. "In about an hour. I talked with Len Fassbinder and elicited a promise that after it's all over and successful—and of course it *will* be successful because he's doing it—he'll let Marie come see her son."

"So who are you representing here? All Souls or Marie Racine?" She couldn't help smiling; he was so uncomfortable, being caught doing something lovable.

"I like the kid."

"Edouard?"

"No, Marty, not Edouard, as you damn well know. Marie. I like Marie. Okay?"

"It's certainly okay by me. She's a lovely girl."

He heaved a sigh. "I know, I know. Tell me the truth, Marty, do you think I'm being a foolish old cradle robber?"

"None of the above," she said, picking up the chart. She noticed a new IV. "Excuse me a minute."

She checked with the head nurse, who told her it was meaningless. He was being fed Intralipid to put some badly needed fat on his skinny little body.

None of this was going to be easy to explain to Marie. The

baby had problems, pretty typical for a preemie, but he could be here for a while. Marty turned to enlist Clive's help but he had left. She'd find him later. In the meantime, she put a gentle finger on the little cheek. Christ, he was small, smaller than the baby doll her mother had given her one Christmas, the only doll she had ever owned. Edouard's entire body, stretched out, would fit between her elbow and her hand. The respirator kept him breathing and radiant heaters kept him warm. He really shouldn't be out here in this cold cold world yet, Marty thought.

Back in her office, she played back her messages. There was a sexy one from Paul, who ought to know better, but it made her smile. Then Max's voice, reminding her of the meeting later today. And then a strange female voice with just the hint of an accent.

"Excuse me, Miss Lamb, I am calling you for Shayna Brown. She wishes to see you . . . she *must* see you, she says. I am here with her and there is nobody else. Shayna's father . . . he believes her to be sick. She says to tell you she is not. Not sick. She simply wants to talk to you. Please come at noon and I will open the door to you. Oh. My name is Selma, I believe we have met."

At last, a chance to see Shayna. It was nearly noon now. She hurried out the Hamilton Place entrance to the clinics and turned down Van Dam to the Browns' building.

Selma buzzed her in instantly and opened the door, wringing her hands. "I don't know what he will think, if he finds out." Another woman who didn't find it necessary to say who "he" was, Marty thought, even as she said, "He won't find out. Don't worry Selma, he won't find out."

Selma wanted to stay with them but Shayna waved her off. The older woman bent her head and obeyed. The moment the room was empty, Shayna began to talk in a hoarse whisper.

"Something has happened to him, Marty. My mother's death . . . we all mourn her—" She broke down, wept. "But he . . . he is crazed. I don't exaggerate, he's gone crazy.

"He . . . he bought a gun, Marty. No, don't look at me like that. I know what I'm talking about. A handgun, a pistol? A revolver? I don't know the difference. I saw it."

"Gun?" Marty repeated. "I believe you. But . . . why? What for?"

"I'm afraid, Marty. I don't know exactly what he plans, but I know this—he plans something. He told me to watch Channel 87 last night at ten, and I did. Did you see it? No? I only hope not many people saw it. He hates you, he hates Dr. Zee, he hates the hospital. After all the years you've been taking care of us! Now he's saying every *goy* is an anti-Semite . . . that Mama *really* died because she was Jewish."

"Shayna, that's crazy. Your mother had lupus and she thought she had to abort her baby and a religious fanatic killed her by accident. In fact, we didn't have any idea she was coming in for an abortion. You believe me, don't you?"

"I believe you, of course I believe you. But do you think the truth could ever change my father's mind? He says you encouraged her to disobey the laws of the Almighty. We know who the Almighty really is, though, don't we? Ezekiel Brown!" She tried to laugh but it quickly turned into a kind of sob.

"Shayna . . ." Marty sat close to the girl and put an arm around her shoulders.

"I don't know what he's thinking anymore! He's different! And he keeps me locked up here in my room! Oh, if I only had braces, if I only had crutches . . . even a wheelchair!"

Marty took the girl's hand in hers. "I admit, it's worrisome, that he's bought a gun. And he's not saying nice things on TV. But he's not a vigilante kind of guy." She kept her tone light. "He's grieving and he's angry and he's looking for someone or something to blame. But he's an intelligent man. He'll come to his senses."

"Maybe before my mother died. But now? I don't know *what* kind of man he is now. Marty . . . Marty . . ." Shayna hesitated, bit her lips, looked at the floor, then blurted out: "He came into my room last night, he wanted to lie down next to me in my bed. He missed the warmth of her body, he said. I was so frightened. I said, 'No, Papa, you cannot.' He came over to the bed anyway, he kept saying he would not touch me, it was only a human warmth that he wanted. But I was afraid. So I said, 'You are suffering terribly. But if you do not leave my room immediately, I will tell everyone about this. *Everyone*, do you

understand me?' And he began to cry, like a child, saying over and over again that he meant no evil, and then he left me, lying in a puddle of my own sweat."

Shayna reached for Marty's hand, clutching it tightly. "But who knows? Who knows what he will do . . . the next time?"

"There won't be a next time. We'll make sure of that. Can someone come and stay with you? I mean night and day." The girl nodded. "Tell Selma . . . tell her you're having dreams about your mother and you need a woman to be there for you. Tell her anything, but make sure someone is here *living* with you."

"I wanted to go with my brothers. They are staying with Selma and her husband, such nice people. They have no children of their own. Her husband, especially, he's so happy to have them, even for a little while. But of course, my father wouldn't allow *me* to stay there. Then everyone would know the shame that is Shayna! But there is no way he could refuse to let someone stay with me. Several people in the congregation have already said I should not be here without a woman to care for me."

Marty hugged her. "Things will get back to normal. He's in shock, Shayna. It was all so sudden."

"Do you imagine that it wasn't sudden for *me*? She was my mama, she was my one true friend! You haven't seen him, since. He is . . . unhinged. And I cannot protect myself from *anything*.

"When I think that *he* kept me this way! I hate him for it. I hate him with all my heart. And I am not afraid that God will punish me for my thoughts. I am already punished. . . ." She gestured to her lifeless legs.

"I could have gone to school, to college, maybe to medical school. I'm smart, I could have made a life for myself. But he ruined me. My father made me spoiled, only half alive, rotten, no taste to me, no use to me—except that I can bear sons to some man! I can give grandsons to him so that he can keep pretending there's nothing *really* wrong with me. Here is what I say to my father!" She spat onto the floor and began again to weep.

Marty was astonished at first, at the depth of Shayna's anger.

But then, who was she kidding? She knew about fathers and fury, and she knew—though she put her arms around Shayna and murmured comforting words into her ear—that there was no comfort for Shayna, no real comfort at all.

She spoke with Selma before she left, with orders that there be a woman to live in the house with Shayna. Selma agreed, saying it was a *shandah*, a shameful thing, for a young beautiful girl to be alone with a man, even if that man were her father. "I myself will stay with her," Selma promised. Even so, it was with a heavy heart that Marty headed back to work.

At four o'clock when she walked into the committee meeting, they were all there, sitting around the big, polished rosewood table. She slid into her chair, noting the envelopes, one sitting before each place around the table. Except for Julia's usual place. And she wasn't in her chair, either.

"Where's Dr. Zee?" she asked.

"We are all wondering that," Max said. "We thought . . . you two being such good friends . . . you might have been told. No? Well, then . . ." He turned to Messinger.

"Yes. Yes. It seems Dr. Zachary-Felsen gave these envelopes to Max this morning, to hand out to the committee. So. Before we begin the business of this meeting, I suggest we see what she has to say."

Marty ripped open her envelope and unfolded the paper. The typed message was brief and to the point. Dr. Zee was resigning, effective immediately. She would clear her office and be out within the week. "I feel I can no longer care for my patients as I would like," the message ended. It was signed by hand.

They were all surprised, Marty could tell by the amazed look on every face. Every face but Dr. Messinger's. He seemed unsurprised and undismayed, even though Julia had been a major rainmaker for this hospital for years.

Marty said, "I hope you're not going to accept this resignation, Dr. Messinger."

"On the contrary," he said. "I have great respect for Dr. Zachary-Felsen's intelligence. If she feels she can no longer serve her patients as she would like, I must respect her decision."

"Without even asking her why?"

"Now, Marty," Dr. Dimwit said, in his best conde-scending manner, "you mustn't let your friendship with Dr. Zee cloud your good sense. Obviously, she hasn't been well lately. She's lost weight and can't seem to shake this virus that's been bedeviling her the past month. You have to figure she knows best."

Dammit, she couldn't argue with him. He was actually *right*. Her eyes slid automatically to where Dr. Zee would nor-mally be sitting. Only, of course, Dr. Zee wasn't there.

"If we have finished with this topic?" Messinger queried. "Shall we go on?" He lowered his eyes and shuffled a couple of papers and then said, "I have been in touch with our attor-neys. The hospital is not responsible for Mrs. Brown's death. In fact, there isn't even anything to show that she came here for an abortion. She hadn't made an appointment—her name is nowhere to be found."

Not responsible. Was that all that mattered? "But of course," Marty said, "all of us here *know* why Miriam was there. This wasn't the first time she came here for an abortion."

Messinger gave her a baleful look. "Yes, Marty, we are all aware of that. I am speaking from the legal point of view. And, from the legal point of view, Rabbi Brown has already said enough on a public television station to be sued for slander."

"No more than he deserves," Len Fassbinder said. "Damned nerve, calling us murderers. I say sue."

"Right now, Len, only a few people, relatively speaking, have heard him," Joel used his most calming voice. "Channel 87 isn't exactly NBC, you know. It's widely known as the nut channel. Nobody pays it much attention. Sue the rabbi, and you *could* attract attention. Why not just let it go, let him vent his anger."

"I agree," Dennis said. "We only dignify his rantings by sending in the lawyers."

"Maybe . . . maybe . . ." Messinger ruminated. There was a prolonged silence, and then he announced, "No more abortions."

"Excuse me?" Marty said. Where in hell had *that* come from?

"We don't want trouble. No more trouble. No more abortions."

"You're asking me to close the entire clinic?"

"No . . . not the clinic. Just stop the abortions."

"Abortions are legal, Dr. Messinger. We're the only ones for miles who do them. We can't just . . . *stop*."

"Oh yes we can. And we will, before anything else happens. I leave it to you to get the word out, Ms. Lamb."

"I won't."

He frowned and pushed his lips in and out, in and out. Her heart was thudding nervously but she didn't care. Abortion clinics were being threatened all over the country; nobody *else* was just laying down and giving up! "We owe it to our patients, Dr. Messinger, we can't just suddenly—"

He waved a languid hand. "You'll think of something to say. . . . Um, we're doing needed renovations in order to keep our accreditation, how's that?" He smiled. "And it might well be true."

"It's not true," Marty said, her voice tight with anger. "And I'm not going to lie to my patients."

Leaning forward in his chair, Messinger said, "Are you being deliberately obtuse, Ms. Lamb? First of all, if we close the abortion clinic—temporarily, let us say temporarily—the rabbi will be satisfied and he will stop his ravings. Secondly, if we are no longer giving abortions, the Life Saviors will no longer gather in front of the building. *Nobody* will have any reason to gather in front of the building. And we will be able to—" He halted.

"Sell ourselves to the highest bidder." It just burst out of her.

Every face at the table turned to her, looking startled. Hell, *she* was startled. "Until you force me, I'm not closing that clinic. We're not going to stop."

Messinger stared at her with no particular expression. Even his voice was mild. "Nurses lose licenses," he said.

"Are you threatening me? In front of all these people?"

"No. Just stating a fact."

"You *are* threatening me! I don't react well to threats."

Was that a smile or a snarl? Whatever it was, it was wintry. "Not a threat, Ms. Lamb. A warning, perhaps. This hospital is

not in the business of giving political or religious groups a place to voice their positions. It is in the business of treating sick people. I would try to remember that, if I were you. This meeting is over."

He banged the table with the flat of his hand, rose, and left.

27

It was hard to get the morning meeting going. Everyone already knew about Dr. Zee leaving; and they were all trying to talk at once.

"How could they let her leave?" . . . "She's the best doctor they've got!" . . . "Yeah, and everyone loves her!" . . . "She's the only doctor who understands nurses!" . . . "Dummy, she was a nurse before she was a doctor." . . . "No kidding? I didn't know that!"

"People! People! Can we try to calm down here?" Marty said. "If we could put the hospital grapevine to work for the good of humanity," she added, with a laugh, "there would be no more secrets and no more wars. Now, I spoke with Dr. Zee last night. Maybe you'd like to know what *she* has to say."

There was instant quiet and everyone turned to her, expectant. "She's staying—no, Izzy, don't get your hopes up—she's staying until after the accreditation team has come and gone. And she's going to suggest that Dr. Giordano become acting chief."

"Does she say why she's leaving us, all of a sudden?" Emilio asked.

"I guess it's not really all of a sudden. Once or twice, she's dropped a hint in my direction—which I ignored. She says she's exhausted—and why shouldn't she be? After a full day in the hospital, she *still* makes house calls at night, and everyone

on the late shift knows they can call her in an emergency and she'll come right over. So, we should try to put a brave face on—what is it, Kenny?"

Kenny was frowning and obviously upset. "Where's the drug sign-out book?" he said. "Come on, I saw it last night, because I needed some Demerol. Who else used it?" Silence and shrugs greeted his question. "Right," he said bitterly, "nobody knows. We could all get into trouble if it doesn't turn up, you know."

"Wait," Virgie said, "No, no, I didn't take it but I saw Norma using it and, just for fun, I peeked. She took out a dose of Fentanyl."

"Fentanyl!" Marty was a little surprised. Black-market Fentanyl was sometimes a popular street drug; but they used very little of it here. Its normal use was in conjunction with short-term anesthesia that had started to wear off. "What for? And why was Norma down here signing out drugs, anyway?"

"Because," Crystal answered lazily, "she was assisting me with a difficult birth. Everyone else down here was tied up. I asked her to get it for me."

Marty studied Crys for any sign of evasion or nervousness, but she was Ms. Cool.

"Do you think she took the book?" Izzy asked Crystal. Then she turned to Marty. "Do *you*?"

Marty was thoughtful. She had caught Norma taking extra gloves last week, stuffing them into her pocket. Norma had tossed them back into the box, saying, "Well, I like to double glove. And, in the clinics, *triple* glove." Having insulted the entire patient population of CCC, she had stomped off.

"Do I think Norma took the drug sign-out book? No, I don't. What possible use could she have for it? It's just been misplaced, Kenny, we'll find it."

"I hope the mischief isn't starting again," Sonya said. "We have enough to deal with around here."

"I'm just happy the poison pen messages seemed to have stopped," Marty said. "They *have* stopped, haven't they?" She made eye contact with each one of them, including Crystal, whose enigmatic cat eyes told her nothing. The rest all nodded or said yes, they had stopped.

"Okay, then. As you all know, the JCAHO people will be here in two weeks . . ." She paused to let them groan. ". . . and practically nothing's been done. As usual. But we *have* been painted, and I hope you all noticed how nice and shiny all the floors are."

"Noticed!" Kenny laughed. "I nearly fell on my ass a couple of times."

"We expect to suffer for the sake of beauty," Marty said, smiling. "Now. Here's what we're going to tell the committee when they come sniffing around and notice that the building is *still* over a hundred years old and doesn't have corridors wide enough for two wheelchairs to pass. . . . Oh, and that reminds me, workmen will appear at some point today to put handrails in all the toilets and all the showers." There was a ragged cheer.

"And then, right after that, workmen will appear to widen the corridor down here." Now there was an eruption of protest and complaint.

"Hey, we're already overcrowded." . . . "Do you realize what that'll do to the waiting rooms?" . . . "Anybody want to tell me how we're gonna put all those patients . . ."

She let them grouse for a few minutes and then pounded the desk for quiet.

"Look, people, I know, I know, I know. I agree. It's a some-what stupid idea. . . . Never mind the comments, Emilio, we're *all* in this leaky vessel together, and we'll all sink together if *something* isn't done. Maybe if we widen the corridors, they won't notice how old the air conditioners are . . . or how all the pipes are beginning to leak. I know it's going to be a major pain in the ass, but we don't want them to shut us down, do we? It's the fastest way to compliance. And everyone make sure all the clinics are squeaky clean, especially the bathrooms. Look for droppings and report them immediately to Maintenance. Sorry, people, but rats are here to stay, in this city. No drop-pings, understood?"

"Can you believe this group of health care professionals is sitting here discussing rat doo-doo?" Crystal snorted. "Well, if there's nothing else . . ." She got up, preparing to leave. If she thinks she's going to escape from me forever, Marty thought, she's crazier than I thought.

Virgie said, "Remember what happened to Kings County, Crys."

Emilio laughed. "Brooklyn! Hey, what do you expect, from Brooklyn? And anyway, isn't Kings County, like, older than ancient Greece?"

"Never mind the jokes about Brooklyn," Marty said. "I remember Dr. Zee telling me that when she began her first-year residency, she was praying she'd be taken by Kings County because Kings County got *everything*. It was a plum assignment, people, and the reason it's become a joke to some is because Kings County is a public hospital and the money ran out. All Souls is private, which means we have a fighting chance to stay open and viable. So will you all please greet our workmen with big smiles? Yes? Okay. Class dismissed."

Crystal was first out the door, but Kenny hung back, wanting to talk. He began by discussing one or two patients, and finally got to what he really wanted to say. "Marty, do you think we'll make it? What if we don't? Are we all out?"

Marty was saved from having to admit she was clueless by the phone. It was Carmen, saying, "You're needed at the Birthing Center. Pronto, you know what I mean?"

Marty ran. She could have found her way by following the sounds of lament. Marie Racine was being released today and apparently did not want to go. She was dressed to leave, sitting on the edge of her bed, clutching her leather purse in both hands, tears pouring down her cheeks, wailing. Crystal sat next to her, trying to talk to her, but it was doubtful the girl was even aware there was anyone there.

Poor Marie. She'd been okay after Clive explained about the operation, subdued and of course very upset, but okay. They had moved her into a bed as far away from the new mothers as they could. But somehow she'd got the idea she could take the baby home with her once he came out of the O.R. And now, apparently, she'd found out that he'd be staying in the Neonatal nursery for a week or so, because she was shrieking *"Non, non, non!"* at the top of her voice.

"I've tried to explain," Crystal said, when she saw Marty. "I called Fassbinder, but he was in the O.R. so I had Dr. Dimwit come downstairs to reassure her, he's so good with the girls,

you know. He talked to her for quite a while. He excused *me* . . . 'That's all right, Nurse, we can handle this ourselves.' There was nothing I could do about it.

"I flunked French, but she seems to think something went wrong with the baby because she didn't have a *doctor* at the birth, that bastard Dinowitz."

Dryly, Marty said, "If you don't know French, Crys, you shouldn't guess."

"What the hell *else* could it be about? She keeps saying *docteur*. Even an ignoramus like me knows that means doctor."

Then Marie looked up and saw Marty. She cried out, *"Madame le docteur!"* and Crystal looked startled, almost disappointed. But she said nothing, just motioned Marty to take her place next to the distraught girl.

In their own way, Marty and Marie managed to communicate. Marie told Marty she had given the baby a name, and the birth certificate lady printed it out the way she said. He had a name, he was her son, she wanted him, and she wanted him *now*. She did not want him to stay here, he was too small and surely he would die. She began to cry again.

"I thought Dennis talked to her a long time. Didn't he explain why the baby has to recuperate here, where he can be watched?"

"He probably did, Marty, and she might have nodded and smiled and only understood half of what he said. She does that, you know."

Marty turned her attention back to Marie, who, having given her problem over to *madame le docteur*, now waited trustingly for Marty to do something about it.

"Marie, Marie. *C'est dommage*, but *il est necessaire que* . . . he needed that surgery, or he certainly *would* have died," she finished, frustrated at her lack of French. Marie shook her turbanned head, the tears leaking from under closed lids.

"But Marie—are you listening to me?—Marie, little Edouard will come home soon. . . ." Damn, she couldn't seem to remember any of her French right now. Maybe that's because she wasn't completely sure that little Edouard would *ever* be able to go home. She'd always had a hard time lying in English. In French? Impossible. It was true that a lot of the pree-

mies got better and went home and were fine. But when an infant needed surgery so soon, in her experience, it was often just the tip of the iceberg.

Marty looked deep into Marie's tear-filled eyes and felt like crying herself. To think that maybe you would never hold your own sweet baby in your arms . . . Now Marty *was* puddling up. Very unprofessional, she scolded herself, blinking back the tears.

"*C'est vrai?* He will get better? He will come home to me?"

Shit. "*Je l'espère.* I hope so. The doctors will do everything—*toute*—to make Edouard better."

Suddenly, Marty felt how tightly Marie had been clutching her hands. Carefully, she pulled them away, putting a hand on Marie's shoulder.

Marie looked off into the distance for a moment, then took in a deep, noisy breath. "*Oui.* Yes. Okay. *Monsieur le docteur,* he say I come *demain* . . . tomorrow. He will allow that I *visite avec mon enfant.*" Slowly she stood up. "Now, I go home."

"You really okay, Marie?" That was Crystal. She and Marty were having the same thought. Who knew what might be going on behind the lovely, brown, expressionless face with its large liquid eyes? Marie might be planning to go back to her apartment, close all the windows and turn on the gas stove. It had happened. "Why don't we all have some coffee?"

"*Non, merci. Pas de café.* I am . . . very tire."

By unspoken agreement, both nurses walked Marie out, through the swinging doors and into the main lobby. Crystal kept up a steady stream of talk, about nothing, about everything, making soothing noise. Marie, her back straight and her head, wrapped in its bright yellow turban, held stiffly erect, looked straight ahead.

Just before they reached the lobby, Marty noticed Crystal's hand tightening on the other woman's arm, and she wondered what little movement had alerted Crys. Then, just before they got to the door, it happened. Marie let out a wail that sounded like the end of the world. She wrenched herself away from Crystal and turned to face them both.

"You cannot cut him into pieces. No, I cannot allow! You must give me my baby, where is he? I want my *bébé!*" She

lunged, beating with her fists on them both, their arms, their shoulders, whatever she could reach.

"Marie! No! Stop!" The girl was beyond hearing anything, and her blows were beginning to hurt, but she was moving so fast, it was hard to get a grip on her. Finally, Marty managed to grab her, holding on tightly against Marie's frantic movements. And then, suddenly, Marie went limp, falling to her knees, taking Marty crashing onto the marble floor with her.

They were holding onto each other, struggling to get up, when Gilbert rushed in, asking, "You okay, Marty?" He began yelling at Marie to calm down.

Marty didn't know who to deal with first. "Gilbert, I'm fine, please, we're both fine." And then, "*C'est bon, Marie, c'est bon.* It's okay, I forgive you." Because Marie was sobbing her apologies to *madame le docteur* for her stupidity, her foolishness.

"Shall I call a cab for her, Ms. Lamb? Or do you want her back downstairs?" Gilbert asked.

"I'll get her a cab, thanks, Gilbert," Crystal said.

"I don't think she ought to be alone, Crys, not when she's so shaky."

"Well, I don't know who could—" Crystal stopped speaking abruptly, her eyes on the front entrance, where Clive Moses had just entered in a rush.

"What's happening over here? *Marie, comment ça va?* Is she okay?" Marty couldn't help noticing that he and Crystal avoided looking at each other.

"I should see to my other patients, Marty," Crystal said, her face stony. She left, very quickly.

After a moment's silence Clive said, "As I was saying, what seems to be the problem over here? Can I help?"

"Marie's baby has had surgery, and she didn't realize, or didn't understand, that he has to stay in the NICU for a while. She thinks they've cut him with knives, or are going to. Something like that. Anyway, she's very upset because she thought she'd be able to take him home today. Dinowitz talked to her, and I thought I'd explained it all. Now I'm not sure. My French is fairly spotty."

"Well, mine's not." He took Marie's hand and, stooping just

a little so their eyes would be even, talked softly and rapidly. Marie relaxed visibly as he spoke and then began to nod. Marty heard her say, *"Oui, c'est ça, oui, oui."*

Clive turned back and smiled. "Leave this to me. I'll explain about the balloon-whatever procedure after she's calmed down. Right now, we're going shopping at the Baby Boutique for a crib and sheets and . . . you know, all that baby stuff. I'm sure we can find some money somewhere." It occurred to Marty that "somewhere" was probably Clive's wallet.

In a minute it was all smiles—although Marie's were a bit damp—and fond farewells. Marty watched Clive and the girl as they made their way down the long front walk to the street, his shoulders bent in a protecting curve over Marie. Maybe it was true love, she thought, walking back to the clinics. That would be so nice for both of them.

The loudspeakers invited her to please come to the front desk immediately. Oh Christ, what now? She'd had enough excitement for one day. "There's someone waiting for you in your office, Marty," Carmen told her, in a particular tone of voice.

Marty's chest began to hurt. It had to be Owen. Dammit, couldn't he stay away? When she opened her office door, the entire room was afloat with extra-large helium balloons, shiny silver, painted in bright colors with huge flowers and the words "I love you." There must have been twenty of them; they nearly filled the whole space.

Owen, looking pleased as punch, was sitting in her chair, twirling in it, a goofy smile on his face. He looked like an aged child. She exploded.

"Owen, you cannot come here like this! And get out of my chair!"

He looked at her blankly. Of course, he didn't move. "Hi, Marty. I'm ready to come home now."

"Well, *I'm* not ready! I'm never going to *be* ready! Get the *hell* out of my chair! *Now!*"

Again, that bland, blank stare. "I bought these balloons for you. I'm ready to come home."

"My place is not your home, Owen."

"I bought these balloons for you."

She took in a deep breath. It would not look good if she killed him in her office. She had to calm down.

"I see the balloons you bought for me."

"Don't you say thank you?"

"Thank you." Through gritted teeth. "And now, you have to leave, Owen. This is my office. This is where I work. You must go. Do you understand?"

Tears filled his eyes, and of course she instantly felt guilty. He is not my responsibility, she told herself, repeating it like a litany. "I bought these balloons for you. I'm ready to come home," he repeated.

She clenched her fists at her sides and prayed for patience. "Thank you, Owen. The balloons are very . . . pretty. But you are *not* going to live with me. No more. You have your *own* home."

There was silence for a moment. She was prepared for him to just keep repeating the same couple of sentences over and over. She'd seen this behavior before. It was as if his brain couldn't take in anything but its own thoughts; she might just as well be talking in Swahili.

Then, like a miracle, he got up from the chair and walked toward her. Feeling ashamed of herself, she backed up, trying to keep the same distance between them.

"But you have to walk me," he said.

"Of course, Owen. Where to? The front entrance?"

"All the way to the sidewalk."

"Let's go," she said, relief sweeping over her. No matter what meds they gave him, she would always be on guard, half expecting his hands to come shooting out to choke her. It wasn't fair, but the way he kept thrusting himself into her life, insisting that he belonged there, was making *her* crazy. Would she *ever* be free of him?

He followed her out; he was very quiet, and she kept turning to make sure he was still there. He seemed sad. She hardened her heart. Gilbert gave Owen a funny look, then opened the door for them to go through, and she could feel his eyes on her back as she and Owen walked, still silent, all the way down to the curb. It was close to noon and the day promised to be typi-

cal late August: hot and humid. She was sweating by the time they ended their journey.

"Good-bye, Marty," Owen said in a lugubrious voice. "I bought those balloons for you."

"Yes, Owen, I know. They're beautiful. Thank you. Good-bye."

She watched him cross the street. Owen turned to look at her and then walked on, his shoulders slumped. And damned if tears didn't come stinging at her eyes.

"Little connubial visit?" The voice at her shoulder startled her.

"Anyone ever tell you it's not polite to creep up on people, Crys?"

"I don't creep. It's my nursie shoes with their crepe soles."

"Yes, well, the visit is over, and why don't we walk together to my office and have our long overdue chat?"

As they strolled back up to the entrance, Marty said, "Where have you been? I left you in the clinics just a few minutes ago."

"More like three-quarters of an hour. I had to run upstairs. So what did he want?"

What damned nerve! Surely Crys didn't expect her to answer any personal questions! "He wanted to hire me to decorate his apartment," she said, and laughed. They were at the clinics now, and before she could say anything else, Crystal looked down at her belt and said, "My beeper." She picked it up, glanced at it, and said: "I've really got to run. Later!"

Marty had not heard the high-pitched beeping. She doubted Crystal had, either. Go ahead, Crys, she thought, keep ducking and dodging. You can't escape the inevitable. In the meantime, at least she hadn't been high for the past couple of days, not at work.

Marty let herself back into her office. If today's visit from Owen had done nothing else, it had galvanized her into action. She went plowing through the undergrowth of papers on her desk and finally came up with the phone number Joel had given her.

"Yes," she said to the voice that caroled, "Law offices of Sarah Fortgang. Can I help you?"

"I am told by Joel Mannes that you do divorces, and that's what I want—a divorce done."

It turned out to be so damned simple! They'd been apart for over seven years, and that was essentially abandonment—just like Joel had told her. And since he'd been hospitalized very recently for mental illness, that mitigated against any reconciliation and so on and so forth. In the end, Sarah Fortgang said, "Great. No problem. I'll fill out the papers, you come into my office in, oh, a week, okay? You'll sign off on everything and I'll do the rest. How's that?"

How's that? Just my freedom, that's all, my declaration of independence. That's a miracle, a magnificence, a munificence, a wonderment, the beginning of the rest of my life.

"That's fine," Marty said. "That's just fine."

She came out of her office, rather dizzy with happiness, looking for someone to tell. And there was just what the nurse ordered: Dr. Zee coming in the front entrance of the clinics, pausing to talk to Carmen.

"Julia!" she yelled, but then in a more urgent tone she shouted it: *"Julia!"* Because, like a very bad dream, Owen was right behind the doctor, pushing the big glass door open, running as fast as he could, shouting something angrily and heading straight for Dr. Zee.

Now she could hear him. "It's your fault! You told Marty those lies! It was you, and now she won't love me anymore!"

Then he saw Marty. He forgot Dr. Zee and headed for her. Marty stood frozen to the spot. What was he going to do? What should *she* do? As he ran past her, Dr. Zee put out a hand to restrain him, and he stiff-armed her. Dr. Zee went flying backward, as light as a leaf, and crumpled to the floor. Marty's head turned, for just one second, her attention on her fallen friend. In that second Owen saw his opportunity and came at her, butting her hard with his shoulder. Down she went, and he stood there for a moment, looming over her. She could hear his rasping breath. She curled up into a little ball, her arms tightly wound over her head for protection, vaguely aware that there was now a lot of shouting, the sounds of footsteps running.

She opened her eyes and peeked out from under one arm. Three or four people were coming after Owen. He whirled

around to run back out the way he'd come in, and he managed to kick her in the side on his way. She hurt but she wasn't knocked out. She was fine, she was fine. It was just that she couldn't seem to make her body move. Many pairs of feet pounded by her.

As she struggled to one elbow, trying to get her legs to follow orders, there were hands holding her, helping her up. Isabelle. Between the two of them she finally got to her feet, gingerly feeling her ribs. He'd really given her a *zetz*. And to think that a few minutes ago she'd been feeling all weepy and *sorry* for him! She was *never*, she thought mournfully, going to get rid of him, never.

"Carmen already called Security," Isabelle reported. "And Gilbert. And the cops. He's not gonna get far. Who the hell *is* he and what's he so mad at?"

"Never mind him! Dr. Zee! How's Dr. Zee?"

Dr. Zee was still on the floor, unconscious. Virgie was holding her while Paul squatted by her side, checking her vital signs. Marty pushed through the ring of patients who had inevitably gathered to see what was happening.

"Come on, people, this isn't a show. You all have appointments, go on, get back where you were."

Then Paul turned his head and shouted: "Get a gurney! This woman is ill and needs to be in a hospital bed!" His face was worried.

"Paul! What's wrong?" She looked down at Dr. Zee, crumpled on the ground, looking so frail, so . . . old, suddenly, and her heart gave a bump. "Paul, please tell me, what is it?"

"I'm not sure."

"But you think you know."

"Marty, please. I know you're concerned, but stay calm, okay? I'm not sure, I don't know. Ah, good. Lift her carefully, guys, gentle now." He waited until Dr. Zee was settled onto the gurney by two orderlies, then turned back to Marty. "You'll be the first to know. I promise." He reached out for her hand, gave it a brief squeeze. And then they all went running out toward the elevators and left her standing there, feeling very alone and very afraid.

28

Paul didn't call until nearly five o'clock. She couldn't imagine *what* the hell was going on with Dr. Zee. Well, that wasn't true. The problem was, she *could* imagine. All sorts of horrible scenarios passed through her mind, but—as she told herself firmly each time she got up to go upstairs to see for herself—she simply had to stop scaring herself with horror stories and wait until she heard from him.

She kept checking back into her office while she was making her rounds. Nothing. And then she managed to miss his call when it came. A few minutes later, when she checked again, her phone was blinking. It was Paul, although not saying what she had hoped to hear. It was brief and it was bleak. "Please come to the Family Practice floor as soon as you can, Marty." The tone of his voice told her that the news was not good.

She'd been fighting herself not to go up all afternoon, and now that she'd been called, suddenly she did not want to get up from her chair and find out what was wrong with Dr. Zee. What she wanted to do was turn back the clock, to before any of these ridiculous things had happened. But since that was impossible . . . she forced herself to her feet. A glance in the bathroom mirror showed her a worried frown and frazzled hair. She wet her hands, smoothed her hair back, and made a new ponytail. A little lipstick, a pinch on the cheeks . . . much better. The troubled look, she couldn't do anything about. She slung her handbag over her shoulder and left, so preoccupied that she took the elevator instead of running up the stairs.

On the Family Practice floor she stopped at the nursing station. The group there, all with grave faces, told her the room

number without her having to say a word. One of the young nurses called after her, "Give her our love, okay, Marty?"

Paul was standing at the window, his back to her, looking out, hands in his pockets. From the doorway she could hear the jingle of coins as he nervously clinked them. Whatever it was, it was serious.

Dr. Zee was curled on her side, her cheek resting on her hands. Marty stared hard, to make sure she was breathing. Then she tiptoed in. Paul turned and held out his arms, wordlessly. She was already crying as his arms went around her. It was bad, it was really bad.

After a minute or two he walked them both out into the hallway, closing the door halfway, but standing where he could see the bed.

"I've been thinking and thinking about how to tell you, and I've decided I just have to say it. It's AIDS."

"No! It couldn't be!"

"You know that sore throat that wouldn't go away? Marty, she has thrush."

"Thrush! But nobody gets thrush . . . ! Oh."

"Yes. Oh. HIV-positives get thrush. They get lots of stuff we all thought was gone forever. She doesn't have pneumonia yet, thank God, but still . . . And she's so goddamn thin . . ." He groaned. "I've seen too many good people taken by this damn thing!"

Marty began to leak tears. "But . . . how?"

"Shhhh . . . she's stirring. Come on."

They went in. Julia gave Marty a weak smile, which only made the tears flow faster. "Aw, Marty, I'm sorry. The last thing I want to do is make you cry."

"*You're* sorry . . . because I'm crying? Christ, Julia . . . !"

"Easy. Easy. You can cry if you want. God knows I did enough of it, when I first realized. I've known for a while that I'm HIV-positive. But I was without symptoms for so long . . . eight years. . . . I guess I thought some kind of magic was going to keep me from the bad stuff. But now it's started, and so . . ." She closed her eyes momentarily. "I've made my peace with it. But it's hard to face, I know. I was so worried, that you'd guess what it might be. Well, finally, you did."

"No I didn't. I'm dumb. Paul just told me, and even then I didn't want to believe it. I still don't," she added stubbornly.

"I know. But I'm afraid it's true. I'm HIV-positive, all right." She turned to look directly at Paul. "So. What bug have I got?"

"Just the thrush ... the sores, you know about. No pneumonia."

"Not pneumonia! Good. Then I have some time. And I had a lot of good years—I can't complain. When this so-called summer cold wouldn't go away, then I knew. It was time to leave."

"That's why you resigned. Well, it's not fair!" Marty cried. She couldn't help it; the tears just kept coming. "It's not right! You're a doctor!"

Dr. Zee began to laugh, but it made her cough. "And that makes me immune? Come on, Marty! Look. Let's stop talking about it for a minute. My voice is going." It was true, she sounded more feeble with every word. "There are more important things we have to discuss. First, Isabelle's mother. I'm going to get out of here, and as soon as I do, I'll be ready to go see her. *If* she still wants me. Will you tell Isabelle?"

"Of course." Marty opened her mouth again, closed it, then decided to hell with it. "I'm sorry, I can't stand here and talk about the work you have to do, and just pretend you have a little sore throat, a little cough. How in hell ... ?"

"Did I get AIDS? Oh, lord ..." The eyes closed and Marty had a horrible moment of thinking death had suddenly come. But the doctor was only gathering her reserves. She patted the side of the bed and said, "I'm not sure how long I can gab ... my throat hurts a bit. ... Now, Marty, you have to stop crying. I'm not dead *yet*. I'm going to get back on my feet, you'll see. I'm a tough old bird, haven't you noticed?"

"Okay. I'll be good." She gave Dr. Zee a rather watery smile.

"Okay. Eight years ago, there was a story in the papers about a married man who discovered he had AIDS, yet he denied being gay, and he'd never had a homosexual experience. He said.

"That man was my patient. He came to me, asking about a

discoloration on his chest. . . . I knew right away it was Kaposi's sarcoma, but I had a complete blood workup done, anyway. HIV-positive. He . . . he couldn't deal with it. We were even more panicky about AIDS in 1987. Nobody knew much except that it was certain death. . . ." Dr. Zee's voice trailed off and she closed her eyes again.

"You're tired." Paul leaned over the bed. "We can come back."

"I get tired. But no, don't go." She visibly pulled herself together.

"You said he couldn't deal with it," Marty said. "What did he do?"

"He became obsessed. How could this have happened to him? It was impossible. . . ." She stopped talking, but lifted one hand to tell them to wait. "I knew how. It was his wife. She'd had a one-night stand the year before, the man was AC-DC, and—

"She had no idea. I know that, because they had recently had a baby and *he* was HIV-positive. In fact, when I saw the results on the child's test, that's when I found out. Mother to fetus is one of the sure ways to spread it."

"You *knew*?" Paul was aghast. "And you didn't tell her? You didn't prepare her? You didn't let her *know*?"

"Yes." The doctor looked more than sad, she looked defeated. "The law is that all newborns are tested for the virus, but we are not allowed to inform the parents. I know, I know . . . it's crazy. So . . . I could do nothing. Somehow my patient found out. . . . He went a little crazy. He charged into my office, with a syringe of his own blood, yelling. He didn't make any sense. . . ." She paused to catch her breath. "I decided to be a hero . . . to grab the syringe . . . and . . . it stuck me. Accidentally."

"Oh, Christ, an *accident*!" Marty breathed.

"I put myself on AZT right away and got the treatment against AIDS-related pneumonia. I went to a city hospital downtown," she explained. "I didn't want anyone here to know that I had tested positive before it was necessary. I double-gloved for everything. I was very careful. So much

time went by and nothing happened, no symptoms. I thought I had escaped. And then I actually forgot about it. . . ."

"Who knew it could take so long to incubate?" Paul said. "We were so ignorant. Hell, we still are. It's been so long, and where's the cure, goddammit. Where's the *cure*?"

"How long . . . ?" Marty couldn't finish the sentence.

"Since I was sure? My summer cold. I kept hoping it was only a summer cold." She gave them a wry smile. She was actually looking better, Marty thought. Maybe it *had* been the fall . . . And then she stopped herself. Talk about denial!

"But then the weight kept falling off," Dr. Zee said, looking ruefully at her body, which, Marty noted, barely made a bump in the bed. How could she have thought her friend's sudden weight loss was normal?

"The worst thing . . ." Dr. Zee started. "Yes, the worst. My G.P. was an old friend, Mel Sorensen. We met in medical school. When the sore throat wouldn't go away, I went to him. He took a look and said, 'If I didn't know better, I'd say you had thrush, Julia!' I told him to get his hand away from my mouth, shouted at him. And then I told him I thought it was probably AIDS."

She paused, drawing in rasping breaths. "As soon as I said the dreaded word, he . . . retreated. He actually backed away from me, as if my very breath was contaminated. In a way, I couldn't blame him. But still . . ."

There was another very long pause. Neither Marty nor Paul moved a muscle. "And then Mel said, 'Of course, Julia, under these circumstances, I can't treat you. I can't take any chances with my other patients. You understand?' I understood." Beat. "But why couldn't we be friends? He never even answered my phone calls. Well. I'm not so sure I would have behaved any better."

"And I," Marty said stoutly, "am sure you *would* have. Paul and I are not going to desert you . . . we'll see you through to the—" She choked on the word *end*. "As everyone else around here will do, too!"

"We'll see, won't we," Dr. Zee said, "once the word gets out?" She gazed at them, leaving both of them with nothing to say.

Marty and Paul walked down the stairs to the clinics together, hand in hand, not talking. What was there to say? It was horrible. Marty's thoughts kept veering away from the central fact. She wondered what had become of the man who had infected Dr. Zee. She wondered if their baby had died already. Everyone died of AIDS, everyone. It was only by a tremendous effort of will that she kept herself from bursting into tears.

Still not speaking, they both went into Marty's office. Her answering machine was blinking. The message was from Max, advising her to make herself available for an emergency meeting tomorrow afternoon at five-thirty. She had a sinking feeling that this particular emergency was spelled D-O-C-T-O-R-Z-E-E.

Paul said it aloud. "Dr. Zee, I bet."

"And I bet it won't be to give her an award for her years of service," Marty said. "You should be at the meeting, Paul. After all, she named you acting chief."

"But I'm not acting chief yet. Anyway, I wasn't invited."

"They probably don't want anyone who might be on her side."

"Whoa, Marty, you don't know what they're going to say or do."

"Oh yes I do. And so do you, and you know it."

"We're only guessing. And you're getting emotional already, before you even know—"

She smiled a bit grimly. "That's the difference between doctors and nurses. We allow ourselves to *feel*." She was instantly ashamed; what a stupid thing to say. "Please forget I said that. I apologize."

"I'll give you a chance to really make up with me, where making up is the most fun."

She smiled and took his hand, but she wondered if she could make love tonight. She was feeling so bereft. She'd already lost her mother. She didn't know how she could stand it happening again.

"I can't stay here. I can't bear looking at papers," Marty said. They left her office and immediately spotted the two cops

up front near Carmen's desk, the growing crowd around them. They both ran.

"What's going on?" Marty said. "I'm the director."

The two policemen were both young and both a bit out of breath. One of them said, "We chased him. The guy who came running out of here earlier, the guy who attacked the director. Oh. I guess that's you."

"You chased him and—"

"He ducked down into the subway. Vaulted over the turnstile, I don't know how, it's supposed to be impossible, and caught a train downtown. We called it in. The transit cops all looked for him. But the subway . . . He could be anywhere now. Sorry."

Marty took in a deep breath. "I'm sure you did your best, officer. And don't worry, he'll surface. He's kind of obsessed with me . . . he's mentally ill."

"One of your patients?"

"No. He's . . . I know him. I used to know him."

"You want to make a complaint?"

Marty looked at Paul. He shrugged. Did she want to make a complaint? Yes. No. Oh hell. "If he turns up here again, officer, I'll call. How's that?"

"Up to you, ma'am." As the officers left, Marty turned to the group of onlookers and said, "That's all, folks. Back where you belong, please."

This place was getting on her nerves. "I'm outta here," she said to Paul. "How about you?"

"I'm with you." They left, walking slowly up Van Dam Avenue, hand in hand. The evening was heavy with impending storms, but at least there was a cool breeze.

"Do you realize? It's almost the end of summer," Marty remarked. "And to think, I was afraid it would never end. We have only two weeks until the accreditation team arrives, and nothing real has been done."

"So what else is new?" Paul said, trying for a light tone. "The hospital doesn't have the money. And with the national health plan falling to pieces, everyone's busy hedging their bets, treading water until they see which way Congress'll go."

"Everyone is worried about *their* unit, *their* patients, *their*

job. Me, too, I guess. If CCC goes . . ." She didn't finish the thought out loud. Maybe this time she and Paul would make it work. She waited for him to say something, something like, "If CCC goes, you'll always have me." *Anything*. But he was silent. So she quickly revised her thoughts: maybe she'd head back to New England, see what was doing in Middletown or maybe a hospital in Newport, give herself a brand-new start. She didn't need a man to make her complete, she told herself bravely. No, she didn't; but she was very afraid that she *did* need Paul Giordano, only she couldn't take any chances this time. This time she was going to keep herself safe from heartache.

She almost walked by the Brown apartment, without looking for the beautiful face in the window. But Shayna's voice, even pitched as low as it was, got her attention.

"Wait, Paul. Shayna's calling me."

"I'll go home and start dinner," he said, holding his hand out for her keys, asking no questions.

"Shhhh . . ." Shayna warned when Marty had edged herself past the shrubs, close up against the opened window. "We have to whisper. Did you get my message? Selma promised me. She promised she'd call from a pay phone."

"I didn't get it, but don't be mad at Selma. Someone—" She stopped. Shayna didn't have to know. "I haven't been getting all my messages."

"Saturday night, when the Sabbath is ended, he is giving a party. For me. For my . . . *betrothal*." Even whispered, the word was laced with acid. "So soon after Mama's death! I tell him it is shameful. He says it is in her memory, in her honor, do you believe it?"

"Oh, Shayna, I'm so sorry. I really am." Marty was ashamed of her next words, even as she spoke them. "He thinks he's doing something good for you . . . normalizing your life. It's an act of love." And who knew? Maybe it was even true.

She could see Shayna's lips curl in disdain. "He doesn't love me, Marty, he only wants to get rid of me so I'll be somebody else's problem. And . . . well, I did something a little stupid. But I was so mad at him!"

"What, Shayna?"

"I told him that wasn't the first time Mama went to the hospital for an abortion. I told him—never mind, I said things I shouldn't have. That's when he announced to me that I will be betrothed on Saturday. He is punishing me, Marty."

"But Shayna, surely your husband will find out. And quickly."

"This man ... Sammy Halpern ... he's ... not exactly normal, Marty. Even if he goes to his father to complain, his father won't do anything. You don't understand—they worship the sainted rabbi. Nobody will tell on him. And I—" Her voice broke.

Marty stood under the window, her hand up on the screen, feeling helpless and angry. "I wish ... is there anything I can do?"

"No, no, I have it all planned. At this betrothal, I'm going to do it. I'm going to tell them all my horrible secret. Can you imagine his face?"

"Please don't, Shayna, he's very ... excitable lately."

"You think I care if he shoots me with his gun, Marty?"

"Don't destroy your own life just to spite your father. Think about what you're doing, okay?"

"Believe me, I've been thinking. And it's not just for spite. If you met my husband-to-be, you'd understand I'm doing this for my sake. There's something wrong with Sammy, Marty. My father who loves me so much is giving me to a mindless idiot."

If only she could do something, Marty thought. Anything. But the rabbi wouldn't let her in. And for this kind of assault, you couldn't call the cops.

"Don't do anything stupid, okay? And remember, I'm just a couple of blocks away. Send someone to get me, if you need me. They can't *all* be blind to your feelings."

Without warning Shayna turned away from the window, calling out "Just a moment! I have no clothes on! None at all!" Then she turned back to Marty, smiling. "He's gone. You see, Marty? I am clever, in my own way. And he'll have to leave soon, so he can talk on television again." She gave a low laugh. "He is in love with that television studio, Marty. He tells us all about it, the hot lights, the cameraman, the hand signals to

speed up or slow down. The electronic pulpit, he calls it. He thinks he is a prophet or something." Her head turned again. "He wants to see me before he goes. You'd better leave. Don't worry, I'll be fine. Go, go."

Marty went. Walking home, she tried to convince herself that Shayna was right, that she'd be fine. But Marty had a feeling that no good could come from the betrothal party on Saturday night, no good at all.

Paul buzzed her in and she found him putting together a very creditable *salade Nicoise* when she walked into the apartment. The sight of him warmed her. So big in the tiny kitchen, a bath towel wrapped around his waist as an apron, totally concentrated on his chore, humming along with Billie Holiday singing "In My Solitude." He was so dear. He was so dear to *her*. How could she have doubts?

She marched into the kitchen, grabbed him and gave him a great big smooch. "You look so cute when you're cooking," she said. "I couldn't resist."

"Hey, if this is what I get, I'll cook every night. Glass of our best red?"

"Lay it on me."

"Later," he said, and they both laughed.

Actually, later, although they *were* lying in her bed together, covered by as little as possible, they were not making love, as planned. Instead, they shared a pint of Ben & Jerry's Cherry Garcia, passing it back and forth, their eyes glued to the TV screen where Rabbi Ezekiel Brown was haranguing his invisible audience from Channel 87. Marty wondered what he was going to do with the information Shayna had given him. One thing was sure, he wasn't going to ignore it.

The rabbi was sitting, and viewers only saw him from the waist up. The viewpoint never changed, the camera never moved closer or pulled away. Marty couldn't help thinking that this was exactly how he let the world see his daughter. He spoke directly to the camera, and surprisingly, he spoke quietly and very earnestly.

". . . it is, of course, a question of *respect*," he was saying as they tuned in. "Do our doctors and our hospitals have any

respect for those who have faith in the Holy One, the creator? I am sorry to say, the answer is no.

"I don't care who you pray to," he said, leaning forward a little, "it is to God, and God hears all prayers. I don't care what you believe in, because you believe in God and God accepts all beliefs. Science and medicine . . . *they* are the narrow-minded ones. They accept nothing outside their narrow creed, their so-called proof . . ."

It was all very calm and a bit boring, she thought. She'd been wrong about his using anything he could to discredit the hospital. She was about to suggest to Paul that they change the channel, when Zeke's voice took on a sharper edge. "In my congregation, life is sacred. The Almighty, blessed be He, gives life and He alone takes it away. Abortion is abomination!" With every word, he was becoming more intense, and he had begun to pound a fist softly on the table in front of him, for emphasis.

"A woman carries new life within her body. This is her sacred task. To murder this life is against divine law. Murder was the first crime in the Bible, brother against brother . . . and the Lord put a mark on Cain's forehead to set him apart from humanity. Why? Because he was now subhuman! And if a mother should murder her child, is she not also subhuman?"

Marty was becoming restless. "What the hell is Messinger talking about: slander? What slander? It's just the usual: a man who thinks he knows what God is thinking. Why don't we—" And then she stopped because she heard the words All Souls.

" . . . a hospital dedicated to saving lives, you say? I say a hospital dedicated to abomination. They turned my own wife away from her husband, her beliefs, her society. They made her less than human. They told her to murder her unborn children, not one, not two, but *many*!" He was now ranting in his Rabbi Voice, his dark eyes fierce in their anger. "And then, when they thought she would tell me, they killed *her* . . . Dr. Milton Messinger, Dr. Dennis Dinowitz, Dr. Julia Zachary-Felsen, Nurse Practitioner Marty Lamb . . ."

She and Paul looked at each other, a bit stunned. Having ended his list of guilty parties, the rabbi sat back a bit and, once again in his reasonable voice, suggested that All Souls be

forced to close down. "Not just because it is filled with the god-less, but because of its many health violations. This hospital could kill *you*." He lifted a sheaf of papers and shook them like a rattle. "I have the figures and the facts." His eyes shifted, and apparently he had been given the signal to stop, because he added, "Until next time," and the camera shifted from him to another talking head, this one a woman who wanted to discuss the Nazis on the Board of Education.

"Okay," Marty said, turning the set off. "Now I see what Dr. Messinger was talking about. Zeke is out of control! Isn't there a lawyer in the Survivors who could tell him about the laws of libel and slander?"

Paul, thoughtful, said, "Maybe he knows exactly what he's doing. Maybe he *wants* a lawsuit. Then he gets a whole new audience."

"I think he's gone off the deep end. And I'm worried for Shayna—" She stopped. She hadn't told him about her recent conversations with Shayna. "You know, he recently bought a handgun."

"Him and everyone else in New York. You know what your trouble is, Marty?" he asked, nuzzling her neck. "You worry about everybody. You worry too much. Let me take your mind off the rabbi and the hospital." His hands began a slow and expert journey around her body, and sure enough, she stopped thinking about anything at all.

29

She was going to be late to the meeting and Messinger wasn't going to like it, but tough, Marty thought. She wanted to see Dr. Zee first. Anyone could guess what the meeting was going to cover, and she wanted as much ammunition as

she could muster. The word was out that Dr. Zee had AIDS, and so, of course, a lot of the patients had gone ballistic. Some of the staff, too. It was understandable, maybe, but it still made her mad.

Carmen told her, her voice thick with outrage, that many of Dr. Zee's patients, "Oh yeah, the very ones who last week called her a saint and kissed her hand," had been jamming the phone lines, castigating CCC for not knowing, for letting a sick doctor practice here, for keeping it a secret.

"What I want to know, Marty, is how the hell can we not know and be keeping it a secret, both at the same time? And how do they find out how long she's been HIV-positive? How come they can list her every symptom, true or not? They know Dr. Zee. They should know she would never take a chance—" Carmen shook her head at the perfidy of the human race. "It's a damn shame. What, she's any different a person today than she was last week? What, she doesn't know what precautions to take, a smart doctor like her? She never heard of double gloving? What is their *problem*?"

Marty had no answers for Carmen; she was sick over the whole damn thing herself. You could tell people over and over that they weren't going to catch the HIV virus with a handshake or even a hug and kiss . . . you could explain and explain. They still panicked. In any case, procedure in the Family Practice clinic meant that doctors never gave shots or took bloods; the nurses did that sort of thing. But Marty knew that none of that mattered now. In the end, dread and terror always took over.

Well, let's see if she could find something to say on Dr. Zee's behalf at this meeting. Dammit, a medical career spanning almost half a century couldn't just be dismissed with the snap of Messinger's fingers!

But when she got upstairs, Dr. Zee was sleeping, and the duty nurse said no way was she waking her, she was still very sick. "It's like the bad old days," the nurse said sadly, "when patients came to the hospital to die. I'm sorry, Marty, I didn't mean she's necessarily—oh, never mind, I'm sorry. She's a tough old bird, right?" The nurse looked around for a piece of wood to knock on for luck.

Marty dashed off to the meeting and was a little bit out of breath when she opened the door to the Conference Room; but it seemed they had all decided to wait for her. No business was being transacted, and in fact all conversation came to an abrupt halt when she appeared.

"Ah. Ms. Lamb. You are late."

"Sorry." She wasn't going to say what had delayed her.

"Let us begin, then." Dr. Messinger looked down at some papers in his hand, but not before he slid her an enigmatic look. "I had planned to discuss Rabbi Brown and his excursion into, ah, the public eye. But we have more urgent matters to take up. I will say that our lawyers are preparing a complaint against him. Libel, I believe."

"You're forgetting," Joel Mannes put in, "the part about Dr. Zee." Marty turned her gaze on Messinger, and he nodded for Joel to go on. "Late this afternoon, Rabbi Brown went on Channel 87 for fifteen minutes. During which time, he wanted the public to know that All Souls is quote a house of corruption unquote, since Dr. Zee is carrying a plague and the hospital is covering it up. Oh, and then he added, 'as usual.' Isn't that about it?" Joel finished, addressing Messinger, who nodded again.

They were all looking at her, Marty noticed, waiting for her to tell them what they should do about the rabbi. She didn't own Zeke Brown, she wasn't his confidante, and she certainly didn't have any influence over him. Nobody did!

"You want to know what I think about Rabbi Brown? I think he's dangerous. I think he's behaving irrationally. I think we should go to the apartment and get his crippled daughter the hell out of there!"

"Excuse me, Marty, but we aren't a social service agency, you know," Aimee said.

"Nor the police," Fassbinder grumped.

"He has an agenda of his own, and it doesn't include Shayna's well-being, I can tell you that! She's a sick girl, a very sick girl, who needs special care, and he's been denying her that care since her birth! He's an unfit parent!"

"Aimee is right; we are not here to do social work, Ms. Lamb." Messinger's lips had thinned with irritation. "If you

think the man is abusing his daughter, I suggest you call the proper authorities."

Marty wanted to laugh. "Are you referring by any chance to a city agency? You can't be serious."

He leveled a look at her that could topple tall buildings. "Totally serious. And now, the next item on the agenda."

She looked down at the brief typed list at her place. Of course. *Julia Zachary-Felsen.*

"I think we will all agree that Dr. Zachary-Felsen should be moved as soon as possible to the St. Clement's AIDS Hospice—"

"Move her! What for? Everyone here knows and loves her! And she's still an attending in this hospital!"

Messinger was maddeningly reasonable. "Now, Marty, Dr. Zee has tendered her resignation. And in the present situation—"

"Now that we know she has AIDS, you mean. We're all medical professionals in this room. We know you can't catch it by touching her. Or even kissing her."

She caught a little shudder, not only from Messinger but from Fassbinder and from Dr. Dimwit and, yes, Aimee Delano, too. The tremor made its way around the table and was gone.

"Marty, we all know how fond of Dr. Zee you are," Dennis Dinowitz said in a kindly tone that set her teeth on edge. "We know that you two have a deep friendship, outside of the hospital setting. And we all understand your concern. But please, be reasonable. People are terrified of AIDS, and for good reason." She couldn't look at him. It was all true, of course, but at the same time it was completely beside the point.

"We *can't* keep her here," Len Fassbinder huffed. "Patients would run screaming from the hospital."

"Oh, Len, that's just not true. Dr. Zee is beloved."

Fassbinder regarded her sadly. "Patients are calling in, cancelling their appointments. Not just with her, with many of the doctors. And we're getting a lot of complaints."

Messinger spoke, in a much harsher tone. "Personally, I find it unconscionable," he said, "that one of our attending physicians, knowing herself to be HIV-positive, would allow herself

to get sick and never discuss it with anyone. Not even with you, Marty, isn't that right? She had an obligation to her patients, and to this hospital."

Marty opened her mouth, but his basilisk stare stopped her. He was right. They all were. Why had Julia kept it such a secret, why hadn't she confided in *someone*? What could she have been thinking?

Joel spoke. "All of this is true. But perhaps we *are* over-reacting. Surely Dr. Zee can remain upstairs while she is sick and bedridden. When . . . if . . . she recovers from this bout of infection, I'm sure she will, ah, cooperate." He shot Marty a look, as if to ask, *How'm I doing?*

"Yes," Marty was eager to agree. "Can't we just wait until she recovers?"

Messinger looked around the table and then gave a nod. "Very well. Meanwhile, we are following her suggestion to have Dr. Giordano step in as interim chief until—well, until we know better what's happening with the hospital."

"Excuse me," Marty said, grateful for the change of subject. "But just what does that mean, Dr. Messinger? What *is* happening with the hospital?"

"I was of course referring to the arrival in two weeks of the team from JCAHO, either the Monday or the Tuesday." He looked at her briefly, then away. "This will interest all of you. They will begin by looking over our policy and procedure manuals and then proceed with investigations of our entire operation. I needn't tell this group that there are problems, many problems. But we have complied on many levels. For instance, every member of the Medical Staff has agreed to rescind their recent, ah, raise in pay." He paused, preening a bit and looking every bit as if he expected applause. "We do have plans to cut certain . . . ah, frills. Later, Ms. Lamb, there will be time later to hear your objections—if any. There *will* be certain, ah, cuts, but nothing you need concern yourself about." Fat chance, Marty thought, but she kept her mouth shut. *That* ought to get some applause.

She felt eyes boring into her and she turned. Joel was staring a message at her. Probably he had something interesting to pass on to her.

"And so. Back to Dr. Zachary-Felsen. We should decide how to divide her private patient load so there is a minimum of disruption ..." Messinger's voice droned on, giving away pieces of Dr. Zee first to this service and then to that one. It wasn't fair. And they were moving so *fast*; Julia was in a bed upstairs, for Christ's sake! Marty could hardly wait for the meeting to be over. When it was, she scraped back her chair, making as much noise as she could, and stomped out. Childish, yes, and it didn't even make her feel better.

The cafeteria was pretty quiet. It was seven-ten. Marty got herself an iced coffee, extra strong, and made herself sit down and *sip* it. It took four and a half minutes to finish the damn thing and she was still annoyed. Damn them, didn't they have any loyalty to a colleague, a comrade? She blinked back tears. She was doing too much crying lately. An older nurse had told her, way back when she was first in training in Boston: "This is a job full of tears." Marty remembered how she had thought the nurse was too old to be working, that she had lost it. How old could that nurse have been? Forty? We mock the thing we are to be, she thought. Who said that? And then she remembered and it made her laugh out loud. Mel Brooks, as the two-thousand-year-old man. Not some philosopher or great thinker, but a comedian.

"I thought you might be here. So tell me what's funny. I need a good joke." Joel slid into the chair opposite her.

"No joke, Joel. Just me, remembering when I thought a nurse in her forties was an old fogey. Suddenly, I'm closer than I'd like to be."

"Aren't we all. Old fogeydom lurks around the corner. Look. Sorry about Dr. Zee. But you can see that the hospital has to—"

"Yes, yes," she interrupted. "I do understand. I really do. I just hate it, that's all."

"Anyway, even if it were possible, do you think she'd like to come back to find her patients shrinking back from her? Or just not showing? You think she'd enjoy the sheepish, defiant looks she'd get from those who left her for another doctor?" He put a hand over hers.

"You gave me a look in the meeting," she said, changing the

subject. "Something juicy?" If he told her he was having an affair with Crystal, how should she react? Surprised? Calm? Nonjudgmental? None of the above. She was going to be straight with him. An old dear friend deserved that much. And if he wanted her advice, she knew what she was going to tell him: get away and stay away. He'd want to know why she was so adamant, and then she could tell him what she'd been figuring out. Now, at last, she'd be able to tell him her fears and, especially, her suspicions, about Ms. Crystal Cole. She had to talk to *somebody*; it was beginning to add up to such a creepy conclusion, she didn't want to face it alone.

But he didn't mention Crys. "Remember how mad you were when the Medical Staff got all those perks, and more money, to boot?" he asked.

"You bet I remember."

"Here's how it happened. Well, when the Medical Staff first asked Messinger for higher fees and all that stuff, Messinger said sorry, we can't afford it. So dear Dennis had a closed-door meeting with the boss man. You know that Dennis is president of the Medical Staff, right? And Dennis told him, 'Here's the cost to you if you roll over and give us what we want. Here's the cost if we all leave this hospital and go to Harmony Hill, and all your admissions go to Harmony Hill *with* us.' "

"He didn't mean it, did he?"

"Do *I* know? Probably not. But Messinger made a quick decision to pay us off. Well, you know what's been going on with the stock market, and the real estate market, and the supermarket. Everything plummeting down. So suddenly there's no money and reimbursements from the state and the fed funds are cut, and here's Messinger with a deal he can no longer afford.

"So he called a meeting last week with the Medical Staff and told us he'd thought of cutting hours; but hey, the JCAHO is on the job. What'll *they* think? Of course, we could always fire some nurses and hire nice cheap nurses' aides—now Marty, don't hit me, *I* didn't say it, Messinger did. I even argued against it, and surprise surprise, so did Dimwit.

"That didn't leave many ways to cut costs except givebacks from the Medical Staff. Dennis said no way. Messinger said he

could fire us all. Dennis said we could just all walk out and that would be the end of All Souls.

"And that, my dear, is why Dr. Messinger suddenly got so cozy with Eliot Wolfe of Harmony Hill. He called Dimwit's bluff! 'You won't play ball? I'll sell the ballpark.' Isn't it beautiful? And then he called Dennis back in, and this time, of course, the Medical Staff was willing to capitulate. It may be too late, though. It could be we won't have to walk out, we'll all be out of work anyway! Or at least demoted, made to serve and sweat under Harmony Hill's slavemasters."

She gave Joel a wan smile. "I can't really appreciate the irony right now, not with Dr. Zee on my mind. Actually," she added after a moment, "I don't find the thought of being a satellite of Harmony Hill so awfully awful. Eliot Wolfe strikes me as pretty damn smart. He won't fire everyone, because that would be stupid." She could see Joel was a bit puzzled by her reaction; he had expected her to enjoy thinking of Dennis with egg on his face. Well, her relationship with Dr. Dimwit had undergone a small but significant change. But she couldn't very well talk to Joel about it, not without opening up his own can of worms. And that had to be *his* job, not hers.

"Sorry, Joel, but I really have to see Julia. Later!" She blew him a kiss and hurried for the elevators, praying that Dr. Zee would be awake this time.

Dr. Zee was not asleep. In fact, she was coming out of the bathroom by herself, a bit weak, a bit shaky, grabbing onto furniture and walls as she made her way around the room, but nonetheless getting there.

"Julia! We have a brand-new thing in this hospital. It's a call button. You push it and a nurse comes."

"Very funny," the doctor said, her voice a bit weak but no longer hoarse. She sat down abruptly on the edge of the bed, slumping a little. "I guess I'm not quite as tough as I like to think I am."

"You're tough enough, but listen, you just got here. Healing takes time. Paul says you're getting better; why push yourself before you're ready?"

"I'm afraid I may never be ready again. And now I *am* sorry. That was self-serving. I escaped for a long time. I can't com-

plain. I guess a lot of bugs have found me and they're spreading the word. But there are a couple of things I have to do before I go."

Marty took in a deep breath. Then she let it out and told the doctor what had transpired in the meeting—except for the part where Messinger suggested she be transferred to an AIDS facility.

When she had finished, Dr. Zee stared off into space for a minute or two. Then she said, "I'm not surprised. At the patients. I'm really not. The imminence of death is something nobody wants to look at. And I have it, shining out of me like a bright light. Aw, Marty, don't cry, honey, not for me. Help me back into this bed, would you? Tell me the latest gossip. Let's talk about something else, anything else. And then there's something I want you to see."

Marty plumped pillows and settled Dr. Zee against them, still fighting tears. But she'd been asked to make conversation, so here goes, she thought. "Have you been filled in on Zeke Brown and his latest? No? Well, you know he's been buying himself time on Channel 87, giving hell to the hospital for quote killing Miriam and all those babies, for defying God's will, for giving abortions, for quote covering up your illness, Julia. He started fairly slowly, for him, mostly religious talk, very biblical, a lot of rhetoric. But now he's naming names, calling us murderers, and that, apparently, is libelous or slanderous. Or, for all I know, both."

"He's always been a man on the edge, we both know that," Dr. Zee said. "And, you know, he adored Miriam, he really did. Arranged marriage or not, he was madly in love with his wife. If you think about it, he even forgave her the worst sin of all—producing damaged children. Of course," the doctor managed a half smile, "it was *her* genetic material that was faulty. Of course. But still . . . he had every reason to divorce her and he didn't. He loved her."

"It would be nice if he could transfer some of that feeling to his daughter. There's to be a betrothal party Saturday night. And Shayna says there's something mentally wrong with the fiancé."

"Oh, God. Zeke really *is* a brute, isn't he? I don't
suppose . . ."

"There's anything we can do? I can't think what."

"Give me a day or two, maybe I can think of something.
God knows I have enough time up here," Dr. Zee said, her eyes
closing again.

"Shayna has some kind of plan of her own, so she tells me."

The doctor's eyes flew open. "A plan of her own? That's not
good. She hasn't been asking for sleeping pills, has she?"

"Stupid me. That didn't occur to me, that she might want to
O.D. on something. But no. She doesn't seem depressed, just
angry and determined." Watching her friend's eyes close once
more, Marty said, "You're tired and I'm not helping. You go to
sleep. I'll come back later."

But the doctor shook her head, gesturing to the nightstand.
"In the drawer . . ." she said.

The minute she saw the plain gray hospital envelope,
Marty's heart began to beat hard. Oh, no, not Julia, not *now*!
But it *was*. A message from the poison pen writer: a page
copied from one of the medical journals, listing the various
opportunistic infections that struck HIV-positive patients, the
prognosis for each, and how many thousands had died so far.
Nothing was underlined or circled and there was no printed
commentary. "I found this in my office a few days ago . . .
before I came up here," Dr. Zee said, reaching to take a sip of
water.

"She's sicker than I thought," Marty said, half to herself.

"Who?"

"The person who's sending these. She can't even leave *you*
alone. What I can't figure is, why is she so angry at everyone?"

She'd been wanting to discuss this problem with Dr. Zee for
weeks. But looking at the drawn face, the dark circles under the
eyes, she thought, not now. Maybe in a few days. By then she
would have had it out with the guilty party and would have
some kind of proof. She hoped.

"Anyway," Marty finished, "she should be ashamed of herself for picking on you. What I can't figure is, how did she
know? You said it came before Owen knocked you down."

"A lucky guess. Or somebody figured out that my cold and

sore throat was lasting longer than it should. I kept denying it, hoping it would magically go away." Dr. Zee sighed and shook her head. "I can't say I'm surprised to end up here, staring death in the face. In a way, it's my turn." She spoke softly and carefully. "My husband died slowly and horribly. Cancer. And our son . . . muscular dystrophy. Not Duchenne's, not genetic, just, oh, bad luck. He went very slowly, too. They were both . . . so brave." She had been staring out at nothing in particular; now she turned her tired gaze on Marty. "I'm not so sure I can be as brave as they were. I watched it happen, twice. After he died . . . my son . . . I swore I would never allow anyone to die so slowly and painfully, inch by crushing inch. That's why I help people to die, Marty. So now I've said it out loud. I doubt they'll put me in jail. It's a little late for that. And when the time comes, I may ask for that help myself."

Marty did not move, nor did Dr. Zee. They sat without speaking, eyes locked, until a silent promise had been asked for, and given.

30

She could hear them talking, out in the hall. Did he think her ears were crippled? Did he think she was too stupid or too sick to listen? Sometimes, Shayna tried to figure out exactly *how* her father thought of her. Because she had no legs to speak of, did he somehow think she had no mind? Could he be so stupid? He was supposed to be a smart man—brilliant, even. But there he was, standing right outside her open bedroom door, talking in a loud voice . . . and she could hear every word.

"Now, Selma, I'm trusting you with my precious daughter. You understand?" She had asked him for Selma; she told him she missed her mother and that nobody would do but the

woman who had been her mother's closest friend, so Selma
had been called in to care for her. He had stared at her for a
minute or two, thinking, and she was so afraid he would guess
why she wanted a woman to stay with her. Oh please, he
mustn't know what was in her mind. He must never know how
she began to sweat every time he opened the door to her room.
He had such a silent tread. Sometimes in the night she would
hear the old floors in the apartment creaking and groaning, and
she would lie there, holding her breath and praying it wasn't
him, sneaking down the hall. But it never happened again. And
so when she asked for Selma, Selma came. Selma was above
all eager to please.

"Oh certainly, Rabbi. She is precious to all of us."

"Anything you see, this does not go outside these walls, you
understand?"

"Of course, Rabbi. I know my duty."

He meant, *Don't you dare tell anyone that my daughter is
disfigured, blemished, imperfect.* And Selma knew it. But
Selma also knew all about Shayna. All the women had
guessed, or found out, long ago. Only the men—"they don't
see what they don't want to see"—were in ignorance.

Selma had come into Shayna's room a few minutes ago to
take away the breakfast tray. Most of the food sat untouched.
Selma gave the tray a baleful look and clucked her tongue, but
said nothing, just removed it and helped Shayna sit up, putting
five or six plump pillows behind her. The effort of simply sitting had exhausted Shayna—she tired so easily these days. She
let the book Selma had handed to her drop. It was too heavy for
her to hold, anyway. She closed her eyes and tried to think
about nothing.

She might have dozed, it was hard to tell. Since Mama died,
she felt like someone in a state somewhere between sleep and
waking. When she opened her eyes, Selma was tiptoeing
around her room.

"It's all right, Selma. I'm not really sleeping."

Selma jumped a little and looked over at Shayna guiltily.
What did she have to be guilty about? Selma was here to be her
slave. . . . Well, that's what it *was.* She wasn't being paid to
be here all day long, to cook so that he and Shayna could eat.

She was doing it for her beloved rabbi; oh, and of course, in memory of her dear dead friend, Miriam. Just the thought of her mother's name brought tears to Shayna's eyes. She tried so hard not to think about her mother, because she was so tired of crying.

Selma saw the tears and immediately that little furrow of worry appeared between her rather small eyes. "Oh, Shayna!" she cried, wringing her hands. Shayna had of course read many stories where women wrung their hands; but Selma was the very first person she'd ever seen *do* it in real life.

"It's all right, Selma, really. I'm just tired. I probably should be in the hospital, to see what's wrong with me."

"But the rabbi says—"

"I know what the rabbi says. But you know something, Selma? The rabbi doesn't always know best. He's not a doctor or a nurse, you know."

She watched with detached interest as warring emotions battled on Selma's face. She wanted to defend her rabbi, but at the same time it was her job to comfort Shayna. She finally settled for saying, "Yes, well, that's true. He's not a doctor or a nurse," and let it go at that.

"And he's going to be in terrible trouble, because of all those things he's saying on the television. Do you realize that, Selma? The hospital will make him stop."

"Stop! Why should he stop? This is a free country!"

How could a grown woman be so naive? "We aren't free to tell lies, Selma. If we tell lies on television, where a lot of people can hear them and maybe believe ... I'm sure that's against the law." She wasn't exactly sure. If only she could talk to Marty Lamb; Marty would tell her. But there were no more telephones in the Brown apartment—he had unplugged them all—no more visits.

"Against the law! Oh, no, Shayna, I'm sure you're wrong. The rabbi would never—"

"Selma, my father believes he is a law unto himself. Maybe he believes he is the Almighty."

"Bite your tongue!"

Shayna was sorry. She liked Selma and, much as she

enjoyed teasing the older woman, didn't want to make her really uncomfortable. "My little joke," she explained.

"I think we ought to pick out your dress, Shayna. For the betrothal party." She was obviously relieved to talk about something else.

The betrothal party. Shayna closed her eyes again, waiting for the wave of fury to pass over her. How could he, with her mother barely in her grave! What had happened to the traditional year of mourning? He thought he could just change the rules if they didn't suit him! Right now, for whatever reason, he needed to get rid of her, to get her out of his house and out of his sight and out of his life. Who cared if he was dooming her to life in a nightmare? She could feel her heart pounding in her chest and she did not trust herself to speak.

Luckily, Selma took her silence for agreement and went right away to the closet, opening the door and flicking through the dresses, all long-sleeved, high-necked, all with skirts to the floor . . . or, in Shayna's case, long enough to cover up the horrible truth.

"This . . . or this . . . or this? What do you think, Shayna? This white lawn with the tucking looks very . . . well, bridal, don't you think?"

"Too bridal. I'm not a bride yet. Oh, God!" She put her face into her hands and wept.

"Shayna, listen, every bride-to-be is nervous. But, you know, the marriage part, the sex part . . . actually, it can be rather nice."

Shayna's head came up with a jerk and she stared at Selma, nice loyal dumb Selma. "Oh, God! Nice! With Sammy Halpern who burned his brains out on drugs, you think that's going to be *nice*?"

"We don't know that Sammy took drugs, Shayna. Nobody knows exactly what happened."

"Oh, wonderful, so it wasn't drugs, he was born that way? Selma, he can't even count to twenty without getting lost! He can't hold a job!"

Again that clucking with the tongue. "Bite your tongue, Shayna. Sammy has a job!"

"He's the janitor for the *shul*. And you *know* the congrega-

tion made that job for him because his father is the treasurer of the Survivors and does our taxes and stuff. He's a moron, Selma. How will I ever have a conversation with him, never mind him sleeping next to me, putting that thing into me night after night!"

"Shayna! For shame!" Selma's round, rather plain face turned red and she couldn't meet Shayna's eyes. She busied herself, instead, with the dresses in the closet. "So Sammy forgets things sometimes. He's a good boy, and you have to admit, he is tall and handsome and has beautiful muscles. He's very good-natured and he used to be so bright, so his genes are good, and he adores you, Shayna, I've seen the way he looks at you."

"Lots of them look at me that way. It's not adoration, Selma, it's 'I wonder what she looks like without that *shmata* over her knees' . . . without *any* clothes on, for that matter. I read books, Selma, I'm not stupid!"

"No, no, Shayna, he really loves you, you'll see." Poor Selma, she didn't know what to do with this conversation, which was not going where she had expected it to. She forgot the dresses and began to flutter around the room, picking up things only to put them right back down again.

"And what will he do when he sees that I'm crippled, when he discovers I feel nothing below the waist?"

"Oh, that." Selma's face cleared. Here was something she could deal with. "Most of them don't care what the woman feels . . . oh dear, I didn't mean that the way it sounds. I'm sure Sammy—oh dear, oh Shayna, please don't cry. I'm sorry, I'm so stupid to make you cry." Shayna just knew, without looking, that Selma was wringing her hands again.

"You didn't make me cry, Selma. None of this is your fault, it's all *him*. Do you *see*, Selma? He wants me married and out of his house. Yussi Halpern wants Sammy married and out of his house. It's the perfect match," she finished bitterly.

"He is your father. He loves you. He wants you to have a normal life."

"*Normal life!* Selma, you don't know what you're saying! There is no normal life for me. He wants me safely put away,

he wants someone else now to keep the horrible secret, he wants—"

Shayna stopped and took in a deep breath. Selma had backed away, fingers in her mouth, eyes wide. If she really alarmed Selma, then Selma would go running to him, babbling about her craziness. He'd probably marry her off the very next day, forget a betrothal. She had to stay calm. She had to stay calm and make her own plans.

"Selma . . . listen, I'm not feeling so good, actually. I should speak with my nurse-practitioner, you know her, Marty Lamb. Would you go to a phone, the one in the street, on the corner, and call her for me? I'll tell you the number."

"The rabbi has said nobody from that accursed hospital may speak with you or any member of his family."

"It's not an accursed hospital. If anything, we are an accursed family."

"Bite your tongue!" Selma bit her own, and spat three times against the evil eye.

"Think, Selma dear, *think*. You were my mother's dearest friend. For years she put her health, and mine, into Marty Lamb's hands. Until her death. She loved Marty Lamb, and so do I. Marty has been a wonderful friend to me. He . . ." She was about to say, *He has gone completely crazy,* but she'd better not. "He still mourns my mother, and so he blames All Souls, he blames Marty and poor Dr. Zee, who is not to blame for her terrible fate. . . ." No more than I am to blame for mine, she thought.

"Selma, I need Marty's help. I am not entirely well, you know. In fact, right now . . ." She sank back against the pillows and tried to look wan and weak. "I really should have medical advice," she said with half of her voice. "I don't know what my father might think if he finds me not well enough for his betrothal announcement."

Selma was a study in thought. Finally, "I will do it for you. For your health," she said.

"Tell Marty please to come over now, while he's gone. And then, Selma, let her in when she rings the bell."

"I will do it. For your health," Selma repeated, almost like a prayer, and left the room.

She was back very quickly, a puzzled frown on her face. "Shayna. There is no dial tone in that telephone."

Sharply: "The public phone outside? Are you sure?"

"Yes. I even asked a woman walking by, if she would try it. She said it was—what was the word?—vandalized."

"My father did that! I know he did! Oh, that devil!"

"Shayna!"

But she was finished placating the woman's stubborn denial of the truth. He had made it so she would have to do what she had to do by herself. So be it.

"Stop, Selma. Lightning bolts are not coming down to strike me dead. I only wish they would! Then I wouldn't have to marry brain-dead Sammy Halpern." Picturing Sammy's blank eyes and loose wet lips, she shuddered.

"Shayna!"

"I mean it, Selma," she said sharply, in a tone she realized sounded just like her father. "You will stop this nonsense that I may not speak the truth, or you will leave. Have you forgotten entirely that I have lost my mother, that I am a woman alone in this household? That I cannot move? Well, listen to me. My life is empty and hopeless, because my mother is dead, and I am so lonesome I could die. Oh, how I wish I could! *Now* do you understand?"

She pushed herself up against the pillows, feeling a sudden surge of strength. "Now. Let's get on with the preparations. If I am not ready for this . . . celebration, my father will be angry with you. So I suggest you behave in a sensible manner and get out what I want to wear for this . . . this farce. There is a red blouse in the closet, very thin silk, from Israel, with beautiful hand embroidery in white . . . also a red layered skirt, yes, that one . . . and now, a pair of scissors. . . ."

It was highly satisfying to watch Selma, so many years her senior, jump so eagerly to follow her orders. To think she had looked up to this woman for so long, like an aunt, like a wise older sister! When all the time Selma was just a sheep, like the rest of the congregation, adoring *him*, waiting for him to tell them what to do. And now, unquestioning, doing the same for her.

Well, Shayna thought, a little smile curling her lips, it would

be very interesting to see how they all behaved *after* the betrothal party, after she had finished what she'd set out to do.

31

Nearly noon and Marty was walking her beat, looking in on the clinics. Today was Wednesday, a very busy day, a *very* busy day since the word had quietly gone out that abortions were still being done, but shhh, no talking about it, we don't want any anti-abortion nuts coming around again. The Life Saviors had suddenly disappeared from in front of the hospital. Why they had decided to leave, or where they had gone, nobody seemed to know. The rumor was they were gathering down-town, preparing to demonstrate in front of the courthouse where William Blenheim would be tried. Good, she thought. Let them be someone *else's* problem.

The Ob/Gyn clinic was open today, too, and as usual, that waiting room was packed. Dr. Dinowitz was here on Wed-nesday and all the women knew it, so Wednesday was a very popular day. As much as the staff liked to sneer at Dr. Dimwit, his patients adored him. And, in any case, Marty wasn't so sure he was a total jerk anymore.

She continued down the hall, clipboard at the ready. The clinics were all crowded and noisy, but surprise! no fights, no screaming, no emergency. How nice. She was so sleepy this morning. Come to think of it, she'd been longing to take a nap every afternoon, for days. But there was Crystal, strolling up the hall from the Birthing Center; and she thought, Not so nice.

Marty had filled Paul in on some of the Crystal Cole saga, finally. It was good to talk to him, not only because she got to share the burden at last, but he'd gone the addiction route him-self. He kept saying "typical, typical" as she described Crys's

sudden mood changes, guilty tears followed by ice-cold defiance followed just as quickly by self-pity.

"I'm just going to tell her straight out," Marty decided. "I'm putting her on report to both the hospital and the Nursing Licensure Board. After I talk to her, she'll know: she's fired and probably finished professionally. And I'm going to beg her to get some psychiatric help. I know a lot of her behavior is due to all the drugs she's been ingesting. But there's something else. She seems totally without conscience or remorse. It's peculiar. She can be such a good actress. But instead of acting rational and reasonable and maybe convincing me she's worth saving, she takes an almost perverse pleasure in painting herself in the most disgusting colors."

"Oh, it's very possible that she finds herself disgusting," Paul said. "I know I felt that way about myself. When you've got the shakes, though, and your nerve endings are beginning to scream, the self-disgust goes down the drain. The need takes over everything. *Everything.*" He shuddered, and Marty, taking his face between her hands, kissed him tenderly.

"That's done with, Paul. Don't think about it. Do you believe I'm saying that? *Don't think about it?* Forget I ever suggested such a stupid thing."

"Not stupid. Just very very difficult. And by the way," he added in a serious voice, "don't underestimate your friend Crystal. She has the ability to fool you, even now that you know everything. She might just decide to put on her rational act and try to convince you that she's heading straight out the door for detox. Don't you believe it. And don't soften. The woman is in deep trouble and desperately needs help. Hang tough, Marty, okay? Insist that she go into detox and then tie her up and *take* her."

Yes, she decided again, watching Crystal and seeing a stranger. The woman she'd thought she knew had more twists than a pretzel.

"Felicia Cuevas came in, ready to deliver. False labor," Crystal said as they met. "We had to send her home. She was crying. Now I ask you, Marty! A perfectly intelligent woman, and she's crying because she's not in labor. I told her to save

her tears for when there was *real* pain, like when she's really in labor."

How had she missed Crystal's disdain for everyone else's pain? It seemed so obvious now. Maybe she'd been hiding it better.

"Felicia is only twenty-two, Crys, and it's her first baby," Marty said mildly. "You free for lunch? In my office?"

"Goodies from the food machines, I take it?"

"No, actually, I thought we'd call Proto's and order a pizza."

"You're on. What time? One okay?"

"One is fine." Marty watched Crystal, impeccably turned out, as usual, sashaying on down the hall, looking as if she didn't have a thing on her mind. But she must know that she was about to get reamed. Reamed *and* reported. She'd better not try another of her little tricks to put it off. It was *not* going to be put off this time.

Marty had set out once more when an angry male voice shouting her name stopped her in her tracks.

"Nurse Lamb! I want to talk to you!"

How many years since anyone had called her "Nurse" like that? Dennis, naturally, and she couldn't help noting he was a frightening shade of pink.

"Calm down, Dennis, you'll give yourself a coronary. What's the problem?"

"*I'll* worry about my heart, thank you. And *you* had better start worrying about your *staff* . . . Ms. *Cole*, specifically."

"*What* specifically has Ms. Cole *done*, Doctor?" She had to be careful not to copy his habit of underlining every other word with his voice, which he did when he was agitated.

"She has *intruded* into the Neonatal nursery, bothering the nurses, and she had the *nerve* to say the doctors are *stupid*!"

"Please, Dennis. I'm on your side. Take it easy and tell me what happened."

"I've just *told* you." But his voice had dropped down a whole octave and he began to look less apoplectic. "Crystal went into the Neonatal ICU and told the nurses there that Baby Racine is *her* patient—well, to be accurate, she said his *mother* is her patient—and that they were breaking the law. She had the goddamn *nerve* to say that *I* . . ." He paused,

taking in a deep breath, apparently carried away by the enormity of Crystal's crime. ". . . to say that *I* had *overstepped* . . . that *I* had no business allowing the infant's surgery! I had nothing to do with any surgery! I'm a gynecologist, not a neonatologist, for God's sake! What's *wrong* with that woman?" He stopped, breathing hard.

"Well, in fact," Marty said, keeping her voice very even, "Marie Racine *is* Crystal's patient and the mother, and actually, Marie wasn't properly told—" She knew she had to tread delicately here. "Besides, Dennis, you should be able to set them straight, in the nursery, without coming to me."

He looked at her for a minute without speaking. "I know. I'm sorry, I just needed to vent, I guess." He looked around furtively, for all the world like someone in a spy movie. "Come on," he said in a low voice, "Clinic A is empty. I want to talk to you."

Intrigued by his sudden change of demeanor, she followed him down the hall and into the waiting room. Again he looked all around, then shut the door, took in a deep breath and said, "Look. I don't think you know Crystal, not really. She's . . . she's capable of . . ." He turned his head, giving her his elegant profile and a glimpse of tears in his eyes. Christ, what was going on? "She's not a nice person, Marty. She had no business barging into the nursery, upsetting the nurses. They have enough on their minds *already*, God knows, and—" Again he stopped, and she could see his Adam's apple move as he swallowed.

"Dennis, this isn't the first time you've tried to tell me something about Crystal. Maybe it's time you spit it out."

"Oh, God!" He turned to the wall, leaning his head against it, the very picture of dejection and defeat. "I can't! But . . . I have to." He turned back to her, the color rising in his face. "She's evil. You're surprised. It's a strong word, *evil*, we don't use it much anymore. But that's what she is. She and I . . . we . . ." He faltered.

"You were having an affair," Marty supplied. It just came to her, and the moment she said it, she knew it was true. She wasn't the least bit surprised when he nodded.

"An affair," he repeated. "That's a gentle way to describe

what went on between us. She *is* a witch, you know, she's very
... shall we say talented. ..." He turned red again, and Marty
was amazed to realize he was blushing.

"But it's over," Marty said. "Is that why you have it in for
her? Because she won't see you anymore?"

To her surprise, he burst out laughing, a rather overwrought
bray. "I have it *in* for *her*? Oh Marty, if you knew how funny
that is! No, that's not it. *I* ended it and *she* ... she won't let it
go. She's after *me*, she won't leave me alone, she sends me
these horrible messages. ..." He shuddered. "She calls me,
threatens she'll tell Messinger that she was forced against her
will—"

"Raped? I doubt anybody would believe that, Dennis.
Crystal is a tough cookie. And, forgive me, but she could have
any man she wants. Why would she carry on like that over
you? I mean ... well, you're very attractive, of course, but—"
She stopped. "Is she in love with you?"

A bitter laugh. "I doubt she's ever felt anything so human.
No, she's not in love with me. She's ... a control freak." He
clamped his lips together as if words he didn't want said might
fling themselves out of his mouth.

The obscene Xerox copy flashed into her head and she made
it go away. Now was not the time to think about that, not with
Dennis standing right there in front of her in his white coat,
stethoscope in the pocket, every inch the handsome and professional physician. Except for those tears. Poor oversexed Dr.
Dimwit, hoist by his own petard. In a manner of speaking.

"She used me," he went on. "You have no idea how ... how
seductive she can be. Sexually, she's ... gifted. She knows
how to get under a man's skin." He was looking everywhere
but at her, the color deepening in his face. "She's ... it's like a
drug, you know. She thought she had me ... in thrall. She
thought I was her prisoner, that I could never escape her." He
paused. "For a while, I wondered. ... But I did. I told her 'No
more!' She can't stand that. Which is why she wants to—"

Marty didn't know if she could listen to any more. Yes, it
was fascinating, in its own horrible way. But enough! "Look,
Dennis, your private life is just that: private. I don't think
anyone has to know." She was tempted to tell him that Crystal

would be leaving the hospital, but it wasn't really his business, and anyway, he'd find out soon enough. "But I certainly will speak to her about going into the ICU and badmouthing you. She had no business doing that."

The clinic door flew open and, speak of the devil, there was Crystal.

"Oh, there you are, Marty. Why, hello, Dr. Dinowitz, fancy seeing you here in the clinics past twelve o'clock noon."

Marty decided to play it very cool. In fact, she decided to lie. She would pretend she and Dennis had been talking about the Racine baby the whole time. "And Doctor," she said, very businesslike, "will you tell Dr. Fassbinder that Ms. Racine should be reassured about her baby? That she should be told he is recovering? He *is* recovering, isn't he?"

"As a matter of fact, yes, he is. Why shouldn't he be? Len is an acknowledged *expert* in that procedure. And no, I will *not* give him orders from you," he sniffed, turning into the insufferable Dr. Dimwit. "Dr. Fassbinder knows better than any nurse—or any midwife." The word *midwife* was said so poisonously, it was amazing that Crystal didn't shrivel up and fall in a small pile of ash on the floor. But, in fact, she stood in the middle of the doorway, refusing to move an inch, smiling up at him as he tried to make his exit. He finally muttered something Marty couldn't catch and Crys moved aside, but just barely. He must have felt every curve in her body as he was forced to squeeze past.

"What did he want with *you?*" Crystal inquired, her voice as mild as milk.

"He really wanted you, I think. He said you barged into the Neonatal nursery and badmouthed him."

Crystal laughed. "No more than I badmouthed Len Fassbinder. Our Dr. Dimwit has a very fragile ego, Marty."

"You had no business there."

"Oh yes, I did have business there. Marie asked me to check on the baby."

"Checking on the baby is one thing, but telling the nurses how stupid the doctors are is something else."

"Something spelled T-R-U-E." Again she laughed. "Okay, okay, I apologize. I won't do it again." She held up two fingers,

Girl Scout style. "I swear. Next time, I'll keep my mouth totally shut. Well, back to the patients." She started away.

"Whoa!" Marty called. "I thought we had a lunch date, Crys!"

"That's half an hour from now."

"Do me a favor. Be sure you show up."

Crystal shrugged elaborately and sauntered off. Marty wanted to run after her, grab her and shake the truth out of her. She made herself calm down. Wasn't this the country where you were innocent until proven guilty? She had to give Crys a chance to defend herself. And who knew? Maybe it wasn't what she thought. Yeah. Right.

When Marty opened the door to her office at one, Crystal was already there, where she shouldn't be.

"Hi," Marty said. "Am I late or are you early?" Hoping her voice didn't mirror her irritation. Crystal's hand was resting on the answering machine. "Have you been playing my messages?" she asked sharply. It just popped out of her.

Crystal pulled her hand off the machine as if she'd been burned. "No, of course not! Why should I be playing your messages, for God's sake? I brought the pizza in." Sure enough, the big box was sitting on the desk.

"Why don't you pass it out, then." While Crystal busied herself pushing papers aside and clearing a space on the desktop, Marty reached very casually into her bag, quietly clicking the tiny tape recorder to on. She covered the movement by pulling out a tissue and dabbing at her nose. Paul had made her practice doing it with her eyes closed until there was no chance of making a mistake. He had warned her to turn it on the minute Crystal began to talk. Such a small tape would only give them thirty minutes.

"You don't look so good, Marty. I guess you've heard the rumors, too."

"What rumors?"

"That CCC is being closed down."

"Closed down? Hell, no." Do you think, Ms. Cole, that I don't notice how you always change the subject? she thought. Don't you know me any better than that? There was no such rumor. Well, one lie certainly deserved another.

"In fact," she said smoothly, "what I've been told is that we'll probably be the only unit left intact."

"Oh, really?"

"*If* All Souls is sold and that's not a done deal, you know." Marty also noted that Crys didn't ask where she got her information, and thought, Crystal, you're slipping.

But the next words out of Crystal's mouth were, "So . . . who's your source?"

"Dennis Dinowitz." She watched for some kind of reaction, but Crystal's expression didn't change at all. "As a matter of fact, Crys, I had a long conversation with Dennis."

"Suddenly he's not Dr. Dimwit? What happened? He fuck you, finally? Jesus, Marty—sor-*ry!* But everyone knows it's eating him up, that you never gave in to him."

"No. But apparently *you* did," Marty said in a voice of ice. Now she got her startled reaction.

"He told you that?"

"He told me a great deal, Crystal, in great detail."

One eyebrow went up quizzically. "He *did?* I find that hard to believe. Why in hell would he tell *you*, of all the— Well, okay, yes, we had a thing going for a while."

"He says he ended it and you won't accept it. He says you've been harassing him . . . calling him at all hours, threatening him . . . sending him nasty messages." She stared hard at the beautiful bland face.

"He told you *that?* Oh, that bastard! Well, Marty, he's lying. He's such a baby, he just can't believe his nooky's gone! He thinks he's God's gift to women, you know that. We've always joked about it. And, actually, he's pretty good. Can keep it up for the longest time . . ." She paused and giggled.

"Crystal, for Christ's sake! This is serious, don't you realize that?"

"Well, 'scuse *me*, Miz Marty ma'am, if I spoke outta turn. But dat man, he do love his poontang." Crystal laughed and posed, then stopped abruptly and said, in a completely different tone, "The man's demented, Marty. He's the one won't let go. He's a sex addict, has to have it all the time. And he did find it, ah, titillating, if you'll excuse another pun, to prong a woman of color."

It sounded true because it sounded the way they'd always guessed him to be, in the days when they used to conjecture all the time about his sex life—the more loathsome the idea, the better. The good old days. It *did* fit his persona, all of it, including finding an extra thrill in Crystal's slightly darker skin.

Something must have shown on Marty's face, because Crystal visibly relaxed. Leaning closer, she lowered her voice and said, "If you want proof of what a sick bastard he is, I can show you. It's all in his office . . . and *I* have a key."

"What are you doing with a key to his private office?"

"I'll give it back. But not until I get back the pictures he took of *me*. Oh yes, he's pretty disgusting. He not only screws your brains out, he poses you and takes pictures. Keeps a great big drawerful of them. Come on, I'll show you."

"Certainly *not*!"

"Yo, Marty, come off the moral outrage, okay? We were both consenting adults. Anyway, we're history, me and Dr. Dimwit."

"But not before you got a . . . um, picture of *him*, right, Crys? You made that Xerox copy and sent it out, first to Aimee and then to me." And that meant, of course, that Crystal was the author of all the other nasty messages, too. Including those that had been left so neatly in the middle of Marty's desk.

Thoughts began to crisscross each other. The other day, in front of the hospital, Crystal had recognized Owen as Marty's husband. Hadn't she said something about a conjugal visit? How had she known who he was? And how had she found out about Paul? Of course: the night the three of them had watched the newscast at Marty's place. Crys had answered her beeper, in the next room. Who was to say she hadn't hung up and then stayed quietly at the open door, listening while Marty and Dr. Zee had a heart-to-heart? She must have been ghosting around the clinics and the hospital corridors a great deal, listening here, watching there. Who'd notice a staff member, a trusted and well-loved midwife? She was the next best thing to invisible. She was *expected* to be there.

"You don't know I did that. He's a busy boy, our Dr. Dimwit. Who's to say it wasn't the Ice Maiden?"

"Let's just say I know it wasn't Aimee. Anyway, if you

didn't do it, how come you know what I'm talking about?
You're becoming very careless. Sit down, Crystal. Over there,
on the other side of the desk." As soon as they were both
seated, Marty leaned forward and fixed the other woman with
her gaze. "Crystal, you're out of control. You need help. And
if you don't get it—"

The gaze instantly shifted to hurt innocence. "Me? Why
don't you ask Norma McClure how well *she* knows Dennis?
She's a weirdo . . . *she*'s the one who told me about that
Xerox!"

"Give me a break, Crystal."

"Just because Dr. Dimwit wanted a picture of his big cock in
all its glory, I'm rotten? All I did was run the copy machine! *He*
probably tapes it to the wall and worships it! Talk about
needing help!"

"I don't care about your sex life. I care about your profes-
sionalism. I care about our patients. And I care about you being
on drugs. It can't go on, Crys. And it's not going to go on."

Crystal burst into wild tears, putting her face into her hands.
Marty sat quietly. She felt no pity; she felt nothing. Here was a
beautiful young woman, skilled in her profession, with everything going for her. What madness had taken her over? She
waited a minute or two and then said, briskly, "Pull yourself
together, Crystal, or someone will hear and come in to check."

Crystal stopped crying abruptly and nodded. Her face was
streaked with tears; other than that, she looked as cool as usual.
No reddened eyes, no puffy circles beneath. As if they hadn't
been real tears . . . or real feelings, for that matter.

"All right, you win," Crystal said, standing up. "I'll tell you
what was going on. But Dimwit is just as guilty as I am. I want
him reported, too!" She looked at Marty, but Marty said
nothing.

After a moment she said, "Maybe I've got a small drug
problem, nothing I can't take care of in a week or two. I've
done it bef—I had some man problems and I stressed. For a
little while I just, like, ordered phony doses for patients and
used the leftovers. But I figured I was going to get caught one
of these days. Dimwit had been hitting on me for a long time,
so I made a deal with him—sex for drugs. It was so simple. I'm

a woman and he's a gynecologist. He told me to say that I was having bad cramps or some shit like that. All right, all right, he prescribed Percodan for chronic endometriosis. And, you know, it wasn't too terrible paying him off. He's a horny bastard, as we all know. . . ." She smiled a little, still looking directly at Marty. "He's a really good lay, Marty. You ought to try it."

Marty was not going to touch that one. "If you had a ready source, why did you mess with the IVs and the bloods, Crystal?"

"So you guessed that, too." A shrug. "Nothing lasts forever. Well, Marty, my ready source began to back off, the wimp. Dimwit was afraid of getting caught! The pharmacist downstairs was asking questions about all my prescriptions! The DEA was gonna come after him! They were going to catch us doing it in his office! Agh! What a fucking baby!"

Quietly, Marty said, "He dumped you."

"Yeah. He dumped me. So I had to start doubling patients' medications again, to get what I needed. And I had to cover up. So I, you know, made messes and 'lost' things in drawers and cupboards where eventually they'd be found. . . . But I wasn't the one who took the greens. You can't pin that on me!"

"Okay, I'll keep that in mind." She'd better keep a very level tone with Crystal, Marty thought. She didn't want to set her off. Maybe it was the drugs, or maybe something a lot more basic, but Crystal was a woman about to explode.

"You knew Virgil Nesbit, didn't you? At St. Francis Assisi."

"That fairy? Sure. He was one of those bleeding-heart paramedics that comes back to check on every fucking patient he brings in. All the nurses and midwives knew him." Her voice was acid.

"So you're the mystery woman who called Ham Pierce, after Virgie was on television?"

"I didn't know Virgil real well, he left St. Francis soon after I got there. But I recognized him when I came here. Those odd eyes. Not that he remembered me . . . I mean she. I would never have said anything except the bitch took me aside one day and whispered that I should take it easy on the drugs. She said that if I took care of the problem myself, she wouldn't tell.

But how could I believe that? He was cute, you know? As a man, I mean. But he wasn't interested in women, not that wuss." She smiled at Marty. "Not like your pal Mannes. He was *starving* for it!"

"Shut up, Crys. I don't want you to say another word about Joel Mannes, do you understand?"

Crystal tossed her head and stood. Uh-oh, Marty thought, here's where the shit hits the fan. But when she spoke, Crystal only said, in a subdued voice, "Are you going to put me on report for this?"

"For screwing doctors? I don't think so. Fornication between two consenting adults is, as far as I know, not a crime, not even a misdemeanor. But—"

"But you *are* going to do it. For what?"

"Oh, I have quite a wide choice. I could report you for harassing the staff with poison pen messages. Or for being stoned while on duty."

Speaking quickly and sounding desperate, Crystal said, "What if I go into a detox program. You can monitor me. I could quit this job, or you could fire me, if that'll make you feel good. But don't put me on report."

"No deals, Crystal."

"What do you think you've got on me?"

"Got on you? What is this, a cops and robbers movie? I've seen you high when you were on duty, Crystal, and that *is* against any code of ethics, not to mention the law of the state of New York. You kept this facility under siege with your horrible messages. You made Angie Buonanotte *quit*, for Christ's sake! Isn't that enough?"

Crystal eyed her for a moment, then smiled. "You think anyone would believe such a wild story?" she said. "I don't think so, especially after I tell them how I stole your boyfriend Mannes from you and it drove you so crazy you had to make up all this stuff about me." The smile widened.

Marty smiled back at her and shook her head. "I don't think so," she said, copying Crystal's cool tone. "Nobody will believe you after they hear the tape I've just made."

"You didn't! I don't believe you!" Crystal came out from behind the desk. "Show me!"

"I'll play it at your hearing, Crys." In truth, too many other people had been mentioned by name. She could never use it.

"Show me, dammit! I don't believe you! You're just trying to spook me!"

"Believe me, Crys."

Crystal's lips pulled back, baring even white teeth in a snarl. "Bitch!" she said hoarsely. "Bitch!" Her eyes were narrowed to slits. When she moved quickly into the center of the room, Marty pulled back instinctively.

But Crystal had no intention of getting anywhere near Marty. She sped for the door, opened it and was gone, slamming it so hard the pizza box jumped on the desk.

It took Marty five minutes to bring her heart rate back to normal. She had thought she was hungry, but just looking at the cold pizza with its pale layer of coagulated cheese turned her stomach. She couldn't eat. Finally, she reached into her bag and checked the little tape briefly. Rewinding for a few seconds, she hit play and heard, thinly but clearly, Crystal's voice, saying, "What do you think you've got on me?" She turned it off. She didn't want to hear it all again right now.

Then she reached out for the telephone, pushing Joel's office extension. It might be a problem, getting him to make a psychiatric evaluation of a woman he'd been— But he had to be asked. He was Chief of Psychiatry; who else would she ask? His line was busy. She waited a minute and tried again. Still busy. Then she tried Paul, and when the voice mail answered, she hung up. What she wanted to tell him should be said in person. Then she went back to Joel's extension and tried several times before she gave up. She knew from experience how he could talk when he wanted to. She stared at the pizza, trying to think. She could smell it, and suddenly she was starving. She took a slice. But there was a bad taste in her mouth, and even Proto's deluxe couldn't take it away.

Time to get some fresh air. On her way out she dialed Joel's extension at one of the lobby house phones. Still busy? A thought occurred to her and, quickly, she went out and across the lawn to Hamilton Place, past the CCC entrance and into the back. And there was Crys at one of the three outdoor pay phones, her head bent, her body curled in, facing the wall. She

didn't have any idea Marty was walking toward her. When Marty got close enough to hear her talking in a half whisper, she was saying "Please" and "Just for a few minutes . . ." and "Remember the last time, how I"—and then she was threatening: "I'll call Alice. I swear it. I'll tell everyone, I'll—"

Joel. Crystal was giving him a hard time, doing her damnedest to get him to meet her.

When she touched Crystal on the shoulder, Crys gave a little scream and slammed the phone down, whirling around. "Jesus Christ! What the hell do you think you're doing, sneaking up behind people and scaring them half to death?"

"Why don't you leave him alone? He doesn't want you anymore." Marty was angrier than she had realized.

"You think I'm talking to Dr. Dimwit? Well, I'm not."

"Not at all. I know who you were talking to. Joel Mannes."

"Do you really think this is your business, Marty?"

"That's right. Joel is my friend and so is his wife. And I happen to know he doesn't want anything more to do with you."

"Well, he wanted *everything* to do with me in the beginning, in every possible position. He may be your friend, and a shrink, but he's no different than the rest of them. He came crawling and begging for more." She had a smug, satisfied look on her face that Marty longed to slap right off. With effort, she stood where she was, kept her voice calm.

"Believe me, he's no longer interested."

"Oh really? Has he come crying to his Marty mommy? They are such fucking babies, every last one of them. They all think with their cocks. Let me tell you the secret of success, Marty. Give a man a really good hard-on and he'll *kill* for you. Even Dr. M—"

"Enough!" Marty snapped. "I don't need any more true confessions! I'm not even sure any of it's true."

"Oh, it's all true, all right, and I could make you a list of men in this hospital you wouldn't *believe*. All I've got to do is snap my fingers and any one of them will come running and panting. But you want to know something? Not one of them has ever been man enough to make *me* beg!" She looked like a teenager, eyes blazing, lower lip thrust out, defiant and scared

all at the same time. What had happened to her, to hollow her out and leave her so empty? "And I don't know why you should be so high and mighty. Everyone knows you're fucking Paul Giordano."

Without thought, Marty's arm flew out. The crack of her hand on Crystal's face was so loud it startled them both. Once again Crystal burst into tears and began to blubber.

"Oh, Jesus, Marty, I didn't mean that, I'm sorry, I really like you, I don't know what's wrong with me, sometimes I think I'm going crazy. You're right, I need help, and that's why I was calling Joel. I was calling Joel for help. Please, Marty . . ."

Crystal was some piece of work, going instinctively for the jugular, Marty thought. In its own way, it was impressive. Her hand was still stinging and that was all she could feel.

Sharply, she said, "Crystal, quit it. All you're doing is getting yourself in deeper and deeper. Pull yourself together and go home. Every time you open your mouth, you make it worse."

The wild weeping turned off as suddenly as it had the last time. "You'll never prove any of it." Her eyes were as hard and opaque as amber. "You can have your fucking tape. I have plenty of doctor friends."

Suddenly, Marty was tired of the whole damned thing.

"Crystal, I've lost all patience with you. You're sick. You're fired."

"You can't fire me!"

"I can't? I just have! Get out of here, out of my sight, and away from this hospital. You've caused enough trouble! Get out! Go on! And don't let me see you anywhere near All Souls, do you understand?"

"We'll see about *that*!" Crystal said. Her hands were both curled into fists. Marty was aware and waiting, ready for the other woman to make even the slightest move. She took a step toward Crystal, who spat onto the ground, turned and strode away. In a minute she'd rounded the corner and was out of sight. But Marty had a feeling that she had not seen the last of Crystal Cole, not yet.

32

Dr. Zee, holding her breath without realizing it, stood gazing at the door with the familiar white-on-black name plate fastened to the middle panel. JULIA ZACHARY-FELSEN, M.D. How many years had it been there, in that same spot? Well, to hell with counting years. What did it matter? She was leaving. It was not going to be easy, packing up her life; but it had to be done. She was ending her relationship with All Souls, long before she'd ever dreamed she would. Coming in and walking around as if she didn't hear the buzz of gossip and conjecture that followed her wherever she went—that was tough, too. So. She opened the door and began to breathe again.

She stood for a few minutes, not quite sure where to start. Then she just got to it, moving quickly around the familiar surroundings of her office, picking and choosing, putting things into different piles. Pile one: keep. Pile two: maybe. Pile three: give away. Pile four: throw away. She was able to keep pile one down to a reasonable minimum; but pile two . . . ! Like Topsy, it just growed.

How could she get rid of the dozens of pictures drawn by children in her practice . . . the birthday cards they had made by hand . . . the letters they had sent her . . . the misspellings, the *many* backwards z's, the love they wrote down so laboriously? How could she get rid of any of it? This was her professional life, here, in this rather small office with its old-fashioned examining room, the scale with weights—so much more accurate than any of the modern ones, she thought—the growth chart from 1967 and the brand-new shiny Food Pyramid poster she'd put up the day before she'd landed in a hospital bed.

Finally, she carefully put everything from pile two into a

bag, to be taken to her new job. We are all under sentence of death from the moment of our birth, she thought. But that's no reason not to make the most of whatever time we are given. Think of Steven . . . But to think of Steven, her son, always brought tears to her eyes. He had been the most gallant of boys, even facing death. Especially facing death. Braver than *she* had been.

She was lucky. The hospital was giving her a pretty penny in farewell. They didn't think of it as a payoff. It was her pension plus a sweetener—in gratitude for years of devotion and service. She knew better. But now, at least she had enough money for just about any contingency. And she had a new job. She would have suffered terribly from inactivity, more than from the physical symptoms—which were showing up so much faster. With such a short time left, she felt desperate to keep moving, to keep healing; and if healing was beyond whatever medicine she knew, then at least to keep taking care of patients.

She was still young; sixty-three was barely past middle age. Her brain was still functioning just as it always had. Please God, the disease wouldn't take hold of her mind. She had no tremors, no moments of blackout, no loss of memory. Everything was in wonderful shape except, of course, her immune system. Sooner or later, she knew, she could end up in a hospital bed, chronically cold, too weak to hold up a newspaper, her bowels out of control, maybe even lose her mind. No. No, she would not allow *that* to happen. Marty wouldn't allow that to happen.

Marty was the closest thing she had to family; she couldn't count her sister Mildred. Millie had a condo in Vail. She was a lady who lunched—and skied and shopped and cocktailed. She was *not* a lady who came cross-country to take care of an older sister with AIDS. The thought was laughable.

Suddenly, Julia made up her mind. Pile three, or was it four, was pushed wholesale into the outsized trash can she'd dragged in from the back. There! she thought, feeling as if she'd actually accomplished something. Why was she doing this now? Messinger had given her until the end of the month to clear her office for the acting Chief of Service; and Paul Giordano had told her to take her time, he was in no hurry. But what the hell, might as well get it over with, right?

She had come in around six-thirty, thinking she'd have a couple of hours by herself. But first Marty found her and cried. Dr. Zee knew Marty had something on her mind, so she'd suggested they save the tears and talk. But then Sonya Washington came in and cried, and Carmen got in early and came in and cried. She never did get a chance to find out what was on Marty's mind *and* she hadn't got very far with her packing, either.

As she headed for the file cabinets, dreading going through them, a voice behind her said, "Dr. Zee?" and it was Virgie. "Dr. Zee, I just wanted to say what a privilege—" she began and, sure enough, she broke down.

Dr. Zee hugged Virgie and made soothing sounds, saying, "Now, Virgie, now, Virgie . . ." She was in tears, too, of course. If this kept up, her eyes would be permanently bloodshot.

She saw Paul Giordano go by several times, back and forth in the hallway, before she realized that he probably wanted to talk to her. As soon as Virgie began to blow her nose, patting her perfect hair, Julia called to him. "Come on in!" She wondered if he'd cry, too.

"Hi," Paul said, looking as if he didn't quite know what to do. Then he asked, "If I hug you, will you get all mushy?"

She laughed. "No. I promise."

The boy knew how to give a good hug, nothing wimpy and tentative. When he let her go and stepped back, his eyes were all shiny and he was blinking hard.

"I know, I know," he said. "But *I* didn't promise."

"I'm taking all these tears as a compliment, Paul."

"Oh, and you're right. You're going to be missed, you know. Especially by me. I was just beginning to learn all your little tricks of the trade, and now you go and leave." He was trying to smile.

"You don't need any tricks, Dr. Giordano. You're a good doctor. You just need to slow down a little, take a couple extra minutes with each patient, and you'll have it down cold. Most of our patients need to be listened to more than they need a doctor."

"Mrs. Golub," Paul said.

"Mrs. Golub," she agreed. Mrs. Golub, eighty-seven years old, with heart failure, in the hospital at least once a week, had

grabbed Paul's hand, asking the same questions over and over. He'd been wonderfully polite, but he had left before her terror had been assuaged, and the old woman had managed to work herself up into a dead faint. When she came to and saw Paul, she shook her head violently and demanded another doctor. Julia had explained to him that Mrs. Golub clung to her doctors for dear life—literally. She needed that reassurance.

"You mean that's it? That's what makes a great doctor? You listen?"

"Oh hell, what do I know? But it's true that most patients need to talk more than they need medicine."

"I'll remember." He looked around, taking in the huge trash bags, the piles of papers. "How long were you here, Dr. Zee?"

"Too long. Maybe the Catholic Church has the right idea. They don't allow their priests to become too attached to any parish or church or city. In fact, the more beloved the parish priest, the more they know he'd better be moved somewhere else."

Paul considered the idea for a minute. Then he said, "Well, I can see it might be good for the priest. But how about the people who are left behind?"

She grinned at him. "*Now* you're getting it!"

He thought about that briefly and then laughed along with her. He was a good man, and so appealing. She could understand how Marty had carried this particular torch for so long.

"You and Marty, you plan to get married?" she said. One of the nice things about dying: you felt free to say whatever you damn well pleased.

It didn't faze him. He grinned at her and said, "Should I ask you for her hand?"

"Is that a yes?"

Paul turned to leave. "If she'll have me. Which is far from certain. We have . . . some history."

She did *not* say, "Yes, I know." Not that he would have heard it. As soon as the words were out of his mouth, he had beat it. Didn't want to talk about it. Men almost never did.

She turned back to tend to pile two, the maybe-yes-maybe-no stuff; but was saved again, when Isabelle came in, looking

indignant. Isabelle was a woman whose emotions were very close to the surface.

"It just isn't fair!" she exclaimed as she bustled in. "It's not fair!" And burst into tears.

"Izzy, Izzy . . ." She put her arms around the little nurse and hugged her. She was really fond of Isabelle. "Listen, dear, it really *is* fair. Really, Izzy, I expected nothing different. Maybe I hoped, but I didn't expect. So don't get all upset on my account, okay? I'm going to be fine. Really."

After a moment Isabelle sniffled a bit and nodded. "I know, I always overreact. My papi has been yelling at me about it since I was this high." She indicated toddler height with her hand. "But I can't help it. I feel things, you know what I mean?"

"I know what you mean. And that's what makes you such a wonderful nurse, Izzy."

Isabelle beamed. "You think so? You really think I'm a wonderful nurse?"

"Yes, I really do."

"Well, it doesn't change what they're doing to you, making you give up your position and everything and just leave."

"Whoa! *They* didn't do it, Izzy, I did it. Look, people are frightened of AIDS, and really, can we blame them? And you know as well as I do that there's no sense in having me as Chief of Service when patients don't want me touching them."

"Well, *we* want you to touch us," Isabelle said with some heat. "In fact . . . in fact . . ." And then she stopped, her eyes filling.

"Isabelle. Are you telling me it's time? For your mama?"

"It is time, yes. Will you come? Tomorrow night?"

"Of course I will. You're absolutely sure? Your family . . . ?"

"Don't you worry about *my* family. My family listens to *me*."

Dr. Zee laughed. "I'm sure they do. What would you think if I brought Marty?"

"Oh, would you? It would be so nice. Mama likes Marty."

"Well, Marty loves her, too, and she'd want to be there."

"We'll be expecting you . . . ooh!" The last remnants of Isabelle's control left her and she burst into noisy tears. "No, no, I'll be fine," she sobbed, and ran out.

Dr. Zee sat at her desk and put her head into her hands.

Maybe it wasn't such a good idea, trying to clear out the office all in one fell swoop. She'd leave the file cabinets for the next time. She wanted to get set up in her new place, anyway. Yes, it was definitely time to get going. Too many tears here.

She left Marty a message in her office. "Sorry I couldn't stick around any longer today," she said to the answering machine. "I'm wondering if you'd like to come with me to Isabelle's house tomorrow evening. If you can't, please leave a message. Otherwise, why don't you meet me?" She left the directions to where she could be found, smiling as she did because Marty would surely wonder what in the world Dr. Zee was *doing* down there.

33

Marty got out of the cab, looking around. She'd had no idea this neighborhood even existed—if you could call a bleak collection of old garages, junk-littered lots, and meat-packing houses a neighborhood. She checked once again, to make sure this was really what she'd written down. Yes, she was on the corner of Washington and Chelsea streets, where Dr. Zee had told her to come; and if she peered past a dilapidated warehouse, she could see the glimmer of water. That would be Twelfth Avenue, and beyond it, the Hudson River, just as Dr. Zee had described. But what in the world was Dr. Zee *doing* here?

Uneasy at the emptiness of the street, she walked slowly west on Chelsea. And then she saw the sign—MERCY HOUSE—on a small building; the date it was built, 1904, carved into the stone lintel. Once painted pale yellow, it was now mostly grungy brick, except for the front door, which gleamed with a recent coat of brave, bright, cornflower blue.

A hand-lettered sign taped to the door announced *HIV Clinic. Walk Right In.* So she did.

She was in a small open space, which had to be the waiting room, though it had been set up to look like a living room. Everything was a bit shabby and there were bald spots in the faded Oriental rug. But how homey it looked, she thought, with its newly painted furniture and bright circus posters taped to the walls. Music was playing softly out of an old radio in one corner. At the far end of the room, between two doors, was the desk.

Almost all the seats were taken, by patients, mostly men, in various stages of illness. The vast majority had the pasty complexion and skeletal thinness of the very sick. Marty was no stranger to AIDS, but no matter how many times she saw it, she still couldn't get used to it. It was so damned relentless.

Dr. Zee's message had said only that Marty could find her here at five-thirty. But Marty wasn't sure whether she should ask for a doctor or a patient. A middle-aged woman in uniform sat at the desk, busily writing. Salvation Army? Marty went up to her, realizing after she got there that what she had thought was a navy-blue suit, too heavy for August in New York City, was a nun's habit. No mistaking the huge crucifix that hung around the woman's neck.

"Sister, I'm looking for Dr. Julia Zachary-Felsen, and I'm not quite—"

The nun beamed. "You're Dr. Zee's friend. How nice to meet you." She pumped Marty's hand. "Sister Augustine. I can't *begin* to tell you how grateful we are to have her services. It's made all the difference, both to us and to— But here I am, babbling on, when she asked that you be brought in the *moment* you arrived. Please come with me."

The door opened onto a warren of cubicles, built of all kinds of materials: plastic panels, wallboard, old doors. "Everything we have is contributed. Furniture, medications, bedding, even the medical services. So we look a bit like a child's playhouse—a rather mad child, I think—but we get the job done! And here we are . . ."

The cubicle had four beds in it. They were all filled. And there was Dr. Zee, right where she had always been, sitting

next to a bed, holding a patient's hand, listening. The man was so wasted, you could barely see his chest move up and down under the sheet as he whispered to the doctor. In another bed, a gray-haired man was raving, his mind gone, while his next door neighbor, who was hooked up to an oxygen supply, tried to calm him. The vile smell of sickness hung over the room.

Marty thought maybe she'd sneak away and come back more noisily. It wasn't nice to stare at people *in extremis*. She needed to get away from the thought that this was her friend's fate. And she didn't want Dr. Zee to catch her observing; it seemed indecent, somehow.

Just then, Julia looked up and saw her. The smile that spread across her face was so radiant, Marty was ashamed she'd even thought of tiptoeing away.

"I'll be with you in a minute, Marty. Edwin, this is my friend, Marty Lamb, who is a nurse-practitioner. Marty, this is Edwin Cartland. The set designer."

Marty and the patient murmured politely, and Marty stepped out of the room and waited in the hallway. It wasn't long before Julia came out, saying, "This way. They saved me a spot at the very back. I'll wash up and then we'll be on our way."

The "spot" was just that: a space cleared for a desk and two straight-back chairs. Piled neatly all around it were boxes and bags, filled and labeled. PAINKILLERS. DRIED FRUIT. CANNED GOODS. BANDAGES. BLANKETS.

"So," Marty said. "This is your surprise."

"This is my surprise. It's a wonderful place. The Sisters of Mercy—well, there aren't enough superlatives for them. Absolutely selfless and ready to serve. Most of them are trained as nurses, you know, so it makes— What? You're looking at me so strangely."

"You look great," Marty said. And she really did. She was still stick-thin, but there was an almost electric glow around her. She radiated energy and purpose. "So much better, actually. Energized."

Dr. Zee laughed. "I am, I am. It's funny. I'm exhausted, but the harder I work, the more strength I seem to find. It's quite a challenge, working here. Take care of AIDS patients and you soon find there aren't enough hours in the day.

Aside from the fact that many of them have been deserted, they need so *much* care."

She said she was doing rounds from six to eight A.M. every day, then she saw patients in a little examining room until ten, and then she went up front, to see new admissions, readmissions, emergencies. And all the time, charts were coming back and phone calls were coming in. "I'm telling you, Marty, I don't have a minute to feel sorry for myself, with this patient load. Hell, I don't have time to be *sick*," she said.

"Well, we all miss you, but this seems such a good thing for you to be—" Marty stopped and stared. For there, coming into the back room, loaded with stuffed shopping bags, was Norma McClure. "Norma?" she said.

"Oh, God," Norma said, turning red.

"No, I haven't made it to deityhood yet. Dare I ask what you're doing here?"

A whole series of emotions marched rapidly across Norma's round face, ending with amusement, of all the damn things. Norma began to laugh. "Oh, God, I know you all think I'm a nutcase. But, honest, I never took anything that we didn't have more than enough of. And they need it so badly—"

"Norma's sister runs this place," Dr. Zee interrupted.

"Norma's sister is a Sister of Mercy?"

"That's right. And here she is now. Sister Mary George, meet Marty Lamb, from All Souls. She's an N.P."

The clone of Norma, only taller, strode over and shook Marty's hand briskly, saying, "Very pleased. Did you and Norma come in together?" She wore a navy-blue suit and crucifix, just like Sister Augustine.

"Uh, not exactly."

"Sister, Marty didn't know until just now where I've been bringing the samples and—"

"Oh, dear. Marty, are you going to tell on her?"

The phrase from childhood made Marty laugh. "No, I'm not going to tell on her. In fact, when I get back, I'm going to see about making regular contributions to this place so Norma won't have to sneak around stealing aspirin samples and bagels."

"Glory be. All right, sis, let's see what we've got this time.

We're running out of gauze bandage and the tape is all gone. So if you . . ." And they busied themselves, making lists and putting things away.

"I'm ready to go, Marty. I think," Dr. Zee said. She bent for her black bag, then straightened and took in a deep breath. "My stomach is in knots right now. My opponents . . . my critics . . . they think it's so easy. *Easy!* I cry each time. Each time, I'm wrenched beyond description. Not because a person is dying. Dying should be everyone's right. But because we allow people to suffer so terribly and because our society won't take their suffering seriously. I hate our stupid laws! The Inuits had the right idea. When you knew you were dying, you said good-bye to everyone and floated off on an ice floe."

"I know. I know." They walked to the front of the clinic and out into the deserted street.

A small smile. "Nevertheless, I'm going to do whatever Mrs. Vargas wants, law or no law."

"I know." Marty gave her a smile. "I'm glad you asked me to go with you," she said. "I keep picturing Isabelle and her family, her sisters and brothers-in-law, her brother and his wife, the grandchildren, standing watch over her, knowing she'll soon be gone, weeping and weeping—" She choked up and tears slid down *her* cheeks.

Poor Marty, Dr. Zee thought. Maybe this was too much to ask of her. So many things had happened to her this summer . . . incredible. Her schizophrenic husband, suddenly back in her life; her old love reappears; her clinics in jeopardy; and now something nasty about Crystal Cole. It would depress anyone. However, nurses were especially prone to depression, so she'd been keeping her eye on Marty these past weeks, looking for signs of pathology, especially after Marty complained of a nausea that wouldn't go away. But Marty Lamb was too tough to give in to life's vagaries. The sick feeling must have been anxiety, nothing more.

"We think we should get used to death," Julia said, "because he's such a constant visitor. But we don't, Marty. We never do. But we *do* do what we have to do, and if that sounds like a song lyric, it isn't. The car's parked around the corner. Let's go." As

they turned the corner, she added: "I'm sorry I never got back to you, the other night when you called, but I got home too late. What's going on . . . ?"

"It's Crystal. You sure you want to drive?"

"I don't know any other way to get to Queens." Trouble with Crystal. Just as she had thought. Crystal had started like a house afire, all efficiency and lovability. But the past few months there had been a change. All that effervescence had changed into something charged and nervous. Let me guess, Dr. Zee thought. Drugs.

They climbed into her battered old '81 VW Rabbit. Even in the heat of late August it coughed and gargled before starting.

"You ever going to get a new car, or what?" Marty teased.

"Or what." They both laughed. The car grumbled but eventually got going, and they were on their way, heading crosstown and uptown to the Queensboro Bridge.

"Whatever happened to your husband? After he knocked me down, did he ever reappear?"

"No," Marty said. "Not in person. The cops lost him in the subway system . . . I guess that's not too hard to do. But . . ." She sighed deeply. "Owen doesn't give up. I've been getting two or three messages a day on my machine at home. It drives me crazy, although Paul says I should just ignore it. Easy for him to say."

"Marty, I don't have to tell you that Paul Giordano loves you. He seems to feel you don't trust him."

"I know he loves me. I just don't know if that's enough."

"Can I tell you something? From my vantage point? It's enough." When there was no response, she slid a look sideways, but Marty had turned to stare out of the window, and Julia couldn't see her face at all. "Crystal," she nudged.

"Oh Christ, I don't even know where to start. Well, actually, yes I do. I fired her."

"I'll guess because she's on drugs."

"I'm in awe, you know that? Yes, she's on drugs. Would you like to guess what else?"

"She's carrying on with a doctor?"

"You're the one who ought to be called Witch," Marty marveled.

"Not really. I've caught her . . . no, that's not right, I've never actually *seen* anything scandalous. But I kept seeing her in parts of the hospital she doesn't belong in. Once I caught her coming out of a patient's room with that good-looking drug rep. . . . Oh, they were talking loudly about some drug or other, but there was something about them . . ." She chuckled. "So, just for fun, I went back and looked into the room."

"And . . . ?"

"What do you think, Marty? It was empty, of course."

"Oh, Christ!" Marty's voice was so despondent, it was almost comical. "Doug Lavoro, too? What could she have wanted from *him*?"

"Think, Marty! Besides being a handsome devil and quite the man with the ladies, Mr. Lavoro is . . . ?"

"*Duh!* A drug rep. But Dennis Dinowitz told me she was getting drugs from *him*, in exchange for sexual favors."

"Once you have a habit, Marty, it's voracious."

"Which habit? The drugs? Or the sex?"

"Who knows? Dr. Dinowitz, eh? Well, that doesn't come as any surprise."

"And she had Joel on the hook, too! Sweet, funny Joel! Oh Christ, I can't even stand thinking about it!"

They were heading onto the Queensboro Bridge, where the traffic was actually not bumper-to-bumper for a change. And then Julia remembered. August. August was the month all the shrinks in private practice took their vacation, and so did all their private patients. Voilà! The traffic in New York suddenly got cut in half.

They were silent while she negotiated into the lane she wanted. Meanwhile, she couldn't help thinking about poor Crystal Cole, trapped into her addiction, or maybe addictions.

Why, she wondered, do so many doctors and nurses, nurses especially, have this tendency to fling themselves into romantic adventure? Being so close to death so constantly? With rare exceptions, they all did it. There were so many torn marriages and ruined relationships in the world of medicine. Working in a hospital seemed to actually *encourage* casual sex. After Hal, she herself had steered clear of it—once burned, twice shy—but many a time she'd be on her rounds

and come across a pair emerging from an empty room, an unused lab—a closet, even—faces flushed, hair disheveled, eyes sleepy and sated. She knew damn well what went on, had always gone on. It was often nurse and doctor—although, of course, it didn't *have* to be. She'd seen plenty of other combinations in her years at All Souls. Like Crystal and that drug rep. Doug something.

What a thing to be thinking of, on her way to help a suffering woman end her life. Strange, how when death hovered nearby, human beings often turned to sex, or thoughts of it, as a kind of affirmation of life. Right now, for instance, Hal had popped into her mind, and she wondered if he had ever given her one little thought after he ended their affair. *Dumped her,* that's what it was called nowadays. Even though it had all happened in the fifties—1955, to be exact—she still could remember how bruised and sore she had been, as if she really *had* been dumped from a great height.

She knew he was married when they started, so she was damn well aware of what she was in for. But somehow, she had chosen to forget. When Hal abruptly announced that his wife was beginning to get suspicious and it was over—no discussion, no argument, no regrets, just so long, please don't make a fuss it won't do any good—she had been stunned and distraught. Hell, her heart had been broken! And as if that weren't bad enough, here she was, sixty-three years old, still remembering it.

She handed Marty the directions Isabelle had drawn on a prescription pad and said, "Tell me where to turn, okay?" And then she concentrated on making her way through the unfamiliar neighborhood.

Isabelle lived on a pleasant street, right off the river, lined with trees and big old apartment buildings, none of them over ten stories. They weren't erecting skyscraper condos when these had been built. The curbs were lined with cars; the first space she found was three blocks away. That was okay; she wasn't in any hurry to get there. She hadn't said any specific hour, just "this evening," but they would be waiting, and if *she* was hesitant and a little afraid, she could just imagine how they were feeling.

She and Marty climbed out of the car, she locked it, and they walked slowly back toward Isabelle's building. Julia was acutely aware of the medical bag in her right hand. She could almost imagine that it gave out a glow because hidden inside was the release Mama Vargas longed for.

The neat black leather attaché case she carried, a birthday gift from Marty a couple of years ago, was nothing at all like the fat bag her family doctor had always brought with him, creaking as he opened it, smelling faintly of drugs, and inside, columns of fascinating glass vials filled with pills and powders, his stethoscope folded up in the middle. Doc O'Brien: she still remembered his brown suits with vests, always rumpled ... remembered his gruff voice—"Say 'aaahh,' Julia, that's a good girl"—still remembered the alcohol sting when he put the thermometer under her tongue, and his tiny grunt when he heaved the bag up off the floor, to get something magical out of it.

Her bag was light; no pills, few potions, and very little magic. Doctors nowadays did not carry drugs around with them, especially not at night. Doctors nowadays did not involve themselves with patients' families and problems; they treated diseases and wounds, and above all, they did battle with their sworn enemy, Death, doing everything to keep life, any kind of life, even a hated painful life, going.

Well, call her old-fashioned, she didn't believe in that stuff. The AMA, that band of reactionaries, had come out with one of their wonderful dicta, in response to the big rise in assisted suicide. "Medicine is a profession dedicated to healing. Its tools should not be used to kill people." Sounded good, but made no sense. Sometimes, there *was* no healing to be had; some things were unhealable, like Mama Vargas's cancer. Sometimes the only "cure" was death. Every doctor knew it. What was it that made everyone think people should be kept alive at all costs? She didn't get it.

As they got closer to the building, they could smell the river smells and hear the river sounds: the tiny lappings, the boats' creakings as they bobbed from side to side. Dr. Zee stopped and breathed it in. There was something wonderful about nature in the middle of the city, like a gift from the gods.

Isabelle and her family lived in a big old brick and limestone building overlooking the water, once rather splendid but now a bit down at the heels. Marty rang the bell and answered the tinny voice that asked, "Dr. Zee?" The lobby door clicked and Julia pushed it open. Inside, it was dimly lit, damp and faintly dank. An old building that was hard to keep clean.

Julia pressed the elevator button—not wanting to walk up the dark stairway to the second floor, although Isabelle always did—and waited while it came groaning down from the top floor. It was just past seven. The elevator came. She folded back the gate, got in, pushed the button that said B. She wanted to put off the inevitable just one little minute more. Silly.

The whole family was there, in the living room, waiting for them. Tears sprang to Julia's eyes when she saw that everyone was all dressed up, as if for a party. There were white shirts, suits, sequins, spike-heeled shoes, organdy ruffles, patent leather. She wished she had thought to wear something . . . what? Elegant, maybe. Something a bit more suited to the solemnity of the occasion than her sharkskin slacks and silk shirt. She glanced over at Marty. Marty was dressed for work, too, in slacks and shirt. She'd twisted her ponytail into a French knot and had put pearl studs in her ears. Marty looked great; she always did.

"Dr. Zee. Marty Lamb. We're so happy to see you." Isabelle's husband, Pepe, ushered them in. "Mama has been waiting for you, haven't you, Mama?" Mrs. Vargas's bed had been moved a month ago into the living room when she had become too weak to walk—"so she can see everything that's going on," Isabelle had told them. Now she opened her eyes and gave a small smile, but Julia noticed immediately that she did not move her head. In the few days since she had last seen her, Mama Vargas seemed to have faded and shrunk.

"Will you have a glass of wine?" Pepe asked. "We're all having a little wine."

"We'll join you, of course." Dr. Zee smiled at the assembled family; some of them she had met, and some of them she'd seen once or twice, and some were new to her. They all smiled back at her.

She would not go to the bedside, or do anything, until they

asked. Mrs. Vargas might have changed her mind; she'd already done so once. But that time, there had been no cere-monial atmosphere, no candles lighted, no gathering of all the aunts and uncles and cousins. Tonight they were all here, even an ancient, wrinkled crone who sat hunched in a flowered chair, rocking herself back and forth, whispering something, maybe prayers.

"Mama is ready," Pepe said. He reached out an arm for Isabelle, who had been kneeling by her mother's side, her head down. She stood up and came to him, tears streaming down her face. "Thank you for coming, Marty. Dr. Zee. Yes, Mama is ready. She can't even whisper now." They stood aside, leaving a kind of corridor for her.

Julia walked to the bed, sat in the chair that was always there, bent close to the woman. Mrs. Vargas's eyes had closed again; Isabelle had said they were almost always closed now. "Mrs. Vargas. Do you hear me and understand me?"

A voice as light as tissue. "Yes."

"Your daughter and son-in-law say you are ready. Are you ready, Mrs. Vargas? To die?"

No pause at all. "Yes."

"Your family is here to say good-bye. Have you said good-bye to everyone?"

This time the "Yes" was so faint, she might almost have imagined it.

"I'm going to hand you two pills, Mrs. Vargas. Can you take them with water?" A faint smile answered her. "You won't feel anything and soon you'll fall asleep." Her voice was beginning to waver. She must be very careful not to cry. Doc-tors and nurses were not allowed to weep and mourn; it was their job to be strong for all the others. And she often wondered if it was a sign of terrible weakness in her, that she never ceased feeling dreadful about her dying patients. That was the main reason to hold back her tears. If she let herself weep, she'd never be able to stop.

Mrs. Vargas opened her eyes. They were bright with intelli-gence. She summoned all her strength and said, "Yes. Bless. Bless."

She bent to her bag, opened it, took out the caplets, looked

up to find Isabelle, strangely calm, standing there, waiting. She handed over the pills and watched while Izzy gave them, one at a time, to her mother, tenderly proffering the glass with the bent tube. Slowly, slowly, Mrs. Vargas sucked in the water, swallowed. Once. Twice. Her eyes were wide-open and Dr. Zee could see her lips forming silent words, but since they were probably in Spanish, she couldn't guess what they were. Isabelle took her mother's hand.

Pepe came to stand with his wife. The room was hushed, as if everyone had stopped breathing. Julia felt weakness stealing over her, but she forced herself to stand and hold her back straight. Ten minutes passed. Another five. Mrs. Vargas's breathing became heavier and more labored. When she gave a little gasp with a sigh at the end of it, Isabelle began to sob, and then so did Pepe. And then every person in the room. The grandchildren held each other, weeping loudly. Dr. Zee walked over to Mrs. Vargas, to check her vital signs. She didn't have to; she knew death when she saw it. But she checked, anyway. There was no pulse. "She's gone," she said, gently closing the eyes, and closed her own in wordless prayer.

When she opened them, the family was clustered all around her, saying "Thank you, Doctor" . . . "God bless you, Doctor" . . . "I'll remember you in my prayers, Doctor." She tried to smile but could not. And then she, too, began to cry, without sound. And was immediately drawn to the sofa, helped into a seat next to Marty, handed a glass of wine and a box of tissues. Marty's hand shot out to enfold hers, and she was grateful for the touch. "I'm so tired," she murmured, putting her head back and closing her eyes, "so tired."

Dawn was putting a yellow glow around the black skyline when they left and walked to the car. "You fell asleep on Isabelle's sofa almost instantly," Marty told her. "I just couldn't wake you."

"So you stayed."

"So I stayed." She yawned.

"What were *you* doing, half the night? Not sleeping, I see."

"Talking with Isabelle and keeping an eye on *you*."

"Don't worry, I'm not going to die so fast."

"You're tougher than anything, right?"

"Damn straight!" she said, although to tell the truth, every muscle and joint ached. Marty was wonderful company, but still, she couldn't help wishing Lou were still alive; she could have talked it all over with him. He would have made her a cup of tea, his answer to all of life's problems, and he would have held her hand and listened. Lou Felsen, cloakie, self-taught modern art aficionado, fifteen years her senior and good, good, good. She had married him on the rebound, really, but it had turned out well for both of them. He was the one who said she should be a doctor, and if she did the studying part, he'd do the tuition part. She still missed him.

When they reached the car, she handed the keys to Marty and said, "You drive."

On their way once again, she turned to Marty. "Make sure Crystal stays fired," she said. "Don't feel sorry for her. She's broken too many rules and now she thinks she can get away with anything."

She could practically *hear* Marty thinking before she finally said, "Crys is our poison pen."

"Oh?" That woke her up. "You have proof?"

"How's a confession? Well . . . a sort-of confession. She likes to tease me with the details, almost admitting stuff and then backing away, grinning like a demon. Or weeping wildly."

"Not pretty."

"No, it's not pretty. But who knows what problems she has? I keep thinking maybe I should wait until she's tried a detox program. I fired her already, but I don't know . . . I have this funny feeling she'll show up and do something else stupid. I want her to get some help, some therapy. I hate to see her lose her license. . . . I really should try to get Dennis and Joel to add their two cents' worth, but I hate to embarrass them that way. Bad enough they got involved in her sickness, but to make it public . . . ? I don't know. And I can't *force* her to go into a program. The whole thing bothers me. It's like having the power of life and death over someone."

"So double check. Triple check. Embarrass your friends. Or don't. Pray, if that'll help. But Marty, I don't think she's salvageable at this point. I think she's dangerous. You *must* make

sure this woman can't ever get near patients again! Fight those nursing impulses!"

They both laughed, a little, but it was rueful. Very rueful.

34

It was Saturday. By all rights, Marty thought, just a bit resentful, she should be home with Paul, enjoying the weekend, maybe even—what a concept!—*sleeping in*. But, no, here she was, stuck in the office with nothing for company but a million reports, her anxiety about JCAHO, and that horrible nauseated feeling. Once this was all over with, maybe she'd get her appetite back. Paul had made French toast for her this morning, and she'd only been able to get down one mouthful. She *hated* being at the mercy of her psyche! And it was a mystery why, when she was feeling so sick to her stomach all the time, her slacks were getting tight. Must be she was stuffing down more doughnuts and coffee while she worked than she wanted to remember. It had been an endless, anxious week anyway, with Isabelle out, mourning her mother; and Crystal God alone knew where; and Paul up to here with details, as he took command of the Family Practice unit.

Well, she'd accomplished *one* thing—she'd taken Norma McClure to Protozoa for a nice lunch and extracted a promise that she'd stop her petty pilfering. "I know it's for a good cause, Norma, but you can't just *take* things out of the hospital."

Norma had protested. "So much goes to waste, Marty. So much is stashed in a cupboard and just goes bad."

"I didn't mean that your sister's clinic should go without. Make lists and check them with me. Or with Dr. Giordano.

Don't worry, he just *looks* fierce. He's really a nice guy and he won't be hard-nosed."

Just to make things even more difficult, renovation work would be going on at the hospital all weekend, in preparation for the visitors on Monday. In truth, most of these so-called renovations would be cosmetic cover-ups. They'd never done anything about widening the corridors in the clinics, for instance. A couple of guys from maintenance had measured the space. And that was the end of CCC's modernization.

It was not, however, the end of labor—not for workmen and not for staff and *particularly* not for heads of departments. She and Paul had both been at the hospital since early in the morning. They'd been working the whole time, without even a few free minutes to talk on the phone. It was almost eight P.M., her office window had gone dark with nightfall, and here she was, still hunting for a whole batch of patient records, which should be in Crystal's files but weren't. The Birthing Center records were a total mess.

Crys had been a lot sicker than anyone had realized. Now, of course, she wasn't around to answer questions. She wasn't *anywhere* to be found, in fact. Marty had called her several times; not even Crys's machine had answered.

Marty put her head into her hands. Her eyes hurt, her back hurt, hell, her *brain* hurt. A whole day of work and very god-damn little to show for it! Soon those fabulous folks from the Joint Committee for Accreditation of Health-related Organizations, armed with their clipboards and pens and sharp little eyes, would be here. *That* was going to be an exercise in futility for All Souls!

I've done all *I* could, she thought—somewhat defensively since she didn't totally believe it.

"Marty, you all tied up?"

Marty looked up and smiled at Sonya. She'd become quite fond of Sonya—and not only because the midwife had slipped right into Crys's job without questions or whining. She hadn't even asked for a raise. She cared about the patients. She worked long hours without complaint; her appearance here now was proof of *that*. And she saw much more than she ever told.

"Yes, I am, Sonya. I am all tied up in knots, to tell you the truth. We're never going to be ready for the JCAHO. I don't know what Crystal did with all the files from—"

"I do. Yeah, I found 'em. In the back closet."

"In the *closet*?"

"I guess she started hiding them there when she began ordering double doses of painkillers."

"You knew she was getting stoned."

"No, ma'am. I didn't *know*. I guessed. I thought so. I was pretty goddamn sure, to tell you the truth. But you can't go by your feelings; you got to have proof, right?"

"Well, we've got enough proof now." Grimly: "And I'm going to use it."

Sonya nodded. "You gotta do what you gotta do. And don't feel too bad, Marty. If you'd seen her the night Marie Racine's baby was born, you'da done it right then and there."

"Oh, God, Baby Edouard. I haven't seen him since—"

"Not to worry . . . mind if I sit?"

"Oh, Sonya, I'm sorry. Where are my brains? Of course. Sit. Please. Can I offer you a cup of horrible coffee from the machine?"

Sonya laughed. "No, thanks. I've had too much already. You want me to get you one?"

"No. It'll keep me up all night, if my worries don't. You said—about Baby Edouard?"

"I've been keeping my eye on him, Marty. It's not a sure thing, him being so small. But they say Dr. Fassbinder's a miracle worker with preemies—a total asshole, but a miracle worker." They both laughed. "And that *bébé*, he's a tough little fella, opens his eyes wide and looks right at you. He's a fighter, I can tell."

"Maybe Marie can have her happy ending. I don't suppose the father has ever showed up?"

"Nope. Although . . . Well, I don't like to gossip."

Marty smiled. "Come on, Sonya. We *all* like to gossip."

"Yeah. Well . . . I think Marie's just about forgotten that guy. Good riddance, *I* say. When the going got tough, he just got going. She hasn't seen him for a while now, not even a phone call to say good-bye. Nothing. But here comes Clive

Moses, making googoo eyes at her." Sonya rolled her large brown eyes. "That Clive Moses, now! There's a *man*! And he's real good to little Marie. What I think—"

The phone rang. It was Paul, to tell her sadly that he'd be working pretty late tonight. "How I wish Dr. Zee hadn't left," he said. "Not only because I miss her, but for purely selfish reasons. She ran this service for umpteen years, so a lot of stuff is filed in her brain. It must be; we can't find it in the *files*." He laughed but he sounded really tired.

"Can I tempt you with visions of home-cooked pasta?"

"Boy, would I love to. But no. If I want to look as if I know what's going on in Family Practice, I'd better stick around until everything is done." Asked when he thought that might be, he groaned and said, "In 1999?" So she'd be dining alone this evening, which meant, probably, take-out Chinese, or maybe a salad if she had enough in the refrigerator.

She hung up and said, "You feel like grabbing a bite at Proto's, Sonya?"

"Oh, thanks, Marty, that'd be nice. But my mama's waiting on me at home. Lots of times she won't eat unless I'm there. So I'd better get going. You should get on home, too. Don't you worry about those records. I'll get 'em all filed."

After Sonya had left, Marty sat at her desk, unable to summon the energy to move from her chair. Now she knew what bone-tired meant. But Sonya was right; she should get out of here and try to relax. A few minutes later she let herself out by the Hamilton Place entrance, dragging her feet a bit but otherwise okay. The weariness had passed but she didn't quite want to get home. Nor did she want to stay at the hospital. She didn't know *what* she wanted to do; nothing appealed.

As she passed Protozoa she peered into the plate-glass window, hoping to see someone she'd like to spend a few minutes with over a nice cold drink; but the glass only gave her back her own reflection, and *that* person was not someone she felt like spending a few minutes with, not right now. Anyway, at this time on Saturday, the place was always mobbed with singles trying to find their one true love before midnight.

She continued on her way, wondering why she was disinclined to go straight home. Wasn't it her castle? Why was she

feeling so uneasy and out of sorts? Because Crystal had disappeared? Or because Owen kept calling her, or because Dr. Zee was sick with an incurable disease? Or none of the above? All she knew was that there was this huge black cloud of anxiety that hovered over her. Maybe it was just the JCAHO. Worst-case scenario—All Souls wasn't accredited. Did it matter, since they were probably going to be sold anyway? And once they became a tax write-off for a big hospital with lots of money, and the new management decided that poor people could just as easily go to Harlem for their health care—or, more likely, to Hell—well, then they'd see what happened. Only she might not be here to see it. Which was a pretty scary thought.

As she passed Shayna's bedroom window she automatically slowed down, hoping the drapes would be pulled aside and she'd see the girl looking out the window, like in the good old days. No such luck. Whatever Zeke was planning for his daughter—and whatever she was planning for him—it was going on away from prying eyes. And it was none of her business—no matter *how* she felt about it. She hurried on.

Oh Christ, what in hell *was* she going to do if she lost her job? Probably apply immediately to the new hospital, for starters. And if that didn't work? Maybe she *would* go back to school; maybe she'd go back to psychiatric nursing; or take a long vacation; and maybe—

"Shit!" she said aloud, startling a pair of teenagers passing her on the street.

Even half a block away there was no mistaking Owen. The streetlight on the corner shone brightly, making a golden halo of his fair curly hair. He was sitting in the middle of the stone steps leading up to her front door, peering down the street. As soon as he caught sight of her, he began waving madly, shouting her name. She wished she could say a magic word and just disappear. He was *never* going to leave her alone; when she was a little old lady in a nursing home, he'd show up to drive her crazy.

"Where were you, Marty?" he demanded as soon as she was close enough. "I was expecting you five minutes ago."

Her heart sank. How could he be expecting her? She did not

normally work all day and most of the evening on Saturday. He must have seen her on the street. Or . . . "Owen, you've been following me!"

"I have something very important to tell you—"

"I don't care if you come with a message from God Himself. You can't stalk me, that's what they call it and it's against the law. Do you understand. Owen? Have I made myself clear? *What?*" she said, catching a change of expression in his face.

"That's exactly *it*, Marty. God *has* been talking to me . . . it's wonderful, Marty, He has such a nice calm voice, not like the others . . . they're so nasty."

"Well, that's a nice change."

"And God told me you're in danger. I'm not stalking you, Marty, I'm watching out for you. God said I should protect you."

Oh Christ. "Owen, are you sure it's God's voice?"

"Certainly I'm sure. He says 'Owen, this is God. Your wife is in danger from the forces of evil.' So you see, I *have* to know where you are, every minute of the night and day."

He was so earnest, so caring. And so sick. His eyes never met hers, but roved about wildly. He must have stopped taking the Clozapine altogether. She sat down on the steps with him and said, carefully, "Look, Owen, remember the last time you heard God's voice? Remember?"

He didn't answer her until she repeated the word several times. Then he nodded.

"And what was it, Owen?" He shook his head stubbornly, so she supplied the answer: "It wasn't God at all. It was one of your voices, telling you it was God. And he told you to cut yourself, remember?"

"I remember that time," he said. "I remember they told me it was in my head. I remember." She relaxed. "But this time, it's *really* God. I checked."

She closed her eyes briefly. It wasn't going to do any good to lose her temper with him. "Owen, listen, I'm not in danger. I'm fine. But you aren't. You have to take your meds."

"I have been. Yes, really, honest to God."

"Then you have to go to the doctor and get them checked. I

promise you, Owen, when the medication is working, God does not speak to you."

"But I *am* taking them. Really." She sat on the stone step, her tush beginning to go numb, wishing she were far far away. It was possible. Sometimes it happened—the voices broke through the medication, no matter how much the dosage was increased. But it couldn't hurt to have somebody talk to him.

"Will you see Joel Mannes and tell him that God is talking to you and let him check your dosage?"

"Dr. Mannes is out to get me!" he said, his voice suddenly strident. "Dr. Mannes made me leave here and live far away. And you're in *danger*, Marty. You're in danger because I'm not here to protect you and it's *his* fault!"

"Owen, you're shouting. If you keep on yelling—"

"I'll stop, I'll stop, I don't want to go to Bellevue."

She hadn't thought of Bellevue, but now that he mentioned it . . . not such a bad idea. "If you don't want to go to Bellevue, and you won't let Dr. Mannes check you, then come back with me to the hospital and we'll call Dr. Chen."

He didn't want to go back to the hospital. He didn't want to talk to Dr. Chen. "I listen only to God and nobody else! You don't seem to understand what an honor it is, that God talks to me. You're being stupid, Marty." His voice was rising with every word. She got up, hefting the heavy shoulder bag . . . just in case. Owen got up, too, and took a step or two closer to her. He was very agitated and it made her nervous. "Watch it, Marty, because God is telling me to protect you or kill you, one or the other, it's up to you."

Oh Christ. She held a hand out, holding him off, and retreated up a couple of steps. "Owen, you're yelling again," she said in her most reasonable voice. "I think you should try to calm down." Yes, she was frightened. He was capable of anything. She probably should take him upstairs and call Dr. Chen from there, but if she did, she'd *never* get rid of him.

"Owen, if you won't see Dr. Mannes and you won't talk to Dr. Chen, you have to leave! You're trespassing. I've got a lawyer and I'm getting a divorce, our marriage is over and I'm in love with another man. I know you're sick, but I can't take care of you! You have to leave and that's final!"

Her heart was pounding like crazy. What if he took it into his head to bop her one, to keep her from divorcing him? But he just stood there, staring blindly at her. Probably too busy listening to what God had to say. So she went up the steps. At the top, she turned around; he was still in the same spot, in the same position. So she quickly let herself in, hurried inside the apartment, and double-locked the door.

Leaning against the door for a moment, she stood listening. Silence. Maybe he'd gone away. But when she peeked out of her window, he was sitting on the bottom step, slumped in dejection. As she watched, he lifted his head, listening, then answered whatever it was he was hearing. She turned away, and if that made her a bad person, well . . . tough. She was so goddamn tired of him.

The answering machine's little red light was blinking rapidly. Maybe something good. For a change. She poured herself a glass of wine and pushed play. There was a minute of two of raspy silence and then a click. That was it. Crystal, she thought. That was Crystal. For some reason, the nonmessage made her extremely uneasy. She sidled over to the bay window and looked out. For a miracle, Owen had left. Maybe God told him to go downtown. Well, this called for celebration. She really wanted to get out of here, anyway. So she might as well just turn around and head back to Protozoa for pizza and a glass of wine. There'd be someone there with a friendly face, someone to talk to. She left a message on Paul's office machine that maybe he should check the bar before coming home.

As she trotted down the front steps she got the feeling someone was staring at her. She stopped and looked around. Nobody. Owen had made *her* paranoid now. Several times she halted unexpectedly and whirled around, only to find nothing. She must look ridiculous; nevertheless, she couldn't shake the feeling that he was *there*, just out of her line of sight. Oh, to hell with him.

Passing the Brown apartment, she heard a lot of noise, and stopped to check it out. It was the hubbub of a large gathering, with the rabbi's voice riding over everything else, in the singsong cadences of a long-winded toast. Then a lot of clapping and laughter. Oh yes. Shayna's betrothal party, Marty

remembered, and moved on. Here she was, feeling sorry for herself because Owen kept popping up. But she had a thousand options. Poor Shayna was *really* trapped. She felt pity for Shayna but there was nothing she could do.

Protozoa was as crowded as she had feared. Even so, she saw Dr. Dimwit right away. He had—in the way of doctors, especially Chiefs of Service—grabbed a table meant for four and was sitting there in solitary majesty. As soon as he spotted her, he motioned her over. He was drinking a martini. As she slid into a chair opposite him, "I'll have one of those, thank you very much," she said.

He held up two fingers, and within moments Aldo himself delivered two chilled glasses with photogenic little drops drifting down the frosted sides, just like in a commercial. They asked after Aldo's baby, got beams and brags and several Polaroid shots to look at, and then Aldo scooped up his pictures and bustled off, saying, "Busy night, busy night."

"What brings *you* here all alone on a Saturday night?" Dennis asked. "I thought you and Giordano . . ." He grinned and lifted his glass in salute.

She smiled back at him. "You thought correctly. Paul's trying to get a handle on his service before the JCAHO come in on Monday. I'm hoping he'll finish soon. What brings *you* here all alone on a Saturday night?"

He shrugged. "My date cancelled out on me."

They both lifted glasses and sipped. "Ahhhh," Marty said. "Excellent choice, Dr. Dinowitz."

"I salute your brave stand with Len Fassbinder." To her surprised look, he laughed and said, "Oh, he told me all about it—how you *dared* show such insolence—to a *physician*! I told him you did it all the time." He laughed again. "He thought he'd shut you up completely, but you showed him!"

Marty took another sip and regarded the handsome face. Had she ever seen Dr. Dimwit *smile* before, much less throw his head back and laugh? "Dennis, tell me something."

"Fire away."

She grinned at him. "I thought you were . . . well, on *their* side. Len's side."

"I've had to rethink a few things lately, Marty. I've been

taking myself very seriously, maybe too seriously. I thought that's what I had to do. I was considered a brilliant young physician, on the fast track. . . ."

"Surely you still are."

"Maybe. But maybe not." A defeated shrug. "Dammit, Marty, all I need is for *her* to start blabbing and spreading rumors. I'm already—" He stopped, ill at ease.

"Already under disciplinary review, Dennis?"

"Jesus! How do you women *do* it? Find out every goddamn thing?"

She was not going to tell him. "I heard a rumor. And, no, not from *her*."

He moaned a little. "What a mess! It's true. Somebody noticed all the D and Cs and the hysterectomies—"

"It took them long enough! Sorry. You were saying . . . ?"

"They called me in and showed me the list and asked me if I really thought all of these procedures were necessary."

"And you said . . . ?"

"I said of course I really thought they were all necessary."

"And were they?"

"Shit, Marty, you know they weren't, not all. Most were. I'm not a complete scumbag. But . . . Messinger had been putting on the pressure, calling the Medical Staff in every couple of weeks and reading off figures to us, saying we had to do better. 'A hospital doesn't run on healthy people, gentlemen.' " Dennis paused and scrubbed his face with his hand, as if he wanted to erase the worried frown between his eyes. But when he dropped his hand, the two deep furrows were still there. "I . . . I was on the fast track, I couldn't afford to fall behind, so . . ." He held his hands out in surrender. "I've been a shit, I know it. But I'm not doing it anymore. If my . . . if my *liaison* with that witch taught me anything, it taught me not to feel so superior."

"Don't worry, they'll let you off with a slap on the wrist. Isn't that what usually happens to bright young physicians who get into trouble?"

"Well . . . as a matter of fact, yes. Everyone's entitled to one mistake, Marty, even you have to admit that. But Crys—*she* could destroy my career. If the word goes out that a gynecolo-

gist is into sex . . . ! I could lose all my patients." He paused and colored a bit. "A lot of them have, you know, a crush on me." He looked a bit sick. "The only reason she hasn't spread the word is because it will uncover *her* activities, too, and she doesn't want to lose her license."

"I hate to tell you this, Dennis, but she's about to. Lose her license, I mean."

"You're not going to use what you know, are you, Marty?"

"Use what? You and Crystal? Hell, no. Why would I do a thing like that?"

"Well, we haven't always, um, got along."

She laughed. "That's putting it mildly, Dr. Dinowitz. Even so, your personal life is your personal life. Anyway, does anyone care if a doctor and a nurse have sex? It's not like it's unusual or anything."

"Dr. Messinger. I get a powerful feeling *he* cares."

"Well, Crystal's in trouble for being stoned on the job, for leaving patients, and as a matter of fact, she's been—" She stopped. They were beginning to become something like friendly, but he didn't have to know *everything*.

His face froze for an instant. "*I* gave her prescriptions, Marty."

"Don't worry. You weren't the only one."

"She has to be stopped. I mean *stopped* . . . not just put on report and quietly relieved of her job. They already did that, at St. Francis."

"They did? They knew she was on drugs and they never said a word when she came here?"

"She went into a detox program, did very well, too. Seemed to be cured. And she's so good at her job, Marty . . . well, but you know that. But after a while . . . hell, you know addicts. Enough stress and they're at it again. But as far as St. Francis was concerned, she'd learned her lesson, so why tell anyone?"

"And then she came here and did the same stuff all over again. How she must be laughing at naive little me."

"She laughs at all of us, Marty, she thinks she's so fucking superior."

"Typical personality disorder, right?" She lifted her glass to take another sip, surprised to find it empty. Dennis noticed and

up went the two fingers and, once again, their drinks appeared like magic. "When I send the report to the licensure board, I hope I don't have to use you as a backup reference, Dennis. I'd hate to get you into any more trouble."

"Well . . . as a matter of fact, I can think of someone even better than me. I don't think she scares *him*."

Marty gave him an I'm-interested-go-ahead look, but she was thinking, please, don't make it some other doctor I know and like.

But the name he gave was not a doctor at all. "Clive Moses."

"Aha. I've always had a feeling there used to be something between them."

"They were engaged to be married."

"Engaged! What happened?"

Dennis stared off at the faraway wall. Finally, he said, "She's very destructive, you know. She has some sort of sick need to demolish anything nice. I don't know what happened to her when she was a kid but it must have been awful."

"You haven't answered my question."

"I'm not absolutely sure what happened. Although . . . Clive and I are in a regular poker game, you know. Men don't usually confess stuff to each other, but things come up when you play cards. A few comments were dropped . . . and, anyway, I didn't need it spelled out for me. I'd been there. Ask him. Tell him you're going to report her to the Nursing Licensure Board. I have a feeling it'll make him so happy, he'll probably tell you everything."

"Okay. I think I will."

"And you might want to warn your pal Mannes," he said casually, sipping at his drink.

"Never fear. Joel's out from under."

They were leaning over the table, pretty close to each other, so they could talk without being overheard. Marty felt somebody's eyes on her—goddammit, she was going to put Owen back into the hospital herself. She'd get him committed if he didn't stop following her!

She turned, glaring—to meet the startled eyes of Paul Giordano, through the hordes around the bar. She waved to him, excused herself for a second and got up. But Paul was out the

door by the time she pushed through the crowd. What was his problem? Couldn't he wait just one minute to hear what she had to say? She didn't even know if he was jealous, seeing her with Dennis the Make-out Man, or if the furious look she'd prepared for Owen had put him off.

She went back to Dennis, saying, "This has been fascinating, Dennis. Thanks for the martinis. But I ought to be on my way. Do you mind?"

"Not at all. Thanks for listening to me. I am a cleansed man and now I will go and sin no more. Well . . . I'll sin no more if that cute little blonde at the bar who's been giving me the eye turns out to be just cross-eyed."

Marty laughed, leaned over impulsively on her way out and gave him a light kiss that hit a corner of his mouth. Now she was glad she had decided not to tell him what Crystal had been doing with that Xerox copy he had "posed" for.

While she was making her way to the door, saying, "Excuse me . . . excuse me . . . excuse me . . ." and wishing it weren't rude to push, she thought she saw Owen, right outside. She barreled through a group of residents, engrossed in discussing a case, and finally made it out onto the sidewalk, in one piece. Over there, by the lamppost! Owen's curly head! She strode over, ready to give him hell, and of course it turned out to be one of the Pediatrics residents.

Feeling extremely foolish, she once again found herself stalling. She had a creepy feeling Owen would be on her front steps again, waiting for her with his messages from God. *She* had a message for God. "Take Owen Lamb out of my life, please." She thought, very briefly, of going back into Protozoa, but the decibel level was climbing with every minute that passed. What with the crowd, the muggy heat, and the din in there, she decided thanks, but no thanks.

She'd go home, give Paul a big kiss, and take a long bubble bath—preferably with him. Of course, she might have to explain what she'd been doing with Dr. Dimwit first.

She expected to hear the unique sound of the hora or some other Israeli dance coming from the Brown apartment, but everyone seemed to have left. All the windows were wide-open, and there were only two voices to be heard, Shayna's and

her father's, both loud and angry. Alarmed, Marty went into the lobby and started for the front door; then stopped. What business was it of hers? But Shayna was so helpless, and Zeke was so volatile lately.

She rang the doorbell, fully expecting to hear the rabbi's voice on the intercom and not to be let in; but at least she'd have created a diversion. She'd have to call Dr. Zee, and together they could figure out how to get Shayna out of this apartment and away from a man who was plainly disturbed.

To her amazement, Zeke came to the door and flung it open. They both stared, dumbfounded, at each other. Then, his lips curled in a smile, he grabbed her arm and yanked her in, saying, "Marty Lamb, just the one I was hoping to see!" Keeping a grip on her arm, he double-locked the door. That, she definitely did not like. And when she saw the gun in his other hand, she liked it even less, especially since he had it pointed right at her.

"Where are your sons?" Diversion, diversion; it worked with two-year-olds, it worked with mental patients, it might even work with him. She was surprised that her voice sounded pretty normal, considering she could hardly breathe.

He waved his children off. "They're gone. They're safe. They will carry on my work when they grow to manhood."

"Let me out of here, Zeke."

"No, I'm afraid you're staying," he said. "Come. Shayna's in here." He pulled her into the living room, just a few steps away. Shayna had been placed deep into the corner of the over-sized velvet sofa, where she could not move. Her twisted legs stuck out in front of her, thin as sticks, lifeless. What's wrong with this picture? Marty asked herself; and then realized, with a shock, what it was.

"Your skirt!" she blurted. "Shayna, what happened to your skirt?" Miriam had showed it to her, months ago, when it came from Saks Fifth Avenue: many diaphanous layers, red on pink on white on red, long and flounced, edged in delicate lace. A birthday present. Very expensive. But now! It had been hacked with a pair of scissors, and the jagged edges barely reached to Shayna's twisted knees.

"Tell her," the rabbi said. His voice was dangerously calm.

"Tell her what happened to your skirt, Shaynele. Tell her what you have done to your father. God said, *'Thou shalt honor thy mother and thy father!'* " he said in a loud voice that shook with emotion.

"I choose to honor my mother, who loved me."

"*I* love you, Shayna. You are too stupid and too stubborn to see what is true. So. Tell her. Tell your friend the nurse what you have done."

"Marty, I apologize for your being dragged in here like this, into the middle of a personal matter." Shayna's face, a pale oval in the dimly lit room, was set and her voice was steady.

"Personal, she calls it. She has chased away my congregation, all of them. They have run at the sight of her misshapen legs!"

"No, Rabbi!" It just came out of Marty's mouth. "Don't say that!"

His clutch on her arm tightened; she thought he might stop her circulation, and she struggled with him until he loosened his grip a bit. "Tell Marty Lamb what you have done, my darling daughter," he purred. "But don't you try to leave, Marty," he warned, waving the gun a little. "Don't even try to move away from me. I want you to hear this."

"Okay, okay," she placated him. "Shayna, what happened?"

"I took the scissors and I cut my skirt short, so that everybody could see my legs. For love of my mother, Selma brought me the scissors, because *he* has made sure to keep everything away from me that is sharp, or that might cut, that I might kill myself with. . . ."

"Shayna, Shayna, of course I have. I love you. I don't wish you dead."

"Not even now?" she jeered. "Oh, you should see your face! Maybe you would like to kill me yourself, no? Yes, I think he plans to kill us, Marty. Oh, Marty, you came at a bad time!" Her beautiful dark eyes glittered in a way that made Marty shiver.

"After all," the rabbi said, "you have destroyed *me*, haven't you, Shayna?" He turned to Marty. "She hid under the paisley shawl her mother bought for her. She looked beautiful when they carried her in on the big carved chair, beautiful. She

shone! She was like a bright light in a dark world. Everyone gasped at the sight of her. There was a sigh from one side of the room to the other. And then—"

"And then, Marty, I cried out, 'Look, look, everyone, at the beautiful bride-to-be . . . look to see what your beloved rabbi has been hiding since the day I was born!' And I threw off the shawl, and there I was, *all* of me!" She clapped her hands.

"My so-called bridegroom, the idiot boy, he could care less! The same stupid smile stayed on his face the whole time. But his brother, Ezra, he was a different matter, right, Papa? Ezra shouted that they have been wondering about the rabbi lately, he hasn't been himself, and now they knew. 'His is a tainted family and Rabbi Ezekiel Brown is a tainted leader!' Ezra yelled that everyone should get out, *get out*! And they did, Marty, they *ran* out of here! They couldn't wait to get away!"

"An abomination unto the Lord," the rabbi muttered.

"I? I am an abomination? Go look in a mirror, Papa! Just go look, if abomination is what you want to see." Her head swiveled back to Marty. "They took my three little brothers, Marty. They dragged them out of this place, wailing. He let them go. And I? I was happy, at last. I caught sight of my face in one of the mirrors and it startled me. I looked lit from within. Now I know what freedom feels like . . . what freedom *looks* like! Like a great shining!"

It was awful; worse than Marty had thought. "Zeke," she said in her calmest, take-charge voice, "you and Shayna need to talk to someone who can help you both through your anger. Just let me out of here."

"Not on your life." He laughed. "Funny I should say that."

"Why funny?"

"Because we're all going to give up our lives, Marty, give up our lives to prove my point. You are going to call Clive Moses and Ham Pierce and tell them both that I'm going to set fire to this place, and we are all, you and Shayna and I, going to die. And we will be purified by the flames."

"What makes you think I'd do that, Zeke?"

He smirked a bit. "Because if you don't, I'll kill Shayna right now. Or maybe you." He leveled the gun right at her head. "And then I'll set fire to the apartment anyway."

35

"Zeke, you're not making sense."

"It is the Almighty's warning to the hospital ... to the medical profession that has usurped the rightful place of the Lord our God. Those who turn away from the word of God will perish in the fires!"

She had to pretend he was making sense, Marty thought. It was important to keep up some sort of dialogue, no matter how insane. "I know it's been awful for you. But the hospital didn't—"

"The hospital gave my wife abortions ... *abortions!* ... even though the hospital knew it was forbidden." He leaned forward. "Many abortions, Marty. All those babies ... my children ... murdered ..."

"She wanted—"

"*She wanted!* You don't seem to understand the most elementary rules, Marty. It doesn't matter what she wanted! What she wanted was nothing—less than nothing! What the Almighty wants, that is what we listen to."

Shayna interrupted. "And you, of course, are the only one in the world God talks to!"

He turned on her. "Careful what you say, Shayna, you may be struck down!"

"Surely Miriam would not like to hear you say that," Marty said to him, rather desperately. How the hell was poor dead Miriam going to hear him say anything?

But his lips curled in a wistful smile and his angry glare became unfocused. He stood, silent, for a moment, and then said, in a thoughtful tone, "I loved her, you know. It was a sin, the way I loved her. Our marriage was arranged by our

fathers. . . ." He turned angrily to Shayna, deep in a corner of the couch, adding, "That is how we do it, Marty, we of the Survivors. Our fathers, whom we honor according to the laws of Moses and Israel, decide who is the best one for our children, and then we ask God's blessing on our decision. And our children, *if they are obedient*, realize that we know best." His voice was rising rapidly up the scale, as a vein in his temple began to pulse; but before Marty could change the subject, he did it himself.

Turning to her, his voice once again softened by memory, he continued, "Our fathers arranged our marriage, but the first time we saw each other and she put her hand in mine . . . a flame was kindled. A flame, a love that burned like fire, a love that no amount of prayer could smother. I loved her, I *needed* her, and now she is dead and I no longer want to live!"

"Zeke, I know Miriam would never want you to—"

"You know nothing." The words were said so emphatically, she took a step backward. "Nothing. My love for her was so great that I forgave her for . . . for those children, those flawed babies, disfigured and horrible. . . ."

"Zeke! Please! Don't!"

But he was beyond hearing her, or anyone. "The one without a brain . . . you saw him, Marty. Marty, *no brain*! Who ever heard of a Jew without a brain!"

"It has nothing to do with—"

"The Jewish people are brilliant, Marty, where did these monstrous children come from? Not from my seed! In my family, for generations, there is nothing like that. Nothing! But in Miriam's family, what do you see? A father whose foot swells up like a balloon, and from what? From good wine, his own wine! Is that not a curse? Miriam's grandmother. Her hands withered into claws and she was in a wheelchair before she was forty years old. It was in Miriam's blood, there was a curse in her blood. I should have set her aside. I should have sent her away. But I burned for her and so, I kept her, her and her cursed blood. . . ."

"Rabbi, that's not a curse. All those things, they're rheumatic diseases, that's all. Yes, they tend to run in families . . . in fact, Miriam was developing the symptoms of lupus and—"

He chopped off her words with a gesture. "I don't want to hear. More of the curse."

"And here sits the living proof of that curse, isn't that right, Papa?" Shayna's voice rang out. "Well, do whatever you want with me! Do your worst! It can't be more awful than what you've already done to me!"

"Shaynele, can't you see, all I wanted was to give you a normal life." It was as if he hadn't heard himself earlier, calling her repulsive.

Shayna's laughter had a hysterical edge. "You didn't care what kind of life I had. You only wanted to get rid of me. Nobody should know you had produced something less than perfect, hey? Why didn't you strangle me at birth . . . or throw me into the river . . . like they do in China?"

The rabbi shook his head and regarded her sadly. "You know, as well as I, that if anyone knew about you . . . then my sons . . . nobody in the congregation would betroth their daughters to my sons!"

She laughed again. "Well, now they *all* know, Papa. Your terrible secret is out and your adoring congregation knows you lied to them and betrayed their trust. So what now, Papa dear?"

Marty was edging back toward the door, her eyes fixed on Zeke. He seemed so intent on his daughter, maybe she could just open the door and slip out.

Suddenly, he whirled. "Where do you think you're going, Marty Lamb? You cannot leave! God sent you to my door for a purpose. You are the sacrifice he demands, in payment for Miriam."

"What about Dr. Zee, Papa?" Shayna said. "She took care of us. As a matter of fact, *she* arranged for Mama to get those abortions."

"The Almighty has already punished her." His face was like stone. "Blessed be His name."

"You bless God's name for sending a horrible plague upon that wonderful woman?" Marty said. "A good and caring physician? That's horrible! Only a cruel God would accept such a blessing."

"Yes, the Almighty is cruel sometimes. And vengeful. Because His word must be obeyed! My people must see that if

He is disobeyed, someone must perish. As it is written: an eye
for an eye and a tooth for a tooth!"

Shayna leaned forward as far as she could. It was difficult;
he had set her down so far into the down cushions of the couch.
But by sheer willpower she pushed herself farther up into a sitting position, her back ramrod straight, so that she could look
at him directly. "Oh, Papa, they're not your people anymore!
Marty, they *fled* from here. They ran away as fast as they
could."

"At the sight of you!" he snarled. "Marty, cover her legs. It
is not fitting for a woman to display her legs, especially not
those legs." He turned away, distaste twisting his face. So it
was as bad as Shayna thought. As far as he was concerned, his
daughter's spina bifida was not an unfortunate genetic accident, but a disfigurement, a blemish, and most of all, a blow to
his ego. In his mind his beautiful, intelligent daughter was
some kind of *freak*. And all that talk about love and caring—
that was bullshit.

"Now, Marty, you will make those calls, please. Or we all
die *without* the television cameras." He motioned with the gun.

She went to the phone. When totally helpless, stall for time.
"I don't understand. Why do you want to talk to Clive Moses?"

"Clive Moses comes from a God-fearing family. His father
was a preacher. Clive understands the religious viewpoint."

She punched Clive's extension at the hospital and, of
course, his voice mail answered. She held the phone out for the
rabbi to hear that it was only a canned voice, but he shook his
head. "I cannot use the telephone on the Sabbath."

Yeah, right. But using a gun was okay. "I wanted you to hear
for yourself that Clive has gone home for the weekend."

"Hang up, then. Give me that phone. I'll call Channel 12
myself."

"But it's the Sabbath," Shayna said sarcastically. "You
cannot use the telephone on the Sabbath."

"God will forgive me. But who knows what you might do,
Marty Lamb, while I am busy talking? So, no, I will not make
a call. And you will hang up."

Marty's eyes were locked with the rabbi's as she put the
receiver back in place. He backed away until he felt the corner

of the sideboard and stopped there, pointing the gun right at her. Her mouth had gone dry and her mind fastened on the elaborate arrangement of pastel ices on the sideboard, slowly melting into slush. The tiny, shiny barrel of the revolver with the nasty hole in the center was leveled at her heart. The rabbi's lips were still curled in that strange little half smile. He'd gone over the edge, she was sure of that. But the big question was, how *far*? Could he still be reached at all? If not by reason, by self-interest? She was going to have to find out.

"Rabbi, if I call one of the doctors at All Souls, will you talk to him?"

"What, and maybe forget about the gun? No, thank you." His eyes narrowed and he added, very softly, "Of course, you might decide to try to trick me. You might not call a doctor at all. You might call the police instead."

"I don't think I'll have to do that." Outside, on the street, the noise level was building perceptibly. Through the living room windows, Marty could see the revolving red and blue lights on the police cruisers. Flashes and flickers of brightness whirled around onto the floor.

"Get away from the phone!" Zeke ordered. *"Now!"*

Marty obeyed, fighting to keep her face emotionless even as her heart rate began to climb. Almost instantly, the phone rang.

"Who could that be?" the Rabbi said.

"The police?"

"Answer it!"

She picked up the receiver and said, "Yes?"

"This is Sergeant Randolph, NYPD. Is everyone all right?"

"Yes. So far." She made eye contact with Zeke and nodded to let him know her guess had been correct. Instantly, he came to her side.

"Can you fill me in?" Sergeant Randolph said.

"Tell him," Zeke ordered, "that All Souls Hospital is a God-less place where murders take place twice a week, every week!" His voice was very loud. Marty doubted it needed repetition, but she did so, anyway.

"Tell him that Rabbi Brown wants to show the city of New York how All Souls Hospital has ruined his life, taken his wife,

his unborn sons, his daughter's sanity, and his every reason to live!"

Expressionless, Marty repeated every word.

"Tell him 'Vengeance is mine, sayeth the Lord. Ye that live by the sword shall die by the sword!' "

Marty parroted the phrases.

"You wanna translate that for me?" the sergeant said.

"I believe that Rabbi Brown intends to kill us all."

Zeke smiled and nodded at her, as if pleased at a particularly bright student.

"How many people are in the apartment?"

"Three of us. The rabbi, his daughter, and me."

"You're a nurse?"

Automatically, like an idiot, she corrected him: "Nurse-practitioner."

"Whatever. Is he threatening you?"

"He has a gun and it is aimed at me." She licked her lips.

"Ask him if he'll talk to me. Wait. Hold on." The sergeant probably turned his head; she heard his voice, muffled, snapping out orders to others: ". . . to the back, the super's got the basement door open. Guy's got a gun and is extremely agitated. Everyone in the front, back off." Thank God. They were actually believing how dangerous Zeke had become. They were actually *doing* something.

"Rabbi, will you talk to Sergeant Randolph of the NYPD?" Marty asked. All the murmuring and shuffling from the front of the building, she noticed, had stopped, as if turned off. Which, of course, is exactly what had happened.

"I'll talk to Ham Pierce," Zeke said. "Nobody else."

"He'll talk to—"

"I heard. Hey, someone get Pierce! Yeah. I saw their truck drive up! Make sure they stay on the next block! Miss Lamb, are you anywhere near the door to the apartment?"

"Uh-huh . . ."

"No speaking in code!" Zeke snapped. "Or you'll hang up!"

"Now, Zeke, the sergeant is trying to get Ham Pierce, so you can talk to him."

"See if you can move everyone away from there," Sergeant

Randolph said. "We may have to break the door down . . . it could get dangerous."

As if it already wasn't! "The rabbi is right here," she said, hoping the sergeant understood what she was trying to tell him. The phone was mounted on the wall, right next to the door; there was no way she could keep the rabbi talking and still move farther away.

Then she heard Ham Pierce's voice and the cop said, "Put him on, okay? Let's see if we can talk him down."

Pierce's deep basso, so familiar from the television, boomed loudly: "Rabbi Brown? Zeke Brown?" She held the receiver out, so Zeke could hear it. "Rabbi! You there? You want to tell your story?"

The rabbi had been hesitating, but now he seemed to make up his mind. "Get over there, Marty, right next to Shayna, on the couch, where I can see both of you. *Move!*" He waved the gun in a wild way she didn't like at all and his voice rose. She smiled at him—she hoped she was smiling at him—and turned toward Shayna. It exposed her back to him, her vulnerable back, and she could feel her flesh crawling. She could *feel* that pistol pointing at her. In his state of mind, highly excitable, he could decide what the hell, squeeze that trigger and *boom*! She might never know what hit her. Sweat popped out all over her body.

Zeke waited until she was sitting next to Shayna and then picked up the phone. Marty put her hand out and found Shayna's waiting for her. They held onto each other tightly, their eyes fixed on the figure at the telephone. He was so . . . not human. That was the scariest part of it. It was impossible to tell what might set him off.

He said the same things to Pierce that he'd said to her, in almost exactly the same words. Like a recording that had got stuck. It occurred to her that now, at least she and Shayna were safely away from the door. If only there were some way to send a signal. But hadn't the sergeant sent everybody to the back of the building? And Zeke would certainly shoot her if she moved. He was growing more and more agitated, yelling into the phone, quoting the Bible, or quoting something that *sounded* biblical.

And then she heard a kind of rustle, just outside the window.

She concentrated, trying to see out into the darkness. There! A face, the pale skin glimmering out there in the bushes? She blinked and the gleam was gone. Damn. Why the hell didn't they just break the glass and come charging in? But she knew why not. The minute he heard the slightest noise, Zeke was likely to just start shooting. And then she heard it again, the faintest whisper of a sound and the *sensation* that there was a darker bulk out there, invisible against the shrubbery, but *there*.

Shayna's hand tightened on hers. Did she see it, too? Marty didn't dare say anything, not even a whisper.

Zeke ranted on, about retribution, and punishment, and vengeance. He was using his Rabbi Voice, getting into a rhythm, swaying back and forth a little as he shouted into the phone. "And the Almighty has told us, an eye for an eye, a tooth for a tooth, a life for a life. My Miriam is dead, my beloved, my wife, my life's partner. Her death demands a sacrifice. The life of Marty Lamb shall be forfeit for the life of my beloved. A life for . . . *Sit right there. Move and I will kill you.*"

The change in the tone, the timbre, and the pitch of his voice was startling. Marty had only shifted a little on the couch, trying to ease her muscles, cramped with anxiety. Her heart sank further. No matter how hypnotic his chant might sound, he was apparently on the alert for everything.

"Very soon, Mr. Pierce, you will watch this apartment go up in flames. What do you mean, what am I waiting for? I'm waiting for a sign from the Almighty. When He bids me destroy the evil in this house, I shall obey Him . . . I will die but that is unimportant. My life is over. Thanks to All Souls Hospital and the evil that dwells in it, my life is over. I have nothing to live for. Nothing."

Abruptly, he hung up the phone, and Marty could actually hear Pierce's voice from outside, shouting, "Rabbi! Rabbi Brown! Pick up the phone again! Someone wishes to speak with you, someone from the hospital!" She could also hear the wailing of the fire truck's siren as it pulled up somewhere down the street, and the thumps of feet running on the pavement outside.

In the apartment, the quiet was deadly. Zeke Brown leaned against the wall, beginning to smile that weird little smile again.

"This is a waste of my time," he said, almost to himself. "I'm sure you are both frightened, waiting for your deaths. I am a merciful man; the Almighty my Lord is a merciful God and—"

Marty did not like the way he was tightening his grip on the pistol and taking new aim at her. "If the Almighty is really a merciful God, He will not want bloodshed," she pleaded. "He will not want killing."

"Sometimes, the merciful act is to end life, you know that, Marty. Did He not turn Lot's wife into a pillar of salt? The Lord God is omnipotent, omnipresent, omniscient. All powerful, everywhere, all knowing." He was beginning to sweat and he looked uncomfortable.

Outside, there was the sound of scuffling, shouting that was suddenly cut off, whispers, footsteps, curses. The rabbi whirled to face the windows, his eyes widening.

"It's my sign!" he cried. "My sign from the Almighty!"

Suddenly the door shook in its frame and began to splinter. Now the whispers turned to shouts: "Stop, you fool!" and "Get that guy outta—!" a lot of yelling and screaming overlapping so that you couldn't understand anything except that people were mad as hell. Someone was battering at the door with an ax; you could see its sharp edge glinting as it hacked its way through the thick wood.

Suddenly, with a mighty crunch, one of the panels gave way, splintering and groaning, and crashed into the room. Zeke jumped back, to escape being hit by pieces of door or the ax—which now hacked away at the other panels, chopping and ripping and tearing like a demented thing.

Marty prayed wordlessly. The police had made it through the basement and were going to force their way in, hurray for the police. Except weren't axes the province of the Fire Department? Maybe their rescuers were firemen; after all, they rescued kittens from trees, didn't they? Why not her and Shayna from a maroon velvet couch?

The man with the ax stepped into the room and for a moment, Marty could only stare in disbelief. Then she started to scream. "No, no, wait!"

But she was too late. The intruder was swinging the ax, lunging forward. Zeke, bleeding, pulled the trigger and blood

blossomed on the man's chest. Then, with a startled look on his face, the rabbi collapsed to his knees as the other man toppled onto him, blade first. The two men fell onto the floor together, where their blood mingled and spread. They were both very, very still.

Marty took her hand from Shayna's and sprang up. Shayna was crying, "Papa! Papa!" and in a minute, she would probably break down—she'd been holding herself together so tightly—but Marty had to go to the men first. She was positive they were both dead; but as a professional, she had to make sure. She knelt by the carnage, feeling the blood soaking into her slacks, only half hearing the police and the reporters as they began to pour in through the bashed-in door, and put her hand gently onto a curly head she knew so well. He must have been following her every minute.

"Oh God, Owen," she moaned. "Just what did you think you were doing? You crazy, romantic fool! You got yourself killed, do you know that? You went and got yourself killed!"

Then she began to shake. And then she began to cry.

36

Owen was dead. Poor Owen, poor deluded, demented fool. You'd think, after so many years of living with his psychosis, that he'd have realized his voices never gave him good news—or the right advice, either. Marty put her face into her hands and wept for his destroyed life. And yet, in the end, his voices had told him to do something heroic. So there was something noble still in his poor, ruined brain. How clever and quiet he had been, trailing her, creeping behind her, just out of sight. But he always had been able to walk on little cat feet, silent and secret.

She stayed on her knees on the carpet, unwilling to leave him. She could feel the blood soaking into the knees of her pants, but she didn't really care. In a minute she would get up and go to Shayna; but right now, just a minute or two to mourn him—her once-husband—and all the sad, wasted years.

And then, with a great pouring of noise, everyone came rushing in—the cops, the firemen, the paramedics.

"Miss! Don't touch anything!" someone snapped; and she looked up, startled, into the face of a very serious young policeman wearing protective gear. Was he kidding? Nurse or no nurse, no way was she going to meddle with the grisly tangled heap on the floor. Poor Zeke. He was dead, too. Owen's weapon was buried in his throat.

She heard Paul before she saw him, yelling, "Let me by, I'm a doctor!" The magic words. All at once he was right next to her, looking frightened until he saw she was okay, and then he pulled her tightly up and into his arms. "Marty, my God, he could have killed you!"

"Who? Zeke? Oh yes, I think he fully intended to." She thought she might start shaking, but she pulled in a deep breath and made it stop. It felt so good to lean into Paul; it felt so safe. But she had to talk about it. "He was going to kill us all and set fire to the apartment. Oh, Paul!" Her eyes filled. "He was ready to kill his own child!" Suddenly she realized—"Shayna! How is she?"

"She's fine, she's fine. One of the Survivor women is over there with her, and Shayna is crying into her shoulder."

She had to get ahold of herself, Marty thought. Behave like a professional. "How did you know I was here? I hadn't planned to come in. In fact, I thought he wouldn't let me in."

Paul gave a brief unamused laugh. "I was chasing after you. Like I always am."

"You disappeared. As soon as I saw you, I left. And you weren't there. I figured . . . I thought maybe you saw me sitting with Dennis and . . . I don't know . . . leaped to a conclusion."

"I did," he said. "But that wasn't it. The look you gave me . . . it said, 'Stay away, dammit, can't you see I'm busy?' I figured maybe you and Dimwit were working out a deal . . . about

Crystal. I wasn't sure. So I made myself scarce. I figured I'd see you at home and get the whole story."

"You were right about that look, but it was meant for Owen. When I felt eyes on me, I was sure it was him. He's been trailing me, probably for days." Once again her eyes filled.

"Oh God, and I just walked away.... Well, anyway, I bumped into a whole army of Survivors, marching along, very excited. Then I saw Rabbi Brown's boys, but no Rabbi Brown, so I asked them what was going on. Most of them just glared at me, but one man stopped and shouted that the rabbi was a liar and a cheat and maybe even a madman and the whole congregation had left him. So I asked them, 'Where is he now? Where's the girl, his daughter?'

"The guy just shrugged it off, but the woman next to him—she's the one here now—she looked terrified. She was crying. She was the one who told me. 'Please,' she said. 'Do something. Shayna is alone with him, in the apartment, and who knows what he might do. I know he has a gun.'

"I told her I'd take care of it. I hightailed it back to Protozoa—the street phone was broken, of course—and called 911. I told them there was a situation brewing here. I looked around for you, to tell you that Shayna was in terrible danger. But you were gone . . . I couldn't believe you'd disappeared so fast—"

"We must have kept missing each other. Never mind. You're here now."

"Wait. There's more. I spotted Owen. He looked pretty strange. His eyes were glazed and he was talking to himself a mile a minute. When he took off, I followed him. He knew you were here. Inside. Precisely where I didn't want you to be. He pulled the alarm on a firebox and went crashing through the bushes in front of the building. I'm surprised the rabbi didn't hear him."

"I saw him. I didn't know it was him. I thought it was the cops. And he wasn't crashing. He was very quiet." She looked at Paul with tenderness. "I thought for a while that I might never see you again, that we might—" Her voice shook and she couldn't finish. Tears began to streak down her face. Paul kissed them away, and she clung to him as if her life depended

upon it. Maybe it did. "Thank you." It was all she could manage without weeping all over him.

"You're *thanking* me? My God, I thought I'd lost you forever! I love you, Marty."

"I love you. More than I thought possible." Her head was beginning to clear now.

"But?" he said.

"But I have a patient here and she's just been threatened with death and then seen her father killed. I think she needs me worse than I need you right now, and believe me, I really need you right now."

Paul laid a gentle hand alongside her cheek. "It's one of the reasons I love you. You really care about other people's pain. So . . . go to your patient."

He straightened up and helped her to her feet. Where was her bag? She always carried some medical supplies with her, just in case. Maybe Shayna needed a tranquilizer—at least a couple of aspirins. The bag was lying on the floor, where it had fallen when Zeke first dragged her inside. It didn't even look stepped on. She got it and then turned her attention to Shayna. The girl had stopped weeping and was leaning against Selma, wiping the tears from her cheeks with the back of her hand while Selma also swiped at them with a giant handkerchief.

"Marty!" Shayna said. "Are you all right?"

"I'm fine. How are *you*?"

"Oh, but you're all bloody!" Shayna was quite pale, but composed—too composed.

"Not mine." She couldn't bear to be more explicit.

Shayna was intrepid. "His. Yes, and the other man's, too. God forgive me, but I feel nothing for my father right now, not even pity. He shot that man, he was ready to kill *us* . . . who was that man, anyway? I'm sorry I'll never be able to thank him. I've never seen him before. Why would a stranger chop down our door?"

Marty hesitated and then scolded herself. What difference did it make now? "My husband." To Shayna's startled expression, she explained, "We hadn't lived together for years. Owen was . . . mentally ill. He heard voices telling him to do things, usually terrible things, hurtful things. But tonight they told him

to save me. We never know, Shayna, where our saviors will come from."

"A-*men!*" Selma said. "Oh, I will never forgive myself for running off with the rest of them. I begged them all, I said, 'Don't leave Shayna alone with that man.' Miriam's death crazed him, you know. Since Miriam died, he hasn't been the same. And we left this poor child all alone, unable to move! For shame!" She went on, speaking to Marty, "Oh, I knew before tonight, I knew ... about her legs. I always knew. Miriam told me everything. She made me swear I would never tell. 'I don't know what he'd do,' she told me, 'if he thinks anyone else knows.' I should have realized, tonight, that he might—oh, let God forgive him—"

Selma looked as if she could keep on going forever with this litany of guilt and woe; but Shayna stopped her.

"Hush, Selma, you did nothing wrong. And you came back, when it could have been dangerous for you. You're a brave and faithful friend." She sounded so much like Zeke at his best, kindly and forceful at the same time.

"When I heard all the sirens, I left your brothers, may they live and be well, with my husband, and I came. I promised your mother that I would always watch over you."

"And you always have," Shayna said. "But now, you know, it's time for me to take care of myself. I'll have to go into the hospital for a long time—to have my legs fixed, *if* they can be fixed. I have to learn how to walk, Selma. I have to get a wheelchair, maybe an electric one. There's a lady who goes up and down Van Dam Avenue, in a red one with a red pennant flying from it, so everyone can see her coming, even the cars. I think I'd like one like that." Shayna patted Selma's hand in a strange role reversal. "Marty knows what needs to be done for me, don't you, Marty?"

"Yes." Marty inclined her head, and Selma immediately moved to give her room to sit down next to the girl. Marty took Shayna's arm, her fingers on the pulse. Regular and steady, a little slow in fact. It was unreal. She'd bet Shayna's blood pressure hadn't gone up, either. Still in shock, probably.

"Can I still have you and Dr. Zee? I don't care that she has AIDS. You know, he was so delighted to tell me about her, since

it was obvious to him that God had done it for *him*, that God was doling out punishments especially for *him*. Marty," she said after a moment of thought, "my father . . . was he crazy?"

"You mean . . . as in psychotic?"

"Yes."

"No, I don't think so. Sometimes living in a closed community allows you not to let other ideas in, and I think *that's* what may have happened to your father. In the end, he allowed himself to believe that his way was the only way—or at least the only *right* way."

Shayna sighed. Her eyes filled and overflowed. "If only he hadn't . . . But he did . . . Can Dr. Zee still be my doctor? Will the hospital let her?"

"You'll have many doctors, Shayna, an orthopedist, a neurologist, a surgeon—at least one surgeon, if not more—physical therapists and occupational therapists. You'll have more doctors than you know what to do with. But of course Dr. Zee and I will be watching over you and checking on your progress. Look, here she comes now."

It looked like the waters parting, the way the cops and technicians and detectives and media people pulled back to let Dr. Zee through. She didn't have to announce that she was a doctor; she looked like one. She was pushing a wheelchair, a concerned frown on her face.

"Everyone okay here?" In an instant she'd taken in everything. "Dr. Giordano called me. . . . Shayna, you all right?"

"I'm fine, Dr. Zee, just fine."

"Vital signs good," Marty said, giving the doctor a meaningful look. "As you can see, Shayna is quite calm." She did not have to add, *She just saw her father die rather horribly in front of her and here she is, chattering away as if everything was pretty much as usual.*

"I think we'll get you a bed in All Souls tonight, Shayna," Dr. Zee said, sitting down as Marty got up. She held the girl's hand. "Your hand is so cold. Are you feeling faint? No? Well, you've been through a lot. I think I'll give you a sedative so you can sleep, okay?"

"Whatever you say, Dr. Zee. And then, tomorrow, I can see the orthopedist about fixing my legs?"

"If you're up to it." Dr. Zee patted her hand. "We're going to get you fixed the best we know how. And I'll stay with you tonight, in case you wake up and need me." She didn't say, *I want to be there when it hits her,* but Marty knew that's what she was thinking.

Paul lifted Shayna, and when he placed her into the wheel-chair, the look of dazzlement that spread across her face was something to see. "At last," she said. "At last." Tears spilled out of her eyes. Dr. Zee wheeled her out; the fierce look on the doctor's face dared anyone to even *try* to ask Shayna any questions. Except for the murmurs of the police photographer and the detectives, the room was quiet as she left.

"Good-bye," Shayna called out, looking back at Marty. "Soon I'll be walking. *Walking.*" And then they were gone.

Paul materialized once more at Marty's side, and put his arm around her shoulders. She was beginning to feel the strain. Her muscles had been so tense, waiting for the shot that would kill her; even her head felt clenched tight. She was so tired, and at the same time so wired. A short, dark man came over and introduced himself as Detective Casanova, saying he'd like to talk to her.

"I am Ms. Lamb's physician," Paul said in his best doctor voice, "and I can't allow her to be questioned at length right now. She will make a brief statement. Tomorrow morning will do just as well, won't it, Detective? Okay, then. Let's go into the dining room, where it's a little quieter." Oh, Paul, I really do love you, Marty thought. What a nice feeling, being taken care of.

She had thought she wouldn't know what to say, but the words just fell out of her mouth. "Rabbi Brown has been distraught since the accidental killing of his wife by an anti-abortion protester last month. Tonight, he was going to announce the betrothal of his daugher, Shayna. But she disrupted the party and everyone left. I came by to check on Shayna—she is my patient at the Community Care Clinics—and was pulled into the situation."

"And what situation was that, Ms. Lamb?"

"Rabbi Brown was threatening to shoot us and burn down the apartment. He was agitated . . . disturbed . . . not thinking clearly."

"And the man with the ax? Where did he come from? I understand you have some connection to him?"

"He was my estranged husband, Owen Lamb, and he chopped his way in here to save us. He *did* save us." Her voice began to tremble. "If you don't mind," she said, "I'd like to go home now." The detective gave her his card and asked her to come to the precinct and give a complete statement tomorrow. "Call me in the morning and we'll set up a time," he said.

"Even on Sunday?"

"Even on Sunday."

"Okay. I will. Thank you."

She let Paul walk her out of the apartment and into the crowded street. It was an eerie sight, with the twirling, flashing police lights, and by now the bright television lights and cameras had appeared. The TV crews were mostly taking pictures of the crowds of people standing there, pointing at the building, asking each other what was happening, telling each other rumors. They all somehow knew to back away from the couple with their arms around each other's waist, knew enough not to ask questions, even though the woman's pants were caked with blood.

They walked slowly. "Dr. Zee is going to stay all night with Shayna. At some point the poor kid is bound to wake up screaming."

"Yes. She was much too serene."

"Me, too, although I may not be everyone's idea of serenity. I don't think I've dealt with it all yet. It mostly feels like a bad dream. But sooner or later I'm going to wake up screaming."

Paul said, "Well, if you do, I'll be right there to make it all right."

She stopped walking and turned to face him. "Oh, Paul, I hope so. I want so much for you to be there to make it all right."

"Always," he said. He reached out to hold both her hands. "Are you ever going to forgive me? For being an asshole?"

"Depends."

"On what?"

"On how good you are." She managed a smile.

"Oh, I intend to be very, very good . . . if you know what I mean." He tried to look lecherous.

She laughed. She was glad she was still able to laugh. "I know what you mean."

He pulled her against him and his mouth found hers. She closed her eyes and the world whirled around behind her eyelids. She pressed closer to him, for balance. The people on the street were watching them, whistling and cheering. She and Paul broke apart, looked into each other's eyes and laughed. Then, holding hands, they started down the street together, heading home.

Deep into the night, Marty came awake all at once, her eyes flying open, her heart racing and pounding from her dream. What *was* it? And then it came back, in little pieces—the two men attacking each other, only this time there were two axes and they were chopping at each other and she kept waiting for them to fall but they didn't, and then one of them turned to her, his ax raised, and she cried out, "Owen! No, don't!" Only now, awake, she realized that the blood-streaked killer's face in her dream hadn't been Owen's. It was Jerry Kelly. Horrible.

Shuddering and shivering, she moaned aloud, and instantly Paul's arms wrapped around her, holding her close, holding her tight. She clung to him, her nose and lips buried in the sweet, familiar scent of his neck.

"I'm here," he murmured. "Shhhh. Nothing can hurt you. I'm here."

"Oh, Paul!" In the darkness, she lifted her head, seeking his lips. His mouth found hers and they kissed, sweetly at first, then more deeply, tongues exploring. She was part of him and he was part of her. "Paul, I love you so much," she whispered.

"My darling . . ." Pulling away a little, his lips left hers to begin a journey down her body—throat, breast, belly, down and down. She began to quiver, her hips moving to meet his kiss. In a matter of moments she was at her climax, pulsating and groaning in pleasure. And then he slid into her, huge and hard, and she came again. And again and again. Paul stopped moving but she could feel the engorged penis inside her, quivering. For a moment he held himself tensely, trying to hold off. Then, with a groan, he gave in, thrusting into her faster and faster until, with a wordless shout, he finished.

Both sweating and breathing hard, they lay entwined. When Paul began to lift himself up, she held onto him, wanting him to stay inside her, close, almost a part of her body. How could she have ever thought it was over? How could she have imagined there might be someone else for her? There was no one else. It was exactly the same as it had been the first time. He was the one. If he didn't want to marry her, she'd stay single the rest of her life, that's all. Somewhere in the middle of these thoughts, still joined together with him, she fell asleep. There were no more bad dreams.

37

Sunday was a perfect September day, blue and gold, not yet poignant with falling leaves and dying flowers, still summer, but gentler and softer. It matched her mood perfectly, Marty thought, holding Paul's hand as they strolled, reveling in the warm roughness of his palm, coarsened by all the washing with strong soap. The hand of a physician. The hand of her beloved.

The sweet smell of apples followed them as they walked by one of the Korean grocery stores. It reminded her of something. School. This was the way the world had always smelled during the first weeks of school, so full of promise and anticipation. Just like her life now, now that she had Paul back again.

"What?" Paul, walking next to her, put an arm around her shoulders and squeezed. "What were you thinking?"

"Poor Owen," she lied. "He'll never again wake up on a beautiful day like this and think how good it is to be alive." Was she still so afraid of rejection that she couldn't tell him what she was really thinking? Yes, she was.

"Do you think he ever did? Love life?"

"Oh Christ, who knows? He must have, once. When he was a little boy. Before the voices."

"Was it always God, talking to him?"

"No, no. Only once before—that *I* know of. The voices changed, but they were usually well-known personalities. Barbara Walters. Mike Wallace. Joanne Woodward. Funny . . . even though her voice told him nasty things, he said he loved her. . . ."

"And you. He must have loved you, Marty. He saved your life. It's incredible, but the man actually hacked his way through a big, thick mahogany door to save you!"

"Maybe. Owen's love always seemed to be more about him than about me. And remember, God wasn't always saying nice things about Marty. Maybe Owen was coming to chop me to bits."

She stopped and shivered involuntarily. Paul stopped walking and reached out for her, holding her, right there in the middle of the street. He was such a sweetie pie. She gave him a smile. "It's okay, just a little flashback . . . of *them*, the two of them. You'd think I'd be used to the sight of blood and gore, wouldn't you?"

They began to walk again. "It wasn't the blood and gore, babe, and you know it."

She had forgotten how it *felt*, to be in love. She had forgotten the sheer joy of it. Once or twice in recent years she'd flirted with the idea of marriage with some nice, suitable man she was going out with—tested it out, even discussed it a little. But it had never been like this. It might be comfortable . . . warm and cozy . . . yes, even exciting sometimes. But not like this—the certainty, the rightness. She hoped Paul felt the same, but was scared to death to ask him.

She was actually gathering up the courage to say something, when he suddenly stopped. "Look. Up ahead." A large, excited crowd milled about farther up the street, in front of the brick apartment building. They all *had* to see the scene of the crime, didn't they? Hundreds of them—neighbors, police guards, the merely curious. Not to mention Channel 1, Channel 12, every network, all the local New York TV stations. And newspaper reporters, a crowd of them. Well, who could blame them? A double murder—a hero appearing out of the blue, saving the

crippled beauty and the nurse from certain death, killing the bad guy and then dying himself. What a story!

The restless throng filled the sidewalk and part of the street in front of the big brick building on Van Dam Avenue, chattering and pointing, the photographers taking pictures of the blank windows. Why? Marty wondered. Nobody was there; the place was empty. No, she saw as they came closer, not quite empty. Lights blazed behind the windows and a small group of men—police, she guessed—huddled together in the living room, conferring.

"Maybe if we cross the street, nobody will bother you," Paul said; but he was too late. Marty heard a shout of "The nurse!" and in a minute a whole pack of people waving mikes and notebooks were descending upon them, shouting questions.

"How do they know me?" Marty wondered.

"I'll bet you were on late TV last night. When we were busy with other matters." Paul grinned at her, so delighted with himself, she had to laugh.

But she wiped the smile from her face as the reporters surrounded them and said as firmly as she could, "No comment. Not now, please." No use; she couldn't be heard above the hubbub.

"All right, everybody. I know Ms. Lamb. She'll talk to me." Hamilton Pierce, who else? But they did all stop talking at once. Pierce smiled at her and thrust a microphone toward her. "Ms. Lamb, how did your ex-husband know where you were? We hear he'd been stalking you." How did they manage to find out all the sordid details?

"Look, I'll talk—to everyone," she said. "But not until I've given my statement to the police. I'm on my way to the precinct house right now, so I'd really appreciate—"

"When are you scheduled to give your statement?"

"Sometime this morning. Soon. *Right now*," she added meaningfully, and made a move to continue on her way.

That did it: turned them on again, yelling questions and shouting demands for comments. She held up a hand. To her astonishment, they shut up.

"If you'll just be patient," she said. "Perhaps I'll be available later."

"Excuse me, ladies and gentlemen, could I get through?" said a familiar rich basso from the back of the crowd. "I have an important message for Ms. Lamb. Come on, now, give her a break." They grumbled a bit, but the waters parted for yet another Moses. Clive took Marty's arm, murmuring something to Paul, and the three of them moved smoothly through the crowd.

As they hurried away from the clump of newspeople, Marty asked, "Nothing's happened to Shayna? Or Dr. Zee?"

"No, no, nothing like that. But I thought you'd be interested to know that the accreditation team won't be coming in tomorrow morning. It's been postponed."

"*Postponed?* You're kidding."

"No, I assure you. They will not appear tomorrow. We are off the hook."

All that work, she thought. All that worry and all that rush. And they *postpone* at the last minute? "I don't get it."

"I won't repeat a rumor," Clive said with a smile, "unless properly begged, of course."

"Consider yourself implored," she said, puzzled but beginning to figure it out.

So, when Clive said, "A press conference has been called for nine o'clock *sharp* tomorrow morning," she wasn't surprised.

"And will Dr. Eliot Wolfe be at this press conference?"

"Smart girl . . . pardon me, woman. You've got it. Dr. Wolfe and Dr. Messinger, together."

"Good," Marty said. "I *think*."

Something caught her eye and she turned quickly, to see Crystal lurking at the outer edges of the congestion, hiding behind the closely packed crowd. "Back in a minute," she said, and headed quietly toward her. Crys suddenly turned and saw her, then quickly melted into the crowd and disappeared. Go ahead, Marty thought, hide. You can't disappear forever. Although, of course, Crys certainly could—if it ever occurred to her to leave New York. Why *didn't* she hop on a train or a plane and head for the hills?

Marty headed back toward the two men. Clive apparently had seen Crystal, too. His face was bleak.

"Well," he said, making an attempt to sound normal, but

failing. "I've given you the news. I'd better get back to *my* job." And he turned to stride back toward the mass of media people.

"What was *that* about?" Paul asked.

"I noticed Crystal hanging out back there, and so, it seems, did Clive. They had something going a couple of years back, according to Dr. Dimwit, and it went very very bad. Anytime they bump into each other, you can cut the tension with a knife."

"Crystal, here? What's wrong with the woman? She knows she's in deep shit. Why the hell does she come lurking around where she's very likely to be spotted?"

"I don't know, Paul. Maybe she *wants* to be spotted. Maybe she wants to be caught and forced to go into a program."

"You know," Paul said at length, "maybe *I* could help with that. I've been there. Maybe *I* could convince her . . . you know, kindred spirits and fellow addicts . . ."

"Don't joke about it, Paul. You finished with it. She never did. Dennis said she'd been detoxed, quite successfully, after she got caught in her last job. So successfully, they decided not to report her. But eventually she took the drug route again. She may not be treatable."

"Let me try, okay?"

"If she ever shows up long enough, okay. Why are we stopping? Oh," she said, recognizing the ancient stone building with the huge Romanesque archway and the blue lights. "Time for Detective Casanova."

The police station windows were covered with chicken wire and needed a washing, the walls could have used a new coat of Public Building Green, and the furniture was Early Battered. Paul waited while Marty sat at Casanova's desk. The detective didn't have a computer, she noticed, just an ancient typewriter. Which he didn't use; he wrote everything by hand. Even so, it didn't take long to give her statement. Neither of the major players in the tragedy was a stranger to her. She was able to answer all the detective's questions.

"So they had no reason to hate each other?"

"No, Detective. As far as I know, they'd never seen each other before. Before the moment when they killed each other." The scene came back to her and she shivered. "And that reminds me . . ."

"Yes?" His pen was once again poised over the paper.

"No, not a fact. A question. Do you happen to know where Owen could have got hold of a hatchet?"

"An ax. It was an ax, not a hatchet. No hatchet would ever have been able to get through that old door. They really *built* them, in those days. It was a Fire Department ax. He must have swiped it from one of the fire engines. One of them showed up, like, two seconds after we called them. Funny . . . I mean, the Fire Department's fast, but that was, like, instantaneous."

"I saw him—Owen—pull a fire alarm," Paul offered.

Detective Casanova regarded Paul with surprise. "Huh. Yeah, well maybe he was planning to take an ax off the fire truck. You think he was, like, smart enough to figure that out?"

"Owen Lamb was psychotic, Detective, not retarded."

From behind her a familiar voice called out, "Is there a Detective Casanova here? I am Mrs. Lamb. Owen Lamb's mother. I am told that my boy's—Oh, hello, Marta. Of all the places for us to meet, finally!"

Beatrice! For a moment Marty could only stare and blink. The formidable matron had shrunk since their last meeting, and her pale, protuberant eyes, so like Owen's, were sunk in puffiness. She looked elderly, although her voice was exactly the same as it had always been—loud and piercing.

"Hello, Beatrice. My condolences. It was awful. I—"

"Yes, yes, and mine to you. You never did get a divorce, did you? Well, then, you're a widow now, Marta, a much better position to be in than married to a poor soul who never seemed to get better. Widowhood at least has dignity. You do know that Owen's father passed on?"

"No. When? Did Owen know?"

"In July, and I certainly told him. He didn't attend the funeral. I thought it best if . . . At any rate, he was being treated at the Mansion and we were out of town, of course, so it would have been impossible, and if not impossible, difficult at the very least." Marty had forgotten how long Beatrice could talk without taking breath. She glanced over at Detective Casanova, who was looking as if he couldn't quite believe this apparition, and no wonder. Beatrice was dressed for a garden party, com-

plete with wide-brimmed hat. All in tasteful black, of course, with a few small and tasteful pieces of diamond jewelry.

The detective consulted some notes on his desk and said, "Mrs. Lamb? Mrs. Beatrice Lamb?"

"As I have said. I believe you have my poor boy's body. I should like to make arrangements . . . cremation, I think . . . the ashes scattered over the ocean. My son was an English professor, Detective, and a poet—"

Casanova shot an unreadable look at Marty. Then he said, mildly, "I think that'll be all, Miz Lamb. Here. Please read your statement and sign on the bottom. And then we'll talk, Mrs. Lamb." And it was over. Beatrice said not another word to her erstwhile daughter-in-law, just inclined her head graciously in farewell.

"Where to?" Paul asked when they got back outside into the bright sunshine. "It's Sunday and it's gorgeous. The park? The Bronx Zoo? Name it." He paused and then went on. "And you can tell me all about Owen's mother while we're on our way. She's like a dinosaur, isn't she? You've seen pictures of them, but if one actually showed up, it would be so much more frightening than you ever imagined." He laughed.

"She *does* look like a fugitive from the forties, doesn't she? I *can't* tell you all about her, because she was always an enigma to me. I'll bet she was an enigma to Owen, too. . . ." She glanced over at Paul. He had already lost interest. She figured he'd just about had it with Lambs. Except her, she hoped.

"You said, 'Where to?' and here's my answer. All Souls, please," she said. "I know, it's my day off. But I just can't stay away! No, just kidding. I want to see Shayna."

"Stupid me. Of course you do."

Funny, Marty thought. Neither one of them was bringing up the subject of tomorrow's press conference. It could mean the end of her job. It could mean the end of his. Maybe that's why they were staying away from it. Her mind went leaping ahead, in spite of her best intentions. All her thoughts about going back to school or moving up to Rhode Island . . . pure silliness. She didn't want to do either. In any case, she couldn't go *anywhere*, not while Dr. Zee was still alive. She'd made Julia a promise, to be there at the end, to help if needed; and she was

going to keep that promise. And how could she forget Shayna? Who was going to take care of Shayna Brown, if not Dr. Zee and Marty Lamb? And then, there was Paul. *Maybe* there was Paul. He hadn't popped the question, had he? And she answered herself, well, neither have *you*, my good woman. Since when are you a shrinking violet? she asked herself, and before she could think of a good answer, they were at the hospital. Hand in hand, they strolled up the front walk.

"I'll just check into my office while you see Shayna," Paul said. "She might get emotional, and she won't want a stranger looking on."

"You *are* a find," Marty said, giving him a light kiss. "I'll come by for you."

He went into the elevator while she took the stairs, breathing a bit hard when she let herself out by the Family Practice unit and nearly fell over Shayna in a wheelchair, all dressed, a little suitcase sitting on her lap.

"Marty! I just called you and left you a message, and poof! here you are. Dr. Zee is sending me to Harmony Hill Hospital for a complete workup. I wanted to remind you to come see me as soon as they let you. I think I can have visitors the whole time."

"I'm sure you can. Anyway, they *have* to let me in. I'm a nurse."

Shayna smiled. "Nurse-practitioner, you mean."

"Anyway, you don't have to remind me to visit you. Of course I will, every day I can." She smiled. A nurse came up, ready to push the chair, but Marty told her they'd need a minute or two alone. The nurse nodded and disappeared down the hall.

Marty regarded Shayna, smiling. "I'm going to miss seeing you every morning on my way to work. But I'll be happy knowing they're working on your legs."

"I have to be very careful, not to expect miracles. Dr. Zee warned me. He . . . We waited too long, Dr. Zee says, to be absolutely sure how much can be fixed. Maybe I'll always have to be in a wheelchair." The lovely face fell, but only for an instant. "But at least I'm free. *Free.* And, Dr. Zee says, if determination counts for anything, maybe I'll make a miracle." She grinned.

"Well, you know who'll be rooting for you. But . . . who'll

be caring for you? I mean . . . as . . . family," she said carefully.

But the steady smile never wavered. Shayna was still in shock, serenely floating above the terrible events of the past several weeks. "Oh, Selma has said I should come to them, to be with my little brothers. I don't know . . . I'm not so sure I want to be so religious anymore. But . . . Selma, she's been so kind to me . . . to my family. I guess I have to go there, at least in the beginning."

"She has your best interests at heart, Shayna. And you're still very young. Don't make too many decisions right away, okay? Don't try to change everything at once. Take it slow." Marty stopped talking and laughed. "I know you're not going to pay the least bit of attention to that. *I* never did!"

"I do know one thing," Shayna said. "I'm going to go to school, and learn to be a nurse. Then, maybe, I'll think about getting married. I've got time. But you . . . you're getting on," she teased. "When are *you* getting married to that nice doctor?"

"Who says I'm getting married at all?"

Shayna laughed. "Oh, you'll marry him, you'll see. It's *beschert*. Fated."

"I'll let you know. . . . Look, Shayna. About nursing. Nurses are on their feet all day long. Anyway, you don't want to change bedpans and turn people over."

"I want to help people, like you do." The girl's eyes filled.

"I think I know where you'd be perfect, Shayna. Think about genetic counseling." The nurse was bustling back, looking at her watch. "It's time for you to go. I *will* miss seeing you every day. It's not going to be the same without you."

"We'll talk on the telephone. You'll visit me in the hospital. We'll write, oh yes, we'll write! I'll get a book on genetic counseling. And I'm going to learn how to use a computer, a word processor. I'm going to come into the twentieth century! Oh, Marty, it's all so exciting!"

Marty stood by the elevator, waving, even after the doors had closed. A happy ending for Shayna, in spite of all the tragedy.

Now, maybe she could check on Baby Edouard and his mama. The Neonatal ICU was only two floors away, and Marie would be there, visiting. Sonya had said that Marie haunted the place, hovering over the bassinet, talking to him and singing

lullabies. But she hadn't yet held her child in her arms. Well, Marty thought as she took the stairs, if Len Fassbinder was as good as they said, Marie might just get *her* happy ending, too.

When Marty got upstairs, she could hear the wails from all the way down the hall. That had to be Marie's voice. Oh Christ, what now? She began to run.

It was so frustrating, having to scrub and pull a smock over her head, wasting precious time while she could plainly hear Marie's sobs and moans as two other voices tried in vain to calm her down. Where was Clive Moses when you needed him? But she knew where he was—down the street, in front of the Browns' apartment building, doing damage control with the media.

Finally, she was done with the preparations and hustled into the nursery. You couldn't miss Marie, with her brightly tur-banned head. One of the two nurses with Marie was Sonya; she was very happy to see that. It seemed Marie wasn't the only woman who haunted the NICU. As Marty joined the trio by Edouard's bassinet, she saw what the problem was. The bassinet was empty. Marie was wailing, *"Il est mort, ah, non, non, ce n'est pas possible!"*

Marty pitched her voice to penetrate anything. "Marie! Marie Racine! Listen to me, please! *Ecoutez, s'il vous plaît!*" Both nurses jumped back and Marie abruptly stopped sobbing. For a moment there was no sound except the bleeps and peeps of the monitors.

"Madame le docteur! They telling me he is . . . finish. *Il est fini. Mon Edouard, il est mort!"* The heartbroken weeping began again.

Marty took both of Marie's hands in hers. Marie's were cold and clammy and her whole body was quivering. "She thinks the baby is dead," Marty explained.

Sonya answered, in a weary voice, "We know that's what she thinks, Marty. We've been trying—"

"Did you tell her he's finished?"

"Oh, lord! No, we told her—we *tried* to tell her—he's almost finished with his *tests*. He's in the back, they'll bring him out in just a few minutes. He was taken off the respirator this morning and all the vitals are being checked. He's going to be fine."

"He's going to be fine!" the other nurse shouted at Marie.

"It doesn't matter how loud you talk, Adele," Sonya said. "She's too upset to understand English. You parley a little, don't you, Marty?"

"Very little, but I'll give it a shot. Marie, *viens ici,*" Marty said, pulling the girl gently away from the bassinet. "*C'est bon.* No. *C'est bien.* Oh hell, I don't know which is right. *Edouard, il est parfait,*" she finally decided on. Well, maybe he wasn't perfect, exactly, but ... And then she stopped talking, as a broad, delighted smile lit up Marie's face.

"Ah, Monsieur Moses ... Clive," Marie said in a certain tone of voice, smiling through her tears.

Marty turned to see Clive wearing the same goofy-happy grin as Marie. The two walked toward each other and then stopped, inches apart, not touching, eyes locked, speaking in rapid French. Then Clive pulled the girl in, to hug her, and she went happily into his embrace.

Marty slid a glance to Sonya and they grinned at each other. Then Sonya said, "Back in a minute," and moved away. Over Marie's shoulder Clive grinned at Marty. "Hi, Marty, we meet again."

"Small world," Marty said.

"So the little fella's going to be okay?"

"Looks that way."

"She's been worried sick, you know. The uncertainty ... it's awful ... and the waiting."

"I know. And she's so far from home and so alone," Marty said.

"Not anymore, she's not." He tightened his grip on Marie, who gave a little squeak of surprise and then, blushing furiously, extricated herself.

"Oh, Clive, that's—" But Marty never got a chance to finish the thought. Sonya had reappeared with a blanket-wrapped bundle in her arms.

"Edouard!" Marie cried. "Edouard!" She stood very still, her hands tightly clasped together. "Sonya, Edouard is ... okay?"

Sonya's answer was to hold out the baby. "Yes. *Oui.* He's okay. Come get him, Mama Marie."

Marie took the baby from Sonya, cradling him, gazing down

on him, her face glowing with happiness while tears streaked down her face. "*Mon fils! Mon petit fils!* I 'ave wait *longtemps!*" Then she lifted her face and said, in awestruck tones, "Clive, see him, he breathe by alone! He is . . . *si beau!*"

"By himself," Clive corrected. "Yes, I see that. And of course he's beautiful. Just like his mama."

"Marty, come see, look by my son, *mon Edouard!* Clive . . . Sonya . . . *tous* . . . *Mon bébé* . . . he does not dead! *Merci au bon Dieu!*"

They gathered around her and looked down at the tiny face. He was a beautiful baby, Marty thought, his skin the color of pale coffee, his eyes huge and brown with thick eyelashes. There was a black fuzz all over his head and a dimple in his chin. His eyes were wide open, and then, as Marty watched, they suddenly closed and he was asleep.

"You go sit down, Marie," Sonya said. "You can hold him as long as you want. Mr. Moses, *you* tell her." The three women hung back as the little family moved to Edouard's bassinet, Clive's arm around Marie's shoulder.

The ICU nurse murmured to Marty, "The baby really ought to go back in the bassinet and she really shouldn't stay very long. But I can't send her away."

"Rules are made to be broken," Sonya said. "Not to worry. *We* won't tell."

"He *will* be okay, won't he?" Marty asked.

"Oh, don't you worry. The way he's coming along, I wouldn't be surprised if he went home pretty soon."

They all turned to look at the little group—the beautiful young woman sitting, gently rocking the sleeping baby, while the tall, strong man stood behind them protectively. The three of them sighed in unison, and then broke into laughter.

As Marty left with Sonya, she found herself blinking back sudden tears. Now quit that, she scolded herself. You'll have a baby one day. Stop worrying. The next happy ending is definitely yours.

38

Even at eight-thirty in the morning the traffic around All Souls was crowded and chaotic. It always was, on Monday. Holding hands and ignoring the lights, Marty and Paul went racing through the intersection opposite the hospital and landed safely on the other side, laughing. They'd been kidding around and giggling like schoolchildren all the way to work. Marty guessed it was either that or give way to anxiety about the future.

When they got to the front door, Gilbert peered at Marty and said, "Good to see you this morning, Marty. *Very* good."

"Thanks, Gilbert, I appreciate it."

He touched his guard cap with two fingers in a kind of salute. She was warmed. "I'm going to miss this place, you know that?" she said to Paul.

"How do you know you're not going to be here?"

"After this press conference? I'm willing to bet that our clinics will be history!" They walked together through the swinging doors. "It's hard to imagine that I won't be here much longer," she said, feeling very teary. Paul left her at the front desk. He gave her a warm kiss, murmuring, "Never say die," against her lips, and hurried down the hall to the Family Practice clinics.

Carmen, watching with great interest, grinned broadly at Marty and said, "Anything I should know?"

"Like what?" Marty could feel the blush rising in her face.

"Hey! That's great! He's such a doll, and so are you."

"Aw, shucks . . . What?" Because Carmen was motioning her to come closer.

"She's here," Carmen said in a low voice. "Crystal. She came in a few minutes ago, cool as could be, and went back to

421

her office. That is, what *used* to be her office. She's been fired, hasn't she?"

Grimly, Marty answered, "She's been fired, yes. She just came in?"

"Yeah, five, ten minutes ago. I didn't see her leaving, so she must still be back there. But I could be wrong, Marty. The phone's been ringing off the hook since I got in." She rolled her eyes. "The press, mostly, and neighborhood people, too. Is Shayna Brown here at the clinics. Is the director of the clinics here at the clinics. Is it true there's a serial killer stalking the hospital. Is it true the hospital is closing. Do *I* know what the story is. I'm telling you, people just can't mind their own business!"

"Tell me about it!"

Crystal was not in her office, which didn't surprise Marty. She was thoroughly annoyed, however. She wanted Crys out of here, gone for good, not reappearing like a ghost to haunt the place. Until she found Crys, she decided, she'd go back to her office and find something to do . . . *anything* to keep her mind off the specter of the press conference.

Normally, on a day when they were all waiting for news that might be bad, she and Crys would have schmoozed a bit, maybe run over to the cafeteria for some coffee and gossip . . . but *that* was over. And Joel had gone off to Michigan after Alice, to make up with her and set things right. So . . . no Joel, either. No Dr. Zee anymore, and no Paul, for the moment.

And from now on there wouldn't be Shayna Brown sitting at her window on the world, either, calling out to her every morning. Ever since she'd started to work at All Souls, Marty had been stopping on her way to work by that window. She'd watched the pretty little girl change into a gorgeous young woman. More than just beautiful—intelligent and strong. Zeke hadn't been able to break her spirit, at least.

Zeke was gone, too. Miriam was gone. And after this morning's press conference, there might not be a Community Care Clinics program, either. The tight little world she'd made for herself was falling to pieces. Come to think of it, with all these changes, maybe she didn't *want* CCC to stay open. Yeah. Right.

She wandered back out into the corridor and instantly felt

better. For there was Isabelle, running in the front entrance, talking a mile a minute as she approached, waving at her.

"There you are. You look okay. *Are* you okay?" Izzy hardly paused for breath. "I saw the whole thing on television yesterday. I was so worried, I could barely sleep a wink but I didn't want to disturb you, I figured you needed your sleep. I hope you got some. Did you? Oh that poor girl, losing her mother and then her father. What's going to happen to her?" Isabelle stopped talking to look closely at Marty. "You didn't get enough sleep, I can see *that*. Oh God, Marty, that poor child, watching her father fall apart like that, hearing him say he was going to kill her! And you, too! Oh my God, what if you—" She could go no further, but burst into tears.

Marty put her arms around Isabelle. Isabelle was a tiny person, barely five feet tall, and her head just about reached Marty's armpit. The embrace was awkward and even funny, and Isabelle pulled away, laughing, wiping at the tears on her face. "I'm such an idiot, crying over what *didn't* happen."

"If it's idiotic, then why am *I* doing it?" And she *was* crying, the tears leaking out of the corners of her eyes. She swiped at them with her hand. "Anyway, thanks for coming in, Izzy. I know you're still in mourning."

"After that message you left me, that there won't be anyone from JCAHO coming in to make us crazy? And that Dr. Messinger and Dr. Wolfe are calling a press conference? You think I could stay home and just *wait*?" Isabelle smoothed her hair nervously. "They're going to get rid of us, aren't they?"

Marty sighed. "I hope not," she said. It was very much a Director Response, all calm and cool. Which is *not* how she felt.

"How's she doing? The girl, Shayna?"

"She's at Harmony Hill now, getting a complete workup for the first time in her life, and happy as a clam. For the moment, anyway. I don't think that reality has quite hit home yet. But Shayna's pretty tough. She had to be, to withstand her father's brainwashing." Marty paused, remembering. "She asked me if I thought Zeke was psychotic."

"What did you tell her?"

"I told her no. He knew what he was doing, knew it was considered wrong. He just thought his agenda was more

important. We didn't count. His sons, the three little boys . . . he never even gave them a thought, just handed them over. . . . Yes," she said, to Isabelle's look of distaste, "pretty disgusting. I got the impression, from what he said, that he'd been completely besotted with Miriam. She was the center of his universe, and the kids were just . . . incidental."

"Huh!" Isabelle snorted her derision. "Sounds to me like *he* was the center of his universe and everyone *else* was incidental."

Over Isabelle's shoulder Marty noticed the big clock on the wall. "Dammit, Izzy, it's nearly nine. The press conference! We'd better get going."

The crowd that had gathered in the main lobby was mostly staff, with just a sprinkling of media people. Marty knew where the rest of them were. Down the street in front of the apartment building, hoping to catch a sound bite or two. Who cared what happened to a couple of hospitals that wanted to merge? Hospitals were swallowing each other alive, everywhere you looked. But a double killing, committed by two men who both thought God spoke to them? Now there was a *story*.

On the dot of nine Eliot Wolfe and Milton Messinger appeared by the front desk. Dr. Wolfe stepped forward, a sheet of paper in his hand. He looked at ease, dapper in a navy-blue, pin-striped suit. He never looked at his notes as he spoke.

"I am Eliot Wolfe, president of Harmony Hill Hospital. On behalf of my board of directors and myself, I'd like to announce that, as of October first, All Souls Women's Hospital will become part of Harmony Hill Hospital, making HHH the largest general care hospital in Manhattan."

The crowd began to buzz, like a hive of angry bees. There was a smattering of applause. Wolfe kept right on, his voice even. "Many of the services now offered at All Souls will be integrated with Harmony Hill's—and that includes much of the medical and support staff." *Much of.* Those were the words that meant something, Marty thought.

"There is bound to be some natural attrition," Dr. Wolfe continued, unperturbed. "And we all hope that will take care of any excess staff.

"The Community Care Clinics, which focus on primary

care for women and children—families—and most particularly on the very people who will be left out of all the health care plans being argued in Congress—CCC will be enlarged and expanded, encompassing the Family Practice services from both hospitals, and will be housed in the hospital proper. The annex will be torn down. The Community Care Clinics will become Harmony Hill's new Uptown Outreach facility. Harmony Hill believes in moving up and out," he added, smiling. It was a poor little joke, but it was all they had. There was a small ripple of laughter.

"We have made a similar arrangement with St. Barnabas Lying-In Hospital on East Twenty-sixth Street," he went on. At every new sentence, a different sound hummed over the growing crowd of onlookers, only to be cut off by insistent "shhh's" as Wolfe went on. "The St. Barnabas facility—Downtown Outreach—will be called Harmony Hill East Side Center. The All Souls facility, as I have already said, will retain the name Community Care Clinics."

Marty and Paul looked at each other. They both knew the hidden meanings of those carefully selected names. The East Side *Center* was for well-to-do patients who didn't want to have to go crosstown to Harmony Hill in all that heavy traffic. The Community Care *Clinics* conveyed clearly that this was the place of choice for poor and uninsured families.

"We plan to open storefront pregnancy clinics in various parts of our catchment area," Wolfe went on. Marty turned to Paul and whispered, "I sent Messinger a memo about that *months* ago!" He had ignored it, of course. And now it was really going to happen! "Residents at Harmony Hill will spend one day each semester following the nursing staff around, learning what happens *after* the doctor writes his orders. Maybe then there won't be so many casual extra tests, bloods, and surgeries," Dr. Wolfe said.

Marty laughed out loud and Paul said: "Don't tell me. Another one of your memos."

She nodded. She was in shock. It was *all* going to happen! Everything she'd been working for, all this time! She was going to be director of a greatly enlarged community outreach program, and maybe she could hire a Crisis Intervention

Officer. And how about a budget person, an accountant of her
very own? And not have to worry all the time that she was
going to be closed down, or that it was time to work on new
grant proposals? No more begging on bended knees! The realization began to fill her. She felt lighter than air, as if she could
float. Maybe she could have it all. Her program. Her career.
Her beloved—if he ever asked her to marry him. So what was
she waiting for? Why didn't she ask *him*? Well, maybe she
would; yes, she *would*. Right now.

Eliot Wolfe had finished his announcements and was shaking
hands with Dr. Messinger, flashes were going off, and everyone
was applauding. So Marty clapped, too. Then there was a tap on
her shoulder. It was Max, whispering that there would be a brief
meeting in Dr. Messinger's office in half an hour. "You, too, Dr.
Giordano." And then he slid away, to notify the others.

"Why do you suppose we need a meeting? And why the big
rush?" Marty said as they made their way back to the clinics. "I
thought Wolfe covered everything."

"That's because you're safe, Marty. But what about Dennis,
for instance? I doubt that Harmony Hill needs two department
heads in OB/GYN. And Joel Mannes. Wolfe didn't say anything about Psychiatry. Harmony Hill's a big hospital. I'm sure
they're fully staffed. And then there's . . ." He paused.

"There's . . . ?"

"Me, Marty. Dr. Giordano, acting chief of Family Practice
at the no-longer-existent All Souls Hospital."

She hadn't thought of that. Shame on her. "How would you
like to work for me, in this Uptown Outreach down-home
clinic thing? I'll give you a job." She kept her voice light but
her heart was beating hard. If he did lose out, would he stay in
New York? Because she couldn't leave.

He smiled. "Maybe. We'll see. Meanwhile, I plan to behave
as if I were still acting chief and go see to my service." He took
the elevator and she continued on to her office.

When she opened her door, there was Crystal, sitting in her
chair. As soon as Marty appeared, Crystal began to grin. How
odd and inappropriate.

"Well, well," she said. "It looks like congratulations are in
order, Marty."

"Thank you. And kindly get out of my chair."

Crys continued to smile broadly.

"Out of my chair. *Now.*"

The grin faded from Crys's face. She stood up, spreading her hands, turning around slowly.

"See? I've touched nothing, taken nothing. And just to prove it . . ." She handed Marty an official envelope from Messinger's office. "I didn't even open it to look." Was she trying to be funny? The message inside the envelope was brief and to the point. There would be a brief meeting of the Executive Committee immediately after the press conference. The same one Max had told her about. Messinger was taking no chances about *this* message.

Crystal was pacing restlessly, not at all interested in the memo. "You were right, you know. I used to come up here occasionally and . . . ah, rearrange things. Listen to your messages. Erase them sometimes."

"Crys, *why?*"

"Because I'm bad, that's why. My daddy always said so, he said some children are just born bad and I was one of them. I know you think I'm misunderstood or neurotic or something. But it's not that. Sometimes I think to myself, 'Oh I want that' or 'Oh, I wonder what would happen if I changed that' . . . and then I take it or change it. I just do what I want to. I'm bad . . . I'm the *worst.*"

"Oh, I doubt—"

But Crystal didn't want to hear anything. She wanted to talk. She thrust her head forward and stared into Marty's eyes. "Don't you wonder how in hell I chose *nursing*, of all the damn things? Well, here's your answer. I didn't choose it. Daddy did. See, here's what happened. My doctor brother, he committed suicide his first year of residency, couldn't take it anymore. He hated medicine. Hell, he was just like all of us, he hated his fucking *life*!

"Well, no mere child was going to ruin my daddy's plans, no way! I got sent to nursing school. I was right up at the top of my class, you know that? Of course I was. Daddy wouldn't have it any other way." Her tone had turned nasty.

"Well, he must have been proud of you," Marty said. She

knew it sounded dumb, and Crys gave her a disgusted look, then resumed her back-and-forth pacing, looking off into the distance as she talked.

"Daddy's not proud. Daddy's not *nothin'*. Daddy is dead," Crystal said with some satisfaction, "And gone." She smiled at Marty.

"I'm sorry," Marty said automatically, and Crys waved off the words, so she got right to it. "You didn't leave St. Francis because of the commute, did you?" Marty said.

"Hell, no. I was head midwife there, with twice as many patients as I have here! No, they kicked me out for using drugs. I wasn't reported to the licensure board because one of the doctors and I . . . He thought he was all finished with sex, he was in his sixties and having a few little problems. But I showed him how a little hash could keep it nice and stiff." She laughed. "He was one grateful doctor. He got me a good recommendation and then told me he hoped I might drop back there now and again, for old times' sake." She laughed again.

"And yes, you got it, I was the one sent Angie that picture of the baby in the bath. That was the first one. I might have been stoned, I don't remember why I sent it. And when I saw what an anonymous message could do, how much hell it could raise, I just had to keep doing it. It was *fun*. I'm a shit, I know it and so fucking what? I was born mean."

"Why target Aimee? Because she had Dennis?"

"Hell, no. I don't worry about *competition*, Marty. I just wanted to bring her down a peg. You know she's bulimic. You don't? Well, she is. She always takes her little radio with her into the john so nobody can hear her upchuck. Her real name is Amy A-M-Y Duchupnik and she was a chubby kid they called Amy Dumptruck." She grinned at Marty. "Amy Dumptruck," she repeated. "She still doesn't realize she's thin. God, she just couldn't believe her luck when Dr. Dimwit began fucking her! Women are such idiots, you know that, Marty? Aimee is a smart woman—okay, so she has a calculator instead of a heart, but still . . . She should have been able to spot a jerk like Dennis, who figures he's got to fuck every woman in the world before he dies. Hell, is it my fault that Amy Dumptruck thought her dream of getting a doctor was finally going to come true?"

"Why is *she* so dumb? *You* screwed him."

Crystal gave her the oddest look. "It's not the same thing at all, Marty. My heart didn't go all fluttery the first time he suggested we have an after-hours drink in his office. And it didn't beat faster when he locked the door and pulled me into his arms and gave me a French kiss that was supposed to make me faint. Actually, he's a pretty fair lover. Like that battery bunny on TV, he just keeps going and going and going. . . ." She laughed again, then abruptly became serious. "But I wasn't dreaming of a wedding. I was seeing beautiful bottles of pills before my eyes. So I fell to my knees and worshiped at the altar; I knew that would get him. Hell, he thinks his cock is a god, anyway. And *then*, when he came after me, begging for more, I told him my price. I wanted prescriptions from him and I wanted him all to myself until I said it was over. And he paid my price, paid it gladly." Her eyes slitted, so that she looked remarkably like a cat. "And then, the bastard, he told me I was too damned expensive and he wasn't going to lose a good job over a blow job! He thought that was so damned funny, so damned clever." She walked to the window and looked out. "I was sorry to have to hurt *you*, Marty—I really like you—but I couldn't leave you out, could I? It would have been so obvious."

Marty felt as if she were suffocating. She breathed in deeply. "Crys, I'm sending you before the Nursing Licensure Board. I've got everything I need to make sure you can never work in a hospital again."

Crys whirled around. "I thought you'd say that! And what am I supposed to do about a job?"

"You need therapy much more than you need a job. And there's a good program—"

"I don't want a fucking *program*, Marty. I want to keep my license, my livelihood. But you're in charge now, right? So you're going to get even with me!"

"Oh, Crys, it's such a pity . . . for a while, I thought we really were friends."

Bitter little laugh. "People like me never *really* have friends. Although you came pretty close, Marty. There's something about you . . . I don't know what it is, but I always had the

feeling that you'd suffered, too. Even before you told me about your mama." Marty stared at her, unable to think of a response.

"I'm right, aren't I? You've had a real tough time in life. But . . ." Crystal began to smile. "Things are looking up, girl-friend. I noticed as soon as you walked in. You're pregnant, Marty."

"I'm . . . ?" As soon as she heard the words, Marty realized it was true. The nausea in the morning, the sudden weight gain, her new need every afternoon for a *nap*, of all the damn things.

"I'm pregnant," she said, her heart lifting. "I'm pregnant!" How stupid of her not to have known it. She was carrying Paul's child, their child. Joy, like a warm glow, spread all through her. "I see you're still the witch they say you are, in spite of every-thing," she said to Crystal. "But that's doesn't ch—"

There was a knock, and before she could send the intruder away, the door opened and in came Clive Moses, apologizing, to ask if a reporter could call Marty sometime today. It seemed she wanted to write an article for *The New York Times Maga-zine* on spina bifida—featuring the story of the rabbi who hid his daughter's "deformity" as well as several other human-interest stories that had surfaced as soon as the word got out about Shayna. Well, Marty thought, it certainly couldn't do any harm to educate the public about neural tube defects.

Opening her mouth to say so, she became uncomfortably aware of the way Clive and Crystal were pretending they didn't see each other. "She'll have to get permission from Shayna," she said. "Who may not want the trauma of her life spread all over the local media."

"On the other hand, she might love telling her story. But don't worry, I'll have the reporter start with Shayna." Clive paused. "What are *you* doing here?" he asked abruptly, turning to Crystal. "Getting fired, I hope."

"Bastard!" It was spat out.

"I'm the bastard. Right," Clive said bitterly. "We were lovers, Marty, we were in love—or so I thought." He may have addressed himself to her, but his eyes never left Crystal.

"In love! Is that what you call wanting to own someone? Are you *in love* with Marie Racine? I doubt it. But she's absolutely

perfect for you, Clive, young and dumb and with very little English. So how can she tell what a bully you are?"

Color climbed in his face, but he went on. "You keep your filthy mouth off Marie, you hear me? I think Marty ought to know what kind of whore you are. I came into St. Francis, Marty, to pick her up one fine Friday, with an armful of roses and a diamond as big as the Ritz. I found her in her office, with one of the doctors—" His voice cracked and he stopped, breathing hard, his fists clenched. "She'd forgotten to lock the door. Or maybe you didn't forget, Crys. Maybe you wanted me to find you at your worst, so I'd have to dump you."

"That wasn't my worst, lover boy, as you well know. That was my best. And you shouldn't have been so quick to dump me, Clive baby," she added with an odd little smile. "I was pregnant and I had to get rid of your bastard."

"You're lying, Crystal."

"Do I sound like I'm lying?"

"You never sound like you're lying. But you lie all the time."

"It was a boy," she said, tossing her head and grinning at him. "What you always wanted."

So swiftly, it was like a blur to Marty's eyes, he stepped forward and, making a sound somewhere between a sob and a moan, slapped Crystal backhanded across her face. The crack sounded like a rifle shot and Crystal went stumbling backward. For one long moment she stared at him, her hand to her flaming cheek, then suddenly she raced past them.

At the doorway she turned for an instant, shouting, "I've never had a break, not once in my life, but you're *never* going to get me in front of the licensure board. You can't fire me, either, because I quit! And don't bother looking for me, because I'm going so far away, nobody will *ever* find me! I'll show you, I'll show you *all*!"

In an instant Clive was after her, calling her name. By the time Marty ran into the hallway, they were both out of sight. She hustled to the front desk, where Carmen said, "Out the door," in answer to the silent question. Marty paused. She felt she ought to go after Crystal, but what good would that do?

She wanted to tell Carmen she was pregnant—hell, she wanted to get on the public speaking system and tell the entire

world!—but she couldn't, not until she'd told Paul. So she leaned on Carmen's desk and filled her in on the Crystal saga.

"What do you think she'll do?" Carmen asked.

"Your guess is as good as mine. Her behavior's been so volatile lately, it's hard to say *what* she'll do. But if she sticks to her promise never to go before the licensure board, I'd say she'll disappear and surface in some other big city. Boston or San Francisco, maybe change her name."

"Sooner or later, she'll be found out."

"Maybe. Lots of people disappear forever."

"And then someone tells the story to 'America's Most Wanted,' and boom!"

Marty glanced at her watch. "Oh my God, I'm already late for Dr. Messinger's debriefing—or whatever it is."

"Time flies, whether you're having fun or not," Carmen pronounced.

"Thanks for the words of wisdom. I'll let everyone know what's going on as soon as I find out. *If* I find out."

What was undoubtedly going to happen, she thought as she hurried to Messinger's office, was they'd all be reassured that jobs were *not* going to be swept away wholesale, that Dr. Wolfe wanted to keep everything in place for the time being. And then, later, one by one, as the new management took over, they'd be let go. *Excessed*, that was the new word for being dumped. Oh well. At least, that way, everyone would have a job for a couple of months, maybe even into the new year.

They had all waited for her, at the meeting. Even more stunning, when she raced in, they all began applauding. She could feel the heat rise in her face, and when she met Paul's eyes, he sent her a tiny air kiss, and she knew she was blushing an even brighter pink.

"You have proved, Ms. Lamb, to be an exemplary Crisis Intervention Officer," Dr. Messinger said, looking just a bit ill at ease with praise. "You managed to keep the Brown girl and yourself alive, in spite of . . . in spite of everything," he finished, somewhat weakly.

"I thank you all," Marty said, seating herself. "And I'd like to ask a favor." She looked straight at Messinger.

He looked puzzled. "Yes?"

"Now can I please quit that job?"

There was a lot of laughter at that. Messinger harrumphed for a moment, mumbled something, and then, obviously relieved to get back to the agenda, said, "I'd like to say that—"

"I beg your pardon. But this is— May I borrow Marty for just one moment?" It was Clive Moses, a bit disheveled and slightly out of breath. "I do apologize for the interruption. . . ."

"You can have her for one moment, yes."

"It's Crystal," Marty said as soon as the door closed and they were standing alone in the anteroom.

"It's Crystal." He looked grim.

She stared at him, feeling her heartbeat speed up. "She's dead."

"No. No. No, of course not. Did I give you that impression? I'm sorry." He tried for a smile, not quite making it. "She disappeared."

"Disappeared? How?"

"She's a witch, that's how! She was running so damn fast . . . but, hey, I'm no slouch when it comes to speed. One minute she was right ahead of me and I was gaining on her. The next . . . gone. I mean *gone*, Marty. There's no telling where she might go or what she might do."

Marty felt drained, suddenly. "When does it end, Clive? When does it end?"

"Well . . . Right here, right now, let's hope."

"What if she—"

"Are you thinking Crystal might commit suicide? Kill herself?" Clive's laughter was bitter. "Give me a break. That's not for her. She's like a cat, she'll land on her feet. Pretty soon, she'll be making trouble for a whole new group of people."

Paul came out of the Conference Room, saying, "They're wondering what's happened, Marty."

"Crystal came in to visit me this morning and she ran out shouting about getting us all, or all of us being sorry or some such craziness."

"I went after her and she disappeared herself," Clive put in.

"She's not in good shape," Marty said. "Oh Christ, if I hadn't told her I was putting her on—"

She reached out for his hand and took a deep breath. Here goes, she thought. "Okay by me," she said. As he bent his lips to hers, she added, "Paul, remind me later to tell you about a little surprise I have for you."

*Lorrie Morgan was born to be
a country-western music star.*

In FOREVER YOURS FAITHFULLY,
she tells us her tempestuous story of sweet
triumph and bitter tragedy.
From her childhood as a Nashville blueblood
performing at the Grand Ole Opry at the tender
age of eleven to her turbulent,
star-crossed love affair with Keith Whitley,
a bluegrass legend she loved passionately
but could not save from his personal demons,
to her rise to superstardom,
she lays bare all the secrets and great passions
of a life lived to the fullest.

And her story would not be complete without the
music that has been her lifeline.

**A special six-song CD featuring never-before-
released material,
featuring a duet with Keith Whitley,
is included with this hardcover.**

FOREVER YOURS FAITHFULLY
by Lorrie Morgan

Published by Ballantine Books.
Coming to bookstores everywhere
in October 1997.